About the Author

Quite early, Kathrin Brückmann developed an interest in the history of Ancient Egypt. In consequence, she chose to study the exotic combination Egyptology, Archaeology and Judaism.

After giving birth to two children, realization dawned on her that digging Egypt top to bottom and being a single parent might not go together all too well. So she tried something different. In 2011, she started writing and, in doing so, returned to her roots. The novel Sinuhe, Sohn der Sykomore (Sinuhe, Son of the Sycamore, so far only available in German) is about a young Egyptian scribe in Twelfth Dynasty Egypt and tells the famous story of Sinuhe as recorded on numerous papyri. The book was received so well, she decided to become a freelance writer. Some short stories in various genres followed her debut novel, one of which won a writing contest by a well-known publisher.

In 2013, she developed the concept for a historical mystery series about two young physicians investigating murders and other crimes in Ancient Egypt—not exactly of their own free will. *Apprenticed to Anubis* (*Verborgener Tod* in German) is the first novel in this series, now followed by *Shadows of the Damned*. Edith Parzefall translated both books into English.

Read more about it at http://hori-Nakhtmin.jimdo.com/

Also by Kathrin Brückmann

Apprenticed to Anubis: In Maat's Service 1
Historical mystery of ancient Egypt

The Bitter Taste of Death: In Maat's Service 3
Historical mystery of ancient Egypt

Shadows
of the Damned

In Maat's Service
Volume 2

Kathrin Brückmann

Original title: Schatten der Verdammten
Hori und Nachtmin Band 2

Translator: Edith Parzefall
Editor: Les Tucker
Cover design: Hannah Böving

ISBN: 1523723203

ISBN-13: 978-1523723201

MAP OF ANCIENT EGYPT

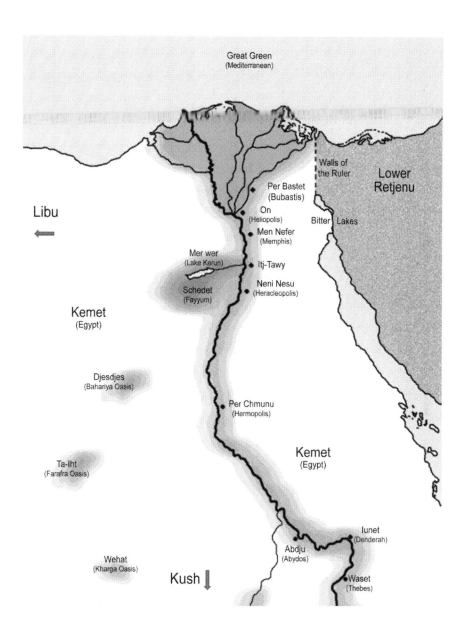

Principal Characters

Historical persons are set in bold, followed by pronunciation pointers in paren-
thesis and the translation of the names in italics. The letter combination 'th' is
pronounced like an aspirated 't'. Certain terms are capitalized in this novel
because they carry a specific meaning or are titles, for example: the Two Lands,
Great Royal Wife, Beautiful West and more.

THE ROYAL DYNASTY

Senusret III. (Senusret) – *husband of goddess Ouseret* – A king who carries a
heavy burden.

Khenmetneferhedjet II (Khenmet-nefer-hedjet) – *joined with the White Crown* –
The Great Royal Wife called Sherit, the younger, carries no weight.

Nofrethenut (Nofret-henut) – *beautiful mistress* – The second royal wife carries
the Horus in the egg.

Senetsenebtisi, Menet, Sat-Hathor, Henut – Senusret's daughters carry on to provide entertainment.

Atef (short for Hori-hetep-em-Atef) – *Horus is content with the Atef crown* – A
royal servant who carries himself without fault.

HORI AND HIS FAMILY

Hori – *name of god Horus* – A physician who can't heal his own heart.

Sobekemhat (Sobek-em-hat) – *Sobek is at the top* – Hori's father and the vizier,
pathologically concerned with his dignity.

Nofret – *the beautiful* – Teti and Puy: Hori's mother and brothers – Sick with worry? Rather not.

Heqet – *name of the frog goddess* – Hori's maid is seriously hurting.

Sheser – *arrow* – Hori's servant and sometimes his stretcher bearer.

Mesu – child, short for Ra-Mesu, child of Re – Hori's lovesick gardener.

NAKHTMIN AND HIS FAMILY

Nakhtmin (Nakht-min) – *Min is strong* – A physician fighting a futile battle.

Mutnofret (Mut-nofret) – *(the goddess) Mut is beautiful* – His battlesome wife who
has much to lose.

Baketamun (Baket-Amun) – *Servant of Amun* – Nakhtmin's cook who fights like a
lioness.

Inti (short for Inen-Ka-i) – *my Ka lingers* – Nakhtmin's servant yields to his wife
without a fight.

AMENY AND HIS FAMILY

Ameny (short for Amen-em-het) – *Amun is at the top* – The second prophet of
Amun suddenly bears great responsibility.

Isis – *name of goddess Isis* – Ameny's wife has a lot to bear.

Huni and Bata – Their twin sons like to bear down on visitors.

At the House of Life

Imhotepankh (Imhotep-ankh) – *Imhotep shall live* – Head of doctors who likes to keep things clear and simple.

Ouseret – *the powerful* – A female physician surrounded by mystery.

In the Amun temple

Iriamun (Iri-Amun) – *belonging to Amun* – The first prophet suffers from old age.

Duamutef (Dua-Mut-ef) – name of one of the four sons of Horus – *Worshipping his mother* – The third prophet quite likes men.

Djedefra (Djed-ef-Ra) – *his perpetuity is Ra* – The fourth prophet suffers a snake bite.

Kagemni (Ka-gemni) – *I've found my ka* – His successor doesn't pity him.

Hemiunu (Hem-Iunu) – *servant of the god Iunu (Ra)* – Head of the priests who dislikes his assistants outflanking him.

Sehetep – *the satisfying one* – Hemiunu's right hand who doesn't always satisfy his superior and must undergo woebegone experiences.

Neb-Wenenef, called Wenen – *master of his existences* – a priest who has much to regret.

Setka (Set-Ka) – *seat of the ka* – a priest who isn't easily suffered.

Neferka (Nefer-Ka) – *beautiful ka* – A priest who takes to his studies with a vengeance.

Bai – *my ba* – a priest easily insulted.

At the House of Death

Hut-Nefer – *beautiful house* – The head of the embalmers keeps dark secrets.

Kheper – *formation, rebirth* – An embalmer who'd like to guard Hori.

Hornakht (Hor-nakht) – *Horus is strong* – An embalmer on his guard.

Nebkaura (Neb-kau-Ra) – *The lord of the kas is Ra* – A lector priest one should guard against.

Merit-Ib – *beloved heart* – His wife guarding herself.

Additional persons

Thotnakht – the king's first scribe.

Tep-Ta – one of the kings personal physicians.

Senankh – head of the Medjay, the king's law enforcers.

Monthnakht – commander of the garrison protecting the embalming compound weryt.

Sennedjem – a palace guard.

Rahotep – his cousin and a weryt guard.

Geheset – a midwife.

PROLOGUE

In the realm of the dead, every sound echoed far too loudly. Rahotep broke out in a sweat despite the consistent breeze from the nearby river. He was supposed to patrol the northern wall of the necropolis looming in the dark, but he didn't dare to move. Oh gods, what had he done to deserve this? Only once in his many years of service with the king's bodyguards did he fall asleep during night watch. And of course, he'd been caught, since the commander had been keeping a wary eye on him already. The man knew no mercy in such cases.

Rahotep thought of his wife and their youngest child, whose yelling kept him from catching up on sleep during the day. The boy sure made a fuss about growing teeth. Dozing off on duty got him transferred to the penal garrison two days ago, and now he had to perform the eeriest service: guard the weryt. Only for a month but that was bad enough.

The previous night he'd suffered through terrible horrors. The noises drifting over from the darkness, the howling of demons in the mountains... The air didn't consist of emptiness here, like he was used to, but was corporeal, palpable, filled with the shadows of the dead. He could feel them creep around his legs, kiss his neck-

A piercing yowl burst through the silence. Rahotep jumped and fled toward the river, where the pier with the life-saving boat lay. At the corner of the weryt wall, he almost bumped into one of his fellow sufferers.

"Back with you!" the guy barked. "You think you can clear out? That's going to cost you if you want us to look the other way, and you'll have to provide a replacement boat."

Rahotep couldn't make out the features of the fellow, but he recognized the voice. "All right, Tutu, I just thought we could have a chat."

The short, fat man laughed nervously. "You're shitting yourself. We all do. Oh well, if you want to."

Rahotep cast an uncertain glance past him to the other figure outlined against the moonlight. At the entrance of the necropolis stood two guards, while one sufficed on each of the other sides, in the south, back and north of the premises. Commander Monthnakht's orders puzzled him. Why should the river need two pairs of watchful eyes? Only a fool voluntarily visited the realm of the dead at night. More likely one of the guards would run off. He felt guilty and at the same time disgusted. Bribery! Some people deserved to do their duty in this place. No, that wasn't an option for him. To desert meant the quarry if caught, and he had a family. "Forget it, I'll carry on. Won't be for long anyway."

"Yeah, good for you," Tutu growled. "I still have a whole year ahead of me."

Reluctantly, Rahotep turned his back on the comforting lights along the opposite riverbank and commenced walking along the wall once more. The farther he ventured into the realm of the shadows, the eerier whispered the voices of lost souls. In an arduous gust, sand whipped against stone and hissed. Like a snake, the snake of the Duat. Soon he'd reach the canal flowing under the wall into the weryt. He dreaded to jump across the water that couldn't be anything but the beginning of the river on which the dead took their journey into the underworld. Demons lurked at the banks. Each time, he feared to land in the gaping jaws of a monster. Did he really have to patrol the other half of the wall? Who knew what awaited him in the pitch-black darkness? But that was his duty! He reached the stone edge and closed his eyes for a moment. Come on, you can do it. He braced himself and prepared to leap.

Puffing and blowing, something broke through the water's surface. A dark shape emerged from the river of the dead! Rahotep froze. He wanted to release his horror in a scream, but his throat constricted, and he couldn't move although his racing heart seemed to shout at his legs: Run, run, you fool! Snarling, the monster climbed from the canal and lunged at him…

Horus in the Egg

Year 2 of Pharaoh Senusret, the third of this name to ascend the throne of Horus. Day 3 of month Ipet-hemet in Shemu, the season of the harvest

"Shsht." Imperiously, the Great Royal Wife placed a finger to her lips, and the chatter of the assembled women ceased. As if he could feel the child's moves better in silence, Hori thought. His hand lay on the barely protruding belly of Nofrethenut, the second wife of the pharaoh. Indeed the calm felt soothing. His fingers found the child's head in the womb, but he sensed no movements of the limbs. After trying in vain for a while, fear grabbed him. He could only hope the gods hadn't cut off the child's breath of life even before it was born. They should have called Nakhtmin, who understood how to peer beneath the skin much better than he did. The pharaoh longed for a son and heir to the Horus throne after Queen Sherit suffered a miscarriage recently. Losing this child would be awful enough, but if his suspicions were correct, the mother was in serious danger. "When did you last sense life in your womb?" he asked.

Nofrethenut closed her eyes and wrinkled her forehead. "I-I'm not sure. Three days?" Her lids snapped open, and she scrutinized him as if he could answer the question.

Hori sighed. This was the second wife's first pregnancy, so she was still inexperienced and therefore scared. Several times he and Nakhtmin had been summoned by nervous palace servants during the last few weeks to check on the queen. As the lowest among the personal physicians of the pharaoh, they were in charge of medical services in the House of Women. Serving as midwives wasn't part of their responsibilities, but in this case Hori was happy to indulge his king. Although Senusret was still young and would surely sire many sons, his loins had so far only produced daughters, while a Horus in the nest would allow the Two Lands to breathe a sigh of relief.

During their previous visits, Nakhtmin and he had always been able to put the expectant mother at ease—and the no-less agitated royal father as well. Calling to Bes, patron of pregnant women, he prayed he wouldn't have to break sad news to the pharaoh. A draft of air pushed through the high ventilation slits and moved the fine gauzy linen hanging from the ceiling around the queen's bed to keep her sleep untroubled by insects. On the breeze wafted the heavy scent of flowers from the royal garden, mixed with the odor of mud drying in the sun, so typical for the season when the river retreated from its banks. It smelled so different, mustier than the fresh Nile mud covering the fields after the season of inundation. All of a sudden he saw the image of a rotting fruit in the mother's womb, which reminded him of the events six months ago. Rotten fruits… Thinking of the child sired in shame with the woman whose name must not be mentioned sent a shiver down his back. However, Senusret dearly loved his fourth daughter despite her ancestry. A beautiful child, but those eyes… There, a flutter. Was that—? No. *Get a grip!* He scolded his heart pounding so hard his fingers throbbed. He had to concentrate on the expectant mother. Maybe he should really call for his friend with the magic hands.

Sensing the women staring at him, he wished they'd leave him alone with his patient. He jerked up to wave them outside and startled one of the maids, still half a child, enough to drop the tablet with refreshments. The clatter set his teeth on edge, but before he could upbraid her, he felt a distinct twitch under his hand. The child lived! Relieved, he burst into laughter. "The little prince had only been napping. Thanks to you, he's now awake and kicking."

Visibly embarrassed, the serving girl picked up the shards.

Queen Sherit let out the breath she'd been holding. "This time you won't get punished, Anat, but you are too easily scared and need to get over that. And now, off with you all!" She gestured for concubines and servants to leave. When Hori was alone with both royal wives, she lowered her head apologetically. "Once again, I've sent for you without cause."

Hori rose from his crouch and smoothed his starched shendyt with one hand. "It's always an honor to serve your majesties." Ouch, that sounded more like he found it an unpleasant duty! He quickly plastered that smile on his face that he knew to melt women's hearts like an ointment cone in the sun. "And of course, it's always a joy for my eyes to cherish your beauty."

Nofrethenut slapped a hand over her mouth and giggled. Quick to forget the fear she'd suffered, she turned back into the young, untroubled woman he knew and whose girlishness hadn't been dampened by two years of marriage to the ruler of the Two Lands. Queen Sherit, significantly older than she and their husband, mockingly lifted her eyebrows, then her gaze wandered to the dates scattered on the floor, some lying in the puddle of palm wine mixed with the remaining shards. "Should I send for something else to eat?"

Hori shook his head. "It'll be dark soon, and I'm tired. I'll just tell the pharaoh all is well with his heir, then return to my estate."

The walk back home didn't take long. His stately property was set in the quarter for officials near the palace. On a whim, he didn't pass through the gate but instead followed the wall to the riverbank, where the dull scent of mud filled his nose. Above the western mountains, the first stars twinkled, and Hori turned toward the city to see if the moon had appeared in the sky already. No, only torches and cooking fires on the roofs illuminated the darkness encroaching swiftly now. Some of the flames seemed to float in the gloom. "Magical," he murmured and shuddered. The power of magic was something he'd learned to fear since his apprenticeship at the weryt, the embalming compound. What was the matter with him today? Why couldn't he shake off the sense of impending doom? He'd been able to reassure the pharaoh but not his own heart. He slipped out of his rush sandals and slid around the end of the wall shielding his property from uninvited visitors all the way down to the riverbank. Around this time of the year, the water level was so low that he reached his garden on almost dry feet. As soon as he left the reeds on the bank behind and felt the gravelly path under his feet, he brushed off the mud and slipped back into his sandals. His servants wouldn't appreciate him smudging the floor in the hall decorated with paintings. His servants… He still hadn't adjusted to having his own considerable household, sometimes a blessing, other times a cumbersome responsibility. His personal servant Sheser, always concerned with a respectable appearance befitting his position, would disapprovingly click his tongue when he saw him. His maid Heqet, however… Hori smiled. The girl readily sweetened his lonely nights. He'd ask her to join him tonight.

Leisurely he ambled toward the lights shining from his house when a whistle from beyond the garden wall made him halt. He approached. "Nakhtmin?"

"Who else?" came the response muffled by the bricks between them.

Had his friend been waiting for his return? Hori groped for the wooden wicket, opened it and stepped through. "I thought you two spent the evening with Ameny." When Nakhtmin's father-in-law invited them, they usually stayed out much longer than dusk. Slowly, he could discern his friend's frame, and now the moon cast pale light into the garden.

The shadows around Nakhtmin's mouth fled from his broad grin into the web of crinkles forming around the corners of his eyes. "Muti is unwell…"

Hori needed a moment to catch on, then gently punched his side. "Well, well, you didn't lose much time. Barley or emmer?"

"Barley." Nakhtmin beamed even brighter. "Let's walk."

One didn't need to be a physician to perform this simple test. If a woman believed she was pregnant, she only had to wet two little sacks of grain with her urine every morning, keeping in one sack barley and in the other emmer. If the grain sprouted, the woman was expecting, and even the gender of the child could be determined, depending on which grains germinated first. Mutnofret would bear him a son.

"Congratulations. Have you told Ameny yet?" He felt rather than saw Nakhtmin's head shake and disturb air as he strolled beside him.

"No, he worries too much, as you know. Where've you been?"

Hori snorted. "Another emergency call from the palace. This time I also feared something might be wrong. The queen hadn't felt the child move for a few days." Falling silent, he imagined to hear Nakhtmin's thoughts as an echo of his own.

"Took her a long time to get pregnant," murmured his friend at last. "Over two years."

The knowledge that women who didn't conceive easily often had problems carrying the child to term hung between them unspoken. Hori picked a blossom from a bush and deeply inhaled the sweet fragrance—jasmine. "Anyway, all was well. A bang woke the little prince."

Nakhtmin laughed halfheartedly. "I'll ask Ameny to make an especially powerful amulet for her. Maybe with a blessing from Amun's wife Mut?"

Another amulet—Hori would rather do more than that. The protection of the gods was important but might not suffice if Nofrethenut's body couldn't bring the fruit of her womb to maturity. However, he couldn't do more than give the queen strengthening potions and enemas to cleanse the metu, the vessels in her body, from deposits of disease. "At least it should reassure her and soothe her fears that might burden the heart of the unborn. May the gods spread their protective wings over the Horus in the egg." Ahead, the contours of Nakhtmin's estate loomed in the darkness. Hori hadn't paid any attention to where they were heading.

"I have a jar of oasis wine stored in my pantry," Nakhtmin announced. "Let's forget those dire thoughts and drink to my son."

Eager to shake off the gloomy mood, Hori nodded.

Quite some time later, when he stumbled into his bedroom, he remembered wanting Heqet to share his bed. But no, he didn't need her tonight.

A booming headache woke Nakhtmin, and he remembered how he and Hori had emptied the jar to the last drop of wine. He scrunched up his face. His tongue, dry and furry, tasted something unpleasant in his mouth. An earthen mug stood on the little table with ivory inlays. He grabbed it with one hand and gulped fresh water. That helped some. Fortunately, Muti still slumbered. She was always frighteningly chipper in the morning, while he, even under normal circumstances, needed some time to shake off sleep. If only there were a potion to wake him up in one fell swoop. As he struggled from his bed and straightened, his head ached even worse. The doorjamb had to serve as support. No sunlight filtered through the ventilation slits catching the northern winds. Good thing, too, because bright light would only hurt his eyes. Dawn approached though.

Groaning, he shuffled down the hallway to the privy. Relieving himself, he heard a door bang and steps padding in the corridor—too heavy for Muti, had to be the cook. If Baketamun was up and about, her husband Inti would be, too. The thought of cold water on his skin drew a languorous moan from Nakhtmin. The bathroom was probably what he most enjoyed in his new house. Every morning, Inti showered him with cold water, shaved his beard and scalp hair off and, if time permitted, massaged him. Yes, that would chase away his headache. He went downstairs.

"Today your weekly visit to the House of Life is due, master. I'm supposed to remind you to pick up some medicine for the sore udder of our goat."

Nakhtmin jerked up. "What?" On the bench under Inti's experienced hands, he'd dozed off again. Slowly the servant's words sank into his hazy mind. "Oh right. I'll remember."

Some of his medical colleagues knew how to make salves and lotions for sick animals. In the end, healing livestock wasn't much different from curing human beings. A broken bone always needed splinting. And didn't animals also have a ka and ba? The heavenly realms were surely inhabited by manifold creatures, or else they'd be rather barren. His thoughts began to blur over these questions. Hori. Hori would know if animals needed mummification to pass the Judgment of the Dead. A name…the animal needed a n…

"Master? You should hurry if you mean to attend the last part of the morning hymn to Amun."

Lifting his numb head, Nakhtmin noticed a patch of spittle on the bench. Embarrassed he wiped his mouth and cheek. He must have fallen asleep again. A stonemason seemed to sit in his head, clobbering his skull with a hammer. Nothing for it but to cure himself at the House of Life before he'd be able to help anyone else. Groaning, he heaved himself from the bench and groped for the wall, while Inti wrapped the shendyt around his hips, hissing in disapproval. The starched linen crackled as he smoothed it. Inti handed him his wig, but Nakhtmin shook his head—which he immediately regretted. No, today he didn't need any additional pressure on his skull. A splendid collar with pearls of turquoise, lapis lazuli and carnelian completed his outfit. Muti was still sleeping when he wanted to say goodbye. Pregnancy was already taking its toll, so he gently kissed her. In the dining room, he ate only some fruit and gulped down more water before he slipped into his sandals and headed off.

The cooling breeze from the Nile woke him up some more. He didn't have to walk far until he turned into the boulevard leading to the Amun temple. The first rays of Ra dipped the human heads of sphinxes lining the road in a rosy glow. The shadows were still long, and under the mighty pylon, darkness enveloped him. In stark contrast, the tip of the obelisk in the middle of the temple courtyard glistened. Senusret's ancestor, Senusret I, had it erected and the tip coated with electrum to reflect the glory and power of sun god Amun-Ra. As wab priest, Nakhtmin also knew that the course of the pointy stone needle's shadow symbolized Amun-Ras daily journey across the sky in his sun bark.

He crossed the courtyard and entered the temple. From its sanctum sanctorum the morning hymns sounded. Every day the first prophet of Amun greeted the god with this solemn chant, which always filled Nakhtmin with a sense of peace and hope. As a priest of the lowest order, he wasn't allowed to enter the sanctum sanctorum, of course, only the four prophets of the god were, and the high-ranking priests who washed Amun's statue after prayers and anointed it with precious oils before clothing it in finest linen and offering the god nourishment and drink. Nakhtmin leaned against one of the richly illustrated columns and let the sounds permeate him. Via a sophisticated system of openings in the upper part of the shrine wall, they filtered unobstructed into the hall and weaved their way between the supports to the ears of the devout.

He wasn't the only physician listening to the hymns this morning. Looking around, he spotted Weni among the attendants. They had trained together, so he nodded at him. As expected, his former friend averted his gaze. Weni giving false testimony against Hori last year stood between them, and probably envy, too. The fellow had always looked down on Nakhtmin because of his lowly origins, and now he likely resented him for his assignment as one of the pharaoh's personal physicians. At least Nakhtmin liked to think so but had to admit—at least to himself—he still felt out of place in this incredibly elevated position, which the pharaoh—life, prosperity and health—had bestowed on him. For that reason he returned to the House of Life once a week to treat the poor although he didn't need to any longer. The times when the head physician could order him to cure no one but those who had only meager compensation to offer for his work were long past. He'd hardly known how to survive back then. Now he regarded his service for the paupers as a sacrifice born of gratitude, because the poor boy from small town Khenmet-Min in Upper Egypt he'd once been now wore fine linen and was allowed to touch the pharaoh.

Weni turned and left. The slapping of his sandals echoed from the walls. Only then did Nakhtmin realize the singing had ended. All around him, the starched shendyts of more priests—wabu and hemu-netjer—swished as they headed to their various tasks. The wabu conducted the lowliest services in the temple, kept the premises clean and looked after the needs of the hemu-netjer priests, from whose ranks the pharaoh selected the four prophets of a god. The rank of wab was also required to study at the House of Life to become a physician, scribe or cleric of the higher ranks. Two priests, deep in conversation about storing sacrificial offerings, passed without paying him any attention.

The first high-ranking hemu-netjer ambled from the corridor leading to the sanctum sanctorum. Obviously the morning ritual had been completed. Bowing and stretching out his arms at knee-level, Nakhtmin looked for the tails of the leopard furs distinguishing their wearers as prophets. His father-in-law was one of them, and he suddenly felt the urge to tell him the wonderful news of Muti's pregnancy. He remained bent over in his uncomfortable pose until all hemu-netjer had passed, none of them flaunting a leopard's tail. The prophets must have taken a different way. His head throbbed again, and when he straightened, he felt dizzy. He shouldn't quaff so much wine in the future, no matter how much fun it was to drink himself silly with Hori.

Leaving the temple, he passed a priest who seemed deep in ardent prayer. Or was he waiting for something? Maybe he hadn't noticed the ritual ending. Well, the principal would make him scurry to his tasks if he caught him. Prayers were for people, priests had to provide for the gods. Nakhtmin smirked as he imagined tat Hemunu letting his stick dance all over the poor guy's back. A piercing pain in his temple dealt him well deserved punishment for his gloating. High time for that potion of willow bark with a pinch of poppy seeds. That should do the trick.

A little while later Nakhtmin's head was cured, and his brooding mood evaporated. While tending to his patients, he completely focused on their ailments. After a couple of hours, he thought of his father-in-law for the first time again and decided to postpone the announcement of Muti's state to another day. His beloved probably wanted to be there when her parents received the news, and upsetting her was not something he liked to risk.

A Mystery

During Nakhtmin's visits in the House of Life, Hori missed his company. "I'm glad you're back," he welcomed his friend and playfully punched him. "How much longer are you intending to serve in the House of Life? Nobody demands it from you."

After entering the palace through the double gate, they directed their steps toward the House of Women. Nakhtmin cast him a surprised glance. "You're going to the weryt once a month for a few days to tend to patients and practice your secret arts there."

Always that snappy tone when he talked about the embalming hall! Was Nakhtmin's volunteer work really comparable to his visits there? "No, that's something completely different. Those *secret arts*, as you like to call them, benefit me as a physician. And you know I can't tell you more." In addition he felt obliged to Kheper, the man who'd become more of a father to him than his real one. Nakhtmin wouldn't understand. After losing his family at a young age, he'd found affectionate substitute parents in Ameny and his wife Isis and led a happy marriage with Mutnofret. Hori didn't feel like quarreling, so he kept his mouth shut.

Right on cue, his brother Teti headed toward them. He too had profited from Hori's adventures last year when his majesty appointed him as treasurer. His gratitude hadn't lasted long though.

"Greetings, brother," Hori said and stopped. Nakhtmin followed suit.

"Hori...?" Teti pushed past them. He had not only gained in dignity but obesity as well.

Hori pressed his lips together. Some things never changed. "All well at home?"

Teti grunted noncommittally.

"Remember me to Mother. And Father..." he called after his fleeing brother's back.

"You should visit your parents occasionally," Nakhtmin stated. "Then you'd know how they-"

Irritated, Hori interrupted him and said what he should've left unspoken for good reason. "What do you know? You with your wife and soon a ch..." Already regretting his words, he caught himself. "Wait! I'm sorry. I didn't mean it the way it sounded. I just wish I had what you have."

Nakhtmin had already rounded the next corner, his gait rather stiff. Tears burned in Hori's eyes. His wallowing in self-pity was really pathetic. His brother was a coldhearted scumbag, but he shouldn't have vented his anger on Nakhtmin, who could be fairly touchy. And he'd been looking forward to their cooperation today! He stormed around the corner and with full force bumped into a man hurrying in his direction.

While Hori rubbed his forehead, the man, whose wig and insignia marked him as a palace messenger, started ranting, "What's wrong with you? Can't you pay attention?" He groaned and also touched his forehead.

Hori felt like he was gazing at his reflection in a pond's surface. "Pardon me," he mumbled. "Let me see the damage. I'm a physician."

The messenger dropped his hand. "Oh. Maybe you can indeed help me. I'm looking for the healer Hori, son of Sobekemhat."

"You've found him." Hori's fingers felt the light swelling above the man's left eyebrow. "Nothing serious, only a lump. I can make a potion to ease the headache if it starts hurting."

"Thank you!" A smile crossed the man's features and fled just as quickly. "Unfortunately, you won't have time for that. My orders are to take you to the pharaoh—life, prosperity and health." His arm stretched out in the direction Hori had come from, the man set off.

"Wait!" Hori called. "Only me, not the physician Nakhtmin as well?"

The messenger stopped and turned his head. "Only you. Now, come on."

The man really was in a hurry to fulfill his orders, What could be so urgent? For a moment he thought to discern a flicker of tear in his eyes. "Um, I'd like to tell someone where I'm off to since I'm expected to take care of my duties."

Even the back of the man radiated anger. Without answering, he marched on. Reluctantly, Hori stomped after him. Really a shame that he had to leave the quarrel with Nakhtmin unresolved. His friend would chew on the insult the whole time like a dog on a bone and not feel any more placid later than he did now. And his leaving without notifying anyone of his absence wouldn't assuage Nakhtmin either, but what could he do? Refuse the king allegiance?

Without hesitating once, the messenger led him through the palace labyrinth. Hori didn't even know half of it and still got lost easily in those corridors with numerous doors leading to offices of the administrators of the Two Lands: tax and province administration, scribes, archive, treasury and much more, not to mention storage rooms and workshops belonging to the royal household. Who could say what was located where from the top of their heads? The Great House was a town within Itj-tawy. However, when he deciphered the label tjati, vizier, on one door they passed, he knew they were getting close to the heart of the Two Lands, the pharaoh's office. Hori turned his head, at the same time hoping and fearing the vizier's door would open because the highest official of Kemet was Sobekemhat, his father. Maybe he too had been summoned to the king. What issues could possibly require Hori's presence? He certainly wouldn't have to provide medical treatment, and he hadn't gotten into mischief. How that sounded—he wasn't a little rascal anymore in need of caning.

"There we are." The messenger opened the door at the front end of the corridor and dumped him like a delivery of straw. While Hori curiously peered into the antechamber, the man dashed away as if the monsters of the Duat chased after him.

Strange. He crossed the room to the gate where Senusret's secretary Atef stood. It was his duty to let you pass or refuse access to the king. However, there were no petitioners sitting on the benches, not even a messenger from one of the far districts of the Two Lands. Usually the king's antechamber swarmed with people, even foreigners, envoys of the desert tribes from faraway Retjenu or Kush. Where were all these people—or had someone chased them away?

Atef had already raised his hand to knock when it finally dawned on Hori who was awaiting him on the other side together with the pharaoh. He entered the simply furnished room, with which he was quite familiar by now, and bowed low before the king. From the corners of his eyes, he'd already spotted the other visitor, whose face showed the features of Anubis, the god of death. That explained the messenger's instant flight and the empty antechamber. The head of the weryt rarely entered the realm of the living, and if he did, he wore the mask of the jackal. The sight of him frightened people in the Two Lands since it felt like encountering the actual god of death.

"Rise and sit down, Hori," Senusret prompted.

"I greet the Strong Bull of Egypt, and you, Hut-Nefer." He pulled up the chair, while questions spun in his mind. What caused the mer-ut to leave the necropolis? Something must have happened in the embalming compound, something serious, or else a message would have sufficed. A disease? A major accident? "Are my medical skills needed at the House of Death?" he burst out, unable to rein in his curiosity any longer.

The king knitted his eyebrows reproachfully.

"It is not the physician Hori we seek, and neither the embalmer Hori," droned Hut-Nefer's deep voice from the mask.

"No?" More questions flared up in his heart.

Senusret seemed tense when he spoke, "An event of immense consequences brings the head of the weryt here. You appear to be the only one able to resolve the mystery."

"What mystery?"

Hut-Nefer cleared his throat in discomfort. "In one of the jars, in which we place the organs of the departed in natron, were two hearts."

"Oh." Baffled, Hori didn't know what to say, then searched for explanations. "A blunder? Did one of the utu put it in the wrong jar?" While he said this, he realized such a mistake was impossible. A hissing snort from the mask confirmed it. Hori knew the workflow of embalming well. Every ut placed the jars with their hieroglyph labels for lung, liver, stomach, intestines beside their table to have them ready before performing the abdominal cut and removing the organs. And with each deceased they started from scratch. After covering the body parts in dehydrating salt, they sealed the jars. Labels with the deceased's name prevented the containers getting mixed up. Therefore, if someone had placed a second heart in the same vessel, the corpse either had two hearts—quite unlikely—or somebody had messed with the jar afterward and sealed it again. Only someone within the strongly shielded weryt could have done that. "Why should anybody do something like that on purpose?" He looked at the two men's faces.

The pharaoh and the head of the weryt had remained silent, probably to let Hori figure things out for himself. Now Hut-Nefer rose and walked a few paces. "That, my dear Hori, is exactly the question. Why should anyone do this?"

"But...there must be a body lacking its heart."

Senusret interrupted. "Before you speak about secrets not even my royal ears may hear, I'll leave you alone." He rose.

"Your majesty..." Hut-Nefer bowed.

The king left the room through a side exit leading to the palace garden as Hori knew. He'd have loved to get some fresh air, too, as the chamber was rather stuffy, and Hut-Nefer emanated the odor of death. The pharaoh surrendering his own office! Only now did he fully realize the seriousness of the matter at hand. This wasn't just about sloppy work.

The mer-ut leaned both arms onto the table and lowered the jackal mask over Hori in a threatening fashion. "The heart entered the weryt alone, without the body in which it once beat, and nobody knows how this could have happened. Every ut has been questioned, even the lector priests. Errors happen, certainly, but everybody within the walls of the weryt knows how important the correct process is. Had someone forgotten to place the heart of a deceased into the respective jar, he would have noticed before finishing work on the corpse and fixed his error in the only appropriate way. No, we need to suspect an intentional act here. Only I can't think of any reason motivating such a deed."

Somebody must have brought a heart into the embalming compound, but that was impossible because nobody from the world of the living was allowed to pass through the gates of the weryt, except the mer-ut and…Hori since last year. Nobody living there received permission to leave the premises except to attend the funeral procession of a relative and that only under strict observation. Hori had made that sorrowful experience last year. Oh, wait! *He* had found a way out… Feeling guilty, he lowered his gaze. "The canal."

The mer-ut slowly shook his head. "After we learned about your loop hole, the king and I immediately ordered guards to patrol outside the walls at night."

Poor guys! With trepidation, he remembered the horror often besetting him during his nightly excursions. The western desert was the realm of the dead, and the shadows of the ostracized and the damned haunted them. He wouldn't spend one night there voluntarily. Maybe the guards had neglected their duties so that somebody managed to dive under the wall. However, only a handful of people knew about this route. Except for those present, only the king, Ameny and Nakhtmin. None of them would do something so terrible. "Then the heart must belong to someone who had been living in the weryt and died," he mused.

The jackal's snout jerked around to him. "Impossible. Nobody's missing. Don't you think that would have been my first guess?"

Hori ducked under the booming reproach. "What exactly do you expect of me?" The mystery seemed unsolvable to him.

"Return to the weryt as if you meant to perform your usual duty. Find out who brought the heart to us and to whom it belonged. You know what happens if the deceased faces Judgment of the Dead without a heart."

Hori gulped. "No afterlife."

Solemnly the pointy snout moved up and down. "We owe the departed to prevent this. You go today. Right now."

Nakhtmin slammed the gate to his estate harder than he intended. The bang didn't ease his still simmering anger at Hori. Night had fallen awhile ago, prone to happen when you had to take over the responsibilities of someone who lazed about— or whatever Hori had done all day. First he begrudged him his luck, then he deserted him. By Seth's balls, what was wrong with his friend all of a sudden?

Inti hurried toward him. "Welcome home, master. Do you need my services tonight?"

Exhausted, Nakhtmin wiped his face and rubbed the spot above the root of his nose with his thumb. "Has your wife reserved a meal for me?"

"Of course."

Yeah, of course, Nakhtmin thought. They were used to him coming home late. A doctor's fate. Nevertheless, guilt nagged at him. He should at least have warned Muti that he'd return quite so late. Since noon he'd known Hori wouldn't lift a finger to help today. And he'd even covered for him by taking care of his patients. If the king found out how he behaved today... No, he wasn't so mean as to tell on his friend. But he needed to have a serious chat with him.

He climbed the stairs to the roof of his house, where Muti and he liked to eat and sometimes sleep during the hot season. From the servants' wing wafted the smell of the dying fire on which Baketamun had cooked their meal. Just now, she and Inti stretched out on the reed mats over there.

Up here, the air was fresher and cooler than in the rooms of bricks, which stored the heat of the day. In the moonlight, he navigated toward the small table, where the leftovers of today's dinner awaited him, covered with a fine cloth.

"A long day, my husband?" Mutnofret's delicate frame rose from her mat. Had she been sleeping or still waiting for him?

Nakhtmin embraced her, then settled on a stool and sighed. "Muti. I was hoping you'd keep me company." He took her hand and pressed it against his cheek.

She lifted the cloth, and enticing fragrances rose. He felt immense hunger, but before he dug in, he told her about the fight with Hori.

Looking confused, she shook her head. "That's not like him. His heart never seems filled with envy because others found happiness." She sat across from him.

Nakhtmin snorted. "Oh yes, there sure are shadows on his heart; I've encountered them before. And he could have any woman he wanted! Only needs to snap his fingers." His voice trailed off. Hori never had to work hard for anything—unlike himself. On top of that, the guy looked brazenly attractive and had a lot more self-confidence than he did. No wonder, since he came from a high-ranking family.

"Don't tell me you envy him although I picked *you*?"

He laughed. "Never." Snarky Muti as he knew her. She was right though. He quickly suppressed his fit of self-pity. "You haven't seen him today?"

"How could I?" She playfully pinched his arm. "Since he was in the palace with you, my overly clever husband." He wanted to counter that Hori had absconded, but Muti continued, "Oh, that reminds me, there's been a message delivered for you. Should still be downstairs. I'll fetch it real quick." She stood, and her dress rustled ever so gently in the night breeze.

The linen was so fine, the moonlight penetrated the fabric and outlined the contours of her body. All of a sudden he only felt appetite for one thing. "Wait." His voice sounded coarse with desire, and he grabbed her.

Pushing his stool away from the table, he drew her onto his lap and kissed her greedily. Not long and Muti had the knot of his belt untied. The length of cloth slid from his hips and exposed his erection. With relish, Muti straddled him. They didn't make it to their bedroom that night.

Having breakfast in the garden, so as not to disturb Muti's slumber, Nakhtmin remembered the message she'd mentioned and asked Inti to fetch it for him. Oh, with an official seal! Struck with horror, he realized this could be important. What if he'd neglected his duties while playing with his wife? However, as soon as he broke the seal, he recognized Hori's writing and frowned indignantly.

"To Nakhtmin, his majesty's personal physician, from Hori, who is his friend. May no shadow darken our friendship. His majesty—life, prosperity and health—has ordered me to the weryt for some time. Health and welfare to you and your wife."

Nakhtmin lowered the note, then read it again without really grasping its meaning. Was that an apology? Almost sounded like one. And it seemed like he didn't show up to perform his duties because the pharaoh summoned him. But since when did Senusret send him to the weryt? Hori went there of his own free will, unlike back when the king sentenced him to serve the dead. Still, he had to remain silent about that mysterious world in the realm of the dead. Anger rose like bile. And now even more secrecy?

When Mutnofret showed her sleepy face, he handed her the letter.

"There you go," she said.

"Yeah, I see. And I still don't understand. But I guess that explains why he disappeared yesterday, and I had to take on all his patients. I wonder what this means though."

"I guess we'll never find out." Muti made a pompous face and imitated Hori's voice, which sometimes did sound a bit bumptious. "You know very well, what happens in the weryt..."

He burst into laughter. "...stays in the weryt, yeah, yeah."

"You think he remembered to let his servants know? I better send Inti over."

"How do you do that, think of everything for everyone?" With affection, he gazed at her and realized what incredible luck he had.

"Years of experience with male negligence." She grinned.

On the way to the palace, he braced himself for once again carrying Hori's burden as well as his own, while the guy visited old friends. Feeling the sting of jealousy in his heart, he couldn't pull it out. While Hori tarried behind the walls of the weryt, he remained locked out. Furtively, he shook his fist toward the west. Hopefully he'd return soon.

RETURN TO THE DEAD

Day 6 of month Ipet-hemet in Shemu, the season of the harvest

The same blue sky as always arched above Hori, nevertheless he woke in a different sphere. Unnecessarily, Kheper's snoring reminded him of that fact. Glad to be staying with his former instructor again, he appreciated even more that Kheper's daughter Nut was now living with her husband a few houses down the lane. Hori used to feel a little uncomfortable here, knowing the ut hoped he'd become his son-in-law. Fortunately, he'd given up the idea when Hori was allowed to leave the weryt. Deep in thought, he regarded the bald head of the old man on the cot beside him and sat up.

Kheper always seemed to enjoy having him although something stood between them now, his being different. He was only a visitor these days, welcome to stay but soon to leave again. Not someone to whom a man passed his knowledge, like to a son. The ut didn't let him feel his disappointment, though. Sobekemhat, on the other hand, never held back with his because Hori hadn't followed the path his father had envisioned for him.

He tore a piece from the interior of the flatbread, which had only been covered with cloth overnight, so it wasn't very soft and juicy anymore. No matter, with a sip of water it slid down his throat just fine. A buzzing fly settled on Kheper's head and explored the shiny surface that no longer required shaving. Merely a thin crown of stubble, more gray than black, had grown overnight. The lids of the sleeper twitched. While the fly crossed the vast barrenness of Kheper's forehead, Hori fingered his own scalp, which was anything but clean-shaven. Yesterday, he'd skipped that part of body care and only slapped on his wig. Today, he'd need to diligently remove every hair on his body before he commenced his services for the dead, or else evil spirits might cling to them and bring death and decay for the living.

The fly had reached his nose, and Kheper slapped at it. "Mh?" Groggily, he sat up. "Oh, oh dear! Why didn't you wake me?"

"I only woke up just now, too."

They'd celebrated his arrival yesterday with beer—and the jug of date wine Hori had swiped at the palace. Kheper wasn't used to staying up late, and likely his head punished him for drinking so much sweet wine, which they rarely received at the weryt.

"You must have forgotten when an ut starts his daily work, you lazybones," Kheper grumbled and tripped over his own feet as he dressed.

Hori grinned. "Wait, I'll get something for your headache."

"Pah, I don't need anything but water. And you better hurry to the ibu." His gaze slid over Hori's hairy legs. "You'll need a long time to get ready. By then Ra's bark will be high up in the sky."

He ushered Hori down the stairs and out of the house. In a trot they hurried to the cleansing hall for the embalmers, which they jokingly called ibu, like the tent for washing corpses. Out of breath, Hori submitted to the skilled hands of a servant and cursed to himself because he had to waste time on regular work with the utu instead of trying to shed some light on the mystery of the surplus heart. Hut-

Nefer'd forbidden him to tell anybody, not even Kheper, why he was here since currently everybody was a possible suspect. But where should he begin? On the one hand, the men would talk more freely with him if they didn't know about his mission, on the other hand, work on the dead bodies was a lonely task. During the day, only the monotone singing of the lector priests filled the silence and the occasional hammering when an ut opened a skull through the nose to remove the gray matter. Either way, chatting with the utu and heriu-heb wasn't an option before the evening. Unfortunately, his last visit to the weryt had only been a week ago, and since then no one else had fallen sick, nobody needed a doctor. As soon as he had the first deceased on the table, the needs of his work distracted him from fruitless brooding, and he rediscovered the excitement he always felt when he was allowed to explore the mysteries inside a corpse with his hands.

In the evening, Hori listened to the men's voices in the ibu, while they all rubbed the grime from their bodies, first with sand, then cold water and some foaming stuff the utu's wives made by cooking oil mixed with potash. He should ask Nut to show him how exactly they created it. Although the substance burned horribly when it got in contact with open wounds, it also seemed to have a healing capacity. At least injuries treated that way rarely got infected or not as badly. However, the stuff smelled pretty bad, so he should talk to Mutnofret if that could be helped with perfume oils.

Hearing the word 'heart' made him prick his ears. What were those guys over there talking about? Hori blinked water from his eyes. Oh, two brothers chatted about a dalliance of the younger one. Hori turned away and once again concentrated on cleaning himself. Hut-Nefer had told him young Hornakht had found the heart, and he lived with his wife in the house right next to Kheper's. Since they were both about the same age, he'd become friends with the ut during the last few months, therefore it wouldn't raise any suspicions if he visited him. Yes, that was a good plan. He dried himself and looked for Kheper, who stood outside on the square before the ibu gabbing with some men his own age.

"Ah, there you are. About time," he called from afar and released his cackling laughter.

Hori joined him. "Hey, do you mind if I pop over to Hornakht tonight for a little chat?"

To his relief, Kheper showed no sign of disappointment. "Oh no, not at all. Nut has invited her old father for dinner, anyway. I was planning to take you along, but you know how women are. First they act as if an unannounced guest was no problem at all, and then they fuss around all evening and don't sit still for one moment until everybody feels uncomfortable." He winked with mischief.

Hori's heart warmed because the old man was so uncomplicated. "Yes, that's how women are. I'm sure Hornakht's wife will also twirl around. Where's the scoundrel? Hey, Hornakht, there you are."

With a wide grin on his face, the lanky fellow ambled over. "Hori! I thought I'd seen your egg head this morning on Kheper's roof."

"I even waved to you, but as always you only had eyes for Amaunet's beauty," Hori retorted. "Would it inconvenience your lovely wife if I dropped by your place for a mug of beer? The old man here is going to eat with his daughter, and my presence might confuse her too much since she just got married."

Kheper bleated like a goat. "I'll tell her that!"

Hori acted appalled. "No, don't do it!" His heart soared, though. Now he felt at home again.

Hornakht linked arms with him and pulled him away. "Hey, you'll join us for dinner, not just a mug of beer. I bet the old billy goat only has dry bread in his pantry."

"Billy goat? I heard that!" Kheper's voice trailed after them.

When Nakhtmin went about his duty in the House of Women that day, a colleague joined him.

"Tep-Ta!" he called in surprise.

The corners of the short physician's mouth drooped even more. Oh no, Nakhtmin didn't even know his real name. Everyone just called him Tep-Ta, head to the earth because of his small size and because he tried to make up for his lack of height by currying favor with his superiors.

"The imi-ra has ordered me to the House of Women during Hori's absence," he rasped. "As your senior, I'll tend to the queens and high-ranking concubines, of course."

"As you wish." Just great! Couldn't the head of the palace physicians choose someone other than this bumptious gnome who thought it beneath him to treat lowly patients? With Hori he could work together, but with this guy, they'd likely work against each other. Unfortunately, there was a strict hierarchy, depending on years of service. Dear gods! If the king himself had informed the imi-ra about Hori's absence, he'd probably stay away for longer than just a week. Nakhtmin's anger over his friend's disappearance paled as his curiosity about the extraordinary circumstances that caused such an arrangement grew.

While Tep-Ta walked through the door leading to the queens' chambers, Nakhtmin took care of the little aches and pains of the other women. Not for the first time did he notice how quiet it was without his friend around. The old Tefnut, whose professed darling Hori was, didn't even show up. Funny how Hori's absence cured her rheumatic pains better than his skilled hands. Nakhtmin grinned to himself.

"You should smile more often," said the girl, whose wounded knee he'd just bandaged. "It suits you."

Surprised, he looked up at the pretty wench with the dark skin of the Kushites, of which much was exposed. The straps of her dress had shifted so that the nipples of her full and firm breasts peaked out. Had she done that on purpose? Her foot resting in his lap answered his question by rubbing against his groin with the desired result. "Oh, um…" Flushing, he peered at the open door. Hopefully, nobody had seen that. He was a married man, after all. Brusquely he rose and dropped the injured leg.

Poor thing. He couldn't hold it against her that she tried. The king might never select her as companion for even one night. There were too many beautiful women here, and Senusret preferred the company of his two queens. Nakhtmin, though, would get in serious trouble if caught giving her that kind of pleasure… After all, every child born in the royal harem was a prince or princess and potentially could ascend the Horus throne someday if the pharaoh's wives didn't give birth to daughters *and* sons. The king must be able to rely on his physicians!

The remaining patients he treated swiftly. Nothing serious, and most ailments were caused by idleness the ladies enjoyed in abundance. The fever of a little prince was the most dramatic case he had to deal with, but the boy was only growing teeth.

When Nakhtmin finished his day's labor, the sun stood high in the sky. For a moment, he wondered if he should check in with the queens, but then the prospect of free time lured him. Tep-Ta wouldn't appreciate his interference anyway.

So he went to the royal bathhouse and let the servants cleanse him scrupulously. The cool water felt great! A muscular Kushite with skin as dark as eyeliner kneaded him thoroughly, then rubbed precious oils over his body. Nakhtmin moaned with contentment. Such a lifestyle sure had its benefits. Having taken care of his duties, he might as well drop by the temple of Amun. Yes, a good idea. Ameny would be happy if he picked him up, and they could stroll together to the mansion district.

He found Muti's father in the green shade of the temple gardens talking to a hem-netjer. Ameny noticed him from afar and waved. When Nakhtmin reached them, his father-in-law placed a hand on the priest's shoulder and said, "I'll weigh your suggestion in my heart. But you have to understand that I can't make this decision alone. For tomorrow evening, I've invited the prophets, as well as all the hemu-netjer of the highest order currently in the residence or able to travel the distance, to my house. You're among those, and I assume you'll attend?"

The priest beamed as if this invitation were extended only to him. "Of course!" He nodded at Nakhtmin and slipped away between two jasmine bushes.

Leaves rustled. The heavy scent of the blossoms filled Nakhtmin's nose. "Who was that, and what did he want?"

"Ah, never mind." Ameny waved dismissively. "That was Setka. He also wants to be considered as successor to the position of fourth prophet."

"Uh-huh. Um…how can he wish to take over someone else's place? What's up with Djedefra?"

"You haven't heard? The man was so clumsy as to have let a cobra bite him here in the garden, yesterday. He's still in sickbed but the doctors are certain he won't survive the night."

Nakhtmin searched the grass around them but found no trace of further poisonous reptiles. Just like it should be.

Ameny's eyes glazed over, and Nakhtmin guessed he remembered the snakes of the former vizier, whose name must never again be mentioned. The man had milked the reptiles and used the poison to kill young women attracting his son's attentions. "A cobra in the Holy Garden of Amun? Did the wabu neglect their duties?"

Ameny clenched his right hand in anger and slammed the fist into his left palm. "How should I know? He was only in office for a year. Do you know how much effort it takes to fill the position again?"

Nakhtmin had no idea, but Ameny probably didn't expect an answer.

"First the head of the hemu-netjer lists all the priests of the highest order, then we prophets check the applicants scrupulously and select the one we deem the best candidate. Naturally, we try to agree on one man to suggest to the pharaoh. After all, we'll have to work closely with him, and he'll get promoted to third prophet when one of us sets out on his journey to the Beautiful West."

That meant Djedefra's successor might become the first prophet of Amun someday and therefore the most powerful priest of the Two Lands. No wonder Setka tried to tip the scales in his favor. "Quite young for such an important office," Nakhtmin murmured.

"Pardon? Oh no, not at all. I was even younger when I was appointed. It's just…"

"What concerns you? Surely not the effort it takes?"

"No, but the timing. Have you seen Iriamun lately? He's been sick for quite awhile now, and I'm afraid he won't last much longer. Basically, I need to look for two worthy replacements, and the applicants are aware of it. Many try to shine in front of the prophets. That's…annoying."

Nakhtmin wouldn't enjoy such a situation either. Pensive, he stared over Ameny's shoulder at the trunk of the tamarind they stood under. "I see. When Iriamun dies, the pharaoh will make you his successor."

"That's custom." Ameny released a nervous laugh. "Although he could appoint someone else."

Nakhtmin shook his head. "He wouldn't do that, and why should he? And Duamutef will likely take over your position, and the fourth-"

"That's exactly my concern!" Ameny interrupted him. "Usually a prophet should get more time to learn the tasks he's supposed to take on. That's what his term as fourth is meant to serve for."

"Every man in Kemet must learn his trade first. No stonemason can mend a broken leg, nor a physician chisel a sculpture," Nakhtmin consented. By the gods, he sounded like the instruction of Dua-Kheti. That wouldn't help his father-in-law.

However Ameny didn't seem to have heard. "Which makes it even more essential to pick the right man. Who knows how much longer Iriamun will be among us?"

"And this Setka-" All of a sudden Nakhtmin remembered where he'd seen the man before: he was the fervently praying priest who hadn't even noticed the end of the morning ritual the other day. "Well, at least he's devotional," he finished the sentence in a different way than he had intended. "How many hemu-netjer operate in the temple?"

Ameny closed his eyes, and his lips moved ever so slightly. "Should be around three hundred," he finally replied.

"That many?" He hadn't expected such a large number.

"Don't forget the temple's assets. They manage those as well."

"Oh, of course." God Amun possessed rich domains spread out over all of Kemet. Fields needed plowing; droves of livestock needed to graze. The crops of those domains supported the priests, and the surplus was sold. Many people were necessary to monitor and supervise and finally to channel the gold into the treasure chambers of the god. "But three hundred? Are you going to host them all, tomorrow? Isis will be delighted."

"Hehehe, then two more hungry mouths won't draw any attention." Ameny seemed to relax. "Just in case you were asking whether you and Muti might dare to raid our pantry before the year ends."

Nakhtmin's cheeks burned with embarrassment. "Uhm, I..." Then he got a grip. "Fortunately, I no longer desperately depend on your supplies, worthy father. However, if the grasshoppers leave you destitute, we'll be happy to share ours with you." He winked, amused and rather proud of himself. Slowly, he'd shrug off the poor boy.

Ameny placed an arm around his shoulders. "You're not paying attention. I told you before that only a few priests of the highest order are under consideration. Hemiunu made a list of good men, but I don't see any of them as a prophet. For example, I'm not sure what to think of Setka. Maybe you and Muti could come over tomorrow because I value your knowledge of human nature. Now though, let's go home before Amun-Ra finishes his journey across the firmament, and our women will give us an earful because the meal has gone cold."

Nakhtmin nodded, pleased with the invitation. Then they could tell Muti's parents about her pregnancy. Not in front of the other guests, but they'd find an opportunity.

Hori rubbed his stomach and praised Amaunet's cooking.

She laughed. "Stop sweet-talking me. Since when do lentils and sour cream compare to the fine meals you must be used to?"

"Sometimes the simple pleasures are what a man's heart craves," Hori replied. Could his hosts even imagine what he usually ate? They only knew life within these walls. He could barely see over the capstones from the rooftop—and only if he straightened up. He hadn't lied, the food was really delicious, but he also didn't want to make his friends long for things forever out of their reach by talking about his life across the river.

"So, out with it, how come you've returned this soon? We didn't expect you for another two weeks." Hornakht stretched out on the rush mat, while Amaunet carried the dishes downstairs. "Bring us some of that nice beer, woman!" he called after her.

Hori had anticipated the question and told him the same as Kheper yesterday. "The pharaoh—life, prosperity and health—requires my presence during the heriu-renpet, so I can watch over the Horus in the egg."

The ut nodded. "An important task. During those days between the years, Sakhmet's messengers carry the plague through the Two Lands. Ah, here comes the beer. Thanks."

"I'll retreat to the bedchamber so my slumber won't disturb your chatter," Amaunet announced.

Hori burst into laughter. "Good night, oh most understanding of all wives." While Hornakht poured the beer through a sieve into a mug, he picked up the topic again that would hopefully gain him some insights. "So I had to reschedule my visit. Apart from that, someone needs to supervise you or you'll keep finding double hearts."

Hornakht lowered the jug and stared at him in bewilderment. "Who told you? That's not something to gossip about!"

"Whoa, easy. I've overheard some talk in the ibu. Everyone knows everything here, news spreads fast."

Hornakht released a nervous laugh. "Well, I'm sure you can imagine how surprised I was. I had sealed the vessel myself, and believe me, there was only one heart in it since the man didn't own more while he was alive."

"Then the seal must have been broken...?" Hori prompted.

"No." Hornakht propped his head on his elbow. "The seal was intact and applied correctly. The mer-ut examined it later. And it was my seal, easy to recognize because it has a small nick."

"So if the heart didn't miraculously reduplicate itself in the jar, only you can have—hey, calm down! There's another possibility: somebody could have stolen your seal."

Hornakht relaxed and sank back onto the mat. "No, it's still there, but anyone could have used it. I keep it under my table."

And the yard where the embalmers removed organs wasn't locked overnight. "Tut, how careless of you."

"Oh, come on, we all leave our seals there, you know that. Don't make me responsible for the mess."

"No, it rather looks as if someone wants you to get in trouble. Tell me on whose toes you stepped."

Hornakht sat up. "You know me, Hori. I'm an agreeable kind of guy. Nobody here holds a grudge against me."

"Sorry, stupid idea. I guess it was pure chance that the second heart turned up in one of your jars. So, whose organ is it? Is one of the dead lacking a heart? Did it grow legs overnight and search for a friend out of loneliness?" He cackled.

The ut squirmed in discomfort. "Hori...I don't want to keep talking about it, if you don't mind. You seem to find this rather amusing but I got into serious trouble. And no, none of the dead misses a heart. Where do you think you are?"

Oh dear, he'd addressed this in the completely wrong way. Usually, Hornakht looked on the bright side of things, but in a case like this, his sense of humor failed him. "I'm sorry, that was really inconsiderate of me." He changed topic but the good mood was ruined. Hori drained his beer and took leave. He wouldn't broach the subject with his friend again. All he'd learned here, Hut-Nefer could have told him, and he at least knew why Hori was snooping around.

Kheper hadn't returned yet, so he'd likely spend the night at Nut's place. Sighing, he unrolled the rush mat on the roof and blinked at the starry sky until his lids drooped.

He peered into the room, where the jars with the entrails were stored during the dehydration phase. There, what was that? The seals broke, the plugs rose. From all vessels, the organs crawled on tiny legs like those some hieroglyphs featured, and they scurried toward him. The intestines slithered over the floor like silvery white worms. Hori stepped aside and they poured out into the moonlight. They seemed to laugh and whisper to each other as if they were celebrating.

Jerking awake, he rubbed his eyes. What a dream! He turned around and glanced over the roof's edge, but of course there weren't any livers or intestines roaming the streets. Kheper's mat still lay rolled up on the floor. He was definitely staying out for the night. Alone in the house, Hori listened for sounds, but all remained silent in the weryt. Around this time of night, he used to risk his nightly excursions through the canal. Maybe he should check that route was definitely barred now. In the near future, he wouldn't get another chance to do so without drawing attention.

In the warm night air, he climbed down the ladder naked and left the house on bare feet. The slapping of sandals might give him away. From Kheper's domicile it took him only a few steps to reach the canal providing Nile water for the ibu. The thick wall towered ahead of him. Before he stepped into the canal, he looked around, but the alley was still deserted. He slid over the edge, immersed himself in the water for a moment, then he took a deep breath and pushed off with his toes to quickly dive through the opening. As always, fear of getting stuck befell him just before he reached the other side of the wall. The next moment, he felt the liberating sense of space above him and broke through the surface.

Gasping for air, he kept the putting and blowing to a minimum, in case the guard was close. He didn't feel like explaining what he was doing here. Cautious, he peered over the edge of the canal, but nothing moved on the sandy ground. In the moonlight, he spotted no traces of recent human presence. All the way down to the narrow strip of fertile land nothing moved. He decided to wait awhile. Soon the guard had to turn around the corner since he wasn't supposed to leave any part of the wall unobserved for long. Time passed and Hori shivered. Where was the fellow?

Resignedly, he climbed out of the canal and sneaked toward the Nile. Surely, there had to be at least two guards patrolling the vast area, more likely four. Maybe the guys were having a little chat. Hori imagined the pier as their preferred hangout, where they'd sit and dangle their feet. Undisturbed he walked all the way to the corner and peered around, but the jetty lay just as deserted under the moonlight. Nobody around! He couldn't believe it. Having slipped past the gate to the weryt, he peeked around the next corner. No guards there either. He cursed his bad luck for heading in the wrong direction. They had to be at the back wall. By the gods, he hated creeping around here at night! And he'd hoped he'd never have to do it again. Breathing raggedly, he reached the end of the wall.

Nothing. Nobody.

Flabbergasted, he leaned his back against the stones. Not one man guarded the weryt although the king himself had ordered the night watch. How could that happen? Gradually, realization sank in that there was still an open gate into the secret world of the embalmers. And the heart without body must have taken that route. But why? What for? The shadows around him offered no answer. Tired, he trotted back to the canal and dove under the wall.

Out of old habit, he reached under a bush clinging to the slightly moister earth by the canal as he stepped out of the water. He dried his face with the piece of cloth he'd always hidden there, then stopped short. That wasn't his rag. He'd picked up his awhile back. What reason could someone in the weryt have for placing a piece of cloth in that exact position if not the same as he once had? Then he remembered one night hearing noises upon his return. He'd thought he was imagining things in his fear of getting caught! He pressed his lips together. Somebody had been watching him after all and now made use of his discovery. Downcast, he went back to Kheper's house. A crime had been committed, possibly one worse than murder. And it was his fault!

New Acquaintances

The next morning, Hori first went to Hut-Nefer's office since the mer-ut needed to hear what he'd found out right away. Fortunately, Kheper couldn't needle him about why he didn't accompany him today.

He knocked and waited a moment until Hut-Nefer's muffled voice called, "Come in."

Hori entered, closed the door and bowed. They were alone, good.

"Ah, Hori. Do you bring answers already?" The mer-ut appeared tense and aged. Worry had deepened the lines in his face, and without the jackal mask he was only a human being after all. He gestured for Hori to sit.

"One answer and many new questions, I'm afraid," he replied and settled on a stool. "Let me start at the beginning." He reported his fruitless conversation with Hornakht.

Hut-Nefer pressed his fingertips together while he listened. Now he placed both hands flat on the table as if he wanted to get up. "You're right. I didn't give you enough information." As he exhaled, his shoulders sank. "I wanted you to form your own impressions but didn't think how little forthcoming those involved would be."

"My starting to work as ut right away probably wasn't the smartest approach either. Usually I take care of the sick first, then add a day of embalming at the end of my stay. However, I came here only a week ago, and nobody was in need of a doctor... People talk more openly with a healer than they might with a friend or colleague."

Hut-Nefer's brows hiked up. "Is that so?"

Oh, that piercing gaze! What did the mer-ut expect of him? Did he want him to betray the secrets of his patients? "Um, I didn't mean to say...I mean—I can't..."

To his relief, a gentle smile showed on Hut-Nefer's face. "I'm sure you'd tell me if somebody confided an outrage."

"Yes. Yes! And I'm not sure at all that I'd have learned more if I'd offered my services as physician yesterday."

"Well, then I better share with you all I know. As Hornakht admitted to you, the seal on the vessel was his own. But, what he didn't notice..." He paused.

Hori bent closer in anticipation.

"The cord wasn't the same as the one Hornakht had wound around all the other jar necks. The thing is, we received new thread reels with the last delivery of provisions, and that yarn is coarser than the one we normally use, not as finely spun. The heart vessel was sealed with the new thread, all the other jars of the deceased with the old one."

"Oh!" Hori blurted. "But couldn't Hornakht simply have run out of yarn just when he wanted to seal the heart jar?"

The corners of Hut-Nefer's mouth twitched. "According to our records, Hornakht removed the organs of that corpse on the twentieth day of month Khonsu. The new reels arrived on the third of month Khenti-khet."

Thirteen days later! "That's interesting. In that case the foreign heart could have been placed in the vessel at the earliest on the evening of that day. Then we can scratch Hornakht from out list of suspects."

"Not necessarily. He could have done the deed anyway, ignorant of the fact the yarn narrows down the time of manipulation."

Of course, his superior was right, no matter how much he'd have liked to acquit Hornakht. Then he imagined the two hearts getting swapped. The deceased might accidentally face the Judgment of the Dead with that of the stranger. Before he could voice his concern, he remembered how much time passed between Hornakht removing the organs and the later manipulation, and he took a deep breath of relief. The fresher heart would still contain far more moisture and therefore would be larger and heavier.

Hut-Nefer interrupted his train of thought, "Everything else you know already. All servants, utu, lector priests, basically everyone in the weryt has been questioned if they saw or noticed something but without result. Albeit, you mentioned having found one answer."

"And the women?" Hori burst out. "Did you ask the women and children?"

The old man shook his head. "They are not familiar with the secrets of mummification, and whoever added the additional heart must have known about our processes. So why should I?"

"Because one doesn't need to understand what's happening when observing someone! The perpetrator won't have messed with the jar during the day under everyone's eyes. The risk of getting caught would have been too high. No, he'd have committed the outrage at night. Think of children jerking awake from a horrifying dream, women soothing their crying children. They could have seen a man creeping through the streets in the middle of the night."

Hut-Nefer groaned. "I'm glad I requested your help! In my zeal to only share what happened on a need-to-know basis, I hadn't thought of that possibility. It will be done."

"Let me take care of it. You sometimes come across as rather... um... intimidating. Back to your question. Yes, I found out something. Last night I dove under the wall to ascertain that route was barred." Now he paused for effect before continuing, "It is not."

"What are you saying?"

"Nobody guarded the walls of the weryt while I walked around. Not one man."

Hut-Nefer jumped up and bellowed, "You must be wrong! The commander of the watch reports all occurrences to me every morning. Today as well. Everything was quiet."

Hori sucked in his lower lip. "I'm sorry to say that, but the man must be lying. I circled the whole weryt. Nobody called to me, nobody stopped me. You should question him, and if he keeps lying, tell him my findings." He grinned.

"What's so funny?" the mer-ut snapped.

"I just thought you might want to wear your mask for that occasion." He pointed to the chest where the jackal face was stored.

"You think it might speed up getting to the truth if Anubis himself asked the questions?" Now Hut-Nefer smiled as well. "You could be right, hehehe. Not a bad idea," he murmured and turned to the chest.

Hori took it as a signal to leave. "In the meantime, I'll see if one of the women or children needs medical services."

Still no news from Hori! Today princess Menet sneaked out of the queens' chambers and complained to him about Tep-Ta being so unfriendly, but what could Nakhtmin do? Instruct his senior in the proper way to deal with the royal family? If the man was dumb enough to alienate the wives and children of the pharaoh, he'd never become first palace physician, but that wasn't his problem. Nofrethenut's health and that of the Horus in the egg surely were, though. From Menet's words he gathered Nofrethenut didn't feel well, and the doctor refused treatment. Even worse, he dumped the strengthening medicine Hori had made for the queen. Strange how rude Tep-Ta acted toward the women, while he liked to fawn on high officials.

In the evening, when he saw him leave the House of Women, ducking and hurrying as if chased, it dawned on Nakhtmin the little man probably had never found much favor with the female sex. Did he hide his insecurity behind a gruff facade because he'd rather be feared than ridiculed? Nakhtmin shook his head. He must be seriously bored if he wasted so much thought on the gnome. Would have been fun to discuss Tep-Ta's behavior with Hori though. At least he could go home now. Still giving his thoughts free rein, he left the palace and walked the streets of Itj-tawy until he realized he'd almost reached the temple of Amun instead of his own house and stopped short. Now he'd have to pretty much retrace his steps. "How stupid."

A young man wearing the clothes of a hem-netjer stepped out of the portico and darted him a baffled look. "You talking about me?"

Nakhtmin's cheeks burned with embarrassment. "Sorry, I just scolded myself. Meaning to go home, I didn't pay attention where I was heading, and thus I ended up here instead."

The stranger laughed. "I know how that happens. Hey, don't I know you? Are you one of the wabu?"

"Wab and physician. I'm Nakhtmin." He relaxed. The guy seemed nice and didn't laugh at him, so he didn't feel quite as foolish anymore.

"I'm Neb-Wenenef. Friends call me Wenen." He draped an arm around Nakhtmin's shoulders. "Shall we walk together?"

Pleased, he nodded but marveled at the geniality of his new acquaintance. "If you're also heading for the palace district."

"O-hooo," Wenen exclaimed. "Don't tell me you've made it that far as a doctor. Or…I guess your father is a government official?" His arm slid from Nakhtmin's shoulder. "My house is in the craftsmen and merchants' quarter. But at least we have part of the way in common."

"Actually, I've recently been appointed a palace physician," Nakhtmin bragged.

Wenen cast him an admiring look. "Wow, that's something! You've got to tell me how you achieved such a feat." His expression darkened. "I'll probably always remain an insignificant hem-netjer."

He might be right, Nakhtmin thought. If he hadn't reached the higher order yet, the prophet positions would soon be filled and with men young enough to survive them both. Wenen's chances of ever becoming a prophet were slim, at least here in the residence. Maybe in a less important temple of the Two Lands? Nakhtmin felt the need to console his new acquaintance. For the first time he regarded himself superior to someone else. "Don't say that. My father was only a simple hem-netjer in Khenmet-Min, and look what I've achieved. And it's not exactly a shabby position you have."

They turned into the hustle and bustle of the fish market, where traders already packed in at that time of day or pitched the leftovers. The place reeked of fish entrails and was very noisy, so he didn't understand Wenen's reply. Only after they'd left the hubbub, he asked him to repeat his words.

The priest showed a crooked smile. "You're right, my heart should be content. I don't have to walk around with Nile mud between my toes, like my father did. He was a papyrus maker. Sobek won't be able to claim me."

Now Nakhtmin regretted his boasting. It was horrible to lose a relative to a crocodile. Without a body to entomb, where would the ka find a home? Without his heart, he couldn't pass the Judgment of the Dead, his ka and ba couldn't meld, and he wouldn't become an akh. Commiserating, he squeezed the man's hand. "My father also set out on his journey to the Beautiful West quite some time ago."

"That's why I became a priest," Wenen explained. "I hoped to make Amun, the king of gods, show mercy on my father's shadow, so they'd allow him to ascend to the heavenly realm." He awkwardly glanced aside. "Even had a grave erected for him, hoping his ba, ka and shadow might find a home there. I visit regularly and bring my offerings."

That wouldn't work, Nakhtmin thought. Separated from body and heart, the ba bird and shadow of Wenen's father were doomed to stray around for eternity. Actually, the priest should know that since he occupied himself far more with these things. However, he refrained from discouraging the man. That wouldn't help, and he took pity on Wenen. "I'm sure your father's ba finds your offerings of food."

At the next fork, Wenen halted. "Here our paths split. I need to go that way. It was nice to meet you, Nakhtmin, palace physician."

That sounded final. He'd have liked to talk some more with Wenen. Their paths probably wouldn't cross soon again. "Why don't you come to my place for dinner?" he suggested spontaneously. "I'm sure my wife would enjoy the company. Or is yours awaiting you?"

Wenen's eyes sparked. "No, I'm unmarried. But are you sure your wife wouldn't mind if I tag along?" He put his arm around Nakhtmin's shoulder and turned his feet toward the palace district.

Suddenly it hit Nakhtmin. "Oh no, that's impossible. I totally forgot that we are invited for dinner." When he saw Wenen's disappointed face, he regretted his blunder even more. "Hey, how about you come tomorrow? Then I can give Mutnofret an advance warning. Our house is the third on the Street of Sycamores."

"I'd be happy to. Very happy." Wenen kissed him on the cheek and hurried off.

Baffled, Nakhtmin rubbed the moist spot but walked the last leg to his house in high spirits. Thanks to this encounter, he didn't feel so lonely anymore.

Arriving at home, he tenderly kissed Muti, who was already groomed to go out. He loved it when she painted her lids with green malachite because that made her almond-shaped eyes shine even brighter. And was that collar new? Must have been expensive! A fit of dizziness seized him, then he pulled himself together. He could afford to adorn his wife although she didn't need it at all. "Your beauty pleases my heart, darling." And it was true. Fascinated he regarded her high cheekbones and full lips often curling into a mocking smile.

"You're in a good mood. Is Hori back?" she asked and grinned.

"That's not the reason," he said and teased her with silence.

"Now, don't tell me your strange colleague…"

"Tep-Ta."

She giggled. "The name's too funny. Has the man stooped to working with you instead of against you?"

Nakhtmin sighed. "That would be nice, but no. I've met someone on the way home, a hem-netjer of Amun, and we got talking. He's a nice young man called Wenen. I've invited him to dinner tomorrow evening at our house. Tell Baketamun we'll have a guest."

She tilted her head and studied him. "That's a bit sudden, don't you think? Usually you don't make friends so fast."

At first he wanted to protest, but then he simply shrugged. She was right. "You'll like him, I'm sure. And I'm glad I have someone to talk to, now that Hori's gone. Who knows for how long?"

"And I'm nobody?" She pouted, crossed her arms and turned her back on him.

"Um…" Nakhtmin cursed his clumsy tongue spilling words faster than his heart could weigh them. Desperate, he searched for a reply that would pacify her. Of course, now his lips were glued together. To his relief, he heard her giggle again. "You snarky woman! Stop teasing me!"

A short time later, they arrived at Ameny's estate where Muti's little brothers, Huni and Bati, charged at Nakhtmin. "Not in bed yet?" he asked.

One of the boys pulled on his belt, the other one on his shendyt until the cloth began to slide.

"Hey, you rascals!" he called and tried to grab the culprits.

Shrieking with delight, the twins dashed away in opposite directions. Sighing in resignation he struggled for a dignified countenance, while he greeted Muti's parents.

The mouth of Lady Isis twitched. "Since the two attend writing school in the mornings, they are exuberant for the rest of the day. I apologize for their behavior." She hugged Mutnofret and offered Nakhtmin her cheek to kiss.

She was still a beautiful woman. Nakhtmin deemed himself lucky, because in her mother he could anticipate how Muti would look later. His father-in-law was also an attractive man—for his forty years or so. He shouldn't say that aloud though! No man liked to be reminded of his aging.

"Great that you've arrived early." Ameny cast a loving smile at his daughter.

"Your other guests aren't here yet?" she asked and exchanged a quick glance with Nakhtmin, while her hand flew to her stomach.

He gave the slightest of nods, which only she would notice, he thought. However, the sharp eye of Isis never missed anything. She looked from her daughter to him and clasped a hand over her mouth. "Ooooh!"

"What is it?" Ameny asked.

Isis wiped a tear from the corner of her eye. "I believe these two have exciting news for us."

The joy over their first grandchild made Nakhtmin wish they could spend the whole evening with Muti's family alone. But the arrival of the first guests—the other two prophets—ended all talk about names for children and plans for the future. Iriamun indeed looked ailing as he leaned heavily on his walking stick. Duamutef, the third prophet, was somewhat younger than Ameny and had fairly soft features. Nakhtmin didn't like him much—he always seemed rather effeminate to him.

Soon, more and more priests poured into the garden of the estate. Some stepped from their barks and ambled over the pier to join the assembly, likely the men living farther away. Pretty strange to throw a dinner party when the unlucky Djedefra was on his way to the Beautiful West. Still, everyone wore yellow as a sign of their mourning.

Additionally, Ameny had forgone everything that usually marked a festive banquet. There were no musicians, no dancers, no meal of several courses, only one long table set with various dishes and drinks, from which everyone could serve himself and eat while standing. It wouldn't have been easy to organize enough tables and seats anyway. Nakhtmin tried to estimate the number of guest and settled for about fifty. Among them he spotted Setka. Of course, keen on the promotion, he wouldn't miss a chance like this to kiss up to everyone.

His gaze grazed Hemiunu, the well-nourished head of the hemu-netjer. The man studied Nakhtmin with an expression of distrust, then waddled over to him. "Do I know you? From which domain are you?"

"Oh, I'm not a hem-netjer," Nakhtmin parried. "My father-in-law Ameny invited me over tonight. I'm one of the pharaoh's personal physicians."

"Is that so? Hm. And what does the venerable prophet expect to gain by asking a doctor to join this assembly? What are you doing here?"

What kind of question was that? As if Ameny weren't allowed to invite him. The man acted like a mother duck protecting her eggs. Did he fear Nakhtmin might usurp someone's position, possibly even his own? "The prophet holds my knowledge of human nature in high esteem," he said and lifted his chin.

"Leave the man alone, Hemiunu, he isn't doing any harm," someone behind Nakhtmin said.

He turned around and saw a hem-netjer of about thirty. "Do I know you?"

"I'm Sehetep, and I know who you are."

"My right hand," Hemiunu growled, obviously not too pleased with the interference of his deputy. Abruptly, he swung around and joined the group besieging the three prophets.

Nakhtmin granted Sehetep a grateful smile. "Your superior wishes a spot in the light of Amun, it seems."

The man burst out laughing. "Slim chances for him. Hemiunu's too simple-minded for such a high office. I think he rather intends to suggest someone else. Hemiunu always makes plans how to influence temple affairs according to his wishes. At least I let him believe they are his schemes." He smiled with self-confidence and jutted out his chin.

That sounded as if Sehetep believed himself to be the lucky one. Nakhtmin seriously doubted that. A simple mind could still burn with ambition, particularly in a man who felt like a spider in the center of its web. Kind of disgusting. Djedefra's body had barely cooled, and they swooped down on his position like vultures. How could he possibly help Ameny make a choice when he didn't know any of those present and their behavior appalled him equally? Without another word, Sehetep turned to other guests.

Alone again, Nakhtmin approached two older men who seemed to be having a good time. Surprising under the circumstances. "May I join in your laughter?" he asked.

The smaller one, whose waistband pretty much disappeared beneath his vast belly, abruptly stopped laughing. "Who are you, eh?" He sounded drunk. His lanky colleague stooped to his ear and whispered something. Both nodded.

"Please excuse my friend Minmose. Grief had him seek solace in the jugs. I'm Sabu." He placed a hand on Nakhtmin's shoulder. "Will you raise your mug with us in memory of Djedefra?"

Minmose invitingly knocked against an earthen vessel, and Nakhtmin raised his eyebrows. The man looked anything but grief-stricken. Nevertheless, he let the priest fill his mug.

Sabu waited until he'd taken the first gulp. "They say you have Ameny's ear. Won't you put in a good word for us with the old sod?" With plump familiarity he playfully punched Nakhtmin.

He'd have loved to simply turn away in disgust, but he was supposed to check out as many guests as possible. Maybe those two weren't even that bad when sober. Who was he kidding? If someone couldn't pull himself together at such a sad and important time, he couldn't be of much use in everyday life. "Sure," he murmured noncommittally and endured a few jokes about Hemiunu before he took leave.

Spotting a lanky priest standing by himself, Nakhtmin joined him. "You too are doomed to watch the blowflies?" he asked.

The guy wrinkled his nose. "Yeah, well put. I'd have forgone all this and spent the evening studying my scrolls. I'm Neferka."

He was a scholar then. Better than the rest of the folks here—not counting Ameny of course. The women had retreated and were probably chatting in the seclusion of Isis's chamber—where he'd love to be right now. "Nakhtmin, physician," he introduced himself. "So, you don't want to take over Djedefra's position, Neferka?"

They walked a few paces along the ornamental pond, where frogs croaked, then the priest replied, "Well, it's not like I wouldn't love to gain access to the most secret scripts… However, the duties attached to such an office would probably keep me from studying them in depth. I am, as they say, indifferent."

Well, if he had no ambition, maybe the guy could tell him more about the others. "What do you think of your competitors? Who'd you recommend if your opinion counted."

"I care little about other members of the temple," Neferka snarled.

A young man approached from the dark. "I can confirm that. Neferka always has his nose in books and deems regular services for the god beneath him."

"How can you say that, Bai?" hissed the hem-netjer. "I take my duties very seriously. But not every company is equally dear to me." With that he strutted off.

36

Hm, not as indifferent as he claimed. Nakhtmin grinned to himself. The scholar sure didn't like being badmouthed. "I'm-"

"Nakhtmin, his majesty's personal physician, I know." Bai's frank grin reminded him of Wenen. "I could tip you off on a few things if you like."

Well-meaning informer or self-serving schemer? He'd find out soon. "Well, well. Go ahead then. So far, I've met Setka, Hemiunu, Sehetep and Neferka, apart from the two drunkards over there, and to be honest, I have no idea who to recommend to my father-in-law."

Bai laughed. "None of those. Setka doesn't like to get his well-groomed hands dirty, but believes his noble origins qualify him for a higher office."

Nakhtmin halted. "Really? What's that about?"

"His uncle is first prophet of Ptah in Men-Nefer, the father had been first prophet of Ra in On."

Nakhtmin whistled. "Not bad. Somebody's got to fill large sandals."

"Correct. Except our friend Setka is the only one to believe he can achieve that. With regard to Minmose and his bosom buddy Sabu, they are good for nothing and won't ever get farther than where they are right now. Similar thing with Hemiunu. He's a competent administrator and trainer, but nobody sees him as a prophet, except he himself. Um, let's move on." Nervously, the young man looked around. Several hemu-netjer strolled in their direction.

Without hesitation, Nakhtmin set off toward the riverbank. "Are you sure he wants the position? Sehetep seems to think Hemiunu is going to recommend him."

Bai snorted. "And cut loose his right hand that takes care of all the cumbersome tasks? Sehetep must be dreaming. Hemiunu would do anything to prevent that. At best, he'd suggest him as the new head of the hemu-netjer if he himself gets promoted." As if to underline the absurdity of Sehetep's illusions, roaring laughter wafted over to them.

"And Sehetep?" Nakhtmin asked. "What do you think of him?" Bai turned out a valuable source of information even if he mostly confirmed his own impressions of the priests. Why did he talk so frankly about negative traits of his competitors? Certainly not without purpose.

"Competent, smart. He'd certainly be able to take on a prophet's office."

Now, that surprised him. Maybe he'd misjudged Bai...

"However, he's quite aware of his qualities."

...or not. "I've already noticed you don't esteem Neferka very highly."

"Well. Extremely smart, erudite. But a prophet needs to lead people and dedicate all his passion to the service for Amun. Neferka's only devoted to his studies. Do you see the youngster over there?"

Nakhtmin peered to where Bai pointed and nodded. "Appears pretty young for a hem-netjer of the highest order."

Bai clapped his hands. "Exactly. That's Meru, another one of Setka's kind, son of an important family."

"And that alone enables him to progress faster? Hard to believe. Ameny wouldn't approve!" he called.

"If you can 'convince' the right people, a lot is possible," Bai claimed and nodded toward Hemiunu and Duamutef. He leaned against a tree trunk and stuck a leaf of grass between his teeth.

Corruption, bribery—at the temple of Amun? That was too outrageous for him to believe. A very different suspicion sneaked up on Nakhtmin, so he stopped in front of the young priest. "And what can you tell me about a certain Bai, except that he has no qualms about denigrating his fellow priests?"

Bai spit out the grass in a high arch. "Seems like there's nothing to say since you've already formed your opinion. I thought you were a decent guy! First, sounding me out, and then holding my frankness against me!" On stiff legs, he stalked into the dark.

Dumbfounded, Nakhtmin stared after him. He'd just meant to make a joke and expected Bai to understand. Of all the people he'd talked to tonight, he liked the young man best, but now he'd ruined it. A nagging inner voice whispered in his ear, 'Or your jocular remark was spot on, and the man is a scandalmonger trying to make himself look better than others.'

The sound of approaching steps drew his attention. Two men were ambling toward him, so he slipped behind a tree. Now he recognized Ameny and—Setka. Looking around the garden he realized most of the hemu-netjer and the other prophets were about to leave.

Ameny said, "Good to know, but you haven't answered my question. You want to fill the position of fourth prophet, and that takes more than a noble line of ancestors. The chosen one must be devoted to the residence, needs a keen perception and knowledge of the temple structures. He must obey orders and be able to give them. Last but not least, he must excel in his studies of the divine mysteries."

"I always do what I'm told. Ask Hemiunu if he can accuse me of negligence," Setka retorted as if Ameny's words had held a reproach.

Ameny's servant hurried over and lit torches along the paths.

"Well, the head of the hemu-netjer has nothing bad to say about you. Unfortunately, you haven't done anything to recommend you for such high office either."

Ouch, that must have hurt. In the light of flickering flames, Nakhtmin watched Setka clench his hands into fists, but to his amazement, the man's features remained completely expressionless. "Hemiunu is a simple man," was his only reply.

Nakhtmin gulped. Quite cheeky to badmouth his superior in front of the prophet. Still, Hemiunu's simple mind had been a recurring topic tonight.

Ameny showed less skill in hiding his anger than Setka had. "Hemiunu has been taking care of his office for a long time and to our full satisfaction." He fell silent for a while, then said, "After the harvest, the administrator of one domain comes and tells you the gains don't meet expectations although the Nile floods neither inundated the fields too little nor too much and everywhere else the barns are full. What do you do?"

Either the flickering light played a trick on Nakhtmin or a smile played around Setka's lips.

"I'll immediately replace the man as domain administrator and accuse him of theft at the kenbet. For he must have embezzled part of the harvest, no doubt."

The corners of Ameny's mouth drooped. "I expected to hear such a response from you. A fourth prophet, though, should first ask why the gains of that domain were so small. Maybe vermin ruined parts of the harvest or predatory Bedouins attacked the farms. Knowing the cause, he would work with the domain adminis-

38

trator on how to prevent such events in the future."

"But that goes without saying," Setka blurted.

"That may be so. Thank you, Setka. It was a long day. We should call it a night." He summoned the servant and asked him to accompany the last guests to the gate.

Nakhtmin stepped from the shadows to his father-in-law. "That was pretty harsh," he remarked as soon as Setka's crunching steps faded.

"Why should I waste my time on him? The man has disqualified himself. Actually, the whole evening was a disappointment. I haven't heard much beyond self-praise and allegations."

"Same here."

"I'm sorry I wasted your time as well. We could have spent a pleasant evening with our wives."

Nakhtmin patted him on the back. "Don't mention it. And if you have doubts about more candidates, let me know and I'll be happy to help. Are you really tired or should we empty a jar?"

Ameny laughed as if the burden of his office had dropped from his shoulders. "By the gods! Let's celebrate my grandson!"

ENLIGHTENING VISITS

Day 8 of month Ipet-hemet in Shemu, the season of the harvest

"Why did you really come to the necropolis? You're asking many questions this time." Kheper eyed him with distrust. "Hornakht has approached me and other men as well because you scared their women with your talk about ghosts haunting the weryt." He took a bite from his slice of bread and chewed deliberately, still keeping his gaze locked on Hori.

Darn, and he'd thought he'd acted rather inconspicuously. But in such a tight-knit community like the weryt inhabitants, his interest naturally drew attention. His mouth opened to spill all he knew when he remembered the king and mer-ut had sworn him to secrecy. Well, he'd talk to the latter in a moment anyway, then he'd ask him to rethink that decision. He cleared his throat. "I didn't mean to scare anyone. Tell the men I'm sorry."

Kheper grumbled, "Better keep your trap shut. People are giving me funny looks because you, who enters and leaves the weryt as you please, also walk in and out of my house. I, however, do not strive to set myself apart from the others."

Shocked, Hori asked, "Should I leave? You don't want me staying with you anymore?" The very idea hurt. If he lost Kheper's friendship, nothing much would compel him to return to the weryt. He never realized the old man made sacrifices for him.

To his relief, Kheper shook his head. "Son of my heart," he mumbled.

Hori's eyes moistened. "I promise you'll soon understand."

The streets of the weryt came alive. Utu and lector priests set out to work. Following the father of his heart, Hori stepped down from the roof and said goodbye at the door. Hopefully he hadn't promised Kheper too much.

Hut-Nefer already awaited him. Since Hori hadn't uncovered anything further, he was eager to hear how the conversation with the watch commander went. He greeted the mer-ut reverentially and sat. "Well?" he asked, feeling tense. "Anything new?"

Rather awkwardly, the mer-ut cleared his throat. "I have questioned Month-nakht. He swears by all the gods that his men reported to him yesterday. The walls were protected all night."

Confused, Hori wiped his face. "In that case his men are lying. I tell you, there was nobody when I took a walk outside."

"I see no reason to doubt Monthnakht's words. I've known him for many inundations as a capable soldier taking care of his difficult duty without complaints or laments, and he has his men under control."

Hori had never thought about it before, but now he wondered, "Do the guards volunteer for this task?"

The mer-ut rose to pace back and forth. "It's a penal garrison. Except for Monthnakht, everyone was transferred to this troop for disciplinary reasons because of defiance or cowardice or any other misdemeanor."

"Oh, well, that explains a few things, doesn't it?"

Hut-Nefer halted. "What exactly do you mean?"

Hori bent forward. "Monthnakht may be honest and competent, but his men are probably not. They could have been dozing somewhere out of sight. I haven't ventured far from the wall. They might even have been hiding out somewhere east of the river, frolicking in one of the taverns. Come to think of it…there was no boat fastened to the pier. But how else could the men have traveled from the garrison at the edge of the city to their posts here? You didn't tell Monthnakht about me diving under the wall, right?"

"I…no. The route under the wall must not be revealed to anyone!" He took a deep breath. "You know how talkative people are. How could he keep such a secret to himself for-"

"All right," Hori interrupted his outpour before the old man started suspecting him of blabbing about his way out. The possibility that someone might have watched him last year already was a heavy burden on his shoulders. How could he have shown so little caution and not notice a spectator? Better to direct Hut-Nefer's wrath toward others just as deserving. "This rabble consists of slackers, and I can't imagine that Monthnakht, capable or not, keeps an eye on them day and night."

"There may be truth in what you say. I just never expected…"

That someone disregarded orders? No, something like that probably never happened in Hut-Nefer's world. And since disobedience lay beyond his imagination's grasp, these guys could do whatever they wanted. Who'd find out? During the night, the gates of the weryt were barred from inside and out. Nobody could enter or leave. The living, though, shied from the realms of the dead—even more when Ra's golden rays didn't fend off the shadows. Until Hori had revealed his escape route to the mer-ut and the king, it wasn't necessary to shield the weryt at night. But neither Monthnakht nor his men were allowed to know the reason for night watch duty. "What are we going to do now?" he asked. "We can't let them get away with it. I'm telling you this must be the way the heart was brought into the weryt." Horror sent a hot bolt through his limbs. "I forgot to tell you that I've found a rag at the canal under the bush next to the opening in the wall—a cloth for a wet man to dry himself. That's where I used to store mine, but that one didn't belong to me. Additional evidence that someone in the weryt knows of the secret passage and makes use of it."

"That's serious. Very serious." Hut-Nefer continued his fretful pacing through the small room. "You had honorable reasons for your transgression-"

"Not to forget that goddess Maat showed me the route," Hori threw in because he felt very guilty for violating the laws of the weryt.

"Sure. Unfortunately, we must assume whoever slips through the canal does it with evil intentions. The secrets of the weryt are in danger—and with them all of Kemet!"

Hori shuddered. Could it really be that bad? What could happen? He didn't understand the rituals which the lector priests performed on the dead because they were composed in an ancient language he couldn't really decipher. In his heart, though, he sensed the terror that might befall the Two Lands. He touched the bracelet on his upper arm, hiding the ankh symbol marking him as one of the adepts of Osiris, the god of the dead. Hori was a keeper of the secrets of the afterlife, and due to his carelessness someone else might betray these now. Hold on! If he didn't understand the rituals, none of the utu would, not to mention women and children. "I think we're looking for a lector priest," he mused. "If we assume the villain strives to betray secrets, he must harbor knowledge worth revealing."

"Not so fast." The mer-ut groaned and sank onto his chair. "How did we move from a surplus heart to sacrilege? Why would anyone commit such a heinous crime? Maybe we are wrong, and nobody left the weryt. One of the priests? Never!"

Hori pressed his lips together, then said, "Can you still believe that despite all the signs pointing in a different direction?" He held up one finger. "The organ does not belong to anyone within the weryt, so it must have come from outside. The walls are not guarded, and the cloth indicates the canal has been used." Finger after finger popped up, while he presented his arguments. "Which leads to the question of why. Since nobody is missing in the weryt, the perpetrator must have returned. For what purpose did he venture outside and come back? What drives him?" Now he jumped up and paced. "Curiosity to see the world of the living? But where did the heart come from? It must belong to a corpse, but none has been found. At least I haven't heard about a body turning up. That's a puzzle I can't solve. Instead of providing answers, my discoveries only raise further questions."

Hut-Nefer waved dismissively. "We know the route of the traitor, so we can catch him when he tries to sneak out again. But what makes you so sure it must be one of the heriu-heb?"

Hori needed a moment to retrace his train of thought. "Oh, right, it's the knowledge of ritual texts. None of the utu would know them." At the same time he realized that he was probably wrong. Even he had heard some of the songs so often that he could recite them by heart. One didn't need to understand in order to repeat. "But what use is it if I don't know what purpose the incantations serve, what they affect…?"

"What are you talking about?"

"Excuse me, I was thinking aloud. The heriu-heb surely don't just memorize the words, but know their meaning. So, if they want to pass on such knowledge, they also have to tell the recipient when they are to be recited and for what purpose. Wouldn't make any sense otherwise, right?"

The smell of food wafted through the ventilation slits. The women were already cooking?

"Our conversation seems to have reached a dead end," Hut-Nefer said. "I need to take care of my duties. So let's figure out what to do next."

Hori remembered Kheper's words. "My host demanded explanations for my strange behavior today. Wouldn't it be smarter if you told the inhabitants of the weryt about the nature of my stay here? We won't be able to keep it secret much longer."

"Reveal the passage? Never!" the mer-ut thundered.

Hori raised his palms to soothe him. "Of course not. Only that I'm supposed to find the origin of the heart. That would enable me to openly ask questions, and the culprit might give himself away by acting suspiciously or by trying to leave the weryt one last time. We definitely need to guard the exit—on the inside. Those guards of the garrison we cannot trust. Once we've caught the villain inside the weryt, you should interrogate Monthnakht's men yourself to find out if they really performed their duty."

The mer-ut sighed. "All right. I'll inform everyone that it's your task to find the villain." The pain of having to admit his inability to govern all things concerning the weryt was etched in his face. But harm had been done and couldn't be undone by silence. "Who's going to protect the passage? The two of us taking turns? I don't trust anyone else. Remember, nobody must learn of the route!"

After a knock at the door, a servant stuck his head in. "The caravan from Sekhet-hemat has arrived with the salt."

Hut-Nefer rose. "I'll be right there." And to Hori he said, "As you see, I can't decide that now."

"No problem, look after the natron delivery. I'll take over the first watch since I know which time of night the culprit will prefer: when all is quiet and long enough before the first inhabitants awaken. Do you grant me permission to tell Kheper about my mission today? Otherwise it'll be tough to sneak away at night."

Turning back at the door, the mer-ut said, "Don't talk to him yet. I'll assemble everyone this evening and let them know. Then he too will learn of your task."

Enticing odors greeted Nakhtmin as he entered his home. Baketamun must have outdone herself. Mutnofret sashayed toward him. "When's he coming, your new friend?" she asked after embracing him.

He laughed. "You're more excited than I am. Yesterday, you showed little enthusiasm."

She tilted her head in a perky way. "I had time to think about it. Except for Hori and my parents, we never have guests, and we don't go out either. Well, sometimes I meet my girlfriends when you're not around…"

Nakhtmin cringed as he remembered the day he accompanied her on such a visit. He didn't understand why she still consorted with such loose women who didn't even refrain from groping under his shendyt. Was she bored? Maybe he should invite a colleague from the palace someday. So far he'd always been too shy and didn't feel the need to foster new contacts.

"It wouldn't hurt if you found more high-ranking friends. We have to think of our son's future," she explained.

"Oh. That's how you look at it." He preferred to pick his company based on his esteem for others not their position in society. Muti had never shown such an attitude before. Her pregnancy possibly prompted such considerations. Or did she fear his own humble origins might cast a shadow over their children's prospects in life? That hurt. At the same time he felt obliged to smooth the way for his child. As a nobody, he'd learned to fend for himself the hard way. And he'd had incredible luck. The scales could have tipped against him easily though, then he'd still be dwelling in a miserable little hut by the river, living by the meager offerings of the poorest. No Muti and none of Baketamun's delicious roasted duck… "Wenen isn't of high rank, nor has he friends in powerful circles, I think. Actually, I got the impression, he…um…" No, he couldn't speak the words: admires me.

As so often, she seemed to know exactly what he meant. "Hm." She crossed her arms. Her mouth took on an austere streak he'd observed in Lady Isis's face before when she scolded her sons. "Is it possible, husband, that he hopes to benefit from his acquaintance with you?"

Nakhtmin sensed that he flushed. "He isn't like that! You'll see for yourself.

Since when are you so intent on such considerations? Wasn't I without a position and lacking connections when you fell in love with me? Didn't your father promise me your hand before he knew how high the pharaoh would promote me soon after? I think our son will do just fine with your father, the second prophet of Amun…" Soon the first. "…and Hori, no less than the vizier's son, supporting him. Not to mention my humble self in an insignificant position as palace physician."

To his surprise, she yielded. "You may be right, but you should use caution."

Caution? Why? Oh, because of the prophet's successor being selected soon? Of course, she'd want to spare him disappointment in case he attached his heart to someone only using him as a stepping stone in his career. However, Wenen couldn't be aware of his connection to the house of the second prophet, or could he?

Their guest's arrival spared him a reply, but he found himself carefully observing Wenen's reaction to their anything-but-humble estate. Could his wife be right with her suspicion that the man just pursued his own advantage? No, in Wenen's face he only read true joy to meet him, the chance acquaintance, again. Why did Muti have to plant such an idea in his heart? Now he felt far more restrained than he'd like to be. To add to his irritation, Muti chatted with their guest in a most relaxed fashion and seemed to enjoy herself very much. Just wait, he thought.

Wenen appeared not to notice his reserved behavior. He was cheerful and laughed a lot. During the meal, Nakhtmin managed to relax.

"Oh, yesterday, Nakhtmin and I had the pleasure to meet several of your colleagues," Muti said. "You weren't there?"

"Me? No way." Wenen laughed. "I haven't climbed to such ranks yet. Second order. How come *you* two were invited by Ameny?" he asked in wonder.

With mischief sparkling in her eyes, Muti winked at Nakhtmin. "He really doesn't know."

Nakhtmin cringed when she bluntly revealed who her father was. Somehow he'd have preferred if Wenen didn't know. Would he ever find out now if the priest sought his company because he actually liked him?

The young man's jaw dropped. "Impossible! Hey, you didn't mention that, Nakhtmin."

While Wenen expressed his surprise, Nakhtmin realized here was another chance to gain information about the priests of Amun. Since his new acquaintance stood no chance to become prophet, his opinions would be honest. He laughed nervously. "We haven't spent enough time together for me to tell you the whole story of my life. Ameny asked me to attend and check out the men who recommend themselves for the high office. Albeit, I had serious difficulties judging who told the truth and who defamed others for selfish reasons. Do you know a priest Setka?"

Wenen's lips curled in amusement. "You mean High-and-mighty? How did such a remarkable encounter come about?"

"He approached Ameny two days ago already when Djedefra was still fighting death. Yesterday evening he attended as well."

The painted brows of his guest danced. "And his noble laziness Setka placed himself at the front of the queue, I assume. Well, I'm aware of my place within the temple hierarchy—and that I still need to learn a lot before I can strive for higher orders. But he thinks his noble birth makes up for his lack of discernment and alacrity. He only does what he absolutely has to, and often enough he finds a fool to take care of it for him." His thumb pointed at his own chest.

Muti laughed aloud at the comical face he pulled. "Oh Wenen, you should have been there yesterday. Then Nakhtmin would at least have had some fun."

Nakhtmin nodded. "He really tried hard to convince Ameny, but in the end showed his true nature like you described it. The best thing is, though, he didn't even realize he'd made a mistake. He probably still believes he had impressed the prophet."

Wenen burst into laughter. When he caught his breath, he wiped tears from his eyes and gasped, "That's exactly the case. You should have seen him prance about today. I guess he's already bought a leopard fur and secretly tries it on at home."

"Dear gods, I'd love to see that," Nakhtmin said. "How come Hemiunu doesn't tell the prophets what Setka is really like? It can't be in his interest if someone like that becomes his superior." Taking a sip from his mug, Nakhtmin remembered that smug comment Setka made and promptly choked on his beer. When the coughing fit subsided, he croaked, "'Hemiunu is a simple man'—that's what the guy dared to say and probably meant the simpleton couldn't appreciate Setka's qualities. Maybe he's right, and Hemiunu can't see his *deficiencies*. By the way, that's something many people said about Hemiunu, him being simple-minded."

To his surprise, Wenen didn't laugh. Instead he turned serious. "We shouldn't joke about that. Hemiunu is a diligent official and good in what he does. However, he too must bend to necessity."

Was that supposed to mean Hemiunu didn't dare to speak with disrespect of someone with such powerful connections? And what about Bai's claim the fat man took bribes from noble families for speeding up their sons' careers? Thank goodness Ameny couldn't be influenced like that. Then an idea struck him. "Who would you recommend if you had the ear of a prophet?"

"Nakhtmin!" Mutnofret hissed.

"Why? He knows the hemu-netjer, at least those who serve in the residence. If you want to know what a man is like, ask his servant."

Wenen released a strange gurgling noise. "Are you calling me the servant of people like Setka?"

Nakhtmin tilted his head and smiled. "You said yourself that you're doing his work."

His new friend featured a crooked smile. "Got a point there... Well, I'd recommend Sehetep and Neferka, both hemu-netjer, who have been serving the god a few years longer than me. Neferka is rather a scholar, well versed in religious scripts, while Sehetep has made himself indispensable to Hemiunu. He's practically his right hand."

"Oh." Nakhtmin faked ignorance. "So, he's good in administration and people management? I think that's the kind of person the prophets are looking for. Hemiunu will surely recommend the man himself." Interesting that Wenen mentioned two of the men he'd met yesterday.

Wenen splayed his hands. "Maybe. However, Sehetep was only recently ordained to the highest order. Anyway, it's late, and tomorrow I have to be at the temple before the first ray of Amun-Ra hits it. I thank you both for an entertaining evening and a delicious meal." He rose.

Nakhtmin felt disappointed. He'd have loved to find out more and preferred to end the evening on a happier note, but he appreciated Wenen's sense of duty that made him place his service for the god before his pleasure.

As soon as they were alone, he burst out, "So, what do you think of him, most distrustful of all women?"

Muti grabbed his hand and squeezed it. "I have to admit you were right. He's nice. I'd love to have him over again."

"All of a sudden the woman is full of praise!" he called with pathos. "Should I be worried?"

"Well, you know, such a clean-shaven head looks rather attractive to the daughter of a priest. And he's quite handsome if a little scrawny. Nofriti wouldn't turn him down."

"Don't you dare speak Nofriti's name in my house! But no, I believe she'd find his teeth too crooked and his nose as well." Or would the slut not mind? In all honesty, he did feel a little flattered by the attention she'd paid him back then although she caused him major embarrassment.

Muti smiled and caressed his chin with her finger, then she turned her back on him and seductively glanced over her shoulder. "Nobody's perfect, my dark admirer from Upper Egypt."

He grabbed her and pulled her to him. "I'll show you what fire blazes through the dark loins of Upper Egypt!"

Her pupils widened with desire.

Afterward, he lay awake for a long time, mulling over recent events. Truly strange, that cobra in the Holy Garden. The reptile's bite had affected the ambitions of the priests like cinder on flames. But what had Wenen meant when he said Hemiunu would only perhaps recommend Sehetep? That sounded like he'd rather not do it. Oh, and Bai had hinted at the same thing. Now he'd completely forgotten to ask Wenen about the young man he'd offended.

An Impressive Appearance

Day 8 and 9 of month Ipet-hemet in Shemu, the season of the harvest

The announcement of Hut-Nefer giving a speech raised much curiosity among the inhabitants of the necropolis. While men and women—utu, lector priests, wailing women and servants—still poured into the square, the head of the weryt motioned for Hori to join him on the small makeshift platform, quickly assembled during the day. As a sign of his trust, Hut-Nefer placed a hand on his shoulder. Hori couldn't remember anything like this assembly happening during the seven moons he'd spent here before, nevertheless people stayed surprisingly calm. Tension hung in the air though.

Hut Nefer waited until everyone had arrived, then waited a little longer. When his deep voice sounded, it commanded such an imperious tone that Hori shivered.

"Inhabitants of the weryt! An outrage has been committed, and the culprit is still among us. The heart of a deceased has not been treated according to the sacred order. You've all been questioned, but the guilty one has not revealed himself. Therefore I asked physician Hori, whom you all know, to investigate this matter, so the heart will be returned to the corpse and the dead can become an akh."

Hori admired Hut-Nefer's skill at making it seem like only the transfiguration of the deceased were at stake here. Intently, he scrutinized the faces in the audience. Did anyone avert his gaze under the pressure of guilt, avoid eye contact? No, it was hopeless. Too many people stood squeezed together. If someone turned, they probably told people to back off.

"I'm asking again who made this mistake," the mer-ut's voice boomed. "He shall come to me or Hori and will not be punished. Alas, should he remain silent, knowing what this means for the afterlife of the poor human being he defiled so horribly, then he must face severe punishment when we expose him. His body will be destroyed, his name committed to oblivion for all eternity."

It appeared to Hori that nobody dared to breathe or look at someone else. At first he couldn't fathom Hut-Nefer would grant the perpetrator pardon, but now he understood. The nameless heart wasn't the only sacrilege the culprit had performed, possibly not even the worst, but the mer-ut only talked about that one. So the perpetrator might indeed hope to get away with confessing this crime, not knowing what else they'd found out.

The words seemed to sink into the hearts of people and weigh them down. Silence hung heavily over the crowd.

"And we will expose the culprit!" With this threat, Hut-Nefer descended the stairs and stepped into the square.

Fear etched into their faces, men and women retreated and made way for him to stride through the crowd. Hori remained up on the pedestal until the head of the weryt was out of sight. Then he realized how silly his hope was that the wanted man would step forward right away, here and now. Revealing himself in front of all eyes would require more courage than he himself would be able to muster. All the gazes now settling on him caused him unease. With haste, he left the platform and headed for Kheper's dwelling. Would the culprit use the chance to cleanse himself of guilt? In all honesty, he seriously doubted it. If he was right and the heart had entered the weryt from outside, the body still had to be out there. Anyone stepping forward would have to admit having left these walls, which was punishable by death and damnation. No ut would prepare the body of such an evildoer for eternity. He shook his head. No, the perpetrator wouldn't take such a risk. More likely, he'd wait for nightfall, his heart filled with terror, to escape one last time under the wall, without intention to return. And with him forbidden knowledge would enter the world of the living. Climbing the stairs to Kheper's roof, he resolved to prevent this at all cost.

The old ut already awaited him. "So that was the reason for all your questions?"

Conscience-stricken Hori lowered his gaze. "Forgive me, I wasn't at liberty to tell you although I really wanted to."

Kheper cackled. "I understand, my boy. Cheer up and dig in before Nut's lentil stew gets cold."

Glad, Hori settled down and scooped food into his bowl. "Mmmh. Say, who takes care of you now that Nut has moved out? You need a woman, at least a maid, who cooks your meals."

The old man coughed. "A maid? For an old dung beetle like me alone?" He was referring to the animal after which he was named, the divine beetle arising from itself.

Yeah, that was a stupid idea. Hori remembered the days when he lived in one of these houses on his own. The staff of the embalming compound had provided him with his daily rations of food, which he had to prepare himself. Only the flat bread was baked in the large communal oven. "Nut won't always be able to keep cooking enough to provide for you as well. Once she has children…"

"Oh come on, one more person at her table barely makes a difference."

Smiling, Hori shook his head. No, he didn't fear for his friend to starve or his daughter to break down under the burden of having to feed him. "Aren't you lonely? A woman would be good for you, and I'm sure there has to be a widow who'd appreciate your merits," he flattered.

"Hear, hear." Kheper's face locked up; he appeared to turn inward.

"Ah, you have already set your eyes on someone!" Hori blurted. "Say, who's the lucky one? Have you asked her already?" He only meant to tease him, but Kheper froze. That didn't look good. His arrow must have hit the target and hurt.

"I loved Nut's mother," Kheper replied curtly. His gaze wandered over the roofs.

The old man still mourning her death years later surprised Hori although it shouldn't. Love was a formidable power, only he had never been allowed to feel it. His maid Heqet satisfied his lust but couldn't fill the emptiness inside him. What would it be like to fall in love? Then he remembered the deeds of the former vizier whose name must not be mentioned. Out of morbid love for his wife, he'd turned into a killer. Hori shuddered. Instead of losing his mind like that, he'd rather stay lonely. Pensive, he scraped the remains from his bowl and set it aside. "Don't worry if I leave the house at unusual times, even at night."

Kheper winked in mischief. "In the service of Maat, I guess?"

Hori laughed. His friend at least knew that he solved a series of murders last year, though he had no idea how Hori had achieved that. "If the goddess of justice calls, I can hardly refuse."

Kheper's snoring had a lulling effect, and Hori had to battle sleep. He must not doze off. Not tonight! At last, all noises from the surrounding roofs ceased, and he dared to set out on his vigil. In the past, when he meant to venture outside through the canal, he'd waited longer so as not to attract the attention of a night owl hearing his steps. Today he had to take the risk lest he arrive too late to catch the perpetrator. Barely making a sound, he sneaked through the alleys of the weryt. To his advantage, no moon shone, leaving the night particularly dark. The spot where he'd have to waylay the man offered little cover for him to lurk behind. Hopefully, the stack of boxes still sat next to the house. He turned onto the path flanking the canal and ending at the wall. Yes, the cases were still there! He quickly slipped behind them and crouched. Now he had to wait.

Time passed. The uncomfortable pose made his knees hurt, and his calves went numb. He shifted his weight—and shouldn't have! Causing an awfully loud scraping noise, one of the crates shifted. Hori held his breath, but nothing happened. With more care, he adjusted his position. Would the man even show up tonight? If the traitor had really watched him dive under the wall—and he must have—he also knew that Hori was aware of his escape route. Wouldn't he expect to find him on watch here? Not if Hut-Nefer's words had fooled him to believe they didn't suspect he left the weryt. The man might still regard himself safe for a little while longer, but at a high risk of exposure. No, Hori was convinced he'd show up tonight—but when? His lids grew heavy.

A noise made him jerk up. Then an all too familiar splash followed. That had to be him! He jumped up and lunged at the shadowy figure standing in the water. "Gotcha, you villain!" he hissed.

His adversary recovered from the surprise fast, too fast. He shook Hori off like an annoying insect and sent him falling backward into the canal. Water splashed over his face. He struggled up and gasped for air once before hands pushed him under the surface again. Desperate, Hori kicked and lashed out trying to free himself of the claw-like grip. Finally, he managed to kick his opponent where it hurt a man most. The guy collapsed, his hands shot to his groin. Hori managed to slide out under him and gulped air, precious air! The other breathed raggedly but released no cry of agony. Hori staggered to his feet. Now he had him!

As he charged at the unknown man, the fellow surprised him again. Fast as lightning, he grasped something at the edge of the canal and lashed out. Sharp pain seared through Hori's head. Something sticky trickled into his eyes. It burned. Again, his adversary struck. Hori's knees buckled. He barely managed to lean to one side lest his upper body sink into the water before his senses dwindled.

What did all that ruckus outside mean, this early in the day? Nakhtmin lowered the pestle he'd used to grind lotus leaves. Then he shrugged and continued to prepare the remedy that increased fertility. Stirred into wine, the women liked to drink it despite the bitter taste because of its additional effect of causing a slight intoxication, which allowed them to forget the boredom of their lives. Footfalls approached the herb chamber. Heavy feet. Now the door was thrust open. Confused, he looked up. It was one of the guards protecting the gate to the House of Women.

"Nakhtmin, you are required at the House of Life. Right away!"

"But I…" With a clumsy gesture, he pointed at the various ingredients he'd meant to concoct into remedies this morning. However, the question of who sent the request caught in his throat. The order could only have been issued by the king. In haste, he wiped his hands on his shendyt and hurried to the door.

"Don't ask me," the armed man said and showed a crooked grin.

Nakhtmin trotted after him, but as they left the House of Women, he realized he should have told Tep-Ta where he was going. "Can you please tell my colleague that I've been summoned if he asks?"

The man snorted. "Him? I don't think he cares."

Probably not, but the gnome could stir up quite some trouble in case one of the concubines required treatment… Interesting comment though, sounded like Tep-Ta was as unpopular with the guards as with the servants. Oh well, none of his concern. Curiosity and anticipation quickened his steps. A medical emergency? Nothing else could give cause for summoning him. Likely a noble patient expecting treatment by one of the king's personal physicians. But why in the House of Life, where many knowledgeable doctors were at hand? Out of breath he passed through the portico of the Amun temple.

To his surprise, Ameny awaited him at the entrance of the building. An expression of relief chased sorrowful concern from his face, a sight to strike Nakhtmin with horror. "Muti!" he burst out. "Is she…the child?"

When Ameny shook his head, Nakhtmin released a wheezing breath he'd been holding. However, the prophet then said, "It's Hori."

Nakhtmin halted. "Hori?" he exclaimed in disbelief. "But he's in the…"

"Sh-shhh," his father-in-law hissed, and Nakhtmin fell silent.

Of course, as few people as possible were supposed to know about his friend's special status although it could hardly be a secret any longer since Hori didn't cross the river in the dark of night now but in broad daylight. Ameny practically dragged him though the familiar hallways of the House of Life until they stopped in front of a treatment room. Hesitant, Nakhtmin entered. His gaze fell onto the still and pale figure on the cot, and he cried out in misery. "Is he…?"

Ameny closed the door behind them. "Only unconscious, but he has suffered a serious head wound. This morning he was found injured in the weryt and brought across right away since they couldn't treat him yonder."

"Oh, Hori, what did you get yourself into now?" Nakhtmin hurried to his friend's side and touched his throat to feel the going of his heart. A faint but regular pounding. "Has he gained consciousness since he was found?"

His father-in-law shook his head. "Is that a bad sign? He must tell us what happened to him."

He worried about more than Hori's health, Nakhtmin realized. What did he know? Was he privy to the purpose of Hori's trip? These questions could wait though. "Not a good one anyway," he murmured. After washing his own hands, he cleansed Hori's head of caked blood. Fresh blood oozed from the gaping wound, and he rinsed it away with clean water. For a brief moment, he saw the skull bone—didn't look fractured, that was good—then more blood obscured his view.

A groan behind him, made him turn. "Ameny?" Just in time, he caught the priest and lowered him onto a stool. "Sit down and don't look if you can't stomach the sight of blood," he said.

Pale around the nose, Ameny nodded. "I'm not that queasy—usually—but that is a nasty wound." Obediently, he closed his eyes.

Nakhtmin carefully felt around Hori's head for any fractures. Luckily he found none. Now he could stitch together the skin around the wound, then he had to hope for the best. The fact that Hori didn't move at all, released no moan or whimper, caused him the most concern.

The door opened and somebody entered the room. A servant, Nakhtmin assumed and didn't look around since he had enough on his hands as he struggled to hold Hori's flesh together while more oozing blood made it slippery. "Hand me needle and sinew," he ordered and stretched out his palm.

A moment later he received what he'd demanded and eased the thin metal into the flesh. Again, the injured didn't even twitch, now or during the other five stitches.

"Nice and clean sewing," said a deep but undoubtedly female voice as he knotted the sinew thread.

Surprised he turned around, and Ameny also opened his eyes to dart the speaker a confused look. She was a slender, tall woman he'd never seen before. Nevertheless, she'd known exactly what he needed and where to find it. "Who are you?" An even better question to ask would have been what the woman was doing here. She towered over him, and that alone intimidated him.

"I'm called Ouseret."

The powerful? How fitting. In general, she had rather harsh features for a woman. Again he noticed the dark timbre of her voice and involuntarily wondered how it might sound when Ouseret surrendered to a man in love-making. To his horror, his penis reacted to his errant thoughts, and he quickly bent over Hori until his erection subsided. When he turned back again, her gaze told him, 'I know exactly what happened.' She smiled, and all of a sudden she appeared overwhelmingly beautiful. Embarrassed he glanced at Ameny, but his father-in-law also stared at this phenomenal woman, mouth agape.

"W-what brings you to me? Um, I'm busy. Please find another doctor to take care of your ailments," he stammered.

"I'm a doctor," she simply said. "The head of physicians has appointed me to tend to this man, but nobody told me that expert hands are already taking care of him."

"Doctor," Nakhtmin echoed and felt incredibly stupid. Of course there were women learning the profession and exercising it although not many felt inclined to do so. He'd never met one before.

"Ah-hrm." Ameny cleared his throat. "I heard of your arrival a few days ago. You were trained in the House of Life at Waset, if I remember correctly?"

She lowered her head. "You are correct."

"What brings you to the residence? Was your husband ordered to come here?" As soon as Nakhtmin had asked the question, he realized how inappropriate it was in the presence of his father-in-law. It sounded as if he wanted to find out whether she was married or not. And Ameny actually shot him a piercing look. However, he'd find it reassuring if this confusing lady were unavailable. Pearls of sweat trickled down his forehead and onto his nose, so he wiped them away. Since she looked in her early twenties, she'd certainly be married.

"Husband? No, I wish to complete my studies here. In Waset, we don't have such vast literature like you do in the House of Life." She said this as if a consort would be rather a nuisance to her, like an annoying beetle. "Now that I have provided exhaustive information about myself...may I ask your names?"

Ameny jumped up. "How unforgivably rude of us! Lady Ouseret, this is my son-in-law Nakhtmin, one of the king's personal physicians. I am Ameny, second prophet of Amun."

Demurely, she bowed. "My heart is delighted. What brings you to my patient?"

Breaking out in a sweat again, Nakhtmin battled his indignation. Why had nobody told him he shouldn't treat Hori? If he were in Ouseret's place, he wouldn't have remained so calm when somebody 'stole' a wealthy patient from him. After all, considering Hori's rank, she could expect a generous fee for her services. "Um, ah, I didn't know...Hori is a colleague and friend. I was summoned from the palace, so I assumed..." He wiped his moist hands on his shendyt and noticed the spots the blue lotus had left on it. Cringing, he closed his eyes. "He's all yours."

As soon as he stepped away from the sickbed, she approached and bent over Hori, who still didn't stir. Wary, he watched her feel his pulse, touch his skin and smell his breath. Afterward she examined his head around the wound and gave a satisfied grunt. "I was afraid I might have to undo your fine needle work to trepan the skull, but the bone is undamaged."

"I know," Nakhtmin retorted. How audacious to suspect a royal physician of such bungling incompetence! Now though, she did something he'd never seen before. She opened one eye lid after the other and scrutinized his eyes.

"Why are you doing this?" Curious, he stepped closer.

She made room for him. "Watch this. When I open the lids of this man-"

"Hori. His name is Hori!"

"Yes, when I open Hori's lid, can you see how his pupil grows smaller?"

"Sure."

"Well, I've had a few patients with head injuries, and I noticed in some of them that their pupils didn't get smaller, but stayed as large as that of a man sitting in darkness."

Pensive, Nakhtmin nodded. "And?"

"Those patients died. Your friend however-"

"Hori."

Annoyed, she lifted her head. "Thanks, I got it the first time! Hori's pupils narrow. It's a good sign. I believe he will recover."

"Really?" He could have kissed her for these words.

"It may take days, though, for him to regain consciousness. Can we take him to a place where he might be more comfortable?"

Ameny rose. "We'll take him to his house. Thank you, Ouseret, for your services. I'll make sure you get compensated, but Nakhtmin can take care of his treatment now."

"Can I?" He blinked and turned to the tall physician. "The pharaoh—life, prosperity and health—won't be able to dispense with both our services. I'd like to hire you to tend to my friend-"

"Hori," she quipped dryly.

He laughed. "Yes, Hori. Would you take care of him while he's sick?" The thought of leaving the House of Life in Tep-Ta's hands alone pained him almost as much as not being able to watch over Hori's health himself. However, this peculiar woman inspired trust. A sudden realization hit him: she reminded him of Hori with her way of observing and drawing conclusions. He smiled to himself.

"What's up?" Ameny barked, likely out of fear for Nakhtmin's marital fidelity if Ouseret lived next door.

"Later. First let's coax a palanquin out of Inpu, so we can transport Hori."

After acquiring a stretcher and two bearers from the head of the House of Life, they watched as Hori, accompanied by Ouseret, disappeared from sight. Only then did Nakhtmin cackle. "I'm looking forward to those two getting acquainted."

Now a grin spread on Ameny's face as well. "Now I understand!"

Nakhtmin scraped his sandals over the stone slabs in the temple courtyard. "You didn't think...? You know how much I love Muti."

Ameny sighed. "That woman! Even I might melt in her hands."

"And she isn't really beautiful either."

"No."

They remained silent for a while until steps behind them caused Nakhtmin to turn. "Oh, there's Wenen!" He waved toward the temple.

The hem-netjer waved back, but rather hesitantly, before stepping closer. "Am I interrupting?" He bowed to the prophet.

"No, not at all. Ameny, you know Wenen?"

"Naturally." Despite his affirmation, he appeared a little confused, but granted the priest a friendly smile. "Does something need my attention?"

"Oh no!" Wenen called. "I only wanted to greet Nakhtmin. It was a lovely evening yesterday. Please give my best wishes to your enchanting wife."

"I'll let her know. You should visit us soon again."

Wenen beamed. "I'd love to. By the way, I often spend my evenings in the tavern *The Apis* at the harbor. Just in case you're looking for me. Or do you know your way around the craftsmen's district? No? Didn't think so. But now I better hurry or else Hemiunu will tweak my ears." After another bow, he rushed off and into the temple.

"You seem to know the man quite well," Ameny remarked, placing emphasis on 'you' and thus revealing that he didn't have a clue who the priest was.

"Not that well. We got talking the other day, so I invited him to our house. He's a nice guy."

Ameny waved dismissively. "Let's talk about it later. I've already idled away enough time. How about I come over to your place tomorrow evening? By then you'll probably know more about Hori's condition—if he hasn't already regained consciousness by then."

He agreed and gazed after his father-in-law rushing off.

Two Women

Knowing Hori in capable hands, Nakhtmin still wanted nothing more than to attend to him on his sickbed. But could he take off the rest of the day? He wouldn't put it beyond Tep-Ta to refuse one of the women treatment because he didn't take her ailments seriously. Better to return to the palace. It was getting late and the little doctor might have finished for the day by the time he got back. Then he could check on the queens himself again, without Tep-Ta noticing that he was interfering. Where did such jealousy come from, or whatever was driving the man? His patients should be more important to him. Quickening his pace, he headed for the Great House when a thought flashed in his heart. In the middle of the street, he jerked to a halt, abruptly enough that someone bumped into him.

"Hey, watch out!"

Nakhtmin barely paid attention because he wondered how, by Seth's all scourging breath, Hori had injured himself so seriously. An accident? No! He'd seen enough head wounds. If a man fell, he hurt himself in other spots. Who managed to hit the ground so that the scalp cracked on top of the skull? Someone must have attacked Hori. A row in the weryt? Although Nakhtmin didn't know much about life behind those walls, he deemed that unlikely. He imagined the existence of an embalmer rather demure and dignified, appropriate for dealing with the dead. Now he remembered his first thought when he saw Hori's wound: his friend must have gotten entangled in sinister schemes again. Crime in the weryt…that would also explain why Hori had been summoned. Nakhtmin groaned. Oh no, not again! And just now when Muti was pregnant and he wanted nothing more than keep life simple and cheerful. He'd sure had enough excitement for a lifetime when Hori had drawn him into solving the series of murders last year. Dispirited, he continued on his way and consoled himself with the thought that this time he wasn't involved. The weryt was Hori's business.

The same guard as in the morning—now Nakhtmin remembered his name: Sennedjem—leaned against the wall next to the door of the House of Women, looking bored. "Is he gone?" he asked.

"You mean the 'Running Nose'?"

Nakhtmin burst out laughing. "Running…who came up with that one? That's even better than Tep-Ta! Just don't let him hear it."

The man snorted. "No wild monkey has bitten me yet! I do like my position. If the gnome files a complaint against me, I might get transferred to the penal garrison." He shuddered.

"Never heard about it, but that sure doesn't sound desirable." Nakhtmin wanted to move on when he realized how pale the broad and scarred guy had turned. "What's wrong with you?"

Sennedjem ran a hand through his short-trimmed hair already showing a little gray. Casting his gaze around, he said, "A cousin of mine met such a fate. Only that one time had he fallen asleep on his shift—could happen to anyone! His superior, though, had been keeping an eye on him, so he got caught and punished." He gulped. "Th-they must guard the necropolis."

"That doesn't sound too bad," Nakhtmin remarked. After all, Hori went there regularly without a demon ever attacking him. Or had exactly that happened to him this time? How could he be so sure a human being had knocked out Hori? But that was of no concern to the guard.

He wanted to turn away when Sennedjem grabbed his arm and held him back. "Not too bad? Evil spirits roam there!"

Nakhtmin suppressed a grin. Rather funny when an old soldier like Sennedjem got weak at the knees. His fear seemed deeply rooted, though, and Nakhtmin restrained himself. Then he remembered how scared he had often been during his nightly journeys to the world of the dead. The eerie howls carrying far across the desert seemed to bounce back and forth between the rocks. His throat tightened. "But during the day…"

Sennedjem grimaced. "Rahotep, my cousin was on night watch. Oh, he told me of the horror that befell him, of the whispering shadows! He begged imploringly for relief from that duty, but in vain. Again he had to venture out into the dark, and since then nobody has seen him. The shadows of the damned took him!" The warrior grabbed Nakhtmin by his shoulders and shook him.

With some difficulty, he struggled out of the man's grip. "That's…that's horrible. You have my sympathy. I'm sure he'll show up again, your cousin." Uttering more vague condolences, he retreated into the House of Women. As soon as he knew the wooden door was between him and the fear-struck man, he leaned against the wall. "Dear gods, what an encounter!" he murmured.

Then he noticed some servant girls busy in the vestibule staring at him with curiosity, so he dragged himself into the room he'd left a few hours ago. The fragrance of lotus blossoms hung heavy in the air. Those he'd have to toss away, just like the remains in the mortar he'd abandoned in his haste. Getting back to work, he mulled over Sennedjem's story. He'd known guards protected the gates of the weryt during the day, but at night? That had to be new or else Hori and he couldn't have met in secret. Oh, of course! *Because* of their forbidden meetings those unfortunate fellows had to patrol the walls during the dark hours now. He'd never considered what the discovery of Hori's escape route had meant for the head of the weryt, and he'd never asked his friend whether he got into trouble for his diving under the wall. Always such secrecy about things concerning the weryt! Naturally, Hori would have answered any questions in the usual way: 'You must not know.' His friend wasn't allowed to share any of those secrets with Nakhtmin.

Whispering shadows? Oh yes, those abounded on the western shore, where everything else remained quiet. Certainly a scary experience, but if *he* managed to overcome his fear—Nakhtmin knew he wasn't a very brave man—why was Sennedjem's heart filled with such terror, which could only be an echo of Rahotep's? Nakhtmin couldn't believe the shadows had taken the poor guy. Sennedjem's cousin probably ran away, once neglectful, always neglectful. He had to be a lazy scoundrel, likely drank too much and then saw the mice dance. Possibly his horror made him jump into the river and drown.

Nakhtmin blew up his cheeks, let the air escape through his closed lips and decided to avoid talking to the guard at the House of Women in the future. To think how funny their chat had started. Running Nose! Grinning, he shoved a box of sweets into the waistband of his shendyt, left the room and told a maid to get rid of the wilting plants. He mustn't forget to order more lotus tomorrow, or else there'd be great agitation in the harem. He headed for the wing of the queens, apart from the other chambers, where the little princesses welcomed him cheerfully.

"Nakhtmin! Nakhtmin is here!"

Even the two-year-old Sat-Hathor, youngest daughter of Senusret and his Great Royal Wife, squealed, "Nammi!" and toddled toward him.

He caught her and swung her around until she crowed with joy. Nakhtmin could barely await the day when a child's laugh would greet him on his return home...

With undisguised expectation, the four girls looked at him, and he patted down the folds of his clothes. "Sorry, I don't have anything for you today."

They charged at him and tore at his belt until the small wooden box poking out of his shendyt dropped to the floor. "Oh, what's that?" he cried. "There was something hiding. But don't tell your nurses lest I get in trouble for ruining your appetite." Grinning, he watched the gang fight over the nuts candied in honey. Knowing he shouldn't do this, he still couldn't resist because he loved to see their eyes gleam. And because of his treats, they more readily swallowed bitter pills he gave them, which they might refuse from Hori's hand.

"I call that bribery," Hori had complained the other day.

"I call that jealousy," he had replied.

A smile on his lips, he entered Nofrethenut's chamber and bowed. "Your majesty?"

She dropped the flax spindle and clapped her hands with joy. "Finally a friendly face. And I feared Hori and you had abandoned me." As if she were alone! Two maids retreated from the bed to a corner of the room where they played senet. Most likely, the three of them had been gossiping about one of the concubines when he interrupted them. The queen spinning flax to gauzy threads was unusual though, and a sign that she didn't cope well with enforced idleness.

"And deprive our eyes of seeing your beauty? Never!" With a quick glance, he took in her protruding belly, the full breasts growing heavy, the warm tone of her skin. The queen had downright blossomed during the last few days; no need to worry about her. "Tep-Ta is looking after you very well." Next to the bed, he discovered several vials on a small table and reached for one. The little doctor may have disposed of his and Hori's potions, but at least he seemed to have concocted his own. The plug gave easily, and he sniffed. No, simply fragrance oil. And he saw several new statues of gods and amulets, strewn about in a careless fashion on various pieces of furniture. "You should wear them," he admonished. "You never know."

She pushed out her lower lip. "Where is Hori? I'm tired of the grumpy gnome looking at me as if I were a disease he had to fight."

Nakhtmin didn't want to upset the queen, so he offered an elusive answer. "He'll soon be back. Do you need company? Should I fetch someone to read to you?"

She waved dismissively. "Tonight there's a banquet at the palace. The pharaoh receives the ambassadors of foreign countries. I better get ready." She got up. "Anat, bring me the dress we've chosen!"

The girl rose in one lithe move and handed Nofrethenut a dress of gossamer linen he could actually see through. "You certainly don't have to attend?" he asked. Blossoming or not, she shouldn't exert herself.

"And miss the delivery of tributes?" She shook her head so vehemently that the braids of her wig flew. "Ostriches and gazelles from Kush they'll bring, and elephant teeth! Have you seen one of those? They are extremely big. Gemstones from Retjenu, myrrh, incense, jewels…" She sighed. Likely this was one of the highlights of the year for her.

"Then I won't be in the way any longer. Enjoy yourself." He bowed and headed for the door.

"Come back soon!" she called after him.

Home at last! No matter how strong the urge to check on Hori, first he wanted to greet his beloved. Since he didn't find her in the house, she probably rested in the garden and enjoyed the cooler air drifting in from the river. He left the building through the backdoor.

Even from afar, he could make out Muti's upset voice. Was she scolding Inti? Oh no, the female doctor stood on his lawn! He couldn't see Muti, but the snippets carried over by the wind spoke of anger over the medical treatment of his friend. Nakhtmin's concern sparked. Had Hori's health taken a turn for worse? Or had he even… He quickened his pace, rounded a tamarisk shrub and saw the two so different women standing near the open aperture to Hori's premises. Ouseret appeared calm and confident. That eased his worries somewhat, while Muti seemed quite agitated. Still, Ouseret should look more affected if her patient's condition gave cause for concern.

"There he is!" Muti called and pointed at him in a rather triumphant gesture. "If anyone treats noble Hori, then certainly not a random stranger, instead he would! Nakhtmin, can you believe it? This woman simply moved into Hori's house and…"

The rest of her tirade buffeted past his ear. Damned, he hadn't even thought of warning her! Three quick steps took him to her side, and he sealed her lips with a kiss. Surprised she fell silent, but he saw the glimmer in her eyes. To err on the safe side, he placed a finger on her lips as he let go of her, so she wouldn't continue spitting insults. "I see you've met physician Ouseret already."

Her eyes widened in surprise. "You know her?"

Ouseret gave a cool smile. "Like I said. Your husband has-"

Since Muti opened her mouth again, likely to protest, Nakhtmin interrupted the doctor's explanation and grabbed his wife's hands. "Your father summoned me to the House of Life this morning, where Hori was lying unconscious. Ouseret had been assigned to take care of him, and since I can't very well tend to him and carry out my duties at the palace, I asked her to accompany him home and become his personal physician until he recovers."

Leery, she scrutinized the tall stranger. "Is she any good?"

Nakhtmin rolled his eyes. "Woman! Would she be here if I didn't trust her skills?" With relief he watched her shoulders sink.

A gust of wind blew a strand of hair in her mouth, which she carelessly wiped away. "I apologize for doubting your words, physician Ouseret. Welcome."

Fortunately, Muti was not only effervescent but also magnanimous enough to admit her mistakes. At least to strangers. Most times. He wasn't always as lucky. Hopefully she wouldn't get jealous of the fascinating stranger. Nakhtmin broke out in a sweat again.

Ouseret gallantly bowed in her direction but looked at him again straight away. "Thank you. Would you like to check on Hori or does it suffice if I tell you his condition is unchanged?"

Darn, now she'd put him in a tight spot. Of course he wanted to see his friend, unconscious or not, but if he demanded that, it looked like he didn't trust the physician after all even though he'd just professed to do so. How much easier the whole situation would be if a male doctor treated him. Nakhtmin found it much simpler to deal with men, and they didn't get insulted so easily. Seeking help, he glanced at his wife.

Mutnofret pressed her lips together for a moment, then she said with that cunning tone he'd learned to fear in her voice, "Of course that's enough. My husband isn't one who always needs to assure himself of his friend, and now we both know him in skilled hands."

"Muti!" he cried out. She made him sound like someone who couldn't do anything by himself. Then he saw the women exchange smiles of understanding and groaned. How did that happen? They'd become allies. Against him! Steaming with anger, he stomped past them, through the gate and toward Hori's house. Women were so difficult! Whenever he thought he'd learned how to treat them, they disabused him.

He found his friend in his bed. Somebody had hung wet linen in the room, so it was refreshingly cool. Heqet surely hadn't done this, it must have been Ouseret. Would he have thought of it? The woman was not only a good doctor, he had to admit, but saw farther than he and his colleagues. Next to Hori's cot stood a jug of fresh water, and he dipped in a piece of cloth conveniently placed beside it. When it was soaked enough, he folded it and exchanged it with the one on Hori's head, not without lifting the pad on the wound and checking it. Looked like it was healing just fine. Why then didn't Hori wake up? He squeezed the limp hand, but his friend didn't stir. Only his chest rose and fell with regular breathing as if he were sleeping. His pulse was stronger too. Nakhtmin rose. Ouseret had done everything he'd have done and more. Most of all, he wished to talk with Hori although he couldn't reply, and their conversation would turn out a monologue. He'd better refrain. What if the women came into the house and heard him? He didn't want to face more ridicule, even less did he dare to return to the garden. Desperate, he clenched his hands. This couldn't be happening—in his own house! Well, in Hori's, but that was almost the same. He got a grip on his heart and sneaked over.

A little later, when he was alone with Muti and sat down at the table with her for dinner, she ignored his ill humor. "We should ask Ouseret if she wants to eat with us as long as she's here," she said.

"Mh," he grunted with little enthusiasm. Did he even have a say in it? Well, at least the physician from Upper Egypt was no Nofriti or one of Muti's other silly friends from the palace district. Maybe he could even discuss medical issues with her.

"When I saw her for the first time...I thought you were standing there dressed like a woman!" She giggled. "Then this deep voice. Isn't she the ugliest woman you've ever seen?"

He choked on his food, and the coughing fit wouldn't ease up. At least he'd be spared her getting jealous of Ouseret. Incredible, how could she err like that? Not that he wanted to yield to his desire, but by Min's phallus... As soon as he could breathe again, he grinned and nodded.

Hori struggled. His opponent was an extremely powerful disease torturing his patient with unbearable pain. Hour after hour, he exerted himself, but all his skills failed. Somebody gave him to drink—a bitter medicine. Hold on, he knew that taste! Grateful, he swallowed, and the patient's pain eased. Finally, he recognized the man lying before him. It was him. Now he could sleep and forget...

Light! It penetrated Hori's lids and pierced his head like a knife. He shielded them with one hand and blinked. A demon bent over him. He gasped and tried to fight it off. The th...... ..... The came to collect him, because he didn't have his heart. Again the potion...

The floor underneath him moved. Ugh, he felt nauseous. Did he drink too much? He rolled onto his side and threw up liquid. A cool hand brushed over his forehead. "Mother?" he mumbled.

"Drink." The voice was deep and sensuous.

He swallowed obediently. Now the woman began to sing, but he couldn't understand the words. Although he was as weak as a suckling babe, he felt yet unknown desire. Isis in the shape of a female sparrowhawk fluttered around him and lowered herself onto his erect penis. Of course! He was Osiris. The mysteries! He had to remember...

When he opened his eyes next time, darkness surrounded him. Where was he? Back in the vault underground, where he became Osiris? He couldn't move. A drum pounded in his head. It must have been beating for hours. He groaned. Something moved beside him. Scraping noises followed by a glaring flash.

He meant to scream, but only a gargle escaped his throat. The pain the light had caused subsided. He blinked.

This was his sleeping chamber, but who was the dark-skinned guy bending over him? "Nakhtmin?"

"My name is Ouseret, and I'm your doctor."

Strange, the man moved his lips, but he heard the same voice that had set him on fire with ecstasy. Could this be a woman? Oh, his head! Soon it would crack like an egg when the chick pecked against the shell from inside. What would hatch from his head? Harried, he closed his eyes.

BARELY AWAKE...

Hori awoke to the singing of a lark and blinked. The room lay in semidarkness, but the position of light strips on the opposite wall told him it had to be early morning. Why was he in his sleeping chamber? Hadn't he been in the weryt just now? Something was wrong here! He sat up to jump out of bed, but the room started to revolve, and he grabbed the bed frame. "By Sakhmet's poisoned arrows!" he mumbled. "Did I drink too much?" He reached for the chamber pot and relieved himself lying back down.

When he put it back on the floor with a slam, something moved on the other side of his bed. Someone. "Heqet?" He couldn't remember spending the night with the girl. Hold on, there'd been something else going on. He'd been aroused...

The woman who'd slept at his feet lifted her head. She was a stranger, that much he realized although he couldn't see her face clearly. "Who are you?"

She rose in one lithe move to amazing height. "I'm called Ouseret." Her features were still in shadows.

That voice! Hori felt like a lyre whose tight strings have been struck. No, that didn't fit. Rather like a cat purring with pleasure. The light played across her dark skin betraying the Upper Egyptian. She was naked and seemed unaware of that fact. When she bent over him, her full breasts dangled in front of his nose. He reached out and cupped the firm pomegranates. He actually did purr now and wanted to kiss his bedmate.

However, she withdrew easily. "I'm your doctor. Let me check your wound."

He was definitely missing something here. "Doctor? Ouch!" What a hangover! He must have done some serious quaffing. Vaguely he remembered the headache and strange dreams plaguing him. Had his trip to the weryt also been a phantasm? Her fingers felt his skull, and without touching it himself, he realized that he had a mighty bump. When she let go of him, he touched the spot carefully anyway. "Did I fall?" Now he could make out her features and recognized the strange 'man' of his nightmare. Well, she did have some rather manly attributes like the dense, dark eyebrows and the angular chin, but now he couldn't understand his error anymore. These finely chiseled lips called for a kiss!

She settled on the edge of his bed—what a glorious butt!—and said, "You were found unconscious and brought to the House of Life. That's all I know. The head of physicians sent me to you, but you have to thank your friend Nakhtmin for the fine stitching of your wound."

Nakhtmin, House of Life? How did all that fit together? His memory was a gaping void. However, if Nakhtmin had already tended to him, what was *she* doing here, this Ouseret? Where did she come from? "Oooh," he groaned. "Why does my head hurt when my heart doesn't know what to make of all this?" The pounding in his head was growing worse again. He sank back. His heart also beat fast.

Her cool hand rested on his ribcage. When she turned sideways, her thighs spread slightly and her feminine odor wafted into his nose. His penis swelled. If only her hand traveled farther down...

A mocking smile played around her lips as she followed his gaze. "Should I fetch your maid, so she can give you relief? By the way, she's pregnant, in case you don't know."

His head turned as hot as his dick. "Thanks, but that's not necessary." Why did it embarrass him that she knew about his affair with the girl? Nothing to be ashamed of. Still he wished she hadn't found out. On top of everything else, he had to find a husband for Heqet now. He owed her that much. Abashed he closed his eyes and pretended to doze off. Shortly after, he really did fall sound asleep.

Next, he woke to male voices arguing in the corridor outside his chamber.

"He cannot get up yet. It's impossible." That was Nakhtmin.

"The pharaoh—life, prosperity and health—ordered me not to return to the palace without my son. It's urgent! The welfare of the Two Lands is at stake."

His father? He was the last person he'd expected to see here. Hori bit his lip. He certainly hadn't dropped by to ask about his health. What was all that about? Was his majesty sick and needed his help? Oh, most likely he was concerned for the Horus in the egg. "Is the queen well?" he asked, but his words turned into a croak nobody heard. Afternoon must have arrived, and he'd slept for most of the day. No wonder his majesty was angry with him, but sending his father—that was a bit much. He grabbed the mug beside him and drank greedily. "Are you going to parlay much longer out there or will you tell me what's up?" This time his voice didn't lack strength. Then he remembered his head injury. Where had the fascinating physician gone? Or had she sprung from his imagination?

Nakhtmin hurried to his side. "Hori! I'm so glad!"

"Tears, my friend?" Hori glanced at Sobekemhat standing in the door frame. His eyes remained dry. "Father, thank you for taking the trouble to come here."

The vizier stepped closer. "My heart rejoices to see you on the path of recovery. I'd just returned from a journey to the south when news of your injury reached me."

That was more emotional than anything Hori had heard from his father's mouth before, and he swallowed. His wound must have been quite serious if austere Sobekemhat showed feelings. Nakhtmin looked like he'd burst with news if he couldn't share them soon. Hori managed a lop-sided smile. As soon as his father left, everything would spill out like grain from a ripped sack. "Where's the woman, that doctor?" he asked.

"She's resting since she'd practically stayed at your side day and night."

At least she really existed! "Day and n… How long?"

"You've been unconscious for almost four days."

Hori cried out in surprise and sat up. The linen slid from his upper body. Sobekemhat stared at the spot on his arm emblazoned with the ankh sign, which marked him as an adept of Osiris. Reverentially, he approached and stretched out his finger to Hori's skin. Of course, his father had never seen the mark before as he hid it under a bracelet during the day. He seemed to know or guess its significance though.

"Um, the pharaoh—life, prosperity and health—demands your advice regarding events in the weryt," he mumbled. Instinctively, he spread thumb and forefinger so fend off evil spirits.

Hori closed his eyes for a moment. Slowly memories returned. "Right, I was there." More he did not know.

Like a mother duck, Nakhtmin intervened. "I've already explained that you're much too weak to get up. It's impossible!"

Hori swung his legs over the edge of the bed, and black spots filled his vision. Heqet jumped to his side and gently lowered him onto the mattress. Where had she sprung from all of a sudden? "Ugh!" He groaned. "No, it's not possible yet."

Sobekemhat's eyebrows bristled with indignation. "Don't be such a w..." He pressed his lips into a thin line and sighed. "What if you were carried in my palanquin?"

Nakhtmin snapped his fingers. "Of course! The stretcher from the House of Life. Maybe it's still here, or else we'll have it fetched. I'll take care of it right away." He left the room.

Hori was alone with his old man. Oh, no, he'd almost overlooked the maid who was now stroking his arm in front of his father. Embarrassed, he withdrew from her.

Sobekemhat cleared his throat and settled on a stool. "Your mother sends her best wishes. She came to see you yesterday and the day before and will be happy to hear you're doing better."

"Oh, thank her in my name for her caring." Nofret had never before visited his new home. Hori suspected his father didn't approve. Could she have rebelled against him for once? A rather mean thought when his father finally showed some concern for him. Maybe they would grow closer? After all, he had proven himself worthy of the king's favor, and now his father even knew of his Osiris status.

Nakhtmin returned. "The stretcher is ready. Our servants Inti and Sheser will carry you. That is, if you feel up to it."

Hori gave a weak grunt. The slightest move of his head hurt. "I doubt I'll be of any use to the king since I don't remember anything about the last few days."

Sobekemhat rose. "Tell him yourself. I'm only supposed to take you to the palace." He appeared like someone rid of an obligation and turned toward the door.

"Father..." Hori bit his lower lip. "Thanks for your visit."

The vizier grunted, then disappeared from Hori's view. A short time later, the steps of the two men with the stretcher sounded in the hallway.

"You know what's at stake!" Senusret called. "You must remember. What happened that night? Did someone knock you out?"

Apart from the king, only the mer-ut was in the room, as usual with the terrifying mask covering his face. Their explanations had helped Hori to shed some light into the darkness of his entombed memories. He knew he'd gone to the weryt to solve the mystery of the surplus heart. And he was aware of what he'd found out already: the absent guards outside the wall, his suspecting a lector priest. Sometimes he thought he could grab the tail of something familiar, but the image usually scattered faster than he could snatch it. Particularly, the night he'd been waiting for the perpetrator was completely lost. The pounding pain paralyzed his mind. There was something, though, a question. No, gone again. It was driving him mad. "I can't help you."

In his agitation, the king paced up and down, and Hori wished he'd stop because it grew strenuous to keep looking at his majesty.

"Hori could simply have tumbled and hit his head," Hut-Nefer remarked.

Senusret halted. "Venerable mer-ut, isn't that wishful thinking? Shouldn't we assume the villain wanted to abscond for fear of getting discovered soon? And when he tried, he encountered our friend here. A fight started."

Fight? The sight of stacked boxes flared up in Hori's memory, but it made little sense. "I...I think that was the case," he whispered and closed his eyes. His strength drained.

"Did you recognize the man? Tell us!"

Hut-Nefer grumbled, "Hopeless. No moon shone that night. However..."

Hori blinked with some effort. The mer-ut lowered his head, giving the impression Anubis himself were distressed, which wouldn't be surprising.

At last, a sigh escaped the pointy snout, "One of lector priests hasn't been seen since that night."

"And you're only telling me now?" Senusret groaned. "It must have been him. Why didn't you alert me right away, as it was your duty? I could have started the search for him then."

For the first time since Hori had known the head of the weryt, his demeanor showed insecurity close to helplessness. "His wife says he's sick and can't come to work."

"Did you ascertain she spoke the truth or simply believe her?" the king asked, his voice sharp like a scalpel.

Drops of sweat trickled down Hut-Nefer's neck, found a way through the decorative pearls in his collar and flowed down his chest. "She claims it's a contagious disease."

Since the pharaoh's face reddened with rage, Hori chimed, "In such a case, the sick have to be isolated or else the illness spreads and rages through the whole compound. Nobody must go near his habitation."

The mask nodded gravely. "That's the rule. And as long as I didn't know anything specific... What reason could she have to lie?"

Hori thought of several. She might know of her husband's ploy or fear he could become a suspect although she thought him innocent. Maybe she imagined her husband hid somewhere out of shame. But where could anyone hide within those walls? Only the mer-ut, the villain and Hori knew of the way out, so she should puzzle over the whereabouts of her husband if nobody found him. "Maybe he's really sick," he pondered although he didn't think it likely.

"Ill or not, the priest must show me his face today!" Hut-Nefer barked and rose. "The heri-heb in question is called Nebkaura."

Hori didn't know the man, but he had little to do with lector priests. Only when one of them needed a physician, he got to know them a little. More often, though, the utu injured themselves when they slipped with a tool, or they needed an unction because their skin turned brittle and cracked from working with dehydrating natron salt. Even servants and women in the embalming compound needed his services more often than heriu-heb who only recited incantations. Contagions however stopped at no one.

"What can you tell me about the man?" Senusret asked the mer-ut. "Has he acted suspicious before?"

"He always took care of his work beyond reproach. Juvenile presumption can't have driven him—if he is the criminal we're looking for—as he has already seen about forty inundations. He's of medium height and shaves his head as it befits a priest." Hut-Nefer's voice trailed off. "The wanted man did not necessarily flee from the weryt. If indeed someone knocked out Hori, he might not have escaped under the wall but reconsidered because he felt caught red-handed. Or he could have returned after achieving what he intended to do." Under the piercing gaze of the king, Hut-Nefer's confused speech in defense ebbed away. "Still, it is probably smart to look for Nebkaura outside the weryt so as not to waste more time."

His attacker had likely fled over all Nile cataracts already. Hori couldn't imagine Nebkaura—or whoever—might be stupid enough to still hang around the residence. Hut-Nefer's reluctance had given the evildoer a significant head start, but he understood the man. In such a tight community as the weryt, any suspicion would have serious consequences for the person at which the finger pointed, and such damage wasn't easy to repair. Last but not least, it must have shocked the mer-ut that one of his people was capable of committing such a crime even when he couldn't deny it any longer. However, sometimes it was hard to look truth in the eye. He cleared his throat. "Do I have permission to consult Nakhtmin in this matter?"

Pharaoh and mer-ut jerked up, so he quickly added, "He already knows of the escape route, and he is well aware of what it means to give away the secrets of the weryt although neither he nor I have any real notion of what exactly Nebkaura might betray. Nevertheless, it always helps me to ask his opinion. He has a different view on things, which often proves valuable, and I promise I will only tell him what he needs to know, only those aspects that don't relate to the actual secrets of the weryt."

When Hut-nefer bowed his head in consent, the king released the breath he'd been holding. "So be it. Mer-ut, return to the weryt and find out if this priest is really sick. As soon as you know more, send one of the weryt guards with a message. And you, Hori, must get well before you can return to the embalming compound. If it will be necessary at all. I'm afraid we need to worry more about the living than the dead these days."

Nakhtmin sat on the jetty of his premises and dangled his feet, impatiently awaiting Hori's return. What made the king summon his friend although he couldn't even stand? He worried about Hori, but at the same time that familiar jealousy pinched him. As usual, he was excluded from the circle of secret bearers.

Behind him, feet crunched gravel, and he turned around. "Darling!" During these last bothersome days, he'd neglected his pregnant wife, spending every free moment at Hori's bed to give Ouseret and Heqet some respite. The two women barely left Hori's side. It had amused Nakhtmin how energetically the little maid defended her patch against the strange woman although Ouseret showed nothing but professional interest in his friend. Mutnofret settled next to him and rested her head on his shoulder. He deeply inhaled her scent of fennel.

"Come inside, my love. You won't be able to see him today," she said. "Tomorrow he'll certainly tell you what it was all about."

"If he's allowed to," Nakhtmin replied more sharply than intended. "But you're right; the strain may be too much for him." With regret, he glanced at the neighboring house.

She followed his gaze and sighed. "Why don't you go out to find some distraction? You could meet with Wenen."

"That's a good idea. That is, if you really don't mind that I leave you alone again."

"Stupid man, what should I do with you when you're so pensive? I know your heart. It will only find peace once you've talked with Hori or gulped down a few jugs of beer."

"Indeed, you know my heart, best of all women." Pretty strange though that she sent him away. He gave her a wary look. "You're not trying to get rid of me, so you can gossip with Ouseret, are you? Now that her patient doesn't need her?"

Mutnofret jutted out her chin, "I never gossip! Women must share knowledge, but you men don't understand that. Walking in and out of the Great House, you catch all the news, while I'm at home all day. Ouseret knows the world out there!" Her eyes sparked.

That sounded as if she felt locked up, unsatisfied. "You want to follow in your friend's footsteps and study at the House of Life?" he teased.

"What if I do? You won't stop me!"

Oh-oh! He envisioned Muti rather as the head of his household and the mother of his children. How could she possibly combine that with stressful studies or the profession of a doctor called for even at the most unusual times of day. Sure peasant women worked the fields, a fisherman's wife sold her husband's catch at the market, but that probably happened out of necessity. At least that's how he imagined it since he'd never asked. "I make enough for both of us, all three of us. You don't h-"

"Of course you'd say that. As if that were the point!" She put her hand on her hips. "Can you imagine that it bores me having nothing to do but to direct servants?"

Other women were content with that and it was an honorable occupation, respected and valued by every man in the Two Lands. "Um, your mother-"

"Don't drag my mother into this! I love her, but I'm not her."

Whoa. "I think I better leave now and meet Wenen." When she was in such a mood, he could only say the wrong thing. Darn Ouseret! Nakhtmin wished she'd never encountered Muti and confused her heart with such nonsense. Or could it be her pregnancy? Did Muti fear the child would tie her to the house? Feeling guilty, he realized that she no longer had much in common with the silly geese she called friends, now that she ran her own household. She should meet other ladies of her age and status. Maybe the wives of Hori's brothers? No, that was a stupid idea. He rose. "Don't wait for me. It might get late."

"Oh, don't worry, I'll be totally occupied with gossiping," she mocked him as he left.

Women! How easy his life had been before he fell in love with Mutnofret! Oh yeah, it was so boring unless the head of physicians tormented him or hunger gnawed at him. And after graduation and his testimony at court he'd stared into an abyss—before him the thugs of the vizier and behind him howling jackals. He shuddered. How fortunate he was now!

At dusk, he reached the harbor district. Familiar odors hung heavy in the narrow alleys where the hot air of the day lingered as if trapped by the warped huts. The area bustled with life at this time of day since many fishermen frequented the taverns to get drunk after the hard work. Wenen probably ate his meals here since he lived alone and had no servant. On every corner, marketeers offered grilled fish, flat bread or vegetables. Nakhtmin's mouth watered. He hadn't enjoyed such simple treats for a long time. Right, and for quite a while he couldn't even afford those.

Although he had eaten at home, he purchased spiced lentils, wrapped in the huge leaf of a water-lily, from an old woman whose mouth turned into a toothless smile when he paid with a piece of a copper deben. Precious metal was rare in this quarter where most people bartered. Savoring the food, he strolled on. The door of the *Golden Ibis* stood invitingly ajar, but although the publican was no longer sleazy Khonsu, Nakhtmin stayed away from that place. That's where it all started, where Hori killed the son of the former vizier. An accident, sure, but with dire consequences. Or fortunate ones, in hindsight. Which tavern had Wenen called his usual watering hole? Ah, yes, *The Apis.*

Only when he stood before the house and stared at the sloppy painting of a bull did he recognize it. That was the place where he'd sat when the little brat approached him with the mysterious message from Hori. What a coincidence! Today the past really caught up with him. Hesitant, he peeked into the dark interior of the dubious tavern. As a hem-netjer, Wenen should be able to afford something better than this. Did his new friend prefer such shady company? In the flickering light of train-oil lamps, he swept his gaze over the heads of the patrons. Over there the flames reflected from the shaved head of a priest. He wanted to call Wenen when he realized the man was engaged in a serious conversation with a shabby guy wearing an ill-fitting wig. Both appeared austere, close to angry. Nakhtmin felt reluctant to join them. He'd come here to get cheered up, not to meet a stranger, so he retreated before Wenen might notice him. Back in the alley, he licked the remains of grease from his hands and moved with the flow of the crowd. The beer he craved he ordered at a different inn.

INCURABLY SICK

Although his visit to the palace had strained Hori, he almost felt like his old self the next day. Unfortunately, his memory still showed the same gaps regarding that fateful night, but preceding events became gradually clearer. Nakhtmin had left for the House of Women early in the morning, while Hori was still sleeping. Nobody to talk to. He was bored although Ouseret had agreed to set up a resting place for him in the shade of trees in his garden. Only Heqet sat with him and culled lentils. Her silent presence started to grow uncomfortable because he couldn't talk with her about the things occupying his mind. Since his injury the girl clinged glued to him, and he felt rather besieged. If only he could read something! However, Ouseret had strictly forbidden that. "It would stress your eyes too much and might aggravate the metu in your head."

Hori sighed. When he looked at Ouseret, different juices in his body started to boil. Likely, she was right about reading, but watching the sunlight play on the surface of the pond wasn't very interesting. Again and again he dozed off. In the late afternoon, Mutnofret joined him for a while and made time pass faster with her amusing chatter until he fell asleep once more.

When he opened his eyes again, Heqet and Muti were gone. Instead, the tall physician sat on the lawn beside him, intently studying a scroll. He observed the contours of her face, the straight nose and full lips and felt an ache in his heart. It started slowly and grew stronger until panic gripped him. The organ performed a wild dance in his ribcage. Had his injury damaged it? He gasped in terror.

The sound drew Ouseret's attention. "You're awake," she stated in her deep voice and lowered the scroll.

As she bent over to examine him, he felt better. The going of his heart turned steadier, and the tightness in his chest loosened up. What a relief!

"You are on the mend. It's time for me to return to work at the House of Life. Your servants can take care of you until you're fully recovered."

"No!" he blurted. The rapid whirl began anew. "Just hearing these words makes me get worse. Don't you notice?" Cold sweat broke out of every pore. He wanted to grab her, so she'd heal him. "Please touch me again."

She drew her dense eyebrows together and felt his frantic pulse. Her hands were warm and dry. "It's nothing you need to worry about," she announced in a mocking tone. "It'll pass."

What kind of a doctor was she? He suffered and she taunted him? Still, he couldn't bear the thought of her leaving and abandoning him to his fate. The dull thuds of his heart sounded like someone beating a drum with the skin not tight enough. He'd never sensed something like this, and it scared him. "Don't go!" he pleaded. "I need you here!"

Nakhtmin's return, announced by the squeaking hinges of the gate, spared her a reply. She rose with elegant moves and left him to the company of his friend. He could only glare after her with chagrin. Now she'd spoiled the joy of anticipating their talk although he craved to tell his friend all about the intricate events at the weryt.

"What's up? Did you two quarrel?" Nakhtmin settled in the spot Ouseret had occupied before.

"She isn't a good doctor," he lamented and related his frightening symptoms and her negligent attitude to Nakhtmin.

And he looked shocked, just like he should! "Oh, let me check for myself. Hm, no. Seems all normal to me. You think it might have to do with your head injury? Hard to imagine. Heart palpitations coming and going? Oh..." Realization dawned in Nakhtmin's face, and a slight smile played around his lips.

Hori sat up, irritated and expectant at the same time.

"Look over there," Nakhtmin ordered and pointed at the house without taking his hand from the spot on his neck where the pounding of the heart could best be felt.

Hori did as he was told. In front of the kitchen wing sat Heqet grinding corn on the milling stone. Otherwise, all was calm, just like his heart. That moment Mutnofret stepped through the door between their estates and approached. Nakhtmin pointed at her, and Hori studied her without noticing anything special.

"All's well," his friend announced. "Now let's try something different. Glance at the river."

Groaning, Hori turned his head to see Ouseret's slender figure standing silhouetted against the reeds at the bank. His throat tightened, his stomach somersaulted.

"Ah," Nakhtmin exclaimed.

"What strange game are you two playing?" Muti asked and settled beside her husband, who explained, to Hori's growing chagrin, the symptoms and results of his tests.

He couldn't shake off the feeling Nakhtmin was making fun of him.

"Let's see if you'd make a good doctor," his friend said to her before turning to him again. "You should know, since she met Ouseret-" The sound of her name sent a jolt through Hori. "-she desires to study at the House of Life."

"So?" Hori uttered vaguely. What was all this about? As if Muti could discern what disease troubled him without professional training. Nakhtmin's lack of seriousness and sympathy for his suffering started to upset him.

Mutnofret's mouth twitched. "Should we really tell him, what's wrong with him?"

"It would be cruel not to do so."

"But it's funnier if we don't."

The pair looked at each other and burst into laughter. Now Hori was seriously annoyed. "Oh sure, I might perish at your feet, and you'd enjoy yourselves. This is no joke!"

Nakhtmin got a grip first. "No, your condition is very serious. There's only one remedy: ask Ouseret to marry you."

Mutnofret giggled.

Hori wanted to jump up, storm into the house and slam the door shut, but he wasn't strong enough yet. Tears welled in his eyes. "Why are you doing this? I'm suffering!"

Nakhtmin took his hand and patted it. "I know. You are in love, my friend."

Very slowly, realization sank into Hori's confused mind. His head grew hot like an oven. How often had he smiled down at patients with condescension when they came to him with a similar ailment, and he still hadn't recognized it in himself? Even Ouseret must have seen through him, that woman who held his heart in her long, slim fingers. Woe to him if she squeezed!

Now Ameny entered the premises. "Oh, there you are!" he called.

Grateful for the distraction that should spare him further ridicule, he remembered how much he'd longed for company earlier. Now he craved solitude just as much, so he could mull over this baffling course of events and probe his new condition with great care. In love… Was it always like this, a pain tasting sweet and bitter at the same time? If only it stopped. May it never end!

"Father!" Muti cried out with joy. "Come, sit with us."

Ameny remained standing beside them. "I only wanted to tell you that I have to leave for a few days. Iriamun's health has worsened rather suddenly, therefore I must undergo a few rites."

They all understood what that meant: the first prophet was dying, and Ameny prepared to succeed him. Hori could guess even more than the others because Ameny's gaze drifted to the ankh sign on his upper arm he hadn't yet covered with the bracelet again. The prophet would be initiated into the mysteries of Osiris! A gust of wind rustled the leaves above their heads. Hori shuddered. He wouldn't want to miss the experience of those rites, but by the gods, he did not wish to repeat them.

"What happened with regard to the fourth prophet? Have you decided on a successor?" Nakhtmin asked.

With effort Hori turned his head. Djedefra should be replaced? He didn't even know about that.

"Considering the rapid decline of Iriamun, we had to act faster than we'd have preferred and selected a man named Kagemni, who had so far managed the largest of the temple domains."

"What's wrong with Djedefra?" Hori asked.

"He encountered a cobra in the Holy Garden of Amun." Nakhtmin's face distorted, and Hori guessed the same memories came to their minds, of how they found the woman whose name must not be spoken, bitten by several cobras.

Mutnofret's brow furrowed. "I still find it hard to believe. A cobra this far north?"

Hori found that strange as well. "Nakhtmin, you're the snake expert among us. Don't these animals prefer the dry desert of the south to the shady, moist northern zones?"

His friend shrugged. "Sure, but it's not that unusual. The gardeners, though, should be flogged for their negligence."

Worry lines creased Ameny's forehead. "It couldn't have happened at a worse moment. Kagemni will soon ascend to third prophet without knowing the duties of his position yet, and we'll have to find a new fourth." Now he did sit down after all.

"As long as it's not Hemiunu, Minmose or Setka," Nakhtmin chimed in.

Ameny gave a thin smile. "Certainly not!"

In agony, Hori closed his eyes. "What are you talking about?"

Nakhtmin reported the assembly in Ameny's house. "By the way, there's something I meant to tell you," he said to his father-in-law. "My friend Wenen gave me the names of two hemu-netjer he deems capable and reliable. You surely know Sehetep, Hemiunu's right hand?"

Friend? Wenen? Hori wanted to ask but postponed it. That could wait until he was alone with Nakhtmin.

Ameny nodded. "Didn't he only recently receive the highest consecration? I'd rather choose someone with more experience."

"Wenen said he already excels in administrative things, and I got the impression that much of what accounts for Hemiunu's diligence is due to him. I wouldn't dismiss him for lack of experience since he seems to make up for that with quick wits and hard work. Even if... No, let's not go there. The other one he suggested was Neferka, a man of great scholarship."

Hori felt like he'd been gone for years, so much had happened he didn't know about, as if he were excluded from the circle he once belonged to and didn't partic-ipate in their lives anymore. A new friend? Then Nakhtmin wouldn't need him any longer, and he'd be alone again... Didn't he suffer enough already because of Ouseret?

Pensive, Ameny rubbed his chin. "Sehetep, indeed... Why hadn't Hemiunu rec-ommended him for the position? He should be taken into consideration. What does this Wenen expect in return for suggesting those two? Are they his friends, and he hopes for favors if one of them is promoted?"

Pushing out his lower lip, Nakhtmin looked begrudged. Oh dear, Ameny shouldn't have said that.

Mutnofret jumped in to say, "No, Father, that's what I thought at first, that he might want to take advantage of Nakhtmin, but Wenen isn't like that. I've met him and think he only wanted to help."

With visible gratitude Nakhtmin smiled at his wife. "Exactly. He doesn't seem to be more than acquainted with the two priests. I encountered Neferka myself and doubt he has any friends except the holy scrolls. With regard to your other ques-tion, Wenen suspected Hemiunu might not want to dispense with his right hand. And I wonder if the man is coveting the position for himself."

Ameny grunted angrily. "Head of the hemu-netjer is a highly respected office requiring much expertise. Hemiunu has been holding it for quite some time and to our satisfaction, but he hasn't commended himself for higher honors. He lacks studiousness."

"Which Neferka exhibits in abundance."

"Thank you." The prophet slapped his son-in-law on the back. "I'll examine both men closely. Maybe one of them presents the solution to our problem. And I'll keep an eye on your friend Wenen if both of you hold him in such high es-teem."

Mutnofret rose. "I should let Baketamun know that we'll have guests for dinner. Father, you'll stay, right? I'm sure Hori can eat with us now again? And of course Ouseret! That's Hori's doctor." She clapped her hands with joy.

Hori groaned. The sound of her name alone pierced him with a puncture needle.

"Actually, I didn't plan to...oh, why not? I've already met Lady Ouseret," mumbled the prophet.

With enthusiasm, Muti bent over. "I can send Mother a message, so she knows where you're hanging out." She kissed her father's cheek. "Or even better, I'll ask her to join us. Then she won't have to miss your company on your last evening. That'll be fun."

Fun? Ever since Baketamun had started bitching because she wasn't prepared to feed so many guests and didn't have enough food in the house, Nakhtmin squirmed. All that in front of Isis! The cook's embarrassing rants traveled all the way into the garden, where they'd settled under the wine trellis. The woman would take out her ill temper on her husband for the rest of the evening, who'd in return punish Nakhtmin in the morning with a rough massage. Adding to that Hori's visible discomfort in Ouseret's presence…

Only Muti had fun, teasing the enamored man. The tall physician, however, remained aloof and cool, as if she didn't notice, while Hori's complexion bounced back and forth between deathly pale and alarmingly red. Well, it was kind of funny because he usually acted so superior. At least his friend was doing much better now—not considering his lovesickness—as he managed to sit upright during the meal, often leaning against the backrest though. Would Ouseret yield to his courtship and release his pain? Despite her reserve, Nakhtmin didn't doubt it. No one rejected him for long. Hori's happiness might cloud his own, though. Woe to him if Muti someday noticed the alluring appeal of the tall doctor, which no man could deny. Hopefully, Ouseret and Hori were already a couple by then.

Under the circumstances, he welcomed Hori's suggestion for the men to withdraw to his estate, while the women could enjoy each other's company. As soon as they'd settled around Hori's resting place in the garden, his friend blurted, "A crime has been committed in the weryt."

He'd known it! "Tell us! Um, are you allowed to?" Eagerly, he awaited the response, while his stomach cramped. He could only hope they wouldn't have to face something as dangerous as last year.

"I obtained permission from mer-ut and pharaoh to reveal certain things. Actually only to you, Nakhtmin." He cast an apologetic smile at Ameny. "But since you already know about the escape route through the canal, it won't hurt if you learn of the events. Such knowledge will be safe with you."

"If not, then the pharaoh—life, prosperity and health—should certainly not make me first prophet of Amun. What happened?"

Hori hesitated for a meaningful moment. Only the nocturnal song of crickets and the gentle rustle of reeds filled the silence. Then he said, "Someone else knows the route. The secrets of the weryt are in danger."

"What?" Nakhtmin snapped.

"Are you sure?" Ameny called even louder.

Hori told them about the heart without body and his discovery that the walls of the embalming compound weren't patrolled. "Well, that's all I know about that night," he concluded. "But it stands to reason the lector priest Nebkaure has left the necropolis. He or somebody else."

Dizziness engulfed Nakhtmin. "W-what's that mean?" he stammered and looked to Ameny for advice.

The prophet's face appeared white as chalk in the faint light of torches. "That somebody might sell secret incantations."

"Like those with which to call forth the dead," Hori added. "The shadows of the damned..."

Nakhtmin shuddered. The western shores must be infested with ghosts, all those deceased, who hadn't received a proper burial! He remembered Wenen's father, who'd set out on his last journey between a crocodile's jaws, and other more vicious shadows. "What harm could these specters cause?"

Hori turned to Ameny. "I don't know. Such knowledge is kept secret for a good reason. Presumably, they could take hold of the living, hurt them, maybe even kill?"

Muti's father nodded gravely. "I don't know specifics, but I'm certain we'd all face great danger if someone released the shadows!"

Nakhtmin thought those demons were dangerous enough when nobody tried to use them and remembered the terrified face of the guard at the House of Women. He took a gulp from his mug and closed his eyes. Oh dear! "Sennedjem's cousin!" he exclaimed.

"What are you talking about?" Hori asked and leaned closer. "Do you mean the guy sometimes guarding the House of Women?"

"Exactly! Listen." He lowered his voice. "His cousin was one of those protecting the weryt. Frantic with dread, he told Sennedjem about the terrible noises he heard during his first night there. The next evening, the man had to enter the realm of the dead again. Since then he has not been seen." With satisfaction, Nakhtmin saw horror reflect on the faces of his audience, then flinched when Hori suddenly grabbed his wrist.

"When was that? What's the man's name?"

"Hey!" He jerked his arm away. "How would I know? And why do you need his name?"

"We have to...ugh... That headache! It twists my tongue. He could be the one whose heart is missing."

Nakhtmin didn't comprehend, but Ameny's features showed understanding. "The villain dived under the wall, not suspecting that it would be guarded!"

Of course! Now he too saw the connection and continued the scenario, "They ran into each other, fought, and the guard died. But why would the killer remove his heart?"

"Yeah," Hori said, stretching the word. "That's a good question. Maybe our culprit didn't intend to do evil when he tested the escape route, only meant to satisfy his curiosity. Then disaster struck, and he had to prevent his deeds being disclosed. At the same time, as an inhabitant of the weryt, he abhorred not properly treating his victim's heart. After all, he had to fear the spirit of the dead taking revenge if he denied him the Judgment of the Dead. That would also explain... No, that I can't tell you."

"So, in that case, the corpse of Sennedjem's cousin—Rahotep, yes, that was his name—must be buried in the sand somewhere on the western shore. And you are insinuating he's awaiting last rites to be performed on him?"

Ameny shook his head. "What insanity!"

"However, that doesn't explain everything," Hori murmured. "Why weren't there any guards patrolling the necropolis the other day? The commander of the garrison swears his men did their duty."

A scream made them all flinch. Ameny laughed out in embarrassment. "Only a waterfowl. A nocturnal predator must have stirred up its nest."

"Maybe we should question the men of that garrison," Nakhtmin suggested. "According to Sennedjem, having to serve there is a form of punishment, so I assume they are all obstreperous fellows with an inclination to sink their noses deep into tankards. We'd only need to find out where they tend to drink and loosen their tongues. Then we might find out when exactly Rahotep disappeared. However, he might have simply run away, and to be honest, that seems most likely to me. What's up?" he asked because Hori seemed to mull over something.

"The mer-ut knew something about when the heart must have entered the weryt... Ah, yes, the cord." Nakhtmin and Ameny exchanged confused glances, but Hori continued unperturbed, "The string was delivered to the weryt on the third day of month Khenti-khet. The heart must have arrived afterward. And it was discovered... on the second or third of this month, three weeks later. If Rahotep disappeared within that time frame, everything fits."

Ameny cleared his throat. "Don't jump to conclusions. As Nakhtmin said, the man might simply have run off and could be hiding now because he deserted."

"That's possible. But then we are looking for someone else's body. How likely is it that a corpse on the eastern shore hasn't been detected? Only yonder, in the west, could the dead remain hidden for so long. I'm not taking the river into consideration, because it would make little sense to prepare the heart of the man but leave the body to the crocodiles."

That sounded convincing. Nowhere would a corpse be better protected against discovery than in the realm of the dead. Who'd start digging in the desert sand? "I'll go tom—oh, no! I have to take care of my duties at the House of Life, my weekly volunteer work. If I don't show up, I'll incur Imhotepankh's scorn." The head of physicians still hadn't warmed to him, but he tolerated his regular tending to the poorest since nobody liked to do it. The old man had made it very clear, though, that he would not accept Nakhtmin coming and going as he pleased. The House of Life depended on physicians rendering their services reliably. Aghast, he realized Hori had gotten him involved in another investigation. And he actually felt eager to jump to it.

His friend was saying, "Mh, since this affair is of such great importance and I won't be up to much for a while longer, we should ask the king to relieve you of all your other duties. Not even Imhotepankh can oppose a royal order."

"And who's going to treat the concubines? I can't leave the House of Women in Tep-Ta's hands alone." He giggled. "Running Nose, that's how Sennedjem called him."

Hori burst out laughing and immediately held his head. "Ouch, I hope that pain ceases soon! No worries, I'll probably be able to return to work in a few days as long as I can occasionally sit down on a chair. These investigations, I'm afraid, won't allow for any delay. The king will agree, and if he sends out Medjay, the law enforcers will draw unwanted attention to the matter. We need to avoid that."

Ameny nodded. "That sounds reasonable. But Nakhtmin..."

"Yes?"

"Be careful! For Muti's sake if not your own. Do you understand what you might be dealing with?"

Nakhtmin did not, not exactly. He imagined a nameless, amorphous horror. His mouth felt parched, so he moistened his tongue with a big gulp of beer from his mug. "Tell me," he croaked although he'd have loved to stay ignorant.

Ameny cleared his throat. "As you know, every human being owns a body, khet, and a name, ren. In addition, he has a double, ka, which contains his life energy. After death, the body turns into a mummy, sah."

Nakhtmin nodded. That much he knew.

"The essence of a person is his ba staying in his body as long as that remains alive. After death, it parts from the corpse and rises in the shape of a bird. It stays attached to the mummy, though. Should the mummy be destroyed, the ba loses its home since it can't return to its body. However, the ba too can be caught when it roams, even get killed."

He swallowed. What dreadful dangers lurked even in death! Gradually, he understood why the knowledge fostered in the weryt was kept so secret.

"When the rites are performed on the mummy, ka and ba unify, and the dead is transfigured into the akh. Surely you know: only as an akh, the deceased ascends to heaven and joins the sun god in his journey across the firmament. Both aspects of the soul, however, still exist separately even after they've merged. The ka needs nourishment, that's why we sacrifice food. By calling the name of the departed, we make sure our prayers reach him. A dead person without a name is forever lost."

Although Nakhtmin knew the basics, he now saw the events and processes at work after death in a different light. Quite often people did things out of custom, without thinking of their purpose. Ameny's words reminded him of a father teaching his son. Maybe he'd done exactly that with Bata and Huni recently. Then he remembered Wenen's grief over his father. Without a body he had no chance of transfiguration.

"Furthermore, there's the shut, the shadow of every living creature," Ameny continued. "He who casts no shadow has no substance and therefore cannot exist. The shut accompanies everyone from birth and even past death. It can leave the grave and fly with the ba. The shut also holds the essence of the soul, like a duplicate copy. Explaining the reasons would be too complicated now. You only need to know that it is so and that therefore the shadow contains a part of the human to which it belongs. Usually it exists in a different sphere than the world of the living."

So the shadows remembered life in this sphere? But of course. That was why some people implored the shadows of their beloved not to haunt and torment them in their dreams. Those shapeless beings had to know with whom they were once associated.

"Now, if one of the aspects of a deceased, mummy, name, ka, ba or shut, gets destroyed, death is final. No resurrection into the heavenly realms, no afterlife." Heavy, the words hung in the air.

Turning over these explanations in his heart, he realized Ameny hadn't mentioned the ghosts of the damned. "And the dangers I'll be facing…" he prompted.

"Oh, right. Foremost, beware of the shadows! They have the power to strike people with illness and death. During the five leap days at the end of the year, it may happen that the shadows stray into the world of the living. Usually they dwell on a plane of the western realm invisible to us. Should someone have the secret knowledge of how to command the shadows of the dead, particularly those of the

74

damned and ostracized, who were denied an afterlife for good reasons, we are in utmost danger. Nobody in the Two Lands would be safe."

Hori nodded. "As a physician you know we sometimes need the assistance of priests or magicians if a patient is possessed by an evil demon."

Nakhtmin had seen such hopeless cases where the patient squirmed in torment and lapsed into cramps until death brought relief. "Our craft is powerless against those." And sometimes dark shadows consumed the vitality of a patient...shadows... He imagined an army of dark specters taking possession of the living. Gruesome! "How can I protect myself?" he cried.

Ameny took his hand. "You'll need powerful amulets. Both of you!" He touched the pendants he wore around his neck, then handed Nakhtmin a skillfully crafted ankh of gold with turquoise inlays. "Take this. Upon my return, I'll get you more potent preservation charms. Promise me you won't do more than sound out those soldiers until then! May the gods have mercy on us. Whoever abuses the knowledge of the shadows won't be able to control them."

Nakhtmin promised and wished he could stay out of it all, but that would be cowardly, and he'd never forgive himself if someone he loved were harmed because he shied from the risk. "How will I recognize such a shadow if it has seized a living person?"

"I think you will." Ameny grimaced. "Let's hope you'll never find out."

Drunken Scoundrels

Day 14 of month Ipet-hemet in Shemu, the season of the harvest

At dawn, Nakhtmin set out for the palace. Fortunately, Senusret started his days early. Actually, he also worked until far into the night. Not for the first time, Nakhtmin wondered if the king ever slept. He certainly didn't envy him for the responsibility as helmsman of the Two Lands since he felt overwhelmed already with the few things he needed to worry about: his patients, the Royal Wife foremost, Muti's pregnancy, Ameny's concerns with filling the prophet positions, Hori's investigation, the shadows... How did the pharaoh manage to carry a much heavier burden on his heart? Nevertheless, the Black Land fared well. Everything went according to plan like in a sophisticated watering system when the Nile waters rose. He admired Senusret, barely older than himself, who achieved all that to the satisfaction of the gods and to the cheers of his people. Woe to the Horus throne, should it ever remain vacant!

Ra's solar bark had barely kissed the horizon when he passed the sleepy-eyed palace guards and entered through the large double gate. By now, he'd often enough visited the royal office to find his way through the resounding hallways by himself. Hori always complained that to him each corridor looked the same, but Nakhtmin memorized little things: a crack in the plaster here, a slight wave in a decorative stripe on the wall there. At last he reached his destination and, as he'd hoped, was the first petitioner of the day. Atef cast him an astonished look. "His majesty—life, prosperity and health—is performing the morning rites for Amun-Ra."

Right, beside everything else, the king was also the highest intermediary between gods and human beings. The prophets only served as his proxies since not even the pharaoh could be in several places at the same time. Still, Nakhtmin hadn't been aware Senusret also celebrated daily rituals, at least for Amun-Ra, but it didn't surprise him either. "I'll wait. My request is urgent," he said and sat on the bench.

Atef yawned and stretched. "Must be the case or else you wouldn't have come here..." His gaze wandered to the amulet with the Eye of Horus marking Nakhtmin as a physician. "Doctor..."

Nakhtmin gave his name in hopes the man might remember him.

"Oh, right, one of the palace physicians. Nevertheless, you must wait." After a while, realization and fear dawned in the servant's face. "You serve in the House of Women! Is something wrong with the Horus in the egg?"

"No, as far as I know, her majesty the queen is well. Another matter of great importance for the Two Lands brings me here."

The king's voice sounded muffled through the cedarwood door. "Atef? What's going on out there?"

The servant opened the door a crack. "A doctor named Nakhtmin wishes to speak with you. He says it's urgent."

"Send him in. I'll talk with him."

Nakhtmin entered. The last few times he'd always been here in the company of Ameny whose respect-commanding position had given him some confidence.

Without his support, Nakhtmin sank into a deep bow and stretched out his palms.

"Nakhtmin! Rise, take a seat."

The burden of responsibility had left traces in the king's face: Deep creases ran from the nose to the corners of his mouth, and heavy lacrimal sacs tugged on his eyelids. Maybe he really never slept. Nakhtmin sat down and cleared his throat. "With your permission, majesty, Hori informed me of the issue with the heart last night. Since he is still too weak and needs care, he suggested I question the soldiers of the garrison. That's why I'm turning to you."

"Hold on," the king interrupted. "Which garrison are you talking about?"

Of course he wouldn't know. Hastily, Nakhtmin reported his conversation with Sennedjem and the conclusions they'd drawn yesterday.

Senusret pressed his fingertips together. "Well now. If your assumptions are correct, then the western desert may swallow those lazy scoundrels. Leaving the weryt unprotected! You have my permission to interrogate the men. Should I send palace guards along to strengthen your authority?"

"With respect, your majesty, I believe they'd rather reveal the truth if they didn't suspect someone with authority is asking questions. Besides, my understanding was that as few people as possible should get wind of this matter."

First, the king appeared angry, then he smiled. "Although it displeases me to think these men would lie to an emissary of my majesty, you might be right. What else do you need?"

"It would foster the investigation if you'd officially relieved me of my duties and not only in the House of Women. Today I'm expected to do volunteer work at the House of Life, and I'd rather not alienate the venerable head of physicians."

"So be it." He opened a side door and raised his voice. "Thotnakht!"

In the adjoining room, Nakhtmin spotted the wig of his majesty's scribe, who sat in the typical position on a sedge mat, a fresh papyrus spread across his shendyt. "Master?" he asked assiduously and grabbed the stylus.

With precise, crisp words, Senusret dictated the two notes. Fascinated, Nakhtmin watched the cane in the scribe's hand slide over the sheet. Blotted with sand and sealed with the pharaoh's signet, the messages were handed to a palace servant. Nakhtmin expressed his gratitude. "Hori hopes to recover enough to soon support Tep-T... um, our valued colleague, at the House of Women. For a while, though, he should take things easy."

Senusret looked up. "I sure hope so! The Running Nose isn't exactly the kind of doctor I want to trust with the well-being of the Horus in the egg. Still, I also must accept the demands of hierarchy. As long as you or Hori are present, I know Nofrethenut to be in good hands."

Nakhtmin's jaw dropped, then he burst out laughing. "You know his nickname?"

The pharaoh grinned mischievously. "You should know I don't miss much, and hardly a name ever suited its bearer better." He sighed. "That pompous gnome could do much damage. My wives have already complained about him. I guess I'll soon have to find a position for the man, one that takes him far away, yet is honorable enough to avoid insulting his family."

The king took him into his confidence! That could only mean he valued Hori and himself not only because of their medical knowledge. For a brief moment, his heart wallowed in a sense of pride. How astonishing that the ruler of the Two Lands also had to yield to such pressures. Wasn't the pharaoh a god?

"So you are aware of the events in the weryt," Senusret interrupted his thoughts.

He nodded. "As far as Hori thought it would be safe to enlighten us—um, me."

The king scrutinized him with sharp eyes. "Us?"

Now fear clutched Nakhtmin's heart. And a moment ago he'd prided himself on the king's trust! "Ameny. He was also present last night. W-we thought…since he already knows…" He wiped his moist hands on his shendyt.

The tension in the pharaoh's face yielded to a smile. "That was well done. Once before the three of you revealed an outrageous crime and proved in command of your tongues. Under different circumstances, I'd probably have consulted him myself."

What circumstances? Then he remembered. "Iriamun! The Two Lands will be in mourning when the first prophet sets out on his journey to the Beautiful West."

Senusret's lids closed for a moment. "Many new responsibilities await Ameny, but *that* change doesn't worry me."

In his place, Nakhtmin would also fret over the leadership of the Amun temple. Did the cobra have to show up just now?

"On a different note, I received a message from the head embalmer. The supposedly sick heri-heb has indeed disappeared. Please tell Hori."

"No surprise there." He caught a questioning glance from the king and quickly added, "I mean that man really made for a prime suspect. May Sakhmet punish him with boils!" Imagining what doom the stolen knowledge of the lector priest might bring down on the Two Lands, he shuddered.

"I can think of much harsher curses for that fellow." Senusret clenched a fist. "If only I'd known earlier. The Medjay of the Two Lands received a message with the description of the culprit."

"May the gods protect us! Hopefully he is caught before he can wreak havoc." A gust of wind rustled the leaves in the royal garden, which briefly blocked the rays of sun streaming in through the ventilation slits. Nakhtmin believed he saw shadows dancing across the walls.

For the first time since his injury, Hori managed to get up without the room spinning around him. When he heard Ouseret's steps approach, he quickly leaned against the wall and groaned.

She entered and scrutinized him head to toe with a mocking gaze. "Doctors make the worst patients. I'll leave you today; my things are already packed."

"No!" he cried. "I'm not well at all today! Surely a relapse." How could he conquer her heart if she returned to the House of Life? Terror made him break out in a sweat. He couldn't bear to not see her again. That notion alone hurt so much— letting her go would kill him. His heart would crumble to dust. Moaning, he sank back onto the bed.

"Hm, you look pale indeed." She settled on the edge and touched his skin. "Cold sweat."

"Everything's spinning in front of my eyes," he lamented. "I'm nauseous." Think, Hori, what other symptoms can occur with severe head injuries? Oh, right. "I see everything twofold but blurred."

With a skeptical look on her face, she bent over him and examined first his eyes then the wound, while he deeply inhaled her feminine scent. She picked up the bronze mirror on his dressing table and redirected Ra's rays at his face. He screamed in agony and held a hand over his eyes. "That hurts!" This time he didn't lie. The light pierced him like a knife.

A sigh slipped from her mouth. "All right, I'll stay another day."

He only wished she wouldn't look so disgruntled. If roles were reversed, he'd break his back if it meant he'd be allowed to tend to her longer.

"I'll have to send one of your servants to the House of Life, though, or else they'll expect me to show up today, and the principal already dislikes me."

She left the room, and with her fled light, air and joy. Hori felt more miserable than ever. How did others survive this condition? Nobody could have loved as fervently as he did. By the gods, he was so sick of lying around all the time!

For fear she might discover his deception, he didn't dare leave his bed. Except for his servants hurrying back and forth in the corridor, nothing held his gaze. When Ouseret walked past, he sat up and called, "Please sit with me." Oh how pathetic that sounded, like a whiny child. He'd certainly not win her heart if he kept acting like that.

As soon as she sat next to him, he suggested casually, "Tell me about you. I barely know anything of you." And he congratulated himself on the choice of subject. All people liked to talk about themselves, particularly women. That way, he could assure her presence for a while. He granted her the smile that made women go all soft.

"There's nothing to say about me, except what you already know. I'm a physician." Her voice took on a metallic quality, wasn't soft and velvety anymore.

Had the blow to his head destroyed the power of his smile? He laughed nervously. "I'm sure there are more interesting things about you to find out. Where did your desire to study medicine stem from?"

"Someone fell sick. The doctors couldn't defeat the demon."

"So you wanted to fathom the secrets of medicine yourself to help the person? A relative?".

Her gaze turned icy. "I have better things to do than indulge in idle chatter. Do you need something? Otherwise…" She moved to get up.

If only he hadn't asked. Now she was mad at him. Still, he couldn't restrain himself. "Your family is from Waset? I mean…you worked at the House of Life there, right?"

"Right."

She bent her leg, and her knee touched his hand, sending a jolt though him. Of their own accord, his fingers moved up her thigh. Ouseret's body stiffened. She brushed off his hand like an annoying insect and rose. "Do you need Heqet in your chamber?" Her voice dripped with contempt.

"Ouseret! Wait! I love you!" he called.

"So what?" She rushed off.

Hori felt he would die.

Nakhtmin hot-footed from the palace to the garrison of the weryt guards. The small camp of adobe barracks surrounded by a wall was built just outside the city and had its own pier. Of course, the men had to row across the river to their posts. Pensive, Nakhtmin looked at the weryt on the opposite bank, clearly discernable in the glistening rays of morning light. Apart from the Anubis temple farther upstream, those walls across were the only signs of human habitation. A soldier stood at each side of the gate. According to Hori, they had not been there the other night. When did the guards change? There should be at least three shifts since the king ordered its protection night and day. Likely the first rotation happened early in the morning while the commander of the garrison was still asleep, another in the afternoon and the last one after Monthnakht went to bed.

Nakhtmin didn't really have a clue how to tackle the problem without betraying his intentions. If he did, the hearts of the men would crouch behind walls just as thick as those over there, and he wouldn't learn anything. First he should find out when they were relieved of their duty, so he could approach them at the right moment. However, he felt no inclination to wait here all day. Hold on, surely they didn't always send the same men to serve there, that would be too cruel even for a penal garrison. That meant every single one of them knew the answer he was looking for. Each one, except for the commander, if he really deserved the trust of the mer-ut. Could he indeed be clueless and innocent? That wasn't impossible though it wouldn't shed a favorable light on him if his men lied and neglected their duties without him finding out.

Nakhtmin was about to approach the camp when he saw a wandering ragman on the street, his pannier stacked high. A common view, which made him cringe anyway. By the holy ennead of Waset, he'd almost knocked on the gate, dressed in his fine shendyt and decorated with precious amulets! In this area close to the harbor district, he'd stick out like a cow with three horns. He groaned and scolded himself for not thinking about it earlier. What now, turn back home and change his clothes? Muti would wonder why he wasn't at the House of Life and ask questions. This time she must not learn of his snooping around. The matter was far too dangerous, particularly with her being pregnant... He swallowed and cast a disgusted glance at the dealer. Did he have a choice? Oh, the man would be thrilled to sell the first batch right here. At least Nakhtmin's sandals were worn enough not to draw attention. He hurried toward the man. "Hiho, do you have a threadbare shendyt for me?"

The old fellow gave a bleating laugh. "What's wrong with yours, sir?"

"Do you wish to be paid in answers or copper?" Nakhtmin rebuked the curious fellow.

"Copper?" Under crinkled lids shifty eyes glittered. "Certainly, my lord, at your service." He let the pannier slide from his shoulders and clumsily spread his goods before Nakhtmin. The clothes smelled musty.

Some idlers stopped and made stupid comments. Too much attention for Nakhtmin's liking. Quickly, he grabbed a washed out piece of cloth and used his bronze knife to cut a far too large bit from his soft copper ring. Fawning and cackling, the trader wanted to seize the occasion and sell more of his wares. Praising his assortment as finest linen worthy of a nobleman, he only made the watchers scatter. Nakhtmin snatched a cloth he spotted among the rags. When the old man stretched out his open hand, he lost his temper. "That's covered by the copper I already gave you, you scoundrel!"

He hurried off with his purchases, changed behind the cover of reeds at the riverbank and wrapped his good things in the cloth. Only with reluctance did he take off his amulets and place them inside the bundle, which he flung around his shoulder. Hopefully they protected him even when he wasn't wearing them on his chest. Dressed like a simple fisherman, he headed toward the adobe wall of the garrison. For once, he appreciated his dark skin that made him look like someone working under the rays of Ra all day. He had almost reached the gate when a group of five men left the camp and turned toward the harbor district. Without hesitation, Nakhtmin followed them.

As he'd hoped, the guys ambled into one of the watering holes already—or still—open for business. Right behind them, he sneaked into the foul-smelling darkness of the tavern and settled at the table next to theirs. They were the only guests. Glad to still have the major part of a copper deben on him, he slapped it on the table and shouted with flourish. "A beer for me and five more for my friends over there. I've had quite some luck rolling the dice last night."

The soldiers replied with happy cheers. "Come on over, friend. Sit with us," one of them called.

Nakhtmin grinned. That went just as he'd hoped. The square fellow at the edge scooted to make room for him on the bench. As soon as he sat, the beers arrived. The innkeeper obviously smelled good business here.

"Now, comrades, what drives you this early to the tankards? Did you get a day off?" Nakhtmin asked and grinned oafishly.

"Nah," his seat neighbor announced. "Our shift's over already, and we're off duty."

"Let's drink to that!" Nakhtmin called and took a small sip that should look like a big gulp, while he congratulated himself. These must be the men of the night watch. He'd caught the right ones!

"Hear, hear!" For a while only slurping and swallowing could be heard.

Nakhtmin eyed the mug to his right. Almost empty. "I'm sure your service makes you thirsty. Another round, innkeeper!"

Enthused, the fellows slammed their tankards onto the table.

"So how come you must work when others sleep? What service do you perform?" he asked.

Nonplussed noses sank toward the beer. "Night watch," mumbled the giant sitting opposite Nakhtmin.

"O-ho! You must be protecting something real precious." From the corners of his eyes, he saw one of the men splay thumb and forefinger under the table to fend off evil.

The pudgy one scratched his chest hair in discomfort then drained his mug in one go.

"Hey, innkeeper, more of the same!" Nakhtmin shouted.

The sight of the foamy brew made the cowards cheer up again. For a while, they talked about things, and Nakhtmin twice ordered more beer.

"W-what'cha w-win?" his neighbor inquired with a heavy tongue.

"Ah, should last for another round or three," Nakhtmin tempted. By now he had four full jugs in front of him. Fortunately, his companions didn't notice they were drinking alone.

All of a sudden, the giant bent forward and whispered, "The dead, we guardin' the dead."

Nakhtmin leaned toward him. "You're kidding! Over there on the western shore? At night? The weryt? I wouldn't dare go there. There roam gh-"

"Sh-shhh," the pudgy one hissed. "We ain't doin' it, guardin' the dead. No-hicc-body mus' know!"

Had he heard right? Nakhtmin wanted to jump up and move to the other end of table. "What do you mean?"

"Shut up, Tutu!" the guy across from the fat one barked. "Or you'll end up like Rahotep."

Tutu paled. "Rahotep! They got him, the demons. We ain't stu-hicc-stupid and stay there overnight."

"Nah," Nakhtmin agreed. "You ain't stupid. A smart man avoids the shadows of the dead."

Nodding, the giant babbled to himself.

"You guys row back when nobody notices and hide, right?"

"Who told you?" Tutu shouted and, swaying, rose to his not very impressive height.

Nakhtmin ducked. Time to retreat. That moment, one of the scoundrels grabbed his neck and pushed his face onto the table, toppling one of the full tankards so it spilled its contents onto the wooden top. Drunk or not, the fellow was strong. Now only his tongue could save him. "Hey, you told me yourselves," he gasped while the puddle expanded toward him. The grip on his neck loosened a little.

"Hey, careful with the beer!" one cried out.

"Idiot!" Tutu bawled.

"Who couldn't keep his trap shut? That was you, fatso!"

A dull thud. Fist on puffy cheek? A scream. Nakhtmin, too, caught blows and kicks. As soon as his tormentor let go of him to charge at someone else, he slid from the bench, which soon after toppled over. Nobody seemed to remember why they were hitting each other. The pudgy one grabbed the lanky one by the throat, emptied his mug and hit his comrade over the head with it.

Trying not to draw attention, Nakhtmin picked up his bundle and sneaked to the innkeeper. "Sorry, but I'm going to look for different company." He handed him his last copper and hoped it would cover the broken mugs and everything else.

Unfazed, the man nodded. "Will be over soon. Then they won't remember any-thing."

So he'd better hurry before the ruffians saw him and did recall his questions. At least he got what he came here for: confirmation that they secretly sneaked away instead of patrolling the necropolis. The king would want to know.

Nakhtmin hastened down the path along the river, then turned into the broad boulevard leading to the temples and the palace. Only when he drew disapproving looks from courtiers and priests he passed, did he realize how ragged he looked. And he reeked of beer. No way could he stand before the king like this. Did it even make sense for him to wait for another audience? At this time of day, the phar-aoh's antechamber would be brimming with petitioners. Mulling over it, Nakhtmin chewed his lower lip. Instead, he should find out where the thugs spent their nights in hiding. Yes, a message to the king should suffice for now. As if of their own accord, his feet had changed direction toward the temple of Amun. Now he stood before the gorgeous facade.

Too bad that Ameny was gone. He'd have loved to consult him. His father-in-law might even have offered to accompany him tonight, so he didn't have to lurk in hiding all alone. But what should he do until the afternoon to pass time? If he returned home early, Muti would ask inconvenient questions. The House of Life was no option either since the king's message had excused him. Maybe Wenen was at leisure to chat with him? First though, he had to clean himself up. Fortunately there was a facility at the entrance to the temple premises he could use. Freshened up, cleansed and wearing his own clothes again, he crossed the courtyard and dove into the shadows of the atrium. Avoiding the sanctum sanctorum, where he wasn't allowed—nor was Wenen—he ambled through the deserted hallways of the administrative building. Strange, as usually wabu and priests hurried about, taking care of their tasks. Since he didn't want to simply open doors and peak into the rooms, he retreated rather disappointed. He'd really have enjoyed meeting Wenen again after he couldn't talk with him the other evening.

Already resigned to idly roaming the streets all day, he remembered that Hori was at home. Why not go to him? Of course, Muti might drop by and then he'd be done for. However, the risk seemed small. Determined, he headed toward home. As he approached nobler houses, the howling of lamenting women reached his ears. Somebody must have died, someone important. Curious, he followed the noises through the alleys all the way to the house of the first prophet Iriamun. The gate to the estate stood ajar, and Nakhtmin spotted several priests on the premises, most of them praying, some standing in groups quietly talking. Here they were! Iriamun must have started his journey into the Beautiful West, and the complete priesthood of Amun paid him their last respects. Not being able to join in would pain Ameny. On the other hand, his initiation into whatever was even more important now. Nakhtmin searched the bent backs and bald heads for Wenen in vain. Disturbing him here and now, wouldn't be appropriate anyway. About to leave, he saw a noble palanquin with drawn curtains turn into the alley. Passing it, he recognized it as the king's. Informing the pharaoh of what he found out from the weryt guards wouldn't make much sense under the circumstances. Senusret would have his mind on other things today.

FOUND OUT

Rustling leaves woke Hori from a light slumber. He lifted his head and spotted Nakhtmin wading through the reeds on the riverbank.

"Why are you sneaking about?" he called.

His friend flinched and ran to him. "Psst!" He glanced over his shoulder to the connecting gate between their estates.

"Oh, taking flight from Muti?"

Nakhtmin nodded sheepishly. "She's not supposed to find out about the mission the king sent us on. You know her. She'd want to help us and get herself in danger. Remember her recklessness last year. She almost had to marry Shepses!" He settled next to Hori. "I've found out something."

Patiently, Hori nodded to his friend's report although his thoughts circled around Ouseret. How could he make her stay longer?

"You aren't listening!" Nakhtmin complained. "Don't you understand what that means? The night guards hide somewhere instead of patrolling the necropolis. Tonight I'll find out where they are holing up."

"Sorry, of course that's an important discovery. We already suspected, now we know for sure. I'd come along later if…"

"No, that's all right. You need to rest a lot."

"I'm going to rest myself to death!" A thought popped up in his mind, and he grabbed Nakhtmin's wrist. "If we search the western shore around the weryt we must find the corpse of unlucky Rahotep."

"Don't you even think about crawling around there on your own!"

"No, that's something for the pharaoh's men. Maybe the king could provide his hunting hyenas. They smell a carcass over quite some distance," Hori mused. "Say, what present can I give Ouseret for her services? Any ideas? Something that impresses her?"

"Hori! Can't you think of anything but that woman?"

He sighed. "Who could?"

"The world's been turned upside down, and he pines like an adolescent. By the way, the first prophet died today. The temple of Amun will go haywire. The first dead, his successor gone, the third without experience, no fourth appointed yet. You really should get a grip on yourself, man. There are more important things going on!"

"Oh," Hori said, but the Amun temple wasn't his concern. Of course, Nakhtmin had to take an interest, being so tightly connected with Ameny. He, however, would prefer to know what might please Ouseret. Had to be something special that would open her heart to him. Precious… 'So what?' she'd said! As if his love were nothing. He currently went through the most unsettling sensations of his life. Well, close to that. "Livestock wouldn't be appropriate. How'd she take care of it? Maybe jewelry."

Nakhtmin grabbed the hair of his wig with both hands. "By Min's phallus! Kiss her and get it over with!"

"I've tried," he whined. "Even confessed my love for her, but she wouldn't hear any of it. Now she avoids me, and tomorrow she'll abandon me." He struggled onto his elbows. "Now, don't you act the expert in all matters of love, just because you managed to lure a woman into your house! How did you conquer Muti, eh?"

At that, the guy burst into laughter. While he felt miserable enough to die because of his longing, Nakhtmin rolled in the grass guffawing. Just you wait!

"Huahaha! How could she dare to reject your love! What an evil woman."

"Don't bad-mouth h—By Seth's testicles! Don't poke fun at me when I need help!"

Nakhtmin cracked up several times more until he pulled himself together and wiped tears from his eyes. "Jewelry is good, but she doesn't look the type who likes to adorn herself much."

Hori pulled a long face, "No, not really. Would be cumbersome when bending over patients, too." His friend was of no help. Or was he? "What? You look like Ra's rays enlightened you."

"Present her with a medical toolkit!" Nakhtmin said. "Some of her own tools are crooked and of low quality. Only very few things made me happier than the beautiful kit Ameny gave me."

Oh, that was fantastic, exactly what he'd been racking his heart for. "Thanks! You are a true friend after all."

Nakhtmin displayed a lopsided grin. "I'd like to think so. And since I don't have anything better to do right now: Should I look around the craftsmen's quarters for something suitable?"

Hori considered the offer, then declined. That present he had to choose himself. In his imagination, he already saw Ouseret's eyes glow with love and gratitude, therefore he only half listened to Nakhtmin's chatter about a lector priest.

On his way back to the garrison, Nakhtmin still alternated between amusement and anger over Hori's behavior. Amazing how hard it had hit his friend for once. The timing couldn't be worse though. Right now though, he should focus his heart on the mystery they must solve. Too many worries occupied his own, and the stress of having to lie to Muti didn't make things any easier. Hopefully this would be his last excuse: he'd pretended wanting to spend the evening with Wenen, while in reality he'd spy on the guards of the necropolis. Too bad he didn't know exactly when the guards changed. To be on the safe side, he'd set out right after an early dinner before the sun kissed the western horizon, and this time he wore his father-in-law's protective amulet as well as a few of his own conspicuously on his chest, just to make sure. Fortunately, he was able to lurk on the eastern shore. Under the circumstances, with ghosts running wild out west, neither gold nor good words could lure him to the other side of the river. Shadows of the damned! Instinctively, he splayed thumb and forefinger.

Soon he reached the jetty of the garrison and found a comfortable spot behind a bush. Through the branches he could keep track of the boats. The last rays of the sun god clearly showed the side walls of the weryt unguarded. Tutu and his companions had been five, one for each direction and two for the river side, so this wasn't the night watch yet. During the day, the two men at the gate sufficed since they'd spot anyone approaching or leaving the realm of the dead. When the sun disappeared behind the hills, they stepped into the small boat bobbing in the shallow Nile. Softly, the oars splashed water. A short time later the papyrus dinghy thudded against the pier, and he heard the men chatting. Ah, there was the replacement. Five men entered a larger boat. Craning his neck to see if they were his *friends* of this morning, he thought he could make out fat Tutu. They'd be lucky if their heads didn't ache after that much beer. Nakhtmin observed them reaching the other side. By now it was pretty dark. What were they doing, sitting on the jetty like hens? Likely they didn't dare venture farther into the realm of the dead. He shifted his position slightly, since a rock poked his butt. Hopefully, he wouldn't have to wait long now.

What was that? Heavy steps pounded over the jetty this side of the river. Someone lit a lamp. Maybe a signal. Across the river, a torch flared up and dipped the men in an eerie light. The signaler on this side might be the commander of the garrison making sure they'd reached the western shore. Or did a friend signal the coast was clear? Either way, both lights were extinguished soon after and the steps beside Nakhtmin retreated while the men yonder climbed into the boat, barely making a noise. Nakhtmin quietly rose and followed the path along the bank outbound since he assumed the men would be heading there. The thin sickle of a moon shed little light, which served Nakhtmin well. If he couldn't see anything, he couldn't be seen. And the reeds stood high enough to prevent his silhouette from showing against the fallow fields. He halted and parted the canes. Where were they? Darn, had he taken the wrong direction? A few steps ahead he made out a building so close to the waterfront, it might jut out into the water at higher levels. He headed for it, hoping to get a better overview of the river there.

The edifice turned out to be a ramshackle fishing hut or boathouse and had a skewed jetty. Ideal to… Of course. He ducked at the sound of murmuring voices and the gentle splashing of oars. This was their hideout. He waited until the men had indeed gotten comfortable inside. As soon as light shone through the cracks, he dared to peek inside. Oh, the place was nicely equipped. And they were really his drinking buddies. Some of the men already lay stretched out on mats, two threw the dice. Maybe they were supposed to watch out in case someone came here. Fat Tutu snored, and a black eye adorned his face. The fun must have continued after Nakhtmin left. He'd seen enough. Without making a noise, he crept away and back home.

Hori's hope Ouseret would dine with him on their last evening was shattered when she claimed Muti had already invited her over. Actually, the whole day she had eluded him, except for checking on him that one time and announcing she'd really leave the next day and return to the House of Life for good. Having seen through his act, she even added it made no sense for him to play the ailing man any longer. Since not even Nakhtmin could keep him company, he stabbed at his food with chagrin and cast longing gazes at the roof of the neighboring house. The contours of the two women were barely visible, but Hori's heart knew which silhouette belonged to his beloved.

The unmistakable creaking of the gate to Nakhtmin's estate made him sit up with anticipation. He hadn't expected his friend to return so early. Since the women were busy, he'd likely come over straight away. Oh, Mutnofret left the roof and went downstairs. Raised voices drifted over. Then fast steps on the gravel of the path. The connecting door flung open with a bang. Somebody approached.

"Where is my wayward husband, huh? Come down, right away, Hori, and tell me where he is!"

Mutnofret! And she was very, very upset. Oh dear, what had Nakhtmin done? Slowly, he descended the stairs—after all he still needed to take care—and lit a torch on one of the lamps in a niche. Mutnofret stood on the lawn behind his house, both hands on her hips.

"Calm down! Didn't he tell you? He wanted to meet Wenen," he repeated the lie Nakhtmin had come up with. That ominous Wenen! He'd have to deal with the fellow soon, but for now he'd do just fine as Nakhtmin's cover.

"Oh, really?"

How could a woman's voice sound so sharp? Hori involuntarily tugged his head in.

"And how come his friend Wenen shows up here just now wanting to ask Nakhtmin if he feels like having a beer with him?"

"Good grief!" he blurted.

"Ha! I knew it. You're in on it!"

Hori scratched his neck. Nobody could have expected that. Nakhtmin had thought Wenen would be busy with mourning rites for Iriamun. "Um…" What to do? Oh yes! He put on a smile. "I guess the two missed each other. As far as I know they hadn't arranged to meet."

A stranger stepped into the circle of torchlight. "You must be Hori. I'm Wenen. Greetings to you." He wrapped an arm around Hori's waist and pressed him against his chest with the other.

Hori responded with more reserve and freed himself of the fairly intimate hug. So that was Wenen who'd conquered the hearts of all his friends in no time. An average Egyptian whose smile and pose appeared candid and friendly. Maybe a little too friendly for Hori's taste. After all, he wasn't one of *those* guys.

Now, though, the man put a hand on Muti's shoulder. "No reason to get upset, Mutnofret. I'm sure Hori's right. I only told Nakhtmin in which tavern I like to hang out. Usually, but of course not tonight. That would have been inappropriate." His face turned serious. His Adam's apple danced up and down as he struggled to swallow, then he wiped a tear from the corner of his eye.

His mourning convinced Hori, nevertheless he wondered if the man was really so sad or simply putting on a show to better cover for Nakhtmin. That would be quite an achievement. No, something really aggrieved him, but it didn't need to be the death of the prophet. Either way, he'd bailed out Nakhtmin and him. Although he'd been determined not to like the man, he did. "Of course, how silly of Nakhtmin! The whole country mourns Iriamun." With satisfaction, he watched Mutnofret lower her head in shame.

"My husband really is a yokel sometimes," she grumbled but seemed placated.

"Tonight, I'm no good company for a lady like you since my heart is deeply saddened, and I hoped…"

"I'm sure there's a jug or more to be found in my pantry," Hori chimed in. "A man shouldn't grieve alone. Keep me company until Nakhtmin returns, which should be soon under the circumstances."

Mutnofret's hands slid from her hips. "Please excuse the fuss I made. Since I also have a guest, I'll take leave now. And should this thoughtless, this-" She paused in search for the best word and settled for, "Nakhtmin show his face, I'll send him over to you straight away."

When she was gone, Hori expelled a breath. "Thanks for not betraying him."

Wenen underlined his grin with a wink. "So he really is doing something Lady Mutnofret must not know about? I never imagined Nakhtmin as the kind of man seeking the company of loose women. Or does he have different preferences?"

Hori laughed. Wenen had proved himself quick on the uptake and loyal to Nakhtmin, but he didn't know him well. "Certainly not, neither one nor the other." The very idea was too comical. He led his guest into the house and fetched another jug from the pantry before heading up the stairs. Wrapped in wet cloth, the wine should be cool and refreshing this hot summer night.

While he placed the torch into the holder, Wenen settled beside Hori's cot on the roof. "So if he isn't whoring around, what's Nakhtmin up to then?"

Quite nosy, but since the man had helped them, Hori budged. "Actually, it's official business and possibly dangerous. Nakhtmin doesn't want to worry his wife in her condition..."

Wenen's face lit up. "Oh, wow! They are expecting. I'll have to congratulate later. Do they know-"

"A boy," Hori interrupted, glad to have diverted his attention from the other matter.

"Great!" The priest took a sip and smacked his lips. "That's a nice wine." Out of the blue, his face darkened, and like before, Hori sensed a whiff of sorrow surrounding the man despite his permanent smile. "A man needs a son to make sacrifices at his grave."

Strange. Not the first thing Hori would have thought of when hearing such news. Oh, Nakhtmin had mentioned something about Wenen...? Right. "You're struggling with a hard lot as a son whose father has no grave. That's awful."

Wenen shook his head. "Oh no, my father has a grave, I took care of that. Only it's empty." He gulped. "I perform the sacrificial rites anyway in hopes they reach his ka or ba."

"I'm sure they do," Hori mumbled. What else could he say without robbing the man of all consolation? So, Wenen mourned his father rather than the departed prophet. He could only hope the mood wouldn't stay this gloomy.

To his relief, the young man waved his arm and brushed away the topic himself. "Excuse me. Sorrow over Iriamun's death saddens my heart, and I'm a pathetic guest, but I'll get over it."

After that they chatted about mutual acquaintances, and Hori even forgot Ouseret for a while.

In high spirits because of his success, Nakhtmin entered his estate and climbed the stairs to the roof. "Oh, my heart jubilates at the sight of such beauty!" he greeted Muti and Ouseret. He kissed his wife and winked at the tall physician. "I had-" A nice evening with Wenen, he meant to say, but Muti cut him off.

"How can you be so dumb?"

Confused, he went down on his knees. What had he done wrong now?

"Looking for the poor man in his favorite tavern when he's in mourning? Guess who dropped by earlier, searching for you? You'll find Wenen at Hori's place. They are yearning for you. Off with you, doofus, and please be gentle with Wenen since he is aggrieved."

Nakhtmin groaned. Wenen here? At least it looked like Hori had managed the crisis well and his beloved hadn't found him out. Only Ouseret's lips curled into a mocking smile, and Nakhtmin felt like she saw through him. As long as she didn't tell Muti… Please, not a word, he pleaded with his eyes. To his relief, the imposing head inclined in consent. "Then I'll see if I can cheer up the two. Hori's heart is also in mourning because his feelings are not reciprocated."

Intently, he scrutinized the harsh beauty. Hori's sorrow didn't seem to touch her. That didn't look good for his friend. Strange how well sociable Muti and the reserved doctor got along. Then Ouseret should also take to Hori. But he'd never say that aloud. Actually, he should buzz off before he said anything that might disclose his nocturnal activities.

"Look who's here!" Hori called at his arrival.

Nakhtmin's knees still felt a little wobbly as he got comfortable on the roof with the others. "Hori, Wenen, it's great you two have finally met." He slapped Wenen on the back, while he tried to communicate with Hori through grimaces telling of his success and asking what happened here.

"Are you in pain?" Hori asked.

Idiot! Or was Hori getting back at him, because he'd laughed at his lovesickness earlier? "Me? Nah. Fortunately, I didn't have to wait long for Wenen's appearance." Did he get the message this time? No, now they both stared at him in confusion. "Five guards showed me the way, so I'm back already."

The blow to his head must have somehow slowed the thinking of Hori's heart, but now he seemed to grasp his meaning and said, "Ah, very nice of the five guys."

Wenen gazed from one to the other and moved to get up. "I thank you for your hospitality, physician Hori, but I have the feeling I'm in the way here. I'm sure you two have important things to discuss." He hung his head. "A man whose heart is in mourning doesn't make for pleasant company."

"No, please stay! I'm sorry, I didn't mean to confuse you. I was only worried how Mutnofret had reacted to your showing up here," Nakhtmin exclaimed.

Wenen gave a restrained smile. "She believes it was a misunderstanding. You were looking for me, while I was on the way to your place."

"Exactly, that's what happened! And she understood." Why did Hori grimace at him now? Did he want to imitate him in mockery? Nakhtmin shrugged. No matter. Had Wenen emphasized the word *your* just now? He couldn't shake off the feeling that more than the first prophet's death troubled the priest's heart. Well, it likely wasn't that important. Another day, when they were alone, he'd probably speak up. "Well, Hori, does a thirsty man get wine here or are you going to let me perish?" he asked.

THE KING'S HYENAS

Day 15 of month Ipet-hemet in Shemu, the season of the harvest

At daybreak, Hori's heart broke as well.

Ouseret joined him in the garden, where he took his breakfast in the shade of the pergola. His joy at seeing her ended abruptly when she announced, "I'll return to the House of Life in a little while."

Hori struggled to swallow the piece of flat bread clogging his throat. Horrified, he couldn't utter a word. She slid onto the chair at the other end of the table and picked up a fig, which she skillfully peeled with her long fingers before taking a bite. Not one drop of juice trickled down her chin. How did she do that? Everything she did seemed so controlled and precise.

"You too are a physician and know you need to take things easy for a while longer, but in my opinion nothing prevents you from returning to your duties," she said after swallowing.

His own bite, which had finally arrived in his stomach, wanted to jump out again. "But…what if I suffer a relapse?" he croaked.

Her eyebrows lifted in astonishment. "Not likely, but if that happens, Nakhtmin should be able to deal with it."

Since he couldn't make his friend look incompetent, he didn't know what to say. She knew how he felt for her, why then was she so cold to him? "May I visit you there from time to time?"

"The House of Life is open to everyone, and you're a doctor. How could I forbid you to come?"

"That's not what I meant, Ouseret! I-I…" Oh, dammit, it wouldn't do any good if he once again declared his love for her like an imbecile. "You are a fascinating woman, and I'd like to get to know you better."

She pressed her lips together, then exclaimed, "As I told you yesterday: there's nothing to know about me. You're my patient, I'm your doctor. That's all."

"It doesn't have to be all!" he cried out. "As soon as you leave, I'm no longer your patient, and you're no longer my physician. Do you want to know anything about me? I'll answer every question." He fell silent. What was he jabbering? Every question? There was so much he couldn't tell anyone.

She sighed. "Hori, I already know the one thing that interests me: your treatment has come to a good end. I'm only a guest at the House of Life here to finish my studies about—to intensify my studies. As soon as I've found what I'm looking for, I'll return to Waset. You see, it would be futile to engage in a… um…friendship."

Friendship? Had Ouseret misunderstood his intentions? Impossible. Something else must be occupying her mind. Intensify her studies? No, she was searching for something specific. And she didn't want to share with him what that was. Maybe it had to do with another man. Icy fear gripped his heart. Not that! He'd take on almost any challenge but couldn't bear the thought her heart already belonged to someone else. Ouseret's features told him any more questions and requests would only drive her farther from him. Maybe she'd see him in a different light when he presented her with the reward for her services. With effort, he forced himself to be patient.

When she left his estate, he felt as if a part of him went with her, while he stayed back an empty shell.

Not much later, Nakhtmin strolled over to him. "I'm going to report to the king what I found out. Are you coming along?"

Hori would prefer to set out and buy the medical instruments, maybe have them made specifically for his beloved, particularly beautiful ones. Oh yes, he'd have her name engraved in the handles, or–

"Hori! Am I going to get an answer today? Time's pressing."

"Sorry. Yes, let's go." Later he should find time to look around the smithies. Nakhtmin was right, he shouldn't forget everything else because of Ouseret.

Despite the early hour, the pharaoh's antechamber was already occupied by several priests wearing yellow, the color of mourning. Their bald heads showed traces of ash. Nevertheless, Atef greeted them with the words, "His majesty ordered me to let him know of your arrival straight away." He disappeared through the door. Although Hori knew how much importance the pharaoh placed on the matter they were investigating, it surprised him that the case took precedence over the mourning and burial rites for Iriamun.

Atef soon returned, accompanied by—oh dear—his father. Hori greeted him reverentially and saw Nakhtmin do the same, nevertheless Sobekemhat seemed more irritated than usual. "Incredible! I wasn't done with my report!" he snorted in Hori's direction and wasted no glance at the other people present.

Hori closed his eyes in torment. This affront would be added to the long list of his alleged misconducts.

Atef kept holding the door open for them. "What are you waiting for, doctors. His majesty doesn't have all day!"

The king indeed looked stressed and barely looked up as they bowed deeply. Papyrus scrolls piled high on his desk. "Thotnakht, you can retreat now. Please make two copies of these for the archive and stay close for further work."

"As you wish, majesty." The scribe collected some of the sheets and left through the side door.

Now, the pharaoh directed his gaze at Hori and Nakhtmin. "Rise. What news do you bring? Oh, and I'm glad to see you on your feet again, Hori."

He deferentially lowered his head. "Thank you, majesty. With your permission, I will get back to my duties at the House of Women today even if I have to leave other tasks in your service to Nakhtmin." Uncertain, he glanced at the king's visitor chairs. Unfortunately, they hadn't been invited to sit down. Oh well, he'd cope. At least the dizziness plaguing him the last few days had finally passed. Meanwhile Nakhtmin had started relating his discovery of the weryt guards' hiding place.

"Scoundrels!" Senusret exclaimed. "They'll regret this. Do continue."

Nakhtmin splayed his fingers. "There's no more to say. If you wish, I can show your men later where to find the lazybones. Oh, and I'd guess not only the five I saw desert their night watches. The rest of the bunch must be in it, too." He told the king about the light signals.

Hori added, "I also recommend searching the western shore around the walls of the necropolis for Rahotep's corpse. The fastest way to find him would be if you provided your hunting hyenas—though they need stuffing before the search lest they tear apart the body when they find it." The trained animals were excellent hunting aids but only if they had eaten so much they wouldn't touch the prey. Otherwise it would be suicide to try to take the catch from the animal.

"Good idea! We still haven't found a trace of the heri-heb on the run."

For a moment, Hori didn't understand what the king was talking about, then the shards of his memory slid into place again. So the supposedly sick priest had really disappeared, fled the weryt and now gallivanted somewhere in the Two Lands. "He could be anywhere by now," he groaned and touched the spot where the man had hit him. "Maybe there is no need to worry, because the man honors his oaths and won't do anything." How dangerous was it to summon the shadows of the dead?

"I'm not willing to take any risk for Kemet. Thotnakht!" the king bellowed.

Hori flinched, and the pounding in his head returned. The scribe entered. "Your majesty?"

In brief words, Senusret dictated an order that authorized Nakhtmin to use his hunting hyenas and a second one placing the soldiers of the penal garrison under his command. "Give these to the commander of the weryt watch," the king said, grinning like a jackal.

Nakhtmin's eyes widened in astonishment, and Hori was surprised as well. "But…those guys? Why use them?" he stammered.

"They deserve punishment, and this way they can atone to some extent. Why should I submit brave and decent men to the horrors of such a search?"

Nakhtmin had to persevere in the reeking kennels until the animal keepers, surprised by the royal order, had stuffed six hyenas. Now the beasts tore at their leashes, drooling and panting. Nakhtmin grimaced in disgust. He couldn't stand the carrion eaters and feared them. To his relief, nobody expected him to set out with the animals on his own. Three handlers led two beasts each and seemed to enjoy the deviation from routine. Well, they didn't know their destination yet. They'd find out soon enough.

On the way to the royal pier, Nakhtmin's companions drew quite some attention. Fortunately, the king had thought of providing a suitable boat to cross the river, so he didn't have to lead the salivating pack through the palace, then the town. Under different circumstances, Nakhtmin would have been thrilled to ride on the magnificent bark, but not like this… While the hyenas curled up at the stern of the royal boat or curiously gaped at the water, he settled up front. "Take us to the garrison of the weryt watch!" he ordered the boatman.

The rowers pulled the oars since they had to go north a bit. With the wind always blowing from there and the current going the opposite direction, setting the sails only made sense when heading south. This time of year the river flowed rather slowly, nevertheless they reached their destination fast. When the pharaoh's bark pulled up to the penal garrison's pier, it didn't take long until the commander stumbled out the back gate, followed by several of his subordinates likely lured by curiosity.

Nakhtmin jumped onto the planks of the jetty. As soon as he stood securely, he read the king's orders to the confused commander and gave him time to grasp the content. "Gather your men, we'll cross the river," he ordered. With the royal bark behind him, he felt confident enough to give orders to this high-ranking officer as if he were his servant. And he deserved it. He might have no clue what his men were doing, but he should. Rabble like this needed a particularly strong hand, which Monthnakht obviously didn't possess.

At least he didn't embarrass himself in front of the soldiers by asking questions or doubting Nakhtmin's mission. "So be it," he said curtly, then hollered, "Men! Come here! Get the boats ready."

"We'll probably need shovels as well. Do you have any?" Nakhtmin asked.

The commander gave a snappy nod. "Only a few though. Maybe three."

"That'll do. We don't want to dig up the whole Beautiful West."

At Nakhtmin's words, the man paled. "Bring the gods protect us! What are you planning to do?"

"You'll see." For now, the soldiers needn't know more. Fear of the king's scorn gave the scoundrels wings. In next to no time, Nakhtmin had enough of them available for the search. Since he had the animals, he wouldn't need more than a dozen men. The garrison didn't have boats for more anyway, and he certainly wouldn't let any of those negligent villains set his dirty feet onto the royal bark! In vain, he searched for his drinking buddies. Likely they were still sleeping off last night's beers. Well, tonight he'd teach them obedience and respect for the king's wishes. He was already looking forward to it. Probably a good thing they weren't here now or they might have recognized him and guessed what awaited them.

While he leaned back in comfort, the weryt guards sweated as no awning shaded them. Instead, they had to man the oars under a blazing midday sun. Pretty disappointing that ferrying across didn't take longer, but the river was narrow during this time of year. He gazed at the banks yonder.

The two guards at the gate of the weryt stared at them with curiosity. Not daring to leave their posts and walk to the jetty, they only leaned forward as far as they could. One of them finally thought of knocking at the gate and announcing the visitors of importance. Even the dumbest rascals of the penal garrison must realize this couldn't be the normal transfer of a deceased. Corpses for the weryt were laid on a vessel resembling the Neshmet bark and towed by a boat in which the mourning relatives sat. Therefore Nakhtmin wasn't surprised when the gate opened the moment the royal bark touched the jetty and the jackal-faced man himself stepped out. The crew of one boat froze in horror, and one of the animal handlers looked as if he wanted to try his luck with the crocodiles in the river. "Anubis," he whispered.

Nakhtmin knew better. This was the head of the embalming compound. Had pharaoh thought ahead and announced the search party? Then he realized everyone was staring at him. Oh, of course, he was in command. Now he broke out in a sweat. What if they didn't find anything? He'd disgrace himself.

With as much dignity as he could muster on the rocking bark, he climbed over the railing and walked to the mer-ut. Bowing reverently, he handed over the pharaoh's message.

The man with the mask skimmed it and said, "Welcome to the realm of the dead, Nakhtmin, son of Nakhtmin."

The deep voice sent a shiver down Nakhtmin's back. If only the mer-ut had chosen different words of greeting! The cowards in the boats would be even more frightened now. "Greetings to you. We will search the desert close to the walls of the weryt, where we expect to find the corpse of Rahotep, one of the weryt guards who disappeared weeks ago without a trace."

The jackal snout lowered in agreement. "So be it. Should you indeed find the body of the missing man, bring it to this gate, so he can receive proper burial treatment as every honest man of the Black Land deserves."

"We will," Nakhtmin promised. If Hori was right and the heart really belonged to Rahotep, at least his shadow wouldn't stay homeless.

The Anubis head jerked around and scrutinized the guards in the boats. Nakht-min cast a glance over his shoulder and had to muster all his self-restraint not to burst out laughing at the sight of the fainthearted lot. These guys wanted to be the king's soldiers? Well, he'd been struck with the same terror during his nightly journeys across the river as they were today.

"May your search be successful. May the rays of Ra keep the shadows of death away from you," the mer-ut blessed, then retreated behind the thick walls.

The soldiers still crouched in the boats. The commander stepped onto the jetty first. "Get to work, men!" he barked.

The hyenas barked as well and tore at their leashes. "What's up?" Nakhtmin called to the keepers. "Bring the animals ashore, so we can get started."

Pale with horror, one of them rose. The boat swayed, and he almost toppled over the railing. When he finally found his balance, he lowered his head in shame and confessed, "Sir, we don't dare."

By the gods! Nakhtmin had neither the time nor patience to convince them the mer-ut's blessing would protect them against danger, particularly since he didn't believe in its power to keep the demons at bay. "It's bright daylight!" he shouted. "Ra's rays banish the shadows. Come on, now, or you can swim back. By Sakhmet's scorn, I won't take you with me to the other side. What will it be? Swim or perform your duty?"

Hesitantly, they stepped out, dragged by the baying hyenas. The guards also had alighted now. To Nakhtmin's relief, Monthnakht took over and split his men into three groups to accompany the hyena handlers.

"Very well. You'll search the northern side, you out back and you the south," Nakhtmin instructed. "Start at the walls of the weryt, and once you've walked the whole length, move farther away from it." He'd bet on finding the corpse to the north where the canal offered the only escape route, but one never knew. Besides, he'd better make the best use of the many men and animals he had at his disposal.

"Uhm, sir?" one of the handlers stammered. "What are we to do when we find what you seek?" He sweated profusely and likely not only because of the sun. The waistband of his shendyt was drenched already.

Good question, if posed with an ulterior motive. He probably didn't want to stay here any longer than necessary. Nakhtmin scanned the assembly. "Hey, is there at least one man in each group who can give a loud whistle?" he asked.

And indeed several men's whistles sounded loud and clear.

"All right, let's get to it!" he called, and the men set out, while he and the com-mander stayed with the boats. Why exhaust himself in such heat? The air shim-mered over the desert, and not even the rock walls cast shadows at noon. He snorted. That kind of shadow they'd all welcome.

He settled on the edge of the jetty and dangled his feet. Finding this a good occasion to question the man about the negligence of his soldiers, he said, "Tell me, Monthnakht, why didn't you report Rahotep's disappearance to the pharaoh or the head of the weryt?"

The sturdy man scratched his neck and took a deep breath. "Oh, well. The men are frightened. Even during the day, every noise jolts them. When the pharaoh—life, prosperity and health—ordered the walls to be patrolled at night, they started to become mutinous. It wasn't the first time one of them deserted."

"Oh." Deserted, as if. Nakhtmin didn't believe that anymore, not in Rahotep's case since his family was so worried. The man surely would have sent note of his whereabouts or told them in advance. Interesting, though, that there had been no more. He could only hope they wouldn't dig up piles of bodies here!

"Well, well," the commander continued. "Service in this garrison had always been horrible, with the night watches unbearable. I...I can understand anyone who...um..."

Oh dear. The man might look tough, but his heart was soft as suet. He wanted to keep the Medjay from searching for the renegades, so they could start a new life elsewhere in the Two Lands. One thing puzzled Nakhtmin though: if several guards had disappeared, why did the soldiers only talk about Rahotep as one taken by the shadows? Then the answer dawned on him. Of course, the others would have told at least close friends about their plans to run off. Rahotep however had left without word or trace while he was on night watch. Far off he heard a hyena bark, but it didn't sound like the beast had caught a scent.

"You are rather sympathetic," Nakhtmin said. "Too much so, unfortunately. The hearts of these men are filled with lies and deception. These irresponsible lazy drunkards deserve far worse punishment than what the king in his wisdom and benignity has ordered. Know one thing: while you believe they protect the weryt at night, as is their duty, they sneak away and row to a hideout where they indulge themselves." Now he studied the commander intently.

His astonishment and indignation seemed real. "What did you say? That's... that's...outrageous!" He jumped up as if to run after the rascals.

Nakhtmin held him back. "I followed them last night and discovered their hiding place after fat Tutu—I see you know who I'm talking about—and his companions had shot their mouths off while drinking with me. I wasn't surprised to notice their absence today. I know where they might be. In a tavern at the harbor since they got enough sleep last night."

"Those...those...!"

"Oh, those five aren't the only ones. Yesterday I saw someone on the garrison pier signaling with a lamp. Shortly afterward, the guards left their posts and rowed back."

Monthnakht blushed. "That was me! I meant to check if the scoundrels got there, because the mer-ut had asked me a few times recently if the night watch was in place."

"And that way you showed them when the coast was clear. I assume you go to sleep afterward?"

Guilt etched into his face, the man nodded. "Oh dear, oh dear! So much negligence under my command! What will the king do with me?" A tear trickled down his cheek.

Nakhtmin felt for the man but couldn't excuse his lenience toward the riffraff he should keep on tight leashes. He probably enjoyed a comfortable life far too much. "All inhabitants of the Two Lands are now in danger because of what you neglected to do. His majesty didn't order a night watch on a whim!" Nakhtmin bit his tongue. He must not reveal more. "Believe me, there's far worse punishment for lazybones than patrolling the walls of the weryt. Others end up in the quarries or mines. Think about it."

The man sank onto his knees and sobbed. "Not the mines!" he whimpered.

"Hey, calm down. I wasn't talking about... Come, come, now. Do you want your men to see you like this? I don't think the king will send you to the mines. Your subordinates, though, deserve exactly that."

The commander lifted his head. "You really think the pharaoh will show mercy with me?"

Yikes, the man looked a mess! With the eye makeup smeared, he might be mistaken for a shadow. "Um, you better wash your face," Nakhtmin suggested, and he did. "Yes, that's nice. Maybe there some more." He tapped a finger at his left temple.

A shrill whistle spared him a response to the question whether he believed the king might show leniency. "Where did that come from?"

"Over there!" The commander pointed to the north.

Just like he thought. With grim satisfaction, he grabbed the shovels and trotted off, the miserable ninny following. As soon as they rounded the corner of the embalming compound, he saw the search party at the rock wall, whose darker shadows at night and protection against the wind he and Hori had often used for their meetings and exchanges of messages. Fairly far from the wall... The weryt escapee must have dragged the corpse all the way there although he could have buried it in the loose desert sand. Why?

Walking over the glowing hot sand was excruciating. At last, they reached the men standing in a sloppy half circle around a mound of rubble. With appreciation, Nakhtmin nodded at the hyena handler, who'd already pulled back his animals and now stood by the small copse of trees, his and Hori's landmark.

That moment it dawned on him, why the killer dragged his victim here: The rocks prevented jackals and hyenas from digging up the body. Clever. The heri-heb desperately wanted to disguise his deed. Only the thing with the heart remained a mystery to him. He dropped the shovels they wouldn't need and strode to the improvised burial mound. "What are you waiting for? Get to it!" He rolled off the first rock.

In high spirits, Hori strolled toward the craftsmen's district. Work had done him well after days of lonesome idleness. While Tep-Ta took a lunch break, he'd even sneaked into the wing of the royal majesties and found them all in good health. Now he hoped to obtain a beautiful gift for Ouseret.

He followed the smell of charcoal fires and the clanging of stone on metal until he reached the area with smithies. At the first workshop he poked his nose in, vessels of copper were made here. Not the right place for his purpose. Copper was too soft for medical instruments, he needed a bronze smith. And he found one in the next building, however amulets and statues of gods were cast here. He asked one of the workers, holding a melting pot with long pliers into the fire, where he might find a toolmaker.

"Across the street, two houses down. Are you looking for something specific, sir?"

"Medical instruments."

A broad grin spread over his face. "Then you should go to my brother Iri. He makes the best far and wide. Real works of art, and the blades are sharp as-"

"I believe you. Where do I find this magician of a smith?"

"At the next turnoff, the workshop at the corner. You can't miss it, if you look for an eye painted onto the lintel."

Hori laughed. The eye was the symbol for Iri; maybe the man could even write? But that would be asking too much. "Thanks, I'll tell him you sent me."

Whistling, he ambled on, found the shop without difficulty and ducked under the lintel. After a few steps, he entered an open yard with a large furnace in one corner. Two men energetically fanned the glowing coals with bellows, and despite the open sky above them, the heat collected in the quad. Another worker used pliers to fix a red-hot piece of metal on an anvil and a fourth man hammered at it with might. Between two beats, Hori asked, "Are you Iri, the toolmaker?"

The hammerer lifted his soot-smeared face. "That's me. What can I do for you?"

"Your brother sends me, because you make the best instruments for a physician."

"That's true. I must ask for your patience though."

Fascinated, Hori watched the stick of metal gradually shape into a knife blade. Sparks flew at every blow. No wonder the four workers all wore aprons of thick leather. Of course, that didn't protect their arms. Those were laced with little scars. By the time the smith was finally content with his work, sweat ran down Hori's body in rivulets.

Iri came to him and rubbed his hands. "Medical instruments, indeed. Please follow me." He pointed at a door.

Eager to leave the hot, stifling courtyard, he wondered how the smiths could bear the glowing heat all day long. Inside the house, it was dark and refreshingly cool. Iri lit a lamp, then placed several leather bundles from a board on the wall onto the table beside the door.

He unrolled one sheath, and Hori saw well-crafted probes, tweezers and scalpels. Acknowledging the work, he pursed his lips. "Not bad, but they are for a lady. Maybe something more delicate, finer crafted?"

"A sunut? Oh yes, I've got just the thing. Someone ordered it a long time ago, then never picked it up. Quite annoying. But maybe it had been waiting for you all that time? The gods lead us on strange routes sometimes. Where is it? Oh, that must be the right one. Look."

Artfully crafted, elegant bronze tools with thin handles perfect for Ouseret's long dainty fingers lay spread out before Hori. "Oh, how gorgeous. Just what I've been looking for!" The handles were embossed with a flowery pattern, that likely provided a good grip even when the hands were covered in blood and mucus. "I'll take it. How much?"

Hori regretted his candid enthusiasm when something flickered in Iri's face that made him fear he'd have to pawn his estate. However, the smith spread his hands and said, "Since the gods meant it to be, ten copper deben, five hin sesame oil and three bales of linen. Fair enough?"

He swallowed. That wasn't exactly a bargain, but those tools were certainly worth it, and how happy Ouseret would be... The price was good and the man honest. Hori shook hands on the deal. "Fair enough. I can give you the copper right away, and my servant will bring you the rest later today." Too bad, though, that he couldn't take the present with him right away.

Iri tilted his head. "I see you're one of the sunu from the House of Life."

Hori puffed out his chest. "Even one of the pharaoh's personal physicians!"

"Truly the gods must have sent you!" Iri cried out. "One of my workers injured himself recently, and now Sakhmet's arrows torment him. Will you treat him? Then I'll owe you five hin of sesame oil and three bales of linen."

Hori grinned. "Sure. Take me to the man, and I'll see what I can do for him."

Soon after, he headed to the House of Life, the instruments with him. Without medicine at hand, he'd only been able to provide some relief by directing Iri's wife to wrap wet rags around the man's legs. However, he'd return later today to do more for him. That duty paled at his growing excitement. What would she say?

GHASTLY FINDINGS

Still hesitating, the soldiers slowly followed Nakhtmin's lead and got to work. Soon the odor of decay hung heavy in the air, and some men couldn't refrain from throwing up. In the meantime, the other search parties had joined them and took turns with their comrades getting nauseous. Although Nakhtmin didn't mind the smell so much since as a doctor he often had to bear similar assaults to the nose when a wound festered, he still left the hard work to the soldiers after removing the first boulders. He decided it would only undermine his dignity to plug away like a common quarry worker, and these scoundrels deserved the punishment.

Monthnakht shifted his weight from one foot to the other. "Didn't think we'd find something," he mumbled.

Even if Nakhtmin pitied him, the man had brought it onto himself—literally—by neglecting his duty when he didn't report the deserters. So he only shrugged. "We'll need a stretcher. And a linen cloth to cover the remains." He summoned two particularly pale guards and ordered them to ask for the required items at the gate of the weryt. Relief already bringing some color back to their faces, they trotted off.

"Dear gods!" One of the workers had uncovered the face of the deceased and almost toppled over with horror. A stone slipped from his hands and plonked onto the ground.

Nakhtmin stepped closer. Not a pretty sight. The head was bashed in, which reminded him of Hori's wound. His friend had been luckier than this fellow, though not by much. Parts of the corpse had dried like jerky, in other places it was in a state of mushy decay. "Is this Rahotep?"

By now pretty much everyone still working on the mound gagged, so he gestured for the commander.

At least the man only paled but retained his composure. "Impossible to say. Maybe."

"I recognize his knife!" someone shouted. "It's him."

Now Nakhtmin also spotted the weapon beside the body. A gaping abdominal cut showed what it had been used for. Must have been a bloody endeavor. Why had Nebkaura done that? Maybe Hori could explain, if he was allowed to. Anyway, Nakhtmin didn't need more proof to give the dead his name back. "We've found Rahotep," he announced.

When the men returned with the stretcher, the corpse was exposed enough to place the basketwork on the sandy ground and push it under the remains while two guys gently lifted hip and shoulder with shovels. Nobody wanted to touch the half-decomposed body, and Nakhtmin could understand that. They probably would've been holding only parts. Everyone was relieved when the cloth covered the remains, and thus, Rahotep at long last received a half-decent procession.

Nakhtmin knocked on the gate of the weryt where two carriers already awaited them and took the load off the soldiers. "This is Rahotep, soldier of his majesty," he said and peered past them with curiosity. However, he couldn't see much except a narrow corridor.

A scribe sitting under a thatched roof beside the gate wrote down the name on a small tablet which he fixed to the body. Nakhtmin was content. At least the mystery of Sennedjem's lost cousin was solved now, his mission accomplished. Hold on, not quite. There were still his five friends of last night. And he almost looked forward to that task. The day was nearing its end when they boarded the boats again and crossed the river. Soon the night watch would take over.

Hori had to exercise all his self-restraint not to rush to Ouseret and place his present at her feet, and himself with it. The usher, who noted the names of the ailing, assigned a doctor and called the patients when their turn had come, told him that the tall physician currently had a patient. So he used the time to compile remedies for Iri's worker to ease the pain and hopefully ban the fever demons. The man really had a serious burn. While pounding herbs, rinds and seeds into pulp, he kept the door of the herb chamber ajar and listened for the clapping of doors. He didn't want to miss the moment when Ouseret was alone. Presumably, she was treating her last patient for the day, though he couldn't know for sure. Every time he peeked into the corridor, he was disappointed: only doors to the wrong treatment rooms opened and closed. He'd almost finished his concoction; what took her so long? A horrible suspicion sneaked up on him: did Ouseret meet another man for a tryst? His colleague Shepses had done that, seduced his female patients here in these floors, without anyone getting wind of it. No, Ouseret wasn't like that. He caressed the fine leather covering his present.

He sifted the wine through a strainer to filter the bitter herbs from the liquid and carefully plugged the small jug. Done. He grabbed his things and left the room. Maybe he should eavesdrop at her door? Oops, the head of the physicians stormed around the corner, and Hori reverently stepped aside. To his astonishment, the old man entered Ouseret's treatment room without knocking.

Hori heard Ouseret's deep voice, then the door closed. What was going on? He crept closer but could only make out that the exchange was heated, at least on Imhotepankh's part. If he placed his ear against... That moment the door was flung open again, and Hori almost stumbled into the room. A stranger, surely the patient, stepped out in confusion. He managed to jump aside and could only hope the two people inside hadn't seen him. Now the corridor was deserted again. Another try? He pressed his ear against the wood, but unable to understand a word, he gave up soon. Did he have to? His agitated heart put the pieces together, one after the other.

The old man stemmed from a great and famous dynasty of doctors, however, he wasn't blessed with the reason and empathy distinguishing a good physician. Stubbornly, he insisted on everything written in books and dismissed all new methods of treatment even if they brought visible success. A female physician had to be a thorn in his withered flesh. As much as Hori would enjoy Imhotepankh's discomfort under different circumstances, the lady of his heart was affected this time. Hori knew the old grump well enough to know, he'd do anything to pull out the thorn. In his view, Nakhtmin and he were also troublemakers, and he let them feel it whenever they met. Oh, he'd better not lurk here when the head of physicians stepped out. That could only harm Ouseret.

With an anxious heart, he returned to the herb chamber and waited, though not for long this time. The door flew open with a bang, hurried steps sounded through the corridor, then silence fell again. Hori set into motion. The door to Ouseret's room stood wide open. She leaned onto the cot where patients usually lay and sobbed.

Damn you, Imhotepankh! Hori hurried to her side.

Ouseret's tears ebbed almost instantly, leaving moist trails on her checks to betray her distress, but she didn't go to the trouble of wiping them away. "What are you doing here?" Her voice was steady and calm.

What a woman! So much self-control commanded his admiration. Unfortunately, that also gave her an impenetrable shell, where Hori's attempts to get closer to her shattered. Ouseret remained as aloof as before. He struggled for equal composure, so he didn't feel like a little boy begging his mother for treats anymore. "I still owe you compensation for your excellent services."

She pushed out her chin. "Excellent? Not everybody would agree with you." That sounded rather bitter.

"Did something happen? Can I help you?" He ventured one step closer.

She straightened. "It's none of your business. I'll have to leave Itj-tawy tomorrow, sadly without having finished my studies."

Hori felt as if the floor swayed underneath him. "No!" Then he'd run out of time to court his beloved. He had to stop her! "Why? Because of the head of physicians? What did he do to you?"

Ouseret stepped back, her gaze darting this way and that. Hesitant, as if she had to pick the words off the floor one by one, she said, "Allegedly, patients complained—men—that they didn't want to be treated by a woman."

"So what? They can go to a male colleague." There had to be more to it, and he really couldn't imagine any man minding if Ouseret tended to him. Then he remembered what Imhotepankh had tried to do to him during his exam. Thanks to Ameny, the old man had fallen into his own trap. "That mean old billy goat! He set a snare for you, right? Did some guy molest you? Tell me his name and I'll-"

"Stop it!" After this short outburst, she quickly composed herself again and shrugged placidly, or so it looked. "Yes, likely a trap, but I can't do anything. And you probably shouldn't shout your insults directed at the venerable head of physicians into the corridor." She sidestepped him and closed the door.

Hori couldn't care less who heard him. "He simply kicked you out? We can't let him get away with such behavior. I have significant infl-"

"We?" she cut in again. "There is no 'we', not in this matter or any other. The only person who could intervene for me is the second prophet of Amun, responsible for the administration of the House of Life, but since the first prophet died-"

This time, Hori interrupted. "Then stay at my house until the positions at the Amun temple are filled again. See, I *can* help you."

Her lips curled in disgust. "That wouldn't be proper. People would regard me as your concubine."

"That didn't concern you the last few days," he retorted, desperate to keep her close.

"That was something completely different. You were sick."

"Then marry me! Daughter-in-law of the vizier and wife of a royal physician—not even Imhotepankh would dare to stonewall you!"

101

She paled. "Your father is the vizier of the Two Lands? Sobekemhat?"

"Yes." For once, the old man was good for something. Only…she seemed shocked by this revelation. He took another step toward her.

She raised her hands as if to fend him off. "Enough. You have no idea who… You'd regret such an imprudent decision soon. I'll depart tomorrow." She squeezed past him and left the room.

For a moment he just stood there, numbed. Then he realized he hadn't given her the present yet and ran after her. "Ouseret! Wait!"

She actually did halt.

"Here." He pressed the leather bundle into her hands and hurried off, tears of helpless rage in his eyes. No, he didn't want to see if she liked his gift. It couldn't bring happiness after all that had just passed. He'd thoroughly bungled it after hoping to see surprised joy in her face… The boat taking her from the residence tomorrow would also rip her from his life. She was lost to him. Forever!

Glad to have completed his mission, Nakhtmin returned home and only wanted to sit or lie with his Muti. To his chagrin, he found the tall doctor with her. Again!

"Ouseret has to leave the city tomorrow, it's her last night," Muti said after freeing herself from his embrace.

And she needed to spend that evening with his wife? Why not with—oh! "Does Hori know?"

"He came to see me at the House of Life. He knows." Ouseret's gaze wandered to a leather-wrapped bundle between the two women, like something they'd been studying, and a sad smile played around her lips. "Please give him my thanks for his wonderful gift. It gladdened my heart."

She liked it and still wanted to leave? So Hori couldn't soften her with that. What might have happened? "I'll go see him, so you two can talk," he murmured.

Nakhtmin found his friend where he expected him to be, at rock bottom, though actually he sat in darkness on the roof of his house. With longing, he stared at the two women on top of the neighboring roof and licked his wounded heart. When Hori told him what had passed between them, Nakhtmin could only shake his head.

"What did you think, proposing marriage like a lifeline? That's not how to win a woman's heart!" Then he remembered what happened with him and Muti and shut up. That was something completely different though. Yes, she had blindsided him, but they were in love. "Admit it, you thought you could impress her with your connections, and she'd sink against your hero's chest."

"Well, yeah, kind of," Hori admitted contritely. Then he protested, "But we could have done something for her! Why didn't she let me? She only said I'd regret it."

"Did she now? Interesting." Nakhtmin concluded Ouseret harbored a secret. She'd been eager to study scripts unavailable in other Houses of Life in Kemet. Why then didn't she stay a few days longer somewhere, like at an inn, or Muti could offer her one of the guest rooms. Meanwhile Hori and he could put in a good word for her. "Don't you want to know what she said about you just now?"

Hori jerked up like a willow crop. "She talked about me? What was it?"

Nakhtmin repeated Ouseret's words, but omitted the sad smile. What sense would it make to spark his hopes again? Then he asked, "Maybe you'd also like to hear how my day went? You might recall: pharaoh, mission, Rahotep?"

Hori groaned. "Fine, tell me since you won't stop bugging me anyway."

And Nakhtmin did. In grisly detail, he described the search for the dead in the realm of the dead. "Afterward I led the commander to the hiding place of his night watch. There we found all five of them. Naturally, they started accusing their brothers-in-arms to be just as guilty. That won't do them any good though. The whole garrison is guarded by the Medjay until the pharaoh decides what to do with the scoundrels."

"And the weryt?"

Nakhtmin pulled his head between his shoulders. "Remains unprotected for now. The safest thing would be to add a grate where the water flows under the wall. Should have been done right away, much better than placing guards there."

"And draw attention to the fact that someone dove through the opening in the wall?" Hori grumbled.

"Wouldn't that be preferable to the current situation? Anyway, we've solved the mystery and accomplished our mission." Nakhtmin was very content with himself. Soon, everything would return to normal. Catching the runaway heri-heb should only be a matter of time. "Only the issue with the heart remains a puzzle. At least, body and heart are reunited for eternity now. That's the most important thing, right?"

Hori laughed. "Removed through an abdominal cut, you said? I think I know what he intended. The lector priest is a son of the weryt after all. Despite being a despicable criminal, he couldn't bring himself to leave his victim without an after-life. I guess he wanted to place the heart back with the body after…um, its treat-ment and perform the necessary rites. What madness! Maybe he feared Rahotep's shadow would haunt him if he didn't do it."

Irritated, because once again he only understood half of it all, Nakhtmin wished he could learn more. Hori was probably right since *he* knew the secrets of the weryt. What a gory thing that was today—of course, he had to take care of the dirty work. He lifted one arm into the air to loosen his tight muscles, and some-thing brushed against his hand. He screamed in horror. "Aah, a shadow! There!" He wildly flung his arms.

Hori jumped up. "Where? Where? Oh, you fool! Those are bats."

Indeed. How embarrassing. "Well, why don't you go searching for a corpse in the realm of the dead for a whole day next time?" he grumbled and turned away. Then he had to laugh at his own silliness.

"What?" Hori asked.

"I'm such an idiot! Here I am, resenting that you aren't allowed to tell me about the mysteries of the weryt although I wouldn't want to know after today. Digging up the body was enough. Believe me, I wouldn't have wanted to explore more of its secrets!"

Mutnofret was still awake when he came home, and they cuddled for a while. "You know, it's really a shame," she said.

"Hm?"

"It would be great if Ouseret married Hori, then I'd also have a friend living next door, just like you and Hori."

"Not his fault," he grumbled and stroked her arm.

She jerked away and glared at him. "Whose fault could it be if not his? She told me what he said."

He propped a hand on his hip. "Hey, at least she can't doubt his feelings for her. She, however, has a heart of stone. Um, or not?"

"Men!" Mutnofret shook her head.

Now Nakhtmin was totally confused. If Ouseret liked Hori, why did she act so dismissive? "She told you he asked for her hand in marriage?"

"How could she believe his feelings might last? Hori is a happy-go-lucky kind of guy; we both know that. He's just impregnated young Heqet, then he hops to her, and who'll be next? With a marriage contract, he'd be well off, and she'd be on her own if he divorced her."

Heqet was with Hori's child? What news! And he'd had no clue. Of course, that was awkward but still no reason... Oh Muti! Just like Hori, she was quick to judge and probably didn't hold back with her opinions when talking to Ouseret. No wonder the doctor didn't trust Hori's vows. "Ah, you know him. Why would he want to divorce her? This time, he means it. That's obvious. He suffers terribly."

"He'll survive," she snapped.

Nakhtmin couldn't shake the feeling that she was mad at Hori. But why? Ouseret must have given her the impression her departure was Hori's fault, and that certainly wasn't fair. Tomorrow morning, he'd encourage Hori to try his luck again with Ouseret. The case didn't seem totally hopeless after all.

THE SECRET OF THE WOMAN

Day 16 of month Ipet-hemet in Shemu, the season of the harvest

The arrival of a royal messenger wrenched Nakhtmin's entire household from sleep when the horizon had only started to turn purple. The summons didn't even leave him time for his usual morning rituals, not to mention breakfast. Nakhtmin quickly wrapped a shendyt around his loins, then hurried down to the hall, where not only the messenger waited but Hori as well. Why this unusual hour for an audience with the pharaoh? He'd have reported to him today anyway, but after catching up on his sleep. Hori only shrugged at him.

They trotted to the Great House, where the slapping of their sandals echoed from the walls of the empty corridors. Rather eerie when nobody else was here. Nakhtmin felt like a thief. Hori seemed to cope pretty well with the exertion. As his doctor, he should have insisted on a slower pace, but now they'd almost arrived. This time, they weren't ushered to Senusret's office; behind the gorgeously carved door, through which they passed, lay the private chambers of the ruler. The king sat at a table laden with food, and Nakhtmin's mouth watered. He wasn't alone though. The head of the weryt sat with him. Not one servant attended to the king and his guest. A secret meeting, he thought and bowed together with Hori.

Senusret invited them to sit and forgo all formalities. "The mer-ut has returned to the world of the living to tell us where things stand in the weryt."

While Nakhtmin appreciated the pharaoh's invitation and partook of the delicious treats, the voice of the mer-ut droned from the mask. "The corpse you brought to us, Nakhtmin, did really lack the heart. That is a relief since we now know it's the right body and we can at least send the heart with the deceased to eternity although his other organs are seriously decomposed. I entrusted the work to my best man, Kheper." He nodded at Hori, over whose face a smile spread. "Everything shall be done to atone the iniquity committed by one of us."

Senusret spit out a date kernel and said, "Spare no expense. The man shall receive treatment worthy of a nobleman. I've already ordered builders to erect a small mastaba over an old grave shaft unfinished by previous workmen. Now they'll finish the dig and adorn the aisles with as many paintings as possible within the short time frame. Rahotep will receive his name and in addition everything else to ensure his afterlife even in millions of years."

Nakhtmin swallowed. A princely compensation for which some people might volunteer to get their heads bashed in. Rahotep's burial would cost more than the man ever earned in his whole life and could have earned in the future. His family must be overjoyed.

The king asked for Nakhtmin's report on yesterday's endeavors, which surprised him. Surely Senusret had been informed already. Indeed, he showed the most interest in the condition of the garrison and Nakhtmin's opinion.

After a brief summary, he ended with the words, "The commander is an honest servant of your majesty, but he shows too much leniency for rabble like this. Since guarding the necropolis is of such importance, you should assign its protection to soldiers you can absolutely trust."

The pharaoh's brow furrowed, and the mer-ut shook his long snout sideways.

"Not long, and these guards would desert as well," he grumbled. "Everyone fears the nightly shadows."

"Maybe it would be worth the risk to secure the canal openings with grates," Hori chimed in. "Then the problem would be solved for good. The weryt has already drawn too much att-"

"We can't let anyone know this route ever existed," the king dismissed the suggestion.

Stumped, they looked at each other.

Nakhtmin envisioned the water system and how Hori dove to pass under the wall, and all of a sudden the image changed to the irrigation canals in Upper Egypt. Pensive, he drew a line into the condensed water on the jug filled with cool fruit juice. "What if we cover part of the waterway with slabs of stone? In the south, canals are covered with planks so the water doesn't vaporize so fast in the sun. That could be given as reason for the modifications—or protection against flying sand."

"What would we gain?" the pharaoh asked grimly.

Hori leaned forward. "Of course! That's it! The walls of the weryt are thick and one has to dive under it. People are no fish, though, and must breathe. By lengthening the distance, nobody will manage to leave the weryt and stay alive." He bit into a slice of melon.

"The sand in the air really poses a problem," the head of the weryt remarked. "Majesty, you know for yourself how canals need cleaning every year." He slightly lifted the mask and sucked some juice through a straw.

Senusret took a deep breath and released the air. "Looks like there might be a solution after all. So be it!"

"How's the search for the wanted man going, that Nebkaura?" Hori inquired.

The king shook his head. "Nothing. It doesn't help that nobody in the eastern realm has ever seen the man. Who could we ask?"

Who, indeed? The vague description Nakhtmin had heard fitted everyone or nobody, and strangers came every day to the residence. Thus, the lector priest could have easily mingled with the folks at the harbor and had probably boarded a boat heading north or south. But how did Nebkaura intend to make a living? "At least he hasn't made use of his knowledge," he said.

Anubis fixed him with a stare. "What makes you say this?"

Squirming under the piercing gaze, he offered, "W-we'd have heard. Noticed, um, wouldn't it have been reported?" *He'd* certainly not hesitate to call the Medjay if a shadow lurked somewhere. He imagined the lawmen capturing the shadows and binding their wrists on their backs. What nonsense! As if it were that easy. "What could be done if it happened?" Self-conscious he rolled the soft interior of his bread into a ball.

The king's face turned very serious. "May the gods spare us! Powerful rites would be needed to ban such a horror. And at a time when the Amun temple is without lead!"

And it would remain like this until Iriamun was ceremoniously carried to his grave after the completion of his mummification. Amun, though, was the king of the gods, so his priests wielded the greatest power.

"However, the prophets are only your majesty's representatives," the mer-ut said. "Within you rest the wisdom and skills to stop the shadows."

Senusret nodded but didn't look pleased. "When the welfare of the Two Lands requires it, I'll confront the ghosts." He took a big gulp from his mug. In a cheerier tone, he said, "As our esteemed Nakhtmin said, it seems like the absconder hasn't put his knowledge to ill use."

Again, Nakhtmin wondered how the heri-heb intended to provide for himself when he hadn't learned anything but what he used to do in the weryt, and that surely wasn't something to earn him bread elsewhere. Well, he might work as a scribe, but why take the risk and leave behind wife and children for such a future. Why kill a man?

"Hut-Nefer, you should check if more is missing in the weryt than only the man himself," Hori pointed out. "Incense, myrrh, oils, resins—anything small and valuable."

Astonished, Nakhtmin stared at him. Had Hori read his thoughts? Of course, he should have thought of that. And it wasn't a secret that precious essences were needed to prepare a corpse for eternity.

He glanced at the king, and he too looked like a man having stepped into air. "I'm glad we called you two in," he blurted. "I don't know anybody else who could've shed light on such a dark tangle. Thanks. You have both helped tremendously."

Nakhtmin bowed to hide his blushing at such praise. Without them, it wouldn't have been possible for the secrets of the weryt to be up for sale. "Whatever I can contribute comes from my heart. Um, since there's nothing else for me to do, may I return to my duties at the House of Women?"

"Certainly, you may go."

"Wait, one more thing." The mer-ut turned his long snout to Hori. "If your health permits, I'd like you to return to the weryt straight away to question Neb-kaura's wife."

"You seem relieved," Hori remarked as they ambled though the corridors, Nakht-min on his way to the House of Women and he to the royal pier, where Hut-Nefer usually tied up his bark.

Nakhtmin turned to him in surprise. "Aren't you too? This is not the time for agitation. I don't want Muti to get upset."

He hadn't thought of that. On the other hand, Nakhtmin had been eager to spy on those lazy guards, so he too must have felt the tingle, the excitement of getting at the bottom of a mystery. *He* had missed it. All too monotonous had his days passed recently.

"Didn't you want to say farewell to Ouseret?" his friend asked.

A harsh pain jabbed him, so he stopped and gasped. "I totally forgot!"

Nakhtmin laughed. "Then your feelings can't run so deep if the prospect of an interrogation in the necropolis makes you forget her."

That was mean! The messenger had barely given him time to remember his name in the morning, then one thing chased the other. Maybe he could manage both if he hurried. The royal pier wasn't too far from the harbor district. "See you later!" he called and dashed off.

Rushing through the streets while ignoring the slight pounding in his head, he already suspected he'd come too late. Ra had already set out on his journey across the sky, and most riverboats departed as early as possible to cover a longer distance. The harbor bustled with people. Fishermen returned with the first catch of the day, dockers helped loading and unloading; the smell of freshly cut wood hung in the air. Hori dodged a man who couldn't look ahead as he bent under the heavy weight of a sack he carried. Finally he reached the section of the pier where the ferryboats tied up.

"Has a boat headed south already today?" he asked a sailor.

He spit into the water before answering, "Several."

Far off, Hori saw Hut-Nefer step onto the royal jetty. If he wanted to take a ride with him, he'd better hurry. "Was a tall woman among the passengers?" he blurted.

The man whistled approvingly. "The dark beauty? Oh yes. I'd love to have set my sail for her myself." Then he grabbed his groin salaciously.

What a sleazebag! Fortunately, Ouseret had found someone else to take her to Waset. Still, she was gone now. Yearning for her, he faced south. Would he ever see her again? Despite his impertinence, he'd have paid the guy anything to chase after her with him. If only he could spend his time as he pleased... Sighing, he turned away and sprinted to Hut-Nefer's bark.

When the gates of the weryt closed behind them, the mer-ut removed the mask and wiped sweat from his face with a cloth. Wearing the disguise for so long in this heat had to be awful. Hori followed him to his office. Surely he wanted to talk about things neither the king, nor Nakhtmin, nor the oarsmen were allowed to hear. Full of expectation, he looked at the old man.

"The name of Nebkaura's wife is Merit-Ib," Hut-Nefer began. "Because of her lying, she's currently in detention at her house. With me, she completely locked up when I asked about her reasons or anything else. Hm." His mouth twisted. "You may be right that I intimidate people."

"I'll do my best to get her talking." He wasn't too sure the woman would confide in him, though. After all, she knew Hut-Nefer had tasked him with solving the crime surrounding the heart. "Where do I find the lector priest's house?"

"It's the fifth on the right side. There are two palm trees in front of it."

Hori didn't need to know more; the habitations of the heriu-heb lay separated from those of the embalmers, were a little larger and more comfortable, some even featured little gardens. Before visiting the traitor's house, he headed to Kheper's place, though. Unfortunately, his fatherly friend was already at work, but he was looking forward to talking with him in the evening. Kheper should be able to tell him a few things. Nebkaura's disappearance couldn't have remained a secret in this tight-knit community.

He found the house of the priest without difficulties since a servant lingered in the shade in front of the entrance, making sure Merit-Ib didn't disappear as well. "No visitors allowed," he snarled.

Hori sighed. "You know me. I'm here on orders of the mer-ut. Now, let me pass!"

The servant lifted his eyebrows in surprise but waved him past. Hori practically sensed the man's curiosity following in his wake as he stepped over the threshold, as if it had taken on a bodily shape. He'd prick his ears hoping to find out something. The small entrance hall was deserted, just like the adjoining rooms. Could the woman not have noticed his arrival? "Hello?" he called. "Merit-Ib?"

At the back of the house something rustled, and he headed there. "My lady, I'm Hori," he addressed the back bending over a chest.

She let the lid drop with a bang and turned. "I know who you are."

A beautiful woman, who lived up to the name Beloved Heart. The past days had left traces on her face though. The way she pressed her lips together looked like she wanted to prevent inconsiderate words from slipping out her mouth. She couldn't hold his gaze. He realized she was afraid and angry. At whom? Putting on a smile, he tried harmless chatter. "It's such a beautiful day and so gloomy in here. Why don't we step into your garden?"

She shrugged and took the lead. A wall of more than a man's height surrounded the small yard. That was good. Nobody would be able to listen in on them. "Beautiful gardening," he praised. "You've made the best of the small space."

Her eyes lit up with pleasure. The garden was obviously her pride. In vain, he looked around for children. However, Merit-Ib was old enough that they might have grown up already. He spotted a bench and eased himself onto it. "Come sit with me."

Hesitantly, she did as she was told.

He leaned his head back and stared into the endless blue sky above. "Look, a falcon!" he called.

Her gaze followed his outstretched arm. "Horus. And like his namesake, he's searching for prey," she said bitterly.

"What makes you think I intend to harm you?"

She remained silent and kneaded her fingers.

"Look, Merit-Ib, it's like this: I serve Maat. Once the goddess even appeared to me and demanded retribution for an atrocity. Because if an outrage remains unatoned, the scales of justice are no longer in balance, and Maat gets angry. What can we humans do? We have to strive for balancing the scales again. One good deed may outweigh a bad one. Thus you could make up for your lie by telling the truth now."

Her lips parted as she stared at him in astonishment. "You really think so?"

"The mer-ut assured me, you won't face punishment if you reveal everything you know about your husband's disappearance." Though the old man hadn't promised anything of the kind, Hori was convinced he'd understand the truth was more important than punishing the culprit's wife.

She lowered her head and began to speak, as if she had to convince her hands. "My husband is gone. His heart...had grown wings long before his body did." She paused. "I'm not sure when it started. Once we were happy, and we loved each other. But the years passed, and it became apparent that I couldn't bear him children. Dissatisfied, he began to resent me. Instead of sharing the bed with me, he roamed the streets of the weryt at night."

And on one such occasion he must have seen Hori leave the necropolis. Was childlessness the sole worm gnawing at Nebkaura's heart?

"He feared for his afterlife," she continued monotonously. "Who'd conserve his name for eternity? Who'd recite the spells? Blaming me, he started to beat me."

Hori closed his eyes. With these simple words, she'd unrolled the miserable life the couple had led. Understandable that Nebkaure despaired. Unlike other people in the Two Lands, the inhabitants of the weryt couldn't visit the graves of their ancestors and honor them. The king saw to it that priests took care of this duty, but some spells could only develop full power when the family of the deceased spoke them.

"He took to secretly copying scrolls he found in the library and studied them."

That caught Hori's full attention. Library? He'd never wondered how the heriu-heb were educated within the weryt, but now it dawned on him: there had to be a writing school on these premises, as well as something like a House of Life where the priests learned the chants they recited over the dead. Or did they study at the neighboring temple of Anubis? The mer-ut was also the first prophet of Anubis. Of course, he'd have writings of secret knowledge. Nebkaura might've gotten his hands on some of those. But what could he hope to achieve? Find a magician who'd guarantee him eternal life after death? Such theft made the man's disap-pearance even worse. Hori wasn't looking forward to telling Hut-Nefer. "Are the copies in the chest you just closed so abruptly?"

She nodded, and Hori took a deep breath of relief. At least the miscreant hadn't taken them with him. But he still didn't get it. "He could have divorced you."

She cast her gaze at him, and he regretted his words. Tears welled in her eyes. "If only he could! There aren't many women a heri-heb may marry. The daughters of the utu would rather consort with an ut, and he'd still have had to support me, as the marriage contract demands. Provide a house for me—here!"

Hori saw the man in a different light now. Under these circumstances, a divorce was probably not an option, and the same went for a second wife. Did Nebkaure hope for a new beginning outside these walls? That would explain why so many months passed without him leaving the weryt for good. He needed to steal enough to settle somewhere as a well-to-do man. He couldn't purloin too much at one time lest he draw attention, only a little here and there... After all, precious essences were occasionally spilled. Besides, Nebkaura needed buyers for his stolen goods, and quantities too large might have raised suspicion or at least curiosity. Except in temples or here in the weryt, where would someone get that much? Hori gave a grim nod. The survey of the storerooms would show. Very likely Hut-Nefer had already ordered that.

"During the last few weeks it got worse with him," Merit-Ib continued. "He was always irritable and on edge."

Hori knew exactly why. Because the guy had killed someone!

"And then he was suddenly gone. What could I do?" She sobbed.

"I understand." He wrapped an arm around her shoulders.

The simple gesture of consolation burst all dams. "I couldn't say anything! If he'd returned! Didn't know where he was..."

The poor woman. He had to speak in her favor to Hut-Nefer. She was innocent, and he understood why she hadn't betrayed her husband.

SETKA'S SANDAL CARRIER

Day 16 of month Ipet-hemet in Shemu, the season of the harvest

When Kheper strolled onto the main square together with other utu and spotted Hori, he grinned over his whole face and spread his arms. "My boy! How wonderful to see you back on your feet! You've given me quite the scare."

Hori enjoyed the embrace but also felt guilty. "The mer-ut kept you in the loop about my recovery?"

"He had to! I pestered him every day."

Looking over Kheper's shoulder, Hori saw the curious glances of the other embalmers, and his friend Hornakht lowered his head conscience-stricken, but he approached. Oh right, they'd argued.

"Hey, nice to see you. I'm really sorry about that," he stammered. "If I'd known that of all the heriu-heb it was mine who…"

Now Hori understood his discomfort. An ut always worked with the same lector priest, and Nebkaura had been reciting during Hornakht's organ removal. So the killer had used his seal when he 'bestowed' one of his canopic jars with an extra heart. "How could you have known? If I'd been in your place, I wouldn't have liked being questioned either." Thus he accepted the apology.

"None of us thought him capable of such a deed," Kheper chimed in. "I'd love to know what all this was about." Curiosity sparkling in his eyes, he studied Hori. More and more utu had gathered around the three of them, obviously just as eager to find out something new.

"You have to forgive me, but my lips are sealed. Can you accommodate me tonight?" he asked his fatherly friend.

Kheper lowered his voice. "If you promise not to sneak out to chase some heriu-heb. Wait here, I'll hurry with the cleansing." And off he went.

Reluctantly, the other men now headed for the ibu as well, and Hori stayed back on the dusty square with only a few children playing around him. It seemed like everybody knew who'd knocked him out. How annoying that he'd forgotten to ask Hut-Nefer what he'd told his people about the man's disappearance. They'd only talked about him questioning Merit-Ib. He touched the wound on his head, under which the steady pounding continued. It would do him good to stretch out on a reed mat soon. He hadn't fully recovered yet.

A little later, he enjoyed the simple lentil meal Nut had made for her father, while Kheper roasted a fish over a fireplace. To celebrate his return, he claimed, but also to make the food fill two stomachs.

"Was it really Nebkaura who hit you over the head?"

Hori simply nodded since his mouth was full. Kheper's gaze swept over the roofs of the houses, where the heriu-heb lived; he looked sad.

"What's up?" he asked. "Did you like the man, and now you miss his company?"

"Nebkaura wasn't a good person," Kheper snarled. "We all knew that. I pity his wife. She's had it rough for a long time. And now what? Where can she go?"

So the beatings didn't go unnoticed. Something like that wasn't easy to keep secret in such a close community. Strange that Kheper talked of Nebkaura as if he were dead already. Even stranger because Hut-Nefer had promised him something earlier. "She'll be free. Merit-Ib will be regarded a widow since the mer-ut is going to ostracize Nebkaura. Tomorrow."

Kheper's eyes widened. "Now that's something. That my old bones have to see the day. Poor thing. Who'll take her on? I don't think she has a family she could move in with."

Oh, his friend put a lot of thought into Merit-Ib's well-being. Would he open his heart to the possibility…? "You've got enough room," he mumbled between bites.

"Oh, come off it." Kheper waved dismissively. "One thing I don't understand. How did Nebkaura manage to get over the walls of the weryt?"

"Yeah, I'm sure you'd love to know that. Maybe he's discovered how to turn into a ba and grow wings?" he suggested.

Kheper's chin dropped. "Seriously?" He gazed into the sky as if expecting to see Nebkaura flap about. "Oh my, what nonsense you speak! But you must know something. Didn't he hit you close to the ibu?"

Hori regretted having to keep the truth to himself. "Yes, I was at the canal providing fresh water for the ibu. And then the blow from behind, and I don't remember anything else." He touched his head. "Better not to ask further. Say, are you going to let the fish get just as black on the other side? Then I'm probably not that hungry."

"Oh, darn!"

Nakhtmin still felt elated by Sennedjem's declarations of gratitude. To his surprise, the harem guard knew who'd found Rahotep. The royal messenger must have told him. At home, a note from Ameny awaited him. "He's back?" he asked Mutnofret.

"Otherwise he wouldn't summon you to the temple," she snapped. "What's going on? For days, you had to rush off to one place or another, Hori disappears and reappears half-dead. As soon as he can stand upright, the king's messenger drags us all from our beds…"

He suppressed a groan. It had only been a matter of time before she got suspicious. Quickly he thought up an explanation. "Oh, that! Had to do with the Horus in the egg. The queen was in pain, and the pharaoh worried."

"And of course there are only two doctors to be found downstream and upstream. I too carry a child under my heart, but that doesn't seem to concern you much." She turned away from him, but only so far that he could still see her lower lip push out.

Quickly, he wrapped his arms around her from behind and placed his hands on her stomach, which wasn't protruding at all yet. "Darling…are you unwell?"

She snorted with derision. "I don't throw a fuss over every twinge."

Horrified, Nakhtmin remembered a dragging pain in the abdomen often preceded a miscarriage. "Did you feel a 'twinge'?"

She shook her head. "No, don't worry, but do I really have to talk about twinges for you to ask how I am doing?"

That wasn't fair. Still…he had neglected her, and Muti wasn't one to tolerate that. Actually, her outburst was overdue. Likely Ouseret's company had distracted her until now. How unfortunate that the tall doctor had departed. He'd have loved for her to be close in case Muti did feel a twinge, but then… "You have no idea how much I've been looking forward to spending the evening with you. Only the two of us!" He sighed. "Your father has much to worry about these days. Upon his return, he was hit with the news of Iriamun's passing. I have no idea, though, why he'd want to consult me in matters of the temple."

"Find out and come back home soon." She smiled over her shoulder at him.

"I will."

In all honesty, he could well imagine why Ameny wanted to see him so urgently. Horrible timing with events at the weryt coinciding with the turmoil at the Amun temple. He entered Ameny's office without knocking and was surprised to see someone else sitting behind his desk. "Duamutef! What...? Oh, right."

The man looked up from his reading and furrowed his brow. "If you're looking for Ameny, he's already moved into Iriamun's rooms," the former third prophet said. Or was he still filling that position?

Of course, initiation would only happen after the ritual of mouth opening for eternity had been performed on Iriamun's mummy in front of his tomb. During the seventy days needed for embalming his body, business at the temple had to go on, so the successors had already moved on to their future positions. "Pardon my intrusion," he mumbled and withdrew.

Two doors down the corridor lay Iriamun's former realm. Intimidated, he knocked first this time. He'd never entered the rooms of the first prophet before. No 'Enter' reached his ear, so he opened the door anyway. Made of cedar wood so thick that only a loud noise could penetrate it, he assumed.

Ameny wasn't here either. Then he heard something from the adjoining room and stepped to the opening. His father-in-law stood with his back to him at an open door leading to the Holy Garden of Amun. The light of the low sun outlined his figure. He was filling out around the middle, Nakhtmin noticed and cleared his throat.

Ameny didn't turn but said, "I'm glad you're here."

He inspired a sense of awe in Nakhtmin, which he hadn't felt in the presence of Muti's father for quite some time, so he bowed. "Prophet?"

Now Ameny did spin around. "Why the formality?" With three steps he reached Nakhtmin and drew him into an embrace. "My new office won't estrange us, will it?"

Embarrassed, Nakhtmin shook his head. What was that? On Ameny's left arm a fresh mark shone forth, the ankh sign. "Th-that's the same as Hori's," he stuttered. Hadn't Ameny just been initiated into secret mysteries? Once he'd asked Hori about the mark but received the usual answer that he must not know, so he'd assumed the symbol had to do with the weryt—a false conclusion. But how could Hori have received such consecration before the future first prophet of Amun had? His friend now always wore a bracelet covering the mark. Maybe Ameny would too. So far the tattoo was still a raw wound, though.

Ameny placed a finger on his lips. "I must not talk about it."

As was to be expected. He shrugged. "Why did you want to speak with me?"

"Sit down. It's about your new acquaintance, Neb-Wenenef."

Nakhtmin sank onto the chair in front of Ameny's new desk. He needed a moment to recognize the name. "You mean Wenen. What about him?"

"Well, you know of my troubles filling the prophet position." At Nakhtmin's nod, Ameny continued, "Since he made some interesting suggestions to you, I wanted to ask him about the men he'd named and find out more. However, now your friend doesn't want to remember anything."

"The names? No problem, I recall them."

"Neither the names, nor having given you any."

"Beg your pardon?" Nakhtmin scratched the spot where the wig touched his forehead. That made no sense. Or had Wenen been hit over the head as well?

"Instead, the man suddenly sings Setka's praise." Ameny's lips twisted.

Believing to have misunderstood, Nakhtmin shook his head. "Setka? But Wenen despises the pompous snob!" The buzzing of a fly sounded overly loud in his ear. What had happened to his friend? The other day, he'd also seemed aggrieved.

Ameny leaned back. "His words fell on deaf ears, believe me, but Duamutef insinuated he thinks Setka a qualified candidate."

Now he couldn't remember the name of the hem-netjer, who was to be promoted to fourth prophet within only a few days and would soon ascend to third. "Uhm, what's the opinion of…?"

"Kagemni?"

"Right."

"That's the problem. Kagemni had been away from the temple for a long time and hardly knows the hemu-netjer. Our 'friend' Setka takes advantage of that and kisses up to him. With the help of your buddy Wenen, by the way, who acts as if he'd recently been appointed Setka's personal sandal carrier."

Stunned, Nakhtmin didn't know what to say.

"I'm afraid Setka used my absence to his advantage," Ameny added.

"Doesn't your word weigh more than that of the other two?" Nakhtmin objected. "You have the king's ear. If you tell Senusret what a foul fruit this priest is…"

"You don't understand-" Ameny interrupted and stared ahead. Then his hand slammed down on the table, hard enough to make Nakhtmin flinch. "Ah, gotcha." Pulling a disgusted face, he flicked a squashed fly from his palm. "Custom dictates the prophets present one candidate to the pharaoh, one they all agree on. We'll have to work together for years. Particularly now, the temple cannot afford arguments between the prophets."

"You need the other two behind you, not working against you. I understand." If Ameny pushed his opinion, although the others disagreed, the second and third prophet wouldn't appreciate that.

Brusquely, Ameny wiped aside some scrolls. "So much to do, but I'm not making any progress. Why don't you talk to Wenen and find out what he's up to. I seriously doubt he supports Setka because of the man's amiable nature."

Nakhtmin rose. "I'll do my best. In the light of all this, I assume Muti and I won't be able to welcome you in our house for awhile?"

"Unfortunately not. She is in good health, I hope? Please give her my love."

Wenen had already left the temple when Nakhtmin was looking for him. Strange how his heart didn't want to call him 'friend' anymore but he couldn't believe he'd misjudged the man, either. Why did the young hem-netjer act so differently than before? Something had to be at the bottom of this, and certainly nothing good.

When he reached the harbor district, dusk encroached. Like last time, the enticing scents of the cookshops wafted through the alleys. Since he'd hardly eaten anything after breakfast with the king, he obtained a roasted fish, which the saleswoman wrapped in a large lotus leave. Holding it in his hand, he entered the tavern with the bull emblem and instinctively looked at the table where he'd seen Wenen the other night. A group of noisy sailors sat there tonight, so he scanned the rest of the room. In vain. Wenen wasn't here.

"What shall it be, my lord?" the innkeeper addressed him.

Nakhtmin flinched. "Nothing, thanks. I'm looking for someone." About to leave, he turned back to the man. "Do you know the priest called Wenen?"

"Maybe."

The man actually held out his hand and ogled the deben on his wrist, from which he'd just scraped a flake to pay for the fish. Nakhtmin peeled off the copper ring and slammed it on the table next to him. "Got a knife?" He certainly wouldn't give the scoundrel the whole circlet.

After receiving a piece as thick as a finger, the innkeeper said, "Yes."

"Yes, what?"

"Yes, I know him."

"You think you're dealing with a dumbhead?" Nakhtmin bellowed. "Give me sensible information, or hand back the copper!"

The racket in the tavern ebbed. Everyone stared at him, and the sailors looked eager for some action. So he lowered his voice. "Has Wenen been here today? Do you know where he lives?"

The innkeeper spit on the floor, so close to Nakhtmin's feet that he stepped back. You just wait, I'll remember that.

"No and no. Grace us with your presence soon again."

The patrons roared with laughter at Nakhtmin's impotent fury. He fled outside. Just great, now there were two watering holes in the harbor district for him to avoid. He shouldn't take on more innkeepers. What now? Wenen lived in the craftsmen's district, but that consisted of innumerable winding alleys since everyone built houses wherever they found enough space. Of course, that meant plenty of dead-end streets, and anyone not familiar with the layout got quickly lost. Maybe with some luck, he could ask his way to Wenen's place. But first he gobbled up his simple meal.

Soon only the cooking fires on the roofs illuminated the growing darkness, but their light didn't shine far. He had to tread carefully so as not to trip over refuse. "Hey, there!" he shouted to a man leaning over the roof, probably curious to see whose steps echoed through the lane. "Do you know a priest called Wenen?"

"Nah, sorry!" he shouted back.

"What's up?" his neighbor called.

"He's asking for a priest of the name Wenen. Do you know him?"

"No, but I'll ask around."

From roof to roof, Nakhtmin's inquiry traveled. Fascinated, he stared up at the first man he'd asked. Incredible, this was like throwing a stone in water and watch the ripples spread all the way to the edges of the pond.

"Hey!" someone finally hollered from one of the houses diagonally opposite. "Are you the fellow looking for Wenen?"

"Yes!"

"You'll find his house in the basket makers' lane. The third one after the well."

"Thanks! And how do I get to the basket makers' lane?"

A many-voiced choir replied and carried him on and on through the labyrinth of streets until he reached his destination: the door to Wenen's house. He shouted his thanks up to his invisible guides, but hesitated to knock. What if Wenen had set out for his favorite watering hole in the meantime?

His worries were unfounded. Even before his fist touched wood, the door opened a crack, and Wenen hissed, "Who's there? Who's making that ruckus?"

"It's me, Nakhtmin."

Was that a groan? A cold hand clutched his arm and pulled him into the house, where an oil lamp cast an unsteady light. "What do you want?"

"Why so unfriendly? I tried to find you at the harbor, but you weren't there, so I thought someone might be able to point me to your place and I'd drop by." After all, Wenen had shown up at his house unannounced as well. The flickering light sent shadows dancing across Wenen's features, so Nakhtmin had difficulties reading his face, but the man didn't look well. "Are you sick?"

With a nervous gesture Wenen invited him to sit. "I have beer. Want some?"

"Sure." Nakhtmin slid onto a bench.

The priest rumbled about in an adjoining room before he returned with two jugs. "To your health."

"To yours."

Strange how different Wenen seemed within his own four walls compared to his visit with Muti and him. So…constrained? Nakhtmin found it hard to put his impression into words. Was he ashamed of his humble dwelling? Nakhtmin certainly didn't feel welcome.

"Is your friend doing better?"

"Hori? Oh yes, he's back at work." To bridge the ensuing silence, he sucked on his straw in the mug as Wenen hadn't sifted the brew. What was he doing here? He should be with Muti instead of forcing this awkward conversation. "Ameny is back."

Wenen nodded. "I know."

"He told me something astonishing, which I find hard to believe."

"You better believe it," Wenen grumbled.

Had he misunderstood? How would the man know to what he was referring? "He said you've turned a fervent admirer of Setka."

Wenen placed his hands on the tabletop and half rose. "That's true. I've misjudged the man."

Nakhtmin snorted into his beer. "Are you kidding me?"

Wenen plopped back onto his stool. "Listen to my words. Remember and carry them to Ameny's ear. Setka is great, I have much to thank him for. If anyone deserves ascending to the ranks of the prophets, then it's him." That sounded like a threat.

"Ameny wouldn't agree with you," Nakhtmin said and thought he wouldn't either. "He'll never choose Setka as fourth prophet. Your new-found friend can put that idea right out of his heart. The persuasive manipulations of you two have caused quite some strife. Ameny asks you to stop praising Setka."

Wenen lowered his head over the mug. Had Nakhtmin seen contentment flare up in his face a moment before? That made even less sense than all the rubbish he'd spouted before. As he sucked on the straw, the priest's cheeks caved inward, and his face briefly resembled a skull, his gaze, though, flickered like the flame of the lamp. What was going on in his heart?

"Would you do me a favor?" Wenen asked.

"Sure." The word slipped from his lips before he could catch himself and regretted it straight away.

"Don't get mixed up in matters of the temple."

"Oh. Hm." Nakhtmin would have loved to comply, but it was too late now.

"Thank you."

Nakhtmin leaned back. Wenen seemed to have taken his utterances for confirmation of his spontaneous agreement. He decided to leave it at that. "Shall we go up to the roof? It's stuffy in here."

"No!" Wenen pushed back his stool and thus actually blocked Nakhtmin's access to the stairs. He immediately seemed to regret his brusqueness though. "Sorry, but it's a real mess up there. Part of the roof has collapsed and needs repairing before anyone can go up there."

Could that be true? It wasn't impossible. However, Nakhtmin got the impression Wenen wanted to hide something completely different. "No problem. Next time then." When slurping noises announced he'd reached the dregs, he pushed the jug away. "I should leave before your neighbors go to sleep, or else I might not find the way back."

Eagerly, Wenen jumped up and opened the door for him. "Oh, that's simple. You see the moon? If you head straight in that direction, you'll reach the mansion district."

Nakhtmin had expected Wenen to accompany him for a bit. What kind of friend was that? "I hope I won't get lost. Thanks for the beer."

"Thanks for your visit." Wenen practically shoved him out the door.

Dumbfounded, Nakhtmin stood in the dark. Who was this person? Certainly not the same he'd called a friend. All of a sudden, he remembered the haunted look on the face of his colleague Weni—funny how they almost shared the same name—when he'd been bribed by the former vizier. Or his own shabby behavior. His bad conscience had weighed him down when the powerful man first threatened him and then promised wealth to make him comply with his demands. Setka originated from a great family, so he too had the means to smooth his way to the top of the temple hierarchy with gold. Only, Nakhtmin would never have thought Wenen to be corrupt. Shaking his head, he went home.

WOMEN PROBLEMS

The next morning, Hori said goodbye to Kheper. There was nothing left for him to do in the weryt now that he'd shown his friend the way to possible new happiness in love. He and Merit-Ib deserved it.

An unusually high number of watercraft bobbed at the pier of the weryt in the low Nile waters, among them barges. Looking back from the boat, he saw men working at the canal and smiled. The king lost no time, and that was good. The other canal providing water for washing the dead in the ibu was also covered. The outlets for the wastewater were too small for anyone to dive through under the wall.

Before beginning his service at the House of Women, he hurried home to change his clothes. Heqet greeted him exuberantly as always when he'd been gone for a while, but this time it annoyed him. She kind of acted like the mistress of the house and his heart. Why had he never noticed before? Brusquely, he fended off her caresses.

When she brought him a fresh shendyt and started fondling his groin, he said, "Thanks, I'll dress on my own."

She cast him a questioning look. "This time, you don't wish me to do that?" Her brown eyes glimmered with moisture.

Please don't cry now, he thought and turned away in irritation. "Not today." And never again. Often, Heqet had massaged his phallus on such occasions and given him pleasure he'd rather receive from different hands now, darker ones with long fingers. It would have felt like betrayal to let the maid gratify his lust. Then he remembered what Ouseret had told him, and he glanced over his shoulder at her. "Is it true that you're with child?"

Her shy smile radiated hope.

"I'll find a husband for you. He shall receive a house from me, where you can live. Maybe one of the gardeners?" There were a few young fellows among them. At least one of them would surely be without wife.

At first she looked about to defy him, then she buckled. "As you wish, master." Her lips quivered.

Oh please, tears after all now? The girl couldn't possibly have fostered illusions *he* might marry her! What would Sobekemhat say if he came up with such an idea? The old man's possible reaction made the notion rather appealing, but he couldn't marry the girl just to rile his father. The vizier wouldn't be pleased with a physician as his daughter-in-law either. Happiness didn't matter to the old man. He only cared for his reputation. "Come, come," he tried to console her. "You'll run your own household, doesn't that please you?"

Instead, horror showed on her face, and she went down on her knees and clasped his legs. "I'll do what you want, but please don't send me away from you!"

Annoyed, he tried to struggle free of her, but she clutched him with the strength of despair. What was she thinking? Did she expect his future wife to put up with his former concubine still living in his house? He wasn't that kind of man, and Ouseret would certainly not feel comfortable with such an arrangement. He took her chin in his hand and forced her to look up at him. "Heqet, this won't work. You'll soon bear a child; motherhood and running your own household will require all your attention. Tell me, is there someone among my or Nakhtmin's servants whom you like and who likes you?"

Her look resembled that of a cornered gazelle. Now he did pity her. If she felt for him as he did for Ouseret, her heart would be breaking now. For the first time he could empathize. Except nothing changed the fact that he'd never love her, and the sooner she directed her longing at someone else, the better.

Finally she seemed to understand. "Mesu," she murmured. "If it has to be this way, I choose your gardener Mesu." She pressed against him. "What if I lose the child?"

That neared Hori. Did she intend to...? Midwives and doctors knew means to make a woman lose the fruit of her womb but only resorted to such measures if pregnancy endangered a woman's life. Unfortunately, there were also physicians who did it without need, for whores or if an unmarried woman didn't want to bear a child. However, that was considered a crime, and she was talking about *his* child!

Emphatically, he said, "That wouldn't change anything, Heqet. I'd dismiss you from my services, but without husband and your own household." He could only hope that dissuaded her from doing anything rash.

"Do I no longer appeal to you?" she fought her last stand.

He sighed. "I thank you for all the pleasures you've given me, but my heart belongs to another woman, and since that happened, I only want her."

Abruptly, she let go of him and tumbled to the ground. "It's her! That man of a woman!"

The hatred in her voice shocked Hori and made it even more important to remove her from his household as soon as possible. "None of your concern who it is," he said. "I'll talk to Mesu. Don't make it any more difficult for all of us. Go now!"

Weeping, she fled his dressing room. He wrapped the clean shendyt around his loins, placed the doctor's amulet around his neck and selected a plain collar. Before leaving his estate, he put his plan into action and asked the chief gardener which of his men was Mesu.

Surprised, the man said, "Over there, at the oleander bushes."

Hori sensed his curious look between his shoulder blades, while he turned onto the path leading through the bushes, but this certainly wasn't any of the old geezer's business. Mesu turned out to be a young fellow of acceptable looks. He'd make a good husband for Heqet, and someday the couple would be happy together, Hori told himself. Nevertheless, he felt a little uneasy when he addressed the man. "Hey, Mesu!"

The boy lowered the knife with which he'd been pruning the bushes. "Yes, master?"

"You know my maid Heqet?"

His face lit up. "Oh yes!" Then he started and tried for an impassive expression.

However, Hori had seen enough. Mesu adored the girl and feared his master might disapprove. "What would you say if she moved into your house as your wife."

119

First he looked about to burst out in cheers, then his features darkened. "Um, but…master! I don't have a house yet. I mean…would she like to? Oh. Um, would you allow it?" he stuttered in confusion.

Hori laughed. "Well, at least the thought doesn't seem to appall you. I would present you with a house for you two to call your own. She agreed to accept you as her husband. However, I have to tell you that Heqet carries my child under her heart."

"Oh." His face turned a dark purple, then he beamed at him. "Yes, with joy, yes! She'll give me children of my own as well! That's very generous of you, sir."

"That's settled then. I'll let you know when I've found suitable habitation for you." It would cost him a lot, because he wanted them to live at least in the craftsmen's district, not in some pauper's hut. He probably owed Heqet that much.

"I didn't expect you to show up today," Nakhtmin called with joy when Hori entered the House of Women late in the morning. "What's up? You look troubled. Something in the weryt you couldn't sort out?"

Hori shook his head. "No, all's taken care of there, and we know why the poor woman lied about her husband." He quickly summarized what he'd found out. "Then I had to deal with something rather unpleasant: Heqet."

Nakhtmin pursed his lips. "Because she's with your child?"

"Exactly. I didn't expect her to take it so much to heart, but I guess she's in love with me." Hori pulled a face showing a strange mix of arrogance and embarrassment.

That was so typical of Hori! Even a blind man could see the girl had a crush on his friend, only he didn't notice. "Why don't you keep her with you?"

Hori snorted indignantly. "And Ouseret? If she becomes my wife and moves into my house, should Heqet serve her then? Right now, her heart is filled with hatred for Ouseret. Besides, since I found out what love is, no other woman can tempt me."

Oh, Hori in the know! Initiated into the mysteries of the goddess of love, Bastet. Not that Ouseret seemed to care what Hori did and with whom. Well, it probably was better for Heqet if she left, for her own sake since she'd only keep yearning for Hori in vain. "What did you do?"

"I asked her if she knew a young man she'd like for a husband. After some shedding of tears she named one of my gardeners."

"Mesu?" Nakhtmin blurted.

Hori darted him a surprised look. "You know him? And that…?"

"Oh boy, you really don't notice anything going on around you. She pines for you, and he for her. It's been this way for quite awhile." Nakhtmin couldn't believe how inconsiderately Hori often treated his servants. Had that been part of his upbringing?

"Oh," he uttered.

Nakhtmin snorted. "I assume Mesu is enthused."

"Well, he should be. I promised him a house in addition to Heqet and her growing belly."

He burst out in laughter. "He'd have taken her anyway, believe me."

"Why didn't you tell me earlier?" Hori called.

"Why should I? Would you have cared?" He simply couldn't resist rubbing it in. Time for Hori to lower his nose a little and not look down on people. In that regard, he was just like his father and didn't even notice. "Besides, providing them with a home is the honorable thing to do. Servants are people too, you know."

Hori blushed at least. "I'll try to remember."

Realizing that his friend grew sick of the taunting, Nakhtmin changed the subject lest they end up in another fight. Heqet wasn't worth it. "By the way, I visited Wenen yesterday." He told him about the strange change of mind.

"Bribed," Hori said. "Setka has far reaching connections, you say? That usually means wealth as well."

Nakhtmin chewed his lower lip. "That's what I suspected, it's just that Wenen doesn't seem the kind of man holding out his hand for bribes."

"Well, that's what one might think of many people," Hori said and tilted his head, scrutinizing him.

Nakhtmin's face grew hot. "That was different! N—um, the man whose name must not be spoken threatened me. I thought I had no choice!"

Hori pulled a face, turned away, his shoulders tense.

"Hey, who saved you in the end? Huh?" Now he could see it: Hori's whole body shook with suppressed amusement. Disgruntled, Nakhtmin grunted, "Stop laughing. Wasn't funny back then."

Hori rose slowly and nodded. "For me either." He rubbed his face with one hand, as if to wipe away unpleasant memories. "I thought my last days had come." He punched his arm. "The happier I am to be here with you today."

Soon after, they visited the pregnant queen together. Nakhtmin was glad to be rid of Tep-Ta. Sennedjem, still grateful for his help, had told him of a rumor that the little doctor had been transferred to the country estate of Senusret's mother, where queen Weret never happened to sojourn. So he was going to be the head of doctors only treating peasants there. Nakhtmin found this promotion of the Running Nose well deserved.

Nofrethenut sat up when they entered. "Both my favorite physicians! How lovely that you've recovered, Hori."

"Your majesty, only my heart's yearning to see your beauty again has made me rise from the sickbed."

She giggled. "Your flattery hasn't suffered from your injuries."

Nakhtmin grimaced behind Hori's back because he always had to overdo it. A giggle from the door caught his attention. Two dark pairs of eyes peered through the crack—probably the two oldest princesses Tisi and Henut. Nakhtmin pulled more faces to amuse the two. While Hori examined the queen, he distracted the young majesties although they could be a real pain.

"Your majesty, I declare you in good health," Hori finally concluded. "The birth will happen in the middle of the month Menkhet."

Even though he hadn't expected to hear anything else, Nakhtmin was relieved to get his own opinion confirmed. The most dangerous days of pregnancy, when women most often lost their children, had passed, and if the gods deigned it so, the pharaoh would greet his heir in three moons.

Finally, Nakhtmin could spend a whole evening alone with Muti. He'd missed her company and still missed being able to tell her what occupied his time and heart. Smart as she was, she'd helped him figure out the mystery of the murdered girls, one of whom had been her sister. However, back then she'd thrown herself head first into horrible danger. Therefore she must not learn of the missing heri-heb. But the troubles of succession at the temple of Amun were something he could tell her about. So while they ate in the pergola of the garden, he related Wenen's strange behavior and Ameny's request to sound him out with regard to his sudden change of mind.

"Oh, poor father!" she cried out. "So much chagrin, and while he has to take on new responsibilities."

"That's all you have to say?" he said in surprise.

"My dear consort, why speak the obvious that you already know?" She stuffed his mouth with a chunk of gooseflesh. "Setka desperately wants to ascend to the ranks of the prophets and is willing to do a lot to achieve his goal. Since he couldn't convince Father, he's trying the other prophets—with success. I guess he's learned to act more prudently and somehow made Wenen indebted to him. And certainly others as well, who actually don't like him much."

He washed down the meat with a gulp of pomegranate juice. "You might as well say the word: corruption. I'm so disappointed in Wenen!"

She pursed her lips. "Didn't I warn you?"

Nakhtmin opened his mouth to counter that she'd changed her opinion of the man, but she put a whole date in his mouth. "Mh! Mh-mh-mh?" he mumbled.

She ignored him. "It really seemed strange that he pretended not to know who you are. I'm sure he sought your friendship to benefit from it. He's subtle, I have to admit that. But why's he now smoothing the way for Setka...? Oh, I got it. Maybe they've agreed on a log-roll. First Setka becomes fourth prophet, then he fosters Wenen's career."

This time, Nakhtmin turned away from her before replying, "But how can Wenen hope that Setka can get him a promotion? All high-ranking positions in the temple will be filled with men young enough to stay in office for many years."

Muti shrugged. "Maybe Setka plans to forget his part of the deal. Other-wise...accidents happen every day. Like a snake in the garden of Amun."

He cringed. "You think it wasn't an accident?" A cobra venturing into the Holy Garden was indeed strange, but not impossible. And it could have bitten anyone promenading in the grove or wherever unlucky Djedefra met his fate. No! He shook his head. "I wouldn't go that far. Setka, as I've got to know him, is pompous and driven by ambition but lacks finesse. I don't think him cunning enough to plan something like this." By the gods, he certainly didn't want to solve another mur-der. If she was right though, then Setka posed far greater danger than he'd granted the man. Better to change the subject before she interfered in temple matters out of boredom. "Hey, you've spent a lot of time with Ouseret. Did you ever talk about Hori?"

She grinned. "Certainly. Hori's wound, the color of his urine, his condition..."

"Woman! You know exactly what I mean. Hori's pining for her, but she made it very clear his affection isn't welcome. However...his gift did please her. Do you know more about her? The woman acted rather mysteriously and never revealed anything about herself."

Pensively, she pursed her lips. "True, she was always reserved about her personal life. I got the impression her family must have had some problems."

"What makes you think so?"

"Well, I asked about her father and the reason why she became a physician instead of marrying..." Deep in thought, she plucked a grape.

Curious, he watched her. "And?"

"Nothing. I only learned her father was also a doctor, or still is. I'm not sure if he's still alive. She didn't want to talk about it. Her mother died a long time ago."

Strange that she didn't even open up to Muti although the two women had spent so much time together. What did they talk about then? Well, Ouseret's family didn't interest him anyway, only the woman. "Does she like Hori a little? I fear he'll set out in search of her at the first chance. I wouldn't want him to hit another wall of rejection."

She turned her head away just a bit and smiled mischievously. "You'd love to know that, wouldn't you? I think he deserves to be miserable for a while. Has he told you what he did with poor Heqet? He simply passed her on to that slob of a gardener, as if she were an overripe fruit only good enough for a beggar."

Astonished, Nakhtmin wondered how she'd found out so soon. Then it dawned on him. The girl probably ran straight to Baketamun to cry at her motherly shoulder, and the cook served her mistress the gossip with her meal.

Muti ate a piece of honey cake and licked her fingers with pleasure. "Say, my spouse, whose love life interests you more, Hori's or yours?" She came to him and slithered around him—no other word could describe it better. Pregnancy already made her breasts fuller.

Mouth parched, he croaked, "Mine."

The next day, as he walked to the palace with Hori, Wenen intercepted them. "Hey, you two," he hollered jovially, as if nothing had happened.

"Oh!" Nakhtmin called in surprise. After their last meeting, he hadn't expected to see the priest so soon again.

Hori greeted the man cheerfully. "What's taking you this way? Got lost? The temple's in that direction." Grinning, he pointed his thumb over his shoulder.

Wenen's smile appeared as open and friendly as always, but that had to be a deception because his gaze and posture seemed even more hounded than last time. Now he wrapped an arm around Nakhtmin's shoulders. "Can I talk to you for a moment?"

That sounded conciliatory. Maybe he'd caught his new friend on the wrong foot when he simply showed up at his home. Would the priest reveal today what troubled him? Of course! He'd chosen this spot so Setka wouldn't see them. "Sure," he replied and exchanged a meaningful look with Hori.

For once, he wasn't slow-witted. "Yeah, you two have a chat, while I go ahead."

Wenen's arm remained on his shoulder as they walked down the street. Many people bustled around them, government officials heading for their workplaces, therefore Nakhtmin suggested, "I know a little park where there shouldn't be anyone around this early in the day. So we could talk in peace there."

"Yes, let's go there."

After a short walk, they reached the recreational greens and sat down on a bench in the shade. For a while, the priest brooded in silence. Nakhtmin sensed his deep emotional distress. How could he help him without knowing the cause?

"I'm really sorry about the other day," Wenen began.

Waving dismissively, Nakhtmin sighed. "What troubles you? You can trust me."

Horror flared in Wenen's gaze, then he lowered his lids. "No. I cannot," he said brusquely only to continue in a more placating tone, "It's got nothing to do with you. I don't want to lose your friendship."

"Is it about Setka?" The sound of the name made Wenen gasp for air, so Nakhtmin dug deeper. "You can tell me if he bribed you. It's not that despicable although it would disappoint me. I want to be your friend anyway."

"Do I look like someone who has suddenly become rich? I'd never let that dodgy weasel bribe me!" he cried.

Oh, suddenly the man had turned into a weasel? Earlier it had sounded as if Setka's steps blessed the very earth he walked on. So he'd been right that something smelled fishy here. And it dawned on him what reeked so foul. "He's putting you under pressure. Does he know something compromising he can expose if you don't do his bidding?"

Wenen jumped up and paced a few steps back and forth, as if fighting an inner battle. "Don't ask!" he finally groaned. "Please. I can't tell you. Just be my friend."

To Nakhtmin's horror, the priest knelt before him, embraced his knees and wept bitterly. Helpless, he stroked the twitching shoulders. What should he do?

Scorn at Setka overwhelmed him. Whatever Wenen might have done, the crime of that son of a bitch was worse. How could anyone do something like this to another human being? All of a sudden, Wenen released him, straightened on his knees and pulled Nakhtmin's head closer. Then he pressed his lips on Nakhtmin's, jumped up and ran away. Baffled, Nakhtmin just sat there. What did that mean? They weren't *that* close. A goodbye kiss?

COME QUICK!

Several days passed without finding a trace of the missing lector priest. The mer-ut reported to the king that indeed significant quantities of valuable resins were gone, and the pharaoh told Hori, who shared the news with Nakhtmin. However, since nothing pointed at Nebkaura also selling secrets of the weryt in addition to these precious items, Nakhtmin gladly regarded the bloodcurdling matter as settled. Lurking shadows and the fear of attacks by foes that couldn't be fought off had troubled him more than he even wanted to admit to himself. Weren't there enough other problems keeping him busy, mostly Ameny's?

Today was the tenth and last day of the week, decade day, when all work ceased in the Two Lands. "Let's visit my parents today, yes?" Muti suggested.

That suited him well. "Good idea."

After sending Inti ahead to announce their visit in advance, they finished dressing.

Right at the gate, the cheering twins greeted them. "We're going on a boat trip! Come on, hurry up!"

Bata tore at Nakhtmin's wrist, Huni dragged Mutnofret along. Out of breath, they reached the jetty.

Isis hugged Muti, while Ameny greeted Nakhtmin with more reserve. The ankh sign on his upper arm was now covered by a bracelet like Hori's.

"Great idea to spend the decade day on the river. It's so hot," Nakhtmin said and studied Muti's father. Dark shadows under his eyes hinted at him not getting much sleep lately, and his features looked tense. The day off should do him well.

The two boys had already climbed aboard and, shrieking like monkeys, tried to scramble up the mast.

"Children!" Isis called. "Stop it, you'll hurt yourselves." The rascals didn't pay any attention to her.

"Oh my, those two all day in such confined space? Is that really such a smart idea?" Mutnofret asked doubtfully.

"We'll head downstream to a branch of the Nile where they can swim, play and exhaust themselves." Isis received a basket and two jugs from a servant—provisions. The grownups stepped onto the boat. Bata and Huni fought over who got to untie the ropes, then they quarreled over the first shift at the punt pole until an unusual fatherly outburst silenced them temporarily. Nakhtmin had never experienced Ameny so short-tempered, but he was glad when the bickering stopped. Hopefully, Muti would only give birth to one child for now.

Ameny spread out on the pillows and closed his eyes but didn't sleep since his lids quivered and sometimes blinked. Nakhtmin settled beside him. "You don't look well. Are you sick?"

"Only exhausted," murmured his father-in-law. "It was a tough struggle to change Duamutef and Kagemni's hearts."

"Then you were able to convince them to select a different fourth prophet? Who?"

"We chose Sehetep, much to Hemiunu's chagrin."

The image of the somewhat conceited head of the priests flashed in Nakhtmin's memory. He wondered why the man wouldn't approve of the choice, then remembered: Sehetep was his right hand. Now the fat guy would have to find another gofer. "Is it final then?"

Ameny gave a lazy nod. "We can't waste time. The man needs awhile to get familiar with his new tasks, and it'll take even longer for Kagemni to fill his new office as third prophet. The pharaoh has been informed."

"Setka won't like that," Nakhtmin murmured.

"Why would I care about Setka?" Ameny blurted. "Bad enough that Wenen supported him. Unfortunately, Duamutef has cast an eye on your friend. A very favorable one."

Yes, it had indeed struck him as strange that the third and soon second prophet would listen to– Oh! Heat rushed to Nakhtmin's cheeks. "You mean Duamutef's heart leans toward men? How does Wenen feel about that?" He squirmed. Such relationships were frowned upon, even if pharaoh Neferkare Pepi had supposedly gone to his general at night and did with him whatever pleased him.

When Ameny nodded, Nakhtmin mulled over the question whether Wenen was also like that. After all, the young man lived alone when others of his age already had families. And hadn't he been relieved to see Muti's appeals didn't affect him? Dear gods, the kiss! Wenen had kissed *him*! All of a sudden, he felt the pressure of his touch again. Disgusted, he wiped his hand over his mouth several times until his lips felt brittle. He wished he could wash them with water. That certainly cast a different light on the relationship between Setka and Wenen. Those two could also have been—he hardly dared to think it—lovers. If so, Wenen had shown rather poor taste. He shared his musings with Ameny, however, without mentioning the kiss. Yuck!

Muti came over and sat with them. Obviously, she'd caught his last words. "Oh, my dense husband! Of course Wenen favors men. Didn't you notice? He tried his luck first with you, then Hori, but he always withdrew quickly when you didn't react the way he'd hoped."

Hori? Nakhtmin felt like he'd been hit over the head. "Whe-when had that happened?" A stab of jealousy confused him even more than anything else.

"That evening when you were out looking for him, when he dropped by our house."

Neither she nor Ameny took exception to such behavior, and Nakhtmin felt like a country bumkin, which he actually was, kind of. Was he prudish because the notion appalled him? Not for the first time, he perceived the difference between his small-town upbringing and Muti's far more world-savvy education. "Then Wenen might have found in Setka a…um, bedfellow?" He stared at Bata struggling with the punt pole he'd taken over from Huni. Soon he'd get bored and hand it to the servant. Then they might actually make some headway. The twins simply weren't strong enough to get the work done.

Ameny laughed out loud. "Setka? He isn't gay! Didn't you notice how brazenly he ogled Muti during the assembly at our estate?"

No, he hadn't. The women had retreated early that evening, and he never saw her together with Setka. He sighed. "Then I understand even less."

His father-in-law snapped his fingers. "Maybe Setka found out and applied pressure to your friend. Such relations aren't really accepted, and if disclosed, Wenen could probably forget all promotions, would remain a small mid-level hem-netjer for the rest of his life. Of Duamutef's inclinations, I only learned when he'd already been third prophet for a while. But now please let's talk about something other than affairs of the temple. I'm sick and tired of all that!"

Hori lay in the shade and enjoyed reading his favorite story again after quite some time, the tale of the eloquent peasant. He'd already followed the man of the oasis on his cumbersome journey to the Nile valley, where he wanted to sell his wares. However, as soon as he arrived at the stream, a cunning tenant cheated him out of all his possessions. Now he was reading how the man turned to the superior of the trickster to reclaim his goods. Hori knew how the story continued. The supervisor, a higher administrator of the king refused the duped man an audience. Thereupon the smart peasant had a bill of complaint written up, in which he explained Maat and a just world order and pointed out that poor and rich had the same rights. Hori loved this part in particular, but the sound of the connecting door to Nakhtmin's premises pulled him out of the story. To his surprise, someone hurried through his garden although Nakhtmin and Muti were gone. He peered around a hedge and saw a stranger approach, a craftsman, judging by his clothes.

"Are you the doctor Hori? Next door they said I might find you here."

His first thought turned to the queen, but then he realized the pharaoh would certainly have sent a different messenger. "Yes," he said hesitantly.

The man kneaded his spotty shendyt and shifted his weight from foot to foot. "Pardon my intrusion. It's about a sick priest. He asked for the physician Nakhtmin, but he isn't at home…"

Hori didn't have to think long. "Wenen?" The other day he'd already looked like a gust of wind might blow him off his feet.

The man nodded with visible unease. "You better hurry. He's in really poor health."

"Wait here, I'll just fetch my medicine bag." Hori jumped up and ran into the house. How stupid of him not to ask more questions like: injury or fever? To err on the safe side, he packed everything he could grab.

Already on the way, he did ask the messenger, but he didn't know any specifics. "A neighbor heard him scream and went over. Soon after, he sent me to get the doctor."

Hori followed the man through the maze of alleys. The way seemed endless. Why didn't the king decree regulations that forbade building anywhere and everywhere. On straight streets, it'd be much easier to get somewhere. Since it was decade day, lots of people were out and about. Only a physician never got a day off, Hori grumbled to himself and had to laugh. If he said that to his father, the man would retort, 'If you had listened to me and took on a position at the treasury…'

At long last, Hori's guide stopped and pointed at a house. "In there."

The door stood ajar, so he entered without knocking and climbed the stairs. The building had two floors and the bedroom was certainly on the upper one. Groaning and murmurs drifted from one of the two rooms to his ears, so he went there. "Hey, there. The physician's here," he called.

A man and a woman looked up from the sickbed. "Praise the gods! I've never seen anything like this!" the woman cried. Both stepped back to make room for him.

Despite the darkness in the chamber, Hori discerned straight away that Wenen was indeed seriously ill. "Bring as many lamps as you can find," he ordered and began to examine the patient. The skin felt clammy from cold sweat. No fever, but the man didn't recognize him, didn't seem aware of his presence at all.

Apathetic a moment ago, Wenen suddenly lashed about wildly. "No! No! Don't!" Then he collapsed again.

The couple returned and placed a few oil lamps in the room. "Can we help you somehow?" the woman asked.

"Would you bring water up, please? And wine, if he has any, otherwise beer."

She nodded and hurried off, while her husband watched from the door what Hori was doing.

Wenen's pulse raced unsteadily. Not a good sign. Now Hori could better see the color of his skin: pale. The face looked gaunt like a starving man's or...that of a very old man. Then Hori noticed Wenen's hair and eyebrows had begun growing back and glimmered white, not black! How was that possible?

"Sir?"

He started, but it was only the woman bringing two jars.

"Thanks, put them over there. Now you better go." The disease might be contagious after all.

As soon as they'd left, he spread his medicines on the table, sniffed this and crumbled that between his fingers, without knowing what he should do. Wenen's breathing turned stertorous and wheezy. Ah, he'd heard that before in stone masons because of the dust they inhaled. Quickly, he mixed some herbs and ground them in the mortar before adding them to the beer. Wine would have worked better, but since the woman hadn't brought any, he assumed Wenen had none at home. While the concoction steeped, he lifted Wenen's lids, but his eyeballs had rolled up so he barely saw more than the whites. "By Sakhmet's arrows! What kind of demon possesses you?" he murmured and bent over the chest of the ailing man.

Wenen jerked up so suddenly that Hori tumbled back but caught himself. Then he started screaming, a wail that reminded him of the eerie howls of the jackals prowling in the west at night.

"Wenen! Calm down, I'm here with you. Hori is here." He stepped closer.

A hand clutched his wrist. Wenen's grip was like that of a bird of prey. "Nakht-min...need physician...prophet...Nakht-" He sank back and lay limp as before.

Hori sifted the beer. "Here, drink this." He lifted the man's head a little, held the mug to his lips, and his patient swallowed obediently. Since he'd added poppy seeds to the brew, he expected Wenen to doze off soon, and he did. Hori could only hope that sleep would bring recovery, because he had no idea what else to do for him. And rest would certainly benefit him more than those ghastly fits consuming Wenen's strength. What should he do? He had to send for Nakhtmin but didn't want to leave the patient alone.

He went downstairs and found the neighbor couple standing around on the street in front of the house chatting with other people. Already the term 'evil spirit' made the rounds. The last thing he needed! "Can one of you fetch the physician Nakht-min? He's at the house of the prophet Ameny."

A boy squeezed through the crowd of grownups. "I'll go, noble sir. I know where it is."

Of course, you'd know, little rascal, Hori thought. The urchin looked curious and meddlesome enough to have explored all of Itj-tawy already. He probably expected a reward, and knowing Lady Isis, Hori felt sure he'd get plenty of honey cake, a feast for the boy. When the child bolted off, he returned to the house and went upstairs.

The bed was deserted, the chamber too.

Hori rubbed his eyes. Where could Wenen have gone? He'd imbibed enough poppy to knock out a donkey. His gaze caught on the ladder up to the roof. Oh no! Not there! With haste he scrambled up the rungs.

Wenen stood at the edge of the roof, arms spread like wings. Hori pulled him back. "Boy, what are you think-" He gasped when he saw Wenen's face: pure horror etched into his features, unseeing eyes still rolled upward.

With much cajoling, Hori managed to lure Wenen down the stairs and back into bed, where he fell asleep as if nothing had happened. "What strange disease is this?" he asked aloud. "He should have slept till morning!"

After a while, Hori grew hungry. Furthermore, he wanted to see if there was another jug of beer in the house, so he could prepare more medicine. Wenen slept peacefully, his breathing and pulse much calmer now. Before he dared to leave him alone again, he barred the bedroom door with a chest from outside. While helping himself to Wenen's sparse provisions, he wondered what kept Nakhtmin. Running to the district of mansions and back couldn't take that long.

DREADFUL END

At the onset of dusk the boat neared its jetty. Nakhtmin alighted first and stretched out his hand to pull one after the other onto firm ground. A tug on his shendyt made him look around to scold the twins, but a strange child stood there, likely a street urchin. "What do you want?" he asked in irritation because he was tired and hungry.

"My lord, you must come! A physician sends for you."

"Hori!" he blurted.

Muti looked shocked as well. "I hope he hasn't relapsed somehow."

The boy fidgeted. "No, the doctor's well. He's treating a sick priest. Come on! You've dallied enough."

Such cheekiness left Nakhtmin dumbfounded, while Bata and Huni giggled. Hiding behind Isis's skirt, they peered around her and made faces at the rascal. Mutnofret's mouth twitched as well. She was still holding the basket of provisions and searched through the leftovers. "Here, for you," she said and handed him a piece of crane breast and some cake.

Greedily the boy snatched the food, then again tugged Nakhtmin's shendyt with his greasy fingers. "Now, come on!"

He'd have liked a bite for the road, but trotted off with the urchin. To his surprise, he didn't lead him toward the temple but to the craftsmen's district, and that moment it dawned on him who the patient was.

"I started to think you'll never get back," Hori barked at the rascal when they reached Wenen's house. Nakhtmin became the next target of his foul temper. "What kept you so long? Come on upstairs. Quick."

To his surprise, a chest barred the door, but Hori simply shoved it aside. "I'll explain later." He entered the room and lit the oil lamps spread throughout the room.

Seeing the priest sleep peacefully, he understood the fuss even less. "Why did you have the cheeky brat drag me here as if this were a matter of life and death?"

Hori told him in what condition he'd found Wenen.

"Onto the roof despite the poppy seeds?" In disbelief, he shook his head and touched the chest of the sick man. He was right though: Wenen's heart beat fast and irregularly. He lifted his lids and flinched. Rolled up like Hori'd said. Spooky! A sense of impending doom sank into his heart. No, no. It had to be a normal disease, which neither of them had heard about yet. "I'm at a loss, just like you. I don't see an injury." Then he noticed the silvery stubble on Wenen's head and gulped. "We should send for a priest or magician. I think a charm is at work here. Is the urchin still around?" He went downstairs and out onto the street, where some neighbors still hung around despite the late hour. The boy stood among them.

"Hey, you!" Nakhtmin called. "Run back to the house of the prophet Ameny as fast as you can and bring him here."

A lumpen man placed a heavy paw on the child's shoulder. "What gives you the right to command my boy around like a servant?"

Resigned, Nakhtmin closed his eyes for a moment. That would turn into another trade off even though the urchin had been rewarded generously. "What would compensate you for the absence of your son?" he asked.

The father licked his lips. "A jar of beer? No, wine. Oasis wine!" He grinned.

"What else then!" slipped out of Nakhtmin's mouth. "A shendyt of royal linen?"

"If you have that on offer…"

To Nakhtmin's relief, his wife chimed in. "Let the boy go! You should be glad to help someone. A good deed to place onto the scales after your death. Might remain the only one!" Snorting, she stepped in front of him, and the boy wriggled free of his father's grip.

Fast as the wind, the child disappeared between the adults. Hopefully, Isis gave the boy a reward he would enjoy, not his father. Pensive, he headed back into the house. Never before did he have to fight an illness like the one Hori described. Uneasy, he scratched his neck. Was there a particularly evil demon at work here? If so, where had Wenen caught it? Nakhtmin could only hope he came to his senses soon, because the man owed him a few answers, not only regarding the kiss. Huh, a collapsed roof. As if! What had Wenen been hiding from him so desperately?

On the table in the downstairs room, he found the remains of a meal and remembered he had skipped dinner. It smelled nice, so he scraped out the bowl. With the last bite, he realized that somebody might have poisoned Wenen, possibly with this meal. Quick now, he had to throw up!

Hori came down the stairs as he shoved a finger in his throat. "What are you doing?"

"I ate the leftovers, but Wenen could have been poisoned."

Hori snorted. "I made the meal hours ago. If I'm well, you won't die either."

"Phew."

"But the thought isn't so farfetched. Poison. Let's see—mandrake, oleander?"

Nakhtmin waved dismissively. "Pointless to try guessing. Could have been a mixture of various poisons. And what would it help us if we guessed right?"

"Well, it sure would," Hori said. "Rare substances are difficult to get your fingers on. If we knew what it was, we might find out who did it."

Although he was right, Nakhtmin didn't like where his thoughts wandered. "I'd rather cure him with an antidote than hunt his killer! We should get milk for him, always helps in cases of poisoning, and make a brew of mugwort and acacia."

Hori chewed his lower lip. "You're right. I'll ask the neighbors for milk. Mugwort and acacia are upstairs. Oh, and I should get a jar of wine or beer since Wenen's pantry is quite empty. You'll wait here for Ameny."

Nakhtmin nodded. If Wenen had really been poisoned, Ameny's conjurations probably wouldn't do much good but couldn't do any harm either. Who might want to get rid of the priest? Maybe Setka because the prophets chose someone else for promotion? However, he didn't really think the man so wicked. Wenen had done his bidding, and it wasn't his fault Ameny had decided against Setka. The man himself would have had to act differently to convince his father-in-law, but the snob would never understand that.

He poked around the pantry, but it hardly offered anything. Strange. As a priest, he received quite some corn, oil and other foods, more than one man alone could consume. Looked like Wenen had traded his provisions for other things, but what? Inside the house, he hadn't seen anything of value. Of course, that didn't mean much since he could have sold the stuff for deben—easier to hide somewhere, maybe buried in the adobe floor. Upstairs in the bedroom sat an almost full jug of beer emanating a strong scent of herbs. Hori's sleeping potion. They'd need that later if Wenen had fits again. Currently the patient seemed calm, his face rather cavernous though.

Sounds of the door opening drew his attention, and he gazed down the stairs. "Ameny! Come on up, he's lying here."

"And who is it?"

Oh, right, his father-in-law wouldn't even know who he'd been called to. "It's Wenen. He's critically ill, possibly poison or a demon."

Ameny entered the chamber. "He sleeps peacefully."

Nakhtmin repeated what Hori had told him about Wenen's symptoms and pointed at the hair turned white. "Can you write up some magic spells for him?" he asked. "I do apologize, but I couldn't think of anyone else to call on, this late and on a decade day."

"Does the man have writing utensils?"

He should have checked earlier so that Ameny could have brought his own. "I'll see if I can find something." He opened the chest beside the bed. "Only clothes." Still, he rummaged on.

Ameny said, "I could write on cloth if you find ink and cane." Meanwhile he leaned over Wenen and murmured incantations.

Nakhtmin wasn't ready to give up yet. A priest without writing materials in his house? He'd check the other upstairs room. Ugh, smelled like something had been burnt here. Charred remains lay in a bowl on the table running along the entire front wall. His nose wrinkled. Beside the bowl lay a scroll. Its back was still empty, and he tore off strips. Here he also found a writing palette with ink stone and stylus. He fetched the water jar from the pantry and filled the small vessel for mixing the ink and brought everything into the sickroom. Just then Hori returned.

"Are you going to give me a hand?" Hori called and unloaded his burden of milk, beer and bread. The loaf he'd mainly gotten for himself and Nakhtmin, but the soft interior could be used to knead medicine into and form little balls. Hearing Nakhtmin stomp down the stairs, he said, "Would be better to take the patient to the House of Life or to our homes. I don't really feel like staying for an unknown time." When he saw Nakhtmin's scrunched up face, he quickly added, "I know he's your friend, and I like him too, but if we move him, we'll have everything we might need at hand, and he'd be more comfortable."

Nakhtmin's features relaxed. "Of course you're right, but after all I've learned about Wenen, I'm not so sure he's even worth my friendship."

Oh, quite a change of tune. He pursed his lips. "Is there something I don't know yet?"

"Could be that he…um, likes men," Nakhtmin blurted.

Hori suppressed a laugh. His friend surely was fairly provincial in such matters. "So what? He still needs our care." He sighed. "I guess we can't send the urchin again to fetch two servants with a stretcher from my estate. The House of Life would be nearer, but the temple gates should be closed already."

Contradictory feelings showed in Nakhtmin's face until he finally said, "Fine, I'll go. I hope I'll find the way again." He marched past Hori and shut the door behind him.

Hori ascended the stairs and greeted Ameny, who painted spells on strips of papyrus in the shine of a lamp. "Oh good, we can add these to his medicine." The writing would dissolve in the liquid and reinforce the power of the potion.

That moment, Wenen started to mumble incoherent words in his sleep. Hori couldn't discern any meaning. He bent over the patient and felt his pulse, which seemed faster and unsteadier than before. His breathing was shallow, and the skin looked deathly pale. For the first time, he sensed their efforts were in vain. The would be of the aith can saw al Wenen, as a doctor, he recognized the signs. Gradually the ailing man became more restless. Hori took two of the finished strips and immersed them in the beer jug he'd brought and mixed in all the antidotes at hand. When the herbs had soaked enough, he fed Wenen drop after drop.

A jolt ran through the sick man's body. His eyes flung open, and he screamed as if all the demons of the underworld possessed him. Shocked, Hori retreated, and Ameny gasped. Wenen's head flung around, tongue lolling. It was darkly discolored. Now his jaws cramped.

"Quick! Help me, Ameny, he'll bite his tongue off!"

The prophet jumped up. "What can I do?"

With all his might, Hori tried to keep the clenching jaws apart. "Piece of wood—spoon! Downstairs! Get one."

Moments later, Ameny returned with the desired object, and Hori shouted, "Between his teeth." Again he put all his effort into prying the mouth open a little more. "Now!"

The wild jerking continued, but at least Wenen wouldn't maim himself. Hori held his legs, Ameny his arms. The fit still continued when Nakhtmin returned.

"By the gods, what happened?"

Hori wasted no breath on lengthy explanations. "I gave him the antidotes with one of the spells, then it started. Help me get the sleeping potion down his throat. No way can we transport him like this!"

While Ameny clutched the patient's shoulders, Hori lifted his head and Nakhtmin trickled some of the mixture into the mouth, still held open by the wooden spoon handle. Wenen had barely swallowed when his howling grew even louder, then he went limp and silent. A rumble downstairs, then clanging of the door. Hori stepped down the stairs halfway to see what the noise meant, but there was nobody. "Nakhtmin, didn't you bring carriers?"

"Of course."

"They've taken flight!" he called. Well, he couldn't really hold it against them. Wenen had sounded too ghastly. "I guess we'll have to carry him ourselves." Hopefully the sedative worked long enough. Ameny alone wouldn't be able to keep him in check if the patient began writhing on the stretcher.

Together they heaved the now unconscious man down the stairs and laid him down on the stretcher.

"Hm, maybe we should cut one of his sheets in strips and fix him with those" Nakhtmin suggested.

"Good idea!"

When they were done, the poor guy resembled a mummy. Hori went back upstairs and, after lighting a torch they'd need in the darkness outside, extinguished the lamps. Then he packed up his things and Ameny's remaining conjurations as well as the half-torn papyrus in case they had to try different spells on Wenen. If not, he could use it for other patients. "I've got everything," he called, shouldered the bag and went down.

Ameny, armed with the torch, held the door open for them. Nakhtmin grabbed the front ends of the bearer poles, he the back, and they marched off. At least the streets lay deserted now. They'd inspired enough gossip about vengeful ghosts for one day. "I'm glad you've learned the route by now," he told Nakhtmin guiding them through the dark alleys.

At last, they reached their neighboring estates, and Nakhtmin headed for Hori's gate instead of his own without even asking. Well, in Muti's condition, they really shouldn't upset her. Not to mention the possibility this disease might be contagious, though Hori didn't really think so.

As soon as they entered the house, Ameny took leave. "You should have enough magic conjurations now, and tomorrow I can write more. May the gods be with you." He looked awfully exhausted.

Hori assumed Wenen's state would take a turn in the course of the night, and probably not for the better, but he didn't say that. After putting the patient up in one of the guestrooms, Nakhtmin began settling down as if to stay. Hori dissuaded him, "Go to your wife and tell her what happened. I'll stay with him. Should I need your help, I'll call for you."

He fetched an armchair from the dining room and braced for a long vigil, but since Wenen slept calmly, he too dozed off despite the uncomfortable position and the heat in the room.

He jerked awake and groaned. His neck was stiff, his arm numb. Even worse, he'd dreamed of shadows and demons. "No wonder," he mumbled.

The lamp had gone out, but gray twilight filtered through the ventilation slits in the wall; morning dawned.

"Aaah! No!" sounded a scream from the bed. Wenen bolted upright, eyes wide open, only showing white, as if the man looked into himself. His arms flailed as if to fend off something. "Shu...shu... Aaaah!"

Hori rushed to his side. "Wenen? Boy, it's me, Hori. Calm down, all is well."

A fierce blow sent him stumbling against the wall. His head started pounding again, and he regretted having sent Nakhtmin home. Run over and fetch him? Not while Wenen was in this state. Impossible to leave him alone, not even to wake one of his servants. Hori meant to hold down his arms, but as soon as he grabbed one wrist, Wenen screamed even louder and began snapping at his hand. Startled, Hori let go and stepped back. The priest's mouth foamed. Demons had to be at work since no poison he knew caused such symptoms.

Helpless he watched Wenen's body fall back and cramp once more. This time, his back arched so much, Hori feared the man might break apart. Then the fit ebbed as abruptly as it had started. The spooky eyes were still wide open, the mouth agape, but Wenen lay completely still now. It took Hori a moment to recognize the silence of death.

EPIDEMIC OR POISON?

Day 21 of month Ipet-hemet in Shemu, the season of the harvest

"Dead?" Nakhtmin couldn't believe it. "Why didn't you call me?" The loss hit him even if he hadn't known the young priest for long and found out a few things about the man that didn't sit right with him.

"How could I? He was in a state I couldn't leave him. Flailed his arms, screamed, cramped, and then it all ended real fast," Hori justified himself.

"Maybe I could've saved him!" Now it was too late. Was it his fault because he'd abandoned the man when he needed him most?

"Are you saying I didn't do everything?" Hori turned the other side of his face to him, where a nice shiner glowed.

All of a sudden, he saw the whole scene unfold: the raving, sick man would have been hard to control. Nakhtmin sighed. "Never mind, the poisoning must have been too far advanced already. Did he say anything?"

Hori frowned. "Nothing intelligible. Toward the end, it seemed like he wanted to speak a name, but he didn't get out more than 'Shu'."

"The god of the air? Did he struggle to breathe?" What horrible death. At least Hori had been with him, so poor Wenen didn't have to die all by himself, even if he couldn't ease his suffering.

His friend scratched his chin. "Could've meant that. Or he wanted to say, 'shu-i', 'I'm free'—of pain. Let's go to the temple of Amun and deliver the sad news. They'll want to pick up the body, so it can be taken to the weryt."

Nakhtmin nodded. The temple owed it to Wenen to receive a proper burial, even if he deviated in his sexual preferences. He couldn't simply go to work now and do his duties at the palace as if nothing had happened, and Hori looked like he needed care himself. "We have to tell Ameny. And somebody should examine your head. I'll send Inti to the palace to notify them of our delay."

When they reached the temple, strange tension hung in the air. The wabu strode with unusual haste, not calling out to colleagues as they normally would when they passed them. Their silent bustle struck him as odd. He nudged Hori with his elbow. "Is this a day of mourning for Iriamun, and I forgot?" he whispered but knew better.

Hori shrugged.

Ameny wasn't in his office, so Nakhtmin tried two doors down the corridor, where the second prophet took care of his tasks. This time he knocked, though he still opened the door without waiting for an invitation.

Duamutef wasn't alone.

"Nakhtmin, Hori! The gods must have sent you," Ameny cried when he recognized them. "You're needed at the House of Life. Three more hemu-netjer have fallen sick, and the physicians are at a loss. What brings you to-? Please tell me Wenen is on the mend!"

More had fallen sick? His heart jolted, then beat rapidly. Contagious after all. That was really bad! Far too many people had been in contact with Wenen yesterday. He could fall sick, Hori, Ameny, Muti... Nakhtmin gulped and looked to Hori, who stood just as speechless. Abashed, he lowered his gaze to the floor and left it to his friend to break the bad news.

"Wenen has commenced his journey to the Beautiful West. As you know, we took him to my house last night where he, unfortunately, passed away at dawn."

Both prophets groaned. "What illness is this?" Duamutef asked.

"We don't know. If nobody at the House of Life recognizes the symptoms, we are dealing with an unknown plague." Hori sounded strangely unaffected.

Nakhtmin wanted to shake him because he was so frightened.

Ameny jumped up. "I'll order a thorough cleansing of the complete temple premises with water as well as a spiritual purification. We have to contain the epidemic."

Nakhtmin wanted to say something but only managed a croak until he cleared his throat. "That's good, but will it suffice? Whoever carries Sakhmet's arrows in his flesh will take it from the temple into the city to his family." Muti and the unborn! The Horus in the egg! He went dizzy. It could be too late already.

Ameny seemed to harbor similar thoughts because he turned pale and leaned on Duamutef's desk. "Nobody must enter or leave the temple until we've stopped the plague!" he proclaimed.

"We can't do that," Hori objected. "The House of Life is part of the temple. Who will treat the ailing if all doctors are locked in here? Besides, Wenen fell sick in the craftsmen's district. The disease is already in the city. Clean the temple, make sacrifices to the gods, pray and craft amulets. If we're really dealing with a contagion, only the almighty gods can help us. Oh, and notify the palace, so people will be prepared if Sakhmet's arrows hit there, too." His calmness even surprised himself. "Nakhtmin, let's go to the patients."

Back outside in the corridor, he hissed at his friend, "Pull yourself together! Your face has turned ashen. You can't help anyone if you faint."

"But...Muti– I may have carried the illness into our home!"

Hori didn't know what to say. What a blessing that Ouseret had left town just in time! Poor Nakhtmin had no such consolation. "Come. The sooner we find a remedy, the safer are the people we love."

Imhotepankh did at least show enough prudence to isolate the three hemu-netjer in one treatment room far from others seeking help. The head of physicians for once looked happy to see him and Nakhtmin. "I hear you've already treated a man with the same symptoms," he said. "Then you won't mind taking care of these new cases."

"Are you telling us that until now nobody dared to enter the room? What kind of physicians are you!" Hori shouted in disgust. Oh well, wouldn't serve anyone if he got upset. Calmer he asked the names of the three patients.

The old man unrolled a papyrus he carried with him and read:

"Neferka, Sehetep, Bai."

"Sehetep!" Nakhtmin blurted.

Astonished, Hori asked. "You know the man?"

His friend first shook his head, then nodded and pulled him into the treatment room. Out of Imhotepankh's hearing, he answered, "By the gods! I know all three, met them at Ameny's. More importantly, the prophets just decided to promote

Sehetep to fourth prophet."

"Oh." Hori's heart beat frantically. "That position seems particularly dangerous these days."

Nakhtmin cast him a baffled look. "What do you mean?"

"Let's examine these poor men first, maybe I can tell you more afterward." First the snake, then Iriamun's quick demise, now Kagemni's chosen successor seriously sick—to Hori this appeared like someone went after the prophets as if to clear obstacles out of his path. No, impossible. No living man could plant a disease that afflicted exactly those who he wished gone. Besides, Wenen had shown the first symptoms, not Sehetep. Most likely they were up against a poisoner after all. What winding path was his heart leading him onto? Someone at the temple killing for a loftier position? A grave accusation, and he had no proof whatsoever.

"Strange," Nakhtmin murmured. "Wenen gave me the names of two men he thought qualified to succeed the unlucky Djedefra. Sehetep and Neferka. Both are lying here."

Again, Hori's heart skipped a beat. Could he be right? Was someone smoothing his way to the top of the priesthood of Amun? Then Ameny might be another target. He had to force his attention on the three patients lying motionless on the cots, their breath labored. He bent over the man closest to him. "His heart goes fast but faintly. And yours," he asked.

"Same here. And look!" He pointed at the stubble sprouting from the man's scalp.

"White! Like Wenen's hair!" Hori exclaimed. "We should prepare a poppy seed potion before the cramps set in. It won't cure the men but hopefully ease their suffering. By the way, I still believe it's poison rather than an epidemic."

Nakhtmin's face brightened with hope. "Then Muti would be safe! What makes you think so?"

Hori explained his suspicion while pounding the dried capsules. "Too much of a coincidence that exactly those men, who might be in someone's way, are struck down, isn't it?"

"I could think of a few who might have done it, Setka first and foremost." Nakhtmin clenched his fists. "That mangy bastard! Woe to him if you're right!" Then his shoulders sagged. "No, why should he kill Wenen first; he'd supported him?"

"No idea. Maybe he didn't want to play along anymore when he found out Setka's plans. Hand me the wine." Hori poured the powder into the mug. "Why is he your prime suspect? There must have been more craving higher ordinations."

Nakhtmin nodded. "You're right, my dislike of the priest makes me jump to conclusions. There are many people vying for the position, too many. Hemiunu, for example. Until we know something definite, we should keep silent. Let's try an antidote again. Maybe it'll work better if applied at an earlier stage."

"Good idea! I'll go and ask if they have milk here." He opened the door, but a wab barred his way.

"On orders of the principal, you must not leave this room. Um…until the patients are cured," he stammered and peered over Hori's shoulder into the room— fear in his eyes.

That was outrageous! Imhotepankh deserved a plague grabbing him by his scrawny wrinkled neck. "Then tell the venerable head of the House of Life that we need the following items." He rattled off a list of herbs proven to counteract poison. "In addition, we need milk, food and drinks for ourselves as well as broth for the sick. Oh, and don't forget clean water!"

When the man darted off, Hori didn't hesitate to follow him casually. It would be a miracle if the fellow remembered everything. And he definitely wanted to see how Imhotepankh reacted to his demands. As expected, he found the two in the well-stocked storeroom and leaned against the doorframe, while the wab emitted a desperate stutter. "And they want letters from acacia. Or something like that."

"Maybe lettuce and acacia?" the old man suggested grudgingly.

Hori cleared his throat and repeated his requests, while the complexion of the old man changed from pale to purple. "No reason to get irritated. As you can deduce, my colleague and I suspect poisoning not a plague. However, I fear our help might come too late for these three patients as well."

"And if you're wrong?" the principal raged. "Back into your chamber! Right away! I'll double the guards!"

Hori blocked his way. "Do what you think you have to do, but at least provide us with medicinal herbs and food, venerable head of physicians. Or should I tell the king—life, prosperity and health—next time I see him that Imhotepankh neglected to tend to those in his care?" He stared into the man's eyes until he averted his gaze.

"No, of course not. You'll get what you need. And may the gods be with you."

Nakhtmin soon realized their efforts wouldn't save their new patients, who withered before their eyes. This time, though, he was able to observe the course of the disease, which he so far only knew from Hori's descriptions. When they gave them the antidote concoction, they were seized by cramps and howled as ghastly as he'd heard Wenen do. Coming from three tortured throats, it was hardly bearable. "All we can do is keep them unconscious," he shouted at Hori.

The room was stuffy, and the air just got worse since the ailing couldn't control their excrement. Hori and he washed them, but the dirty rags and sheets piling in the corner reeked. Nakhtmin cursed Imhotepankh's obstinacy, forbidding them to hand the trash to the servants outside. With a real epidemic, he'd be right to isolate them though. Unfortunately, they couldn't prove their diagnosis of poisoning.

The room was already crowded with the three cots, so there were none for them to lie down on and take a nap. Hori already had a restless night behind him. His new bump on the head also caused concern. Nakhtmin hammered against the door. "Hey! Bring us mats. Even doctors must get some sleep."

A short time later, the door opened a crack, through which reed mats were shoved. "You first," he said to Hori. "You need it more than I do."

"Thanks, but I'm not at all tired." Nevertheless, he curled up on one of them and dozed off quickly, judging by his deep, regular breathing.

And just then the patients stirred again. Nakhtmin poured some of the sleeping potion into a mug. First he tried to feed some to Bai. The man couldn't even swallow anymore. Most of the brew spilled from his mouth. Nakhtmin placed a wet cloth on his forehead, where sweat pearled. None of the patients had fever; Bai's skin felt clammy cool. His breathing turned labored, and his eyes rolled upward, flung open as he gasped for air. Nakhtmin lifted his upper body and leaned him against the wall. Now he seemed to breathe easier. Once more he put the mug to brittle lips, and this time Bai swallowed. To Nakhtmin's relief, the body went limp as the drink took effect. "Poor guy," he murmured. "Scandalmonger or not, you don't deserve this."

Nakhtmin turned to Sehetep, but when he touched him, the man began to scream. As if on cue, Neferka joined in with a howl.

Hori jerked up. "What?"

"Take care of Neferka," Nakhtmin shouted and pressed a writhing Sehetep back onto the cot. "Sakhmet have mercy! What demoniacal poison is this?"

The designated fourth prophet bucked like a donkey. "Shuuuuu!" he yowled.

Neferka caterwauled more verbosely. "Dark. Aaaah! Take it away from me. Be gone! Aaaah!" He, too, lashed about.

No way could he get any medicine into him without Hori joining forces with him. "Hori, let go of yours and help me. I'll hold mine and you pour some of the potion into him," he shouted above the ghastly noise.

Hori shook his head. "Too late," he called back. "It'll be over soon."

Impossible! The two were battling the demons inside them. Hori must be wrong. Again, Sehetep arched under his hands, then went limp. Not another sound left his mouth. Relieved, Nakhtmin reached for the mug. "I got him!"

Hori looked up. "Boy, he's dead. Better help me."

Before Nakhtmin could snap out of his stupor, the silence of death also surrounded Neferka. "Holy excrement of the dung eater!" he blurted. "Was it like this with Wenen in the morning?"

Hori nodded.

"What about Bai? Was I able to save him at least?"

Hori went to the priest and touched his throat for the pace of his heart. Surprised he lifted his head. "He's alive! What did you do to prevent the cramps?"

"Only the sleeping potion. You think he might convalesce if we keep him unconscious?" Hope spread within him. Whatever killed these men was horrible and dangerous, but maybe there was a cure. For the first time in hours he thought of his own health. "Do you notice any indisposition? I don't."

Hori waved dismissively. "With regard to Bai, we can only wait and see. Maybe he took in a smaller dose than the others. Do you believe me now that we're not dealing with a normal illness? Somebody made the four men sick intentionally. But how and why?"

"Yes." Nakhtmin sighed in relief. Then Muti was safe. "You said earlier it could be about the promotion. Since Sehetep had been selected and Neferka had at least been considered, that really could have been the reason. Only Bai and Wenen don't fit the picture. In whose way could they have stood?"

Hori sucked in his lower lip. "Good question. That's where we should start. As soon as we get out of here, we have to find out more about the hierarchy and structure of the Amun temple. Fortunately, you have such excellent connections to the future first prophet," he said with a wink. "But now I should really get some more sleep."

"And the corpses? Imhotepankh can't seriously expect us to spend the night with two decomposing bodies!" He jumped up and flung open the door. "Hey! Somebody's gotta take away the dead."

The two wabu pressed their backs against the opposite wall and lifted their hands as if to fend him off. Hm, now there were two? Imhotepankh apparently wanted to make sure his guards didn't get duped again. Nakhtmin managed to convince one of them to fetch the principal, who grudgingly allowed them to move the bodies to the next room.

While Hori soon fell asleep again, Nakhtmin prepared for a long night vigil. Since they had enough space now, he also spread his mat but only sat on it, leaning his back against the wall. This way, he had a clear view of Bai who was also sitting up. Only the faint rise and fall of his chest gave away he was still alive.

At dawn, Nakhtmin's eyes watered with fatigue. The oil lamp began to smoke, then extinguished. He shook Hori's shoulder. "Can you take over? I'm falling asleep."

Hori rubbed his lids and yawned. "Sure. How is he?"

"All quiet."

His friend rose and stepped to the cot. "No wonder. Bai has set out on his journey to the Beautiful West."

The news hit Nakhtmin harder than he'd have expected. A sob escaped him. "In vain, all for nothing!" Under different circumstances, in a time without temple intrigues, he'd probably have gotten along well with him.

Hori sounded calm. "At least he didn't have to face death in such a horrible manner. He is released, and so are we. Come on, let's leave this cursed place."

POKING THE BEEHIVE

Day 22 of month Ipet-hemet in Shemu, the season of the harvest

While Nakhtmin and he undertook a thorough cleansing in the washrooms of the House of Life and donned fresh shendyts, the three deceased were transferred to the weryt in almost inappropriate haste. Hori caught only a glimpse of the relatives placing Sehetep and Bai on imitations of the Neshmet bark, so they could return someday awakened to new life like Osiris. Since Neferka's family lived in a faraway nome and couldn't be notified fast enough, the priesthood of the Amun temple took over this service. The barks were towed by three boats, in which the relatives sat. When Hori returned from the pier, the temple was once again in mourning, but he got the impression the gloomy mood was owed to more than the losses. The hemu-netjer and wabu were afraid, and for good reason. They didn't know yet that no plague spread among them, but a cunning murderer roamed the temple. Together with Nakhtmin, he called on Ameny.

"Close the door," the prophet said instead of greeting them. The creases at both sides of his mouth had deepened.

As if he'd aged overnight, Hori thought as he bowed.

"Is Muti in good health?" Nakhtmin blurted. "Does she know why I couldn't come home?"

"She's fine but worries about you. I too am glad neither of you show signs of the disease. Or do you sense something?" Ameny intently studied Nakhtmin, who didn't look too well after a night of waking. "Have a seat. You must be exhausted."

Hori hurried to put him at ease. "I'm convinced the four men were murdered intentionally, likely with a rare poison." He sank onto one of the chairs in front of Ameny's desk.

Not for the first time, he appreciated the quick uptake of Nakhtmin's father-in-law, who had once before supported them in a dangerous investigation. Now the prophet asked, "You think it's about the succession of Djedefra and Kagemni?"

Hori nodded. "When I heard whom Sakhmet's arrows had hit, the thought struck me, bright and clear like Ra in the morning. Only Bai and Wenen don't quite fit the pattern. However, as Nakhtmin told me, Wenen had been trying to influence exactly that decision recently."

"Since nobody else fell sick, the suspicion is well-grounded," Nakhtmin agreed.

Ameny stroked his shaven head and groaned. "Would have been too cruel a whim of the gods to afflict the most capable of the hemu-netjer with a plague and no one else. But a killer among us? My heart doesn't want to believe it!"

"I can't think of any other explanation," Hori countered. "We need to find out more about the victims. Can you tell us something about Bai?"

"The victims, yes. Bai was well on the way to becoming Hemiunu's new right hand, after Sehetep's promotion to fourth prophet. I'd been in a lengthy discussion with the head of the hemu-netjer and had to promise him free choice in replacing Sehetep. He selected Bai, a promising and smart young man."

And he'd one day fill Hemiunu's position. Also a great honor but certainly not unwarranted. There were always some who stood out because of their industry and attentive heart, and Bai must have been one of them. Therefore, the perpetrator had to fear him like the other men. Or were there other reasons for the deeds, which he simply hadn't grasped yet?

"The best of our priesthood," Ameny moaned.

Nakhtmin rubbed his chin. "Which priests vied for the position of fourth prophet most fervently? I mean…there were so many at your gathering, and they all seemed to buzz around you and your colleagues like flies around a dung h—Oh, forgive me."

Ameny waved dismissively and sipped from his mug. Hori's tongue stuck to the roof of his mouth. Nakhtmin and he hadn't thought it proper to eat and drink with the corpse still in the room. "Do you have something for us as well?" he asked.

"Help yourselves, but it's only water." While Hori drank, the prophet replied to Nakhtmin's question, "Some more men had approached me, some by message from administrators of remote domains. To my surprise, even Hemiunu voiced interest lately…" Pensive, he gazed at his fingertips. "Anyway, they're either indispensable where they serve, because the estates aren't easy to manage, or they're not qualified for the big task awaiting the fourth here. Or both, like in the case of Hemiunu, who is a good head of the hemu-netjer but could never become a prophet spiritually or intellectually."

Hori wiped his lips. "Did you tell him that?" Couldn't have been an easy discussion between Ameny and the man.

"There was no way to spare him the truth after he dismissed my first objection that he does invaluable work as principal of the hemu-netjer and couldn't be replaced."

"Thus he must watch as his underling passes him and climbs the ranks in promotion!" Nakhtmin called. "The domain administrators we can probably disregard as killers. We have to look within the Amun temple of Itj-tawy. We should question Hemiunu." He wanted to storm out the door, but Ameny stopped him.

"Wait! The relatives of Sehetep and Bai asked for the personal things of the two men. Sehetep's mother would also like to know if her son said something. Maybe something that could console her?" Pleading, he looked from Nakhtmin to Hori. "The woman is beside herself with grief. Sehetep was her only surviving child of ten."

Shocked, Hori gazed at his friend, who only shook his head. "Better to spare the woman the grisly details of his struggle. The deaths of the four men were neither easy nor free of pain. The only thing he cried out in the end was 'Shu' as he flailed his arms. That was also Wenen's last word. Maybe he wanted to shoo the demon that possessed him? But that would have been childish. Ameny? What's up, did you just see a ghost?"

The prophet sagged in his chair. "Shu-Ra? Could that have been what they tried to say?"

"Empty mouth? Well, it's possible," Nakhtmin said. "But that doesn't make much sense either. Neferka yelled we should take something away from him. Both died too fast for us to learn more. At least we could spare Bai the horrible cramps with poppy seeds. He didn't say anything before he died."

Hori barely listened to his friend's babbling. "What is Shu-Ra, Ameny?"

"Not what but who! I know that the hemu-netjer gave Hemiunu this nickname because he's always chewing something."

Nakhtmin burst out laughing, but caught himself quickly. Hori could only think: how fitting! Fat Hemiunu was indeed always carrying a bag of treats around. He'd often wondered why the head of the hemu-netjer stuffed himself like a goose. Did the hunger of his heart for higher offices and honors drive him to do so? And now those had been within his reach, but others snatched the prize from him. "Cursed demons of the underworld! Nakhtmin, you're right, we need to take a close look at Hemiunu."

"You have my permission to question whomever you want. But be careful, please. I couldn't bear it if something happened to you," Ameny said.

"Don't worry, we'll pretend to seek the source from which the disease spread. Nobody needs to learn what we know," Hori said and rose

Nakhtmin really didn't envy Ameny his position at the top of the Amun temple. His father-in-law right now faced the challenge of relating recent events to the king. Why did this have to happen when matters in the weryt weren't even completely resolved? He could only hope that no more people fell sick.

Hori and he found Hemiunu in the temple's storerooms, where he handed out freshly laundered mourning garb. He was already dressed in yellow; sprinkling ashes on the heads didn't behoove them within the temple, though, because it had to stay absolutely clean.

Hori addressed the fat man directly. "Venerable principal, I'm Hori, this is Nakhtmin. We've treated the four priests. Prophet Ameny asked us to talk with you about their recent deaths."

Hemiunu sighed. "What a tragedy! Particularly Bai will be missed, and in Sehetep, I lost a friend." His subordinates pricked their ears, and when he noticed, he ushered Hori and Nakhtmin toward the corridor. "Let's take a walk."

To Nakhtmin he appeared truly distraught. Or did he act the grieving man so convincingly? "Sehetep was your assistant before the promotion, right?" he asked.

"Yes, and a very capable one." His fingers reached for the bag of treats at his side but found none.

Had Hemiunu decided to fast although he wasn't a relative of the four men? That too pointed at great grief, particularly in a glutton like him. Or was it a sign of guilty feelings? Nakhtmin found it hard to see a coldblooded poisoner in the jovial man with the wobbly cheeks. "Then you were probably happy for him because his skills were acknowledged by the higher-ups," he dug deeper.

The man's face darkened, and he sniffed. "Not for long could he bask in the light of Amun-Ra. His poor parents! He had such a close relationship with them. His three children... What woe!"

Behind Hemiunu's back, Hori pulled a face and rolled his eyes. Yes, maybe he did overdo the pitying. On the one hand, it fit the simple mind Ameny had attributed to him, on the other, he might just act that part as well. Because he was too lazy to show his abilities? Didn't a frog sit apparently dumb and addled on a lotus leave until a fly whirred past? Woe to the fly if it got within reach of the frog's tongue!

"Now the three prophets must find another replacement for Djedefra," Hori said.

Hemiunu spun around as if he'd forgotten his presence. "What? Oh, yes. Awful.

Last time had been difficult enough to fill two positions in such short time."

"Then it won't surprise you to hear Ameny considers appointing you."

Baffled, Nakhtmin stared at Hori. What made him pretend such a thing? Ameny had told them the exact opposite. Oh, of course! Very clever of his friend. Excited, he waited for the fat principal's reaction.

The man smiled with self-importance. "Not at all. Actually, the prophet had already considered me before, however, he knew my services as head of the hemu-netjer were indispensable. So I suggested Sehetep, who was just as competent as myself."

A blatant lie. Was Hori going to tell him they knew better, to provoke unguarded comments?

No, instead he asked, "No hard feelings because they didn't promote you then?"

Hemiunu shook his head so vehemently the folds of his thick neck wobbled. "How could I harbor feelings of envy when Sehetep was like my own son?"

"What did you think of Neferka?" Nakhtmin inquired. "Was he just as promising a young priest as your right hand?"

Before answering, the principal picked up his waddling pace until they reached the corner of the hallway and turned into a remote aisle where nobody else could be seen. "No great loss," he then grumbled. "But don't tell anyone I said that. I distrust men never lifting their noses from books."

Such an outspoken confession surprised Nakhtmin almost as much as the poor judgment it revealed. "Isn't studiousness one of the columns of faith?"

"We are supposed to serve the gods, not to fathom their mysteries!" Hemiunu hissed. "Who digs too deep may find things not meant for humans to know. You saw where that can lead."

Hori cleared his throat. "Please excuse our intrusion, venerable principal. We've kept you long enough from your duties." To Nakhtmin he said, "Come."

As soon as they were out of hearing, Nakhtmin protested, "Hey, it had just turned interesting. Why did we let him off the hook?"

"That's exactly the reason. Didn't you notice? He blames Neferka for having brought on the mysterious 'disease'. I never considered the possibility one of the four might have evoked such a horrible curse. Or that was a clever diversion."

Nakhtmin stopped short. A curse? Of course, another valid option. "You're right. Hemiunu lied. He still craves the position his assistant had snatched from him, and he doesn't share Ameny's opinion that he isn't qualified. I don't buy into his grief for Sehetep and Bai. Or are you thinking Neferka could have found a conjuration during his studies, which he showed to Hemiunu, and he tested it?"

"You mean an accident by ignorance?"

"Or on purpose. Why these four priests, if not triggered by the wish to smooth the path to becoming fourth prophet? Hm, somehow I don't think he has it in him. If Ameny's right, the man's too simpleminded for such scheming. And I don't really think him capable of murder by poisoning either." Then he remembered what he'd thought earlier. "Or he is very clever and only acts stupid to avoid extra work." An embarrassed chuckle escaped him. "Sometimes I do that when I don't feel like taking care of certain tasks, act as if I were too clumsy until Muti relieves me."

Hori clicked his tongue. "If only we could peer into people's hearts. I'll remember how you deal with Muti."

"Don't you dare!" Nakhtmin cried. "Oh, I just saw Setka over there."

Eager to meet the priest who caused such strong dislike in Ameny, Hori wanted to form his own opinion of the man. "What are you waiting for? We have to question him as well." Basically every member of the temple could have committed the crime, but these two, Hemiunu and Setka, had the strongest motives. Both wanted the position, both were rejected. Hemiunu couldn't accept Ameny's judgment and thought himself the most suitable man. If what Hori'd heard about Setka was true, the same applied to him, only for different reasons. Taking a deep breath, he regretted having to deal with one of those snobs again. Shepses and Neferib had been bad enough to last him for the rest of his life. They'd also thought they could take all the liberties they wanted, just because their father was vizier back then. He hurried after his friend along the corridor.

"Where did he go?" Nakhtmin exclaimed. "He was right here just now." Catching his breath, he halted.

"Maybe he stepped into one of the rooms?" Hori suggested.

His friend glared at him. "Oh really? Only we can't go and pull open all the doors. Who knows what lies behind them? Or are you familiar with this part of the temple?"

He shook his head and peered around the next corner. "Maybe he went that way. I think the library's down there." The huge temple premises around the sanctum sanctorum consisted of many buildings connected to each other, some via corridors and open colonnades, others could be reached through courtyards. There were storerooms, administration offices and utility sheds for maintaining the Holy Garden, the House of Life with its treatment rooms, dormitories for the students and a lot more. "Hey, *you* lived here during your studies!"

Nakhtmin snorted. "I never saw more of the temple than the library. But you might be right. I've just never approached it from this side."

They headed toward the gate at the end of the corridor when a door opened behind them. Steps sounded and grew fainter as someone went the other direction. Nakhtmin looked back. "That's him. Come on!"

Hori felt silly running after the man, so he called. "Hey, Setka!"

The priest stopped and turned around. For a brief moment, it looked like he had no idea who'd called to him, then he recognized Nakhtmin. While they exchanged polite greetings, Hori could observe the ominous priest. He wore yellow clothes, but mourning didn't necessarily reach his heart. In general, he looked like any hem-netjer serving in the temple. So far, he couldn't determine why his two friends found the man so appalling.

"I'm Hori, friend and colleague of Nakhtmin," he introduced himself. "My condolences for your loss. I heard you were a good friend of Wenen?"

Setka furrowed his brow. "Who says that?"

"Wenen told me a few days before his death," Nakhtmin replied. "He held you in high regard."

The painted eyebrows lifted. "Really? Well, I did take him under my wings a little. On his own, he couldn't hope to get ahead because of his lowly origins."

Oh, Setka was indeed one of those guys! All of a sudden, Hori saw his father before him, who liked to speak in the same fashion. Now he understood Ameny and Nakhtmin. "Very kind of you to take care of him. He told everyone how much he appreciated it. His praise of you still rings in my ears."

His self-important smile made Setka look about as light-minded as Hemiunu had earlier. "Least he could do after I bestowed my benevolence on him! Well, well, it's a shame, but he caused his own demise."

Hori exchanged quick glances with Nakhtmin, who seemed just as baffled as he felt. "What do you mean?"

In the diffuse light filtering through the ventilation slits, he believed he saw the man go pale. Did Setka know more? After all, Wenen had been the first to get afflicted by the eerie disease.

"That blighted area where he'd been living," the priest responded vaguely. "Isn't that a hotbed for plagues? You're the physicians. Why do you ask me? Talking of which: Am I safe in the temple or is the air here contaminated? What are you doing to protect me? If my uncle hears that you let your patients die... He has the king's ear."

This time, Nakhtmin cast him an insecure glance, but Hori gave the slightest shake of his head in response. He shouldn't let such bumptious babble impress him. "You're safe here, Setka. One thing we know for sure: there's no danger of contagion. The four priests were poisoned."

Setka's lids flickered. "You're lying!"

At last, Nakhtmin found his voice again. "Oh, are you the doctor now, or what makes you say that?"

Hori placed a calming hand on his shoulder. "Don't get upset. He's just afraid. Although we should be the next ones to be struck down. Come on, let's go to Hemiunu and congratulate him."

Both men stared at him uncomprehendingly, but fortunately Setka couldn't see that Nakhtmin had no clue what he was talking about either. "What could you possibly congratulate that lardass on?" the hem-netjer asked doubtfully.

"Ameny wants to appoint him as fourth prophet. Tomorrow he'll go see the pharaoh to inform him of the decision."

Hori watched realization dawn on Nakhtmin's face. "Oh yes, Hemiunu will soon be a very happy lardass," he confirmed. "That's what he wished for, as you know."

Now Setka had really paled. "They can't do this!" Without another word, he spun around and marched off.

As soon as he was out of sight, Nakhtmin hissed, "What were you thinking to tell him such nonsense?"

Hori grinned. "Just poking the beehive a little to see what flies out. He knows something, didn't you notice?"

"The thing about causing his own demise?"

"Exactly. And instead of answering, he attacked and threatened us both. There's something fishy about the alleged friendship of Wenen and this stinker. First he sounded us out to learn what we know, then he confirmed everything. You're probably right about Setka finding out Wenen's secret preference for men and put on the pressure so he'd recommend him to the prophets." He linked arms with Nakhtmin, and they strolled toward the temple's exit. He needed fresh air and breakfast.

Nakhtmin jerked to a halt. "Man, are you completely crazy?"

"What?"

"If Setka is the murderer, how high would you rate Hemiunu's chances of living to see another day?"

Hori wanted to bang his head against the wall. "I'm such an idiot," he groaned. "Just because I wanted to rile the snotty bastard. I guess we can forget breakfast since we'll have to watch out for fatty."

His friend grinned. "Doesn't have to be us watching, but somebody must. Fortunately, I have good connections to folks at the top of the temple."

A CURSE

Nakhtmin didn't feel all too comfortable using the head of the hemu-netjer as bait for Setka, but how else should they disclose the killer? The arrogant priest certainly wasn't the type to be seized by regret and confess—if he was guilty. Since Ameny should have returned from the palace by now, Nakhtmin headed to his office to report what they'd found out so far, while Hori wanted to 'sound out' more people as he liked to call it.

"Ah, Nakhtmin," his father-in-law greeted him. "What news do you bring? The pharaoh is concerned about what's been happening at the temple. He relieved you and Hori of your duties until either the plague is contained or the poisoner is found." He gestured for Nakhtmin to sit.

"Did you drop by my house? Does Muti know where I am?"

"I sent a messenger."

"Thanks." In brief words he relayed the questioning of Hemiunu and Setka. "Both are suspects. The principal lied to us and still covets the rank of prophet. His grieving for his assistant was piled on too thick to be credible. And he tried to blame Neferka for the deaths. He supposedly discovered a 'curse' during his studies, which could have turned against him."

Now the prophet blanched. "A curse? Go on."

"Setka wasn't honest with us either. He claimed Wenen brought on his fate. When we asked what he meant, he came up with his living conditions, but he must have been thinking of something else. What Hori said next wasn't really smart: that you intend to promote Hemiunu. That misinformation upset Setka."

Ameny snorted. "What made him say that? If it makes the rounds! It would be cruel to Hemiunu to give him hope. Despite all his flaws, he's a good principal with much patience for the whims and pranks of the young priests. I'll have to rectify this right away." He rose.

Nakhtmin hadn't even thought of that. He tried to calm down his father-in-law. "I doubt Setka will tell anyone. However, I fear Hemiunu might be in danger. I still regard Setka as our prime suspect, because his heart is full of selfishness. If he is our man, he'll do anything to get the new rival out of the way." Feeling guilty, he lowered his gaze. "Um, it would be wise of you to assign a guard for him. Shu-Ra should live up to his name today and not eat anything because it might be poisoned."

"Anything else?" Ameny blurted. "Why didn't you think first before you endangered innocent people? As if there weren't enough problems I have to deal with." Before Nakhtmin could protest the unfair accusation, Ameny continued in a conciliatory tone, "Something you said made me think of a completely different scenario. However, before I say anything about it, I have to consult someone. First, though, I should make sure your inconsiderately set snare doesn't strangle the wrong person. Come with me." He stormed out of the room, and Nakhtmin hurried after him. They strode through the corridors until they encountered a wab bowing reverentially before the prophet.

"Gather all wabu and hemu-netjer in the main courtyard," Ameny ordered. "I have to make an announcement."

The man nodded and rushed off.

Surprised, Nakhtmin asked, "What do you want to tell them?"

His father-in-law didn't reveal his plans, but gave four more priests the same order as the first. Then they ran into Hori talking to several hemu-netjer. By now, wabu swarmed in the corridors, spreading the prophet's request, and more and more members of the temple headed toward the largest courtyard.

"Ameny wants to announce something," Nakhtmin explained to his friend. He felt bad because Hori's thoughtless comment angered his father-in-law, and Hori would surely blame him if Ameny now foiled his plot. "You all better come along." He answered Hori's questioning look with a shrug since he didn't know either what would happen next.

When they stepped out into the sunshine, the large courtyard with the obelisk towering in its center brimmed with people. Sounding surprised, Hori said, "I never expected so many folks working at the temple."

"Three hundred hemu-netjer alone, according to Ameny. Some of them don't operate in the residence though," Nakhtmin explained. "Most of the priests here are certainly wabu, doctors or servants." What a crowd! Within these walls worked about twice as many people as lived in his village back home! The temple was a city within the city, and that wasn't the end of it. Numerous domains belonged to Amun; after each successful campaign, the god received his share of the booty, and the kings donated more land to the temple. Ascending to the rank of prophet truly meant power. Until now, the desire for the position of fourth prophet had seemed a little silly to him, but gradually he grasped that there was more to it. Next to the pharaoh, the first prophet of this temple was one of the most powerful men in Kemet.

Ameny beckoned the other two prophets and whispered to them. Together with Duamutef and Kagemni, he climbed the steps leading to the hall next to the sanctum sanctorum and waited. What for, Nakhtmin wondered. When he commenced his speech, it was the exact right moment. All talking had ceased, and all eyes were directed at the three dignitaries.

"Hemu-netjer, wabu, servants. A disaster has struck the temple. Four of us fell victim to it, among them Sehetep, who should have succeeded Djedefra after the burial ceremony of the transfigured Iriamun." He paused to continue in a louder voice. "Is the god angry with us?"

His father-in-law moved the hearts of his listeners, who looked at each other with concern as if seeking an answer from their colleagues. Nakhtmin spotted Hemiunu among the men up front. He nudged Hori and whispered, "Do you see Setka somewhere? Maybe you should keep an eye on him to see how he reacts, while I watch the glutton."

Hori nodded and swept his gaze over the heads. "Got him, but I can't see him too well, because the obelisk half covers him."

That moment, Ameny continued, "Amun, in his wisdom, has revealed to me that he did not direct Sakhmet's arrows against us in scorn. No! A coward is among us. One who craves higher ordination and whose disappointment over not having been selected turned him into a poisoner."

The assembled seemed paralyzed by the news. Only faint murmurs and shuffling feet could be heard. Nakhtmin concentrated on Hemiunu's bloated face, in which surprise, indignation and something like fear showed in turn. A reaction caused by outrage at the deaths of his subordinates or due to his shock over his well disguised deed having been disclosed?

"To make sure no more good men will fall prey to his black heart, I announce on behalf of the prophets of Amun: only after the guilty party has been found will Djedefra's successor be chosen."

What a smart decision! That way Ameny had robbed the murderer of two targets at the same time. Did Hemiunu appear relieved? Hard to tell. Nakhtmin looked to where Setka had stood moments ago, but the man was gone. Following Hori's gaze, he discovered him in a group of hemu-netjer, who gesticulated in agitation. Only Setka seemed completely unaffected. "And?" he asked.

Hori shrugged. "He might as well wear a mask!" he grumbled. "It would tell me just as much. Did you have more success?"

Nakhtmin turned his hand this way and that, to signify the ambiguity of his observations. "Let's talk when we're alone." He pulled his friend in the direction Ameny had gone.

After only a few steps, they saw the prophets standing close to the sanctum sanctorum, but Ameny took part in a passionate discussion with his two colleagues. Nakhtmin chuckled and whispered, "I guess he has much to explain since they didn't have a clue."

"Just like me," Hori hissed. "What's the meaning of it all?" Then he sighed. "No, you don't have to tell me. I guess Ameny wasn't willing to use Hemiunu as bait."

They ambled back to the courtyard. "At least we don't have to watch over fatty now," Nakhtmin said. Then he blinked into the sky. "Is it really noon already? I'm faint with hunger."

"Me too!"

Even before Hori could have his first bite of the day, his servant announced a royal messenger. Swiftly, he shoved a piece of bread in his mouth before beckoning the man.

He gave a sloppy bow. "His majesty—life, prosperity and health—requests your presence at the Great House."

Hori groaned. "Can I finish breakfast first?"

The messenger's lips curled disapprovingly as he cast a meaningful glance at the sun bark. "I cannot allow this. My order is to bring the physician Hori right away."

The guy obviously thought him a dawdler who only just now crawled out of bed and had to expect a royal scolding. He jumped up anyway and brushed the crumbs from his shendyt. "Well then, let's not make the king impatient."

They jogged to the palace, and before he knew it, Hori stood in front of Atef. "His majesty already awaits you." He opened the door to Senusret's office.

Hori entered and called in surprise, "Hut-Nefer!" Beside the king and the head of the weryt sat Ameny. Then he noticed his blunder and sank into a low bow. "Your majesty!"

The pharaoh impatiently waved away the need of formalities. "Sit down, Hori. The venerable prophet Ameny approached me with troubling news, which also requires the presence of the mer-ut."

Shocked, Hori sank onto the offered chair. Was Ameny so angry over him fooling Setka and endangering Hemiunu that they wanted to ban him to the weryt again?

Hut-Nefer's deep voice droned from the jackal mask. "You and Nakhtmin treated the four sick men and know most about their suffering. Could it have been caused by a curse?"

Curse? He too had thought along those lines during their desperate attempts to save the patients, and then... "Oh yes, indeed! Hemiunu insinuated something of the kind with regard to Neferka's studies and him digging up more than humans should know. He might have discovered a powerful conjuration." Hori was so relieved not to be in trouble that his tongue threatened to get in a twist. "I dismissed the possibility as an attempt to redirect our suspicions to someone else. I can't imagine the public library of the temple holding such secret and dangerous scripts. Or...?" The faces of the pharaoh and Ameny looked too grave for a diversion. Of course he couldn't see Hut-Nefer's expression.

Ameny leaned forward and hissed, "Forget the library. I suspect something quite different. What if the fugitive lector priest has sold his knowledge after all, and it found its way to one of the hemu-netjer in *my* temple, who then used the most powerful curse in existence: conjuring the shadows of the damned!"

Horrified, Hori remained speechless. How could he have not seen it? It was so obvious. "Shu—he meant shut!"

Ameny groaned. "Of course. Not Shu-Ra but shut they wanted to say."

The king looked back and forth between them in visible confusion, and Hori hurried to explain. "Neferka's last words were even clearer. He mentioned the dark, asked us to take 'it' away from him. I'm sure a shadow possessed him and darkened his heart." And something else fit in. "The hair of all four had turned white although they were young men."

The jackal snout gave an imperious nod. "I've heard enough and have no doubt: The secrets of the weryt have been revealed. Woe to us! Have these forces been unleashed, barely a power on earth can curb them."

Hori shuddered. He didn't want to imagine the horrors his patients must have experienced. "What can we do?" he whispered and looked at faces betraying the same helplessness and fear he felt.

"The adepts of Osiris must gather," the mer-ut announced. "Will their combined powers suffice? Never before have we attempted anything like it. I'll search the secret scrolls for the right ritual to ban the shadows. Let's hope they don't create further harm in the meantime. No one but us may know of the assembly of adepts, you understand, Hori? Nobody! You and your friend must find the culprit, because only this villain knows where to find the fugitive Nebkaura. To catch him must be our main goal lest he sell his knowledge to others."

"So be it. Messengers will be sent to the first prophets of all gods of Kemet." The king seemed deeply disturbed, and that scared Hori more than anything else. He was the heart of the Two Lands! Could the adepts manage to fend off the danger with their united forces if even the mer-ut and pharaoh harbored doubts? Only the king and first prophets of the major gods were initiated to the mysteries of the god of death, and of course Hut-Nefer was one of them as first prophet of Anubis.

And Ameny too had recently been ordained, as he knew. Hori touched the bracelet covering his ankh sign. By the gods, he was one of the adepts as well! He too would have to fight the shadows…

That disturbing prospect occupied his heart on the whole way home and still gripped him as he settled in his garden at the table where his staff had covered the food to await his return—one bright spot on such a mirthless day. The connecting door opened and Nakhtmin approached. How he'd love to discuss everything he'd learned at the palace with him, but as so often, he had to remain silent about what troubled him most.

"Where've you been?" his friend asked and sat beside him. "I came over earlier but was told you'd been summoned."

Hori swallowed a bite. "To the king. Ameny suspects our four patients really did fall victim to a curse, not poison. The pharaoh called me and the mer-ut to the meeting, and Hut-Nefer confirmed our worst fears. Somebody conjures the shadows and thus curses the living."

"Shu—shut!" Nakhtmin cried. He jumped up and toppled his stool.

"Sit down, man. You're white as alabaster," Hori said although he felt no confidence. "Listen, our mission has become even more urgent. We must find the man who cursed the four priests—alive so he can tell us where the treacherous lector priest from the weryt hides." He quickly put some cold meat in his mouth since he'd probably have to leave his home soon again.

Nakhtmin nodded. His jaws ground in tension. "Chickenshit! Ameny shouldn't have destroyed our trap!"

"Wouldn't have done us much good," Hori objected. "We counted on an attack with poison, which the perpetrator would have had to add to Hemiunu's food or drink. A curse, however, can be performed anywhere. Earlier, while you talked to Ameny, I sounded out some of the hemu-netjer, particularly with regard to Wenen. Since the curse hit him first, he must have been a major obstacle for the murderer."

Nakhtmin popped a grape in his mouth and mumbled, "Or he jush wanted to tesht if it worksh."

Another possibility, which made Wenen a random victim. Hori groaned. That wouldn't help in finding the perpetrator. "Anyway, some marveled at Wenen's sudden friendship with Setka. He must have despised the man before."

Nakhtmin nodded and plucked another grape from the bunch.

"Setka treated him like a lackey, but Wenen bent over backward to do his bidding. In a similar fashion, Hemiunu let his right hand jump through hoops for him-"

"Well, if shu- means shut, not Shu-Ra, we can ignore the fatso, right?" Nakhtmin interrupted.

Hori considered this, then shook his head. "That doesn't change anything. Shu-Ra also craves the position. Too bad that not everyone with ambitions admits to them. I got the impression several of the people I talked to would have appreciated the promotion if offered."

"Strange," Nakhtmin mulled. "Maybe Wenen was the only member of the temple who openly admitted that he wasn't ready for such a responsibility."

He snorted. "People tend to overrate themselves. Maybe Wenen was really the man he appeared to be, or his modesty was an act to catch the prophets' eyes. Who knows?"

To Hori's relief, Nakhtmin didn't take this unfavorable portrait of his dead friend's character personally. "Yeah, I've thought along these lines as well," he admitted instead. "When I realized how I'd presented Wenen to Ameny in the most favorable light, maybe he knew his certain preferences, which apparently everyone recognized except me, would hinder his career. Either way, he wasn't even eligible as a priest of the medium order." Bitterness dragged down the corners of his mouth. "However, Ameny insinuated he'd support the guy after I praised him. Maybe people were right to warn me of his intentions. Why is it so hard to find true friends?"

Commiserating, Hori grabbed his hand. "Never doubt my friendship! And Muti truly loves you—and Ameny." Nakhtmin really shouldn't complain. "At least you have someone to come home to!" Wistful, he thought of Ouseret and wondered if she had arrived in Waset already. Ah, no, she only left seven days ago. The trip should take about two weeks. That long? By the gods! It would take twice that time for all adepts of Osiris to reach the residence from all parts of the country. Too far spread were the main cult sites of the gods of Kemet. What doom might befall the Two Lands until then? And on top of that, the heriu-renpet neared, the days between the years, of which it is said: 'Sakhmet's messengers carry the plague through the Two Lands. Only those who can name the leap days won't go hungry and thirsty nor fall prey to this year's plague because Sakhmet has no power over them. On those evil days, do not work with corn or clothes. Do not begin anything.'

Hori's heart contracted with fear.

THE BEE STINGS

While Nakhtmin slept during the hottest hours of the day because he could barely stand on his feet, Hori once again went to see Ameny. Washed and clad in clean clothes, with a meal in his stomach, he felt more or less up for the task ahead. When he wanted to enter the prophet's office, Ameny asked him to wait, since a priest was with him. Wait? With time so short, there wasn't a moment to waste. Duamutef, the future second prophet, strolled toward him, and Hori seized the opportunity. He bowed. "Venerable prophet, may I ask you a few questions?"

Duamutef opened the door to Ameny's former office. "Please come in." As they both sat down, he added, "Albeit, I don't know how I might help you." He too looked worn out with sorrow and worries brought on by recent events.

Hori thought of the man's entanglement in Setka's scheming and Ameny telling Nakhtmin he was a homosexual. "I heard you were close to Wenen. I'm sorry for your loss."

"Thanks. But close…" He waved dismissively. "I did appreciate him."

Of course, why would he admit anything to Hori? Now he wondered if Duamutef's wife knew. He was married after all. Otherwise he'd probably have raised suspicions. Maybe he liked both sexes, that happened, too. "Um, right, whatever. I was surprised to hear that you suggested a certain Setka as candidate, which rather annoyed Ameny since he doesn't think much of the man. How come you hold him in much higher esteem?" Intently, he observed the changing expressions of the man's face. Disgust? Anger? Relief? If Setka was an extortionist, he might not have had only Wenen under his thumb. And Duamutef had much to lose. However, the prophet wouldn't gain anything from Wenen's death, but everything if Setka died, and he still strutted about.

"Setka…" the man hissed. "Why does that bother you?"

Whoa, a song of praise sounded different. That confirmed his assumption. Duamutef had been forced. "Not at all. It only surprised me because you resisted Ameny for quite some time." At the same time, Ameny stubbornly resisted the pressure of his colleagues to appoint Setka. How did the extortionist react to that? And shouldn't Duamutef fear Setka might expose him now although his secret wasn't that secret? Confused, he rubbed the bridge of his nose. Things didn't really fit.

"I wasn't the only one. Kagemni also spoke up for Setka."

Kagemni, the new prophet. How had Setka strung him along? Not likely that he found out something compromising about the man in such short time to put pressure on him. "Didn't it annoy you two that Ameny disregarded your unanimous decision?"

Yes, now he did display anger. "Mph," was the prophets only comment.

And that was probably a smart reply. Ameny'd be able to tell him more about the relationship between him and his two colleagues. He rose and took leave.

This time, Ameny waved Hori in but seemed even tenser than before. "Since that speech, one after the other comes in to give clues," he sighed. "Have a seat. What are you planning to do next?"

"I've been wondering about that ritual," he admitted his biggest worry. "It'll take at least forty days for all adepts to assemble here. The main cult sites of the big gods of Kemet are scattered all over the Two Lands. From the sanctuary of Satet on the Nile island Abu in the south to that of the snake goddess Wadjet in the double cities Pe and Dep in the north, they'll have to travel to the residence—after the king's messenger has reached them! How are we going to fight the shadows until we can perform the ritual?"

"Oh that. Follow me." Ameny rose and smiled sagely. "Gradually, we'll have to disclose even our biggest secrets to you, it seems." Through a connecting door he went into an adjoining room and from there entered the Holy Garden of Amun.

Curious, Hori followed him to two aviaries with pigeons, whose cooing filled the air.

"We breed these birds," he said and pointed to the left cage. "Those in the other one hatched in various Amun temples and were raised there. Birds with a blue ribbon are from Waset, brown indicates the temple in Khemenu. The thing is, they always return to their homes when we set them free. So if the presence of a prophet from a faraway temple is required in the residence, I send a pigeon, and the bird keeper there knows what it means. Naturally, the king has birds from all the temples and from some of the nomarchs and major dignitaries of the Two Lands."

Fascinated, Hori watched the fowls. How did they manage such a feat, finding their way back home even after years in unknown territories? "But how does the recipient know who sent the flying messenger?"

"Oh, that's simple." Amen even chuckled at Hori's amazement. "Before we set free a bird, we tie an additional ribbon in the color green of the Amun temple in Itj-tawy to its leg. The king's color is of course gold."

"How cleverly devised and handy!" he exclaimed. "And how long does it take a pigeon to fly from here to Waset?"

"Not even a day." Ameny smiled proudly. "After such a mission, the animal can stay at home, and the prophet brings us a young replacement bird."

If only he were a pigeon! Hori could fly to Ouseret and watch her from the sky, maybe even sit on her shoulder…

"Such a message always means the recipient must travel to the residence as fast as possible. Presumably, the king has already sent birds north and south."

"But the adepts had only recently assembled for your initiation!" Hori groaned. "What a shame that they're already on their way back. Then it'll take some time for them to even find out they are supposed to come here again."

"That's no problem either. I'm sure you know Senusret's ancestor Amenemhat, the founder of the dynasty, introduced rowboat relays?"

Hori, who'd never strayed far from the residence, shook his head.

"Unfortunately, it was a necessity back then. There'd been unrest again and again under Amenemhat. Several times, Lower Egypt revolted against his majesty, instigated by traitors who coveted the throne. Because of that, the residence had been moved from Waset to the Balance of the Two Lands, where both parts of the country touch."

"Itj-tawy, 'who rules the Two Lands'. I understand."

"Actually, your father should know all about it since he often uses these speedboats when he holds court in southern parts of the country. Strange that he never told you about them."

Hori thought this a bad moment to elaborate on his relationship with his father, or rather the lack thereof.

Ameny didn't seem to expect an answer anyway because he continued, "In every larger city along the Nile, royal rowboats are on standby to swiftly take passengers to the next station. Thus there are always well-rested rowers available, and a distance that would take a bark two weeks can be covered within a few days. I expect the prophets used them for their return trip so they didn't need to stay away from their temples longer than necessary. They should have arrived by now."

"Excellent!" Hori blurted. "Then we could perform the ritual even before the heriu-renpet?"

Ameny nodded grimly. "I sure hope so. The leap days are dangerous enough."

They settled on a bench in the shade. How peaceful everything seemed here. A mild breeze played with the leaves of trees and carried the scent of jasmine. Hori found it hard to associate dark forces at work with this garden, flooded with sunlight, and the venerable sanctum sanctorum. "The gods demand flawless purity, still there is one among your priests whose heart is filled with black malice. Amun must be irate at such sacrilege."

Ameny studied him intently. "You think the god might reveal the guilty one himself? But how?"

Various ideas swirled in Hori's mind but none of them seemed promising. No, he couldn't believe a lifeless statue only representing the god might point a finger at the culprit. "Were any of the clues you received from your subordinates enlightening?" he asked instead.

"No, I'm afraid in their eagerness they start seeing ghosts. Some accusations seemed to aim at getting rid of a disliked colleague, or people wanted to divert any suspicion from themselves by pointing in a different direction." He snorted a laugh. "The guy who dropped by last actually accused the wab Ini-Herit, because one never knows who he is looking at with his crossed eyes."

Hori trusted Ameny's judgment. So much discord among the hemu-netjer, whose thinking should focus on serving the god! This crisis brought numerous festering conflicts to light, and that wouldn't make Ameny's task to rule the temple any easier. "Did you discuss with the other two prophets whom you might appoint after the current losses?"

The prophet buried his face in his hands. "I don't dare to," he burst out. "Duamutef is a good prophet but blabs too much when a young man sweet-talks him. Many know this and take advantage."

"Hm, I saw him just now. He wasn't very talkative with me. Say, could it be that he didn't speak in favor of Setka not because Wenen praised the man but because Setka threatened to make his favoring men public? I got that feeling."

Baffled, Ameny looked up. "Possible. Oh, indeed! He only yielded to my wish after I casually mentioned that his secret has been known for quite some time, and nobody thought of removing him from his post because of it. Of course! Then he knew the extortionist couldn't harm him."

And that was also why Setka didn't follow through with his threat when he lost the game. Duamutef's behavior was objectionable anyway. Someone yielding to pressure instead of taking responsibility for his actions should succeed Ameny someday? That didn't seem wise to Hori but wasn't any of his business. The first prophet hopefully had many years ahead of him. Gossip, however, thrived in the temple, as he'd noticed already, and within such a tight community small things might get blown up to the size of an elephant. In the morning he'd listened to many little secrets one or the other supposedly harbored, which certainly had nothing to do with the investigation, like Hemiunu's anything-but-secret stash of treats. Wenen's sexual preferences also had been a topic, and several thought the young priest had brought on his own demise—wait, who'd said that? Right, Setka. About that arrogant young man he hadn't heard one good thing, but that alone didn't make him a murderer. "Too bad that the priests don't live in the temple," he mused. "Then we could search their rooms for suspicious scripts."

Ameny straightened. "A search! That's a good idea in any case. The pharaoh will certainly let us use the Medjay since Nakhtmin wouldn't be able to cope with such a big task alone. Besides-" He paused. "It would be ill advised if you two attracted too much attention. The perpetrator might select you as his next targets."

Since morning, Hori had worried about the same thing, so he'd tried to act casual when he talked to the priests. "Fortunately, Nakhtmin has been visiting you often and still works at the House of Life once a week, so he's less conspicuous. Besides, most people should know by now that we treated the four patients, so it's natural for us to come to the temple and ask questions. But you're right, we need to act in a way that the villain doesn't think it necessary to strike again. The thing with Hemiunu was stupid of me. Fortunately, you counteracted my thoughtless words in your speech." He rose. "Nakhtmin should have arrived by now and is probably looking for us. Let's go back inside."

Ameny shook his head. "It's time for the evening ritual, and you'd better hurry or you won't find anyone left to ask questions. The hemu-netjer will gather before the sanctum sanctorum, then head home."

Hori nodded and turned to the door, through which they'd entered the garden, but Ameny strode in a different direction. "This way's shorter."

Nakhtmin knocked on Ameny's door, but no one invited him in. Then he remembered how thick the door was and opened it a crack. A dragging noise sounded, as if something lay behind the door. His father-in-law wasn't in there. Should he wait? Ameny surely wouldn't mind. He entered and, closing the door, he spotted a papyrus on the floor that must have been shoved aside and caused the noise. Looked like someone had pushed it through the gap above the threshold. Curious, he bent down. Hold on, was he allowed to read it? Might concern secrets of the temple. Without meaning to, he deciphered the first words, which perplexed him. No secret but a denunciation. He actually had to know this, so he continued reading. Somebody accused Hemiunu to be the murderer and demanded that Ameny search his office. And the note was signed 'A friend'. Well, that was interesting. Ameny's speech foiled Hori's ploy but brought new insights. But why did the mysterious informer hide his identity? Indecisive, he wondered if he should wait for the prophet or Hori to return. Wasn't this urgent? Where were the two? If they didn't show up, he had to act alone!

Almost out the door, he realized he still held the message in his hand. Should he leave it here so that Ameny would learn of its content? However, it wouldn't be good to leave it lying around here where anyone might stumble upon it. If Hemiunu was innocent, the false accusation would still cling to him—not good in his position. The man struggled enough to gain some respect. Besides, he might run into his friends on the way. Then he could show them the letter.

He headed for the storerooms, where he'd met the fat principle of the hemu-netjer in the morning. Most likely Hemiunu's office was close to those since he managed the stocks. There weren't many wabu around any longer with the workday coming to an end. When he reached the storerooms, the gates were just being closed for the night. He asked the servant where he might find Hemiunu, and the man pointed to a nearby door. Nakhtmin was content with himself because he'd guessed right. Now he only had to wait for the principal to leave his rooms. He lurked in an aisle to one side, so the fatso wouldn't ask him what he was doing here.

Noises in the main corridor made him peer around the corner, but he only saw the three prophets, probably on their way to the evening ritual. Oh, that was perfect! Hemiunu also had to attend. Indeed, a short time later, he heard a door open and slow steps move away. Nakhtmin recognized the broad back. The coast was clear. Since nobody was around any longer, he sneaked to the door leading to Hemiunu's realm and slipped inside. How fortunate that no one locked their doors. Now he could take his time since the principal certainly wouldn't come back, and he didn't have to fear people dropping by.

Again he scrutinized the note for a clue where to start his search, but the accusation was too general. The room was furnished with a table, a mat on the floor— Hemiunu would sit there when writing something—and two chests. A door lead to another room. Cautiously, Nakhtmin opened it. Shelves lined the walls, and numerous scrolls filled their honeycomb-shaped compartments. He groaned. Sifting through all those would take weeks! Would Shu-Ra store his secrets where anyone might accidentally find them? He pulled out a random papyrus and skimmed the listing of a domain's tributes. Another scroll recorded lease agreements with peasants. That didn't get him anywhere.

He returned to the other room and opened the first chest. At a glance, it only contained linen clothes. Nakhtmin felt his way along the layers of fabric to the bottom of the furniture. No, nothing that shouldn't be there. The second chest only contained Hemiunu's seal, some jewelry and more papyri, which he quickly unrolled: Hemiunu's letter of appointment as head of the hemu-netjer, a list of the earnings of his country estate and his marriage contract. Why didn't he keep that at his home? Replacing the scrolls, he paused. The bottom of the chest should be much lower. He knocked on the wood—hollow. His fingers brushed over the panel, feeling for a hole that would allow him to lift it, but there was nothing. Along the edge of the side panel, he had more luck. Two leather straps stuck out between bottom and sidewall, ideal to grip and pull up the board. Now he understood why this box was basically empty. The few items only served to cover the flaps. Nakhtmin squatted, emptied the chest and viewed the greasy leather. The cranny was obviously used a lot. The straps felt sticky to his touch, and Nakhtmin anticipated what he might find there: Shu-Ra's stash of treats.

Underneath the false floor, a compartment held bowls of candied fruit, bags of dried chickpeas, almonds and plenty more snacks. The content of one small bag gave him pause though. These dark seeds were castor beans and not to be eaten! The oil pressed from those was an effective laxative he often prescribed, but the seeds contained a deadly poison. Their teachers at the House of Life had explicitly warned them. They had to carefully filter the oil and make sure no parts of the grain got into the medicine. As if spell-bound, Nakhtmin stared at the shiny pellets and recapitulated the symptoms he'd been taught. Fortunately, he'd never had to deal with a case of such poisoning himself. A burning mouth, dizziness, cramps— that perfectly fit what they'd observed in their patients before they died. Then it had been poisoning after all! Nakhtmin wanted to cheer in relief. So much better than a shadow curse!

When he heard a noise from the door, he froze. Somebody came in! Could he sneak to the adjoining room and hide? No, too late!

The entering man halted in surprise. It was Hemiunu. His gaze darted across the scene: his scattered treasures, the raided hiding place. Then he hollered, "What are you doing here? Who do you think you are?"

He slammed the door shut and took a step toward him, while Nakhtmin jumped to his feet. How could he explain? But why should he justify his actions? He bent to pick up the informer's note and held it under Hemiunu's nose. "This prompted me to search your rooms. Read for yourself!"

The principal snatched the papyrus and skimmed the lines. Nakhtmin saw him go pale and took it for a sign of guilt. "Apparently the one who points his finger at you is right. Or how do you explain that I found lethal poison in your secret trove?" He grabbed the bag and proffered it like a servant might present food to his master. "With this poison you killed four men."

"No!" shrieked Hemiunu. "No!"

The fat man shoved him hard enough for Nakhtmin to tumble back. Groping for something to hold onto with his left arm, he clutched the seeds in his right hand, then he tripped over something and hit his head against the wall. Numbed, he sank to the floor. Through the haze before his eyes, he saw his attacker bend over him. No, no! Now his last hour had come! Hemiunu only had to put one of the castor beans in his mouth…Unconsciousness settled over him.

IN THE DARK

Hori only picked up more unfounded rumors from the few priests he managed to question. When the men of god deserted the premises, he also left since soon the temple would be locked for the night. In vain, he watched for Nakhtmin among the people pouring out. Thinking his friend probably overslept when taking his nap, Hori headed home.

Eating dinner alone, he got a little miffed because neither Nakhtmin nor Heqet kept him company. He liked to chat during his meals even if it was only shallow babble. The girl couldn't possibly hold a grudge against him just because he wanted her to marry the gardener. He'd worked his way to the fruit when finally the connecting door between their estates opened. However, not Nakhtmin but Muti approached.

"What? You're at home?" she called. "And where did you leave my husband?"

A bite caught in his throat. "Nakhtmin isn't with you?" Darn, she looked pale, close to fainting. "Sit down."

"He wanted to meet you at the temple. Hours ago." She sank onto a chair.

Hori shook his head. "We must have missed each other." But where was he then? Icy fear clutched his heart. He could only hope his friend hadn't investigated on his own and stepped on the wrong man's toes. Nakhtmin a victim of the shadows? No, please! He noticed Muti's scrutinizing gaze and pulled himself together. She must not perceive his fear. "He probably accompanied Ameny and forgot to send you a message, that country yokel." The explanation calmed her somewhat, and it could have happened.

In Muti's eyes well-known scorn flashed. "Woe to him! He'll get an earful when he returns."

Hori laughed. "Have mercy on him. He's a man and of the crude bumpkin kind, he can't help it. Should I hop over and fetch him?" He wanted to make sure anyway.

She waved dismissively. "No need to. I'm exhausted and will go sleep now. I'm sure you're right. Good night."

"Night, Muti. Rest well," he said and watched her slender figure until she closed the gate behind her. Then he bolted up and dashed through the dark garden to the front entrance of his estate and along the alleys of the mansion district to the house of the prophet.

Fortunately, the gate wasn't barred for the night yet. He circled the house on the gravel path and, as he'd hoped, light shone through the slats of the backdoor to Ameny's den. The prophet was still up and Nakhtmin probably with him. Gently, so he wouldn't wake the entire household, he knocked. A moment later, the door swung open.

"Hori?" Ameny gaped at him. "What brings you here at such a late hour?"

He peered past the man but couldn't see anyone else in the room. "Um, is Nakhtmin here?"

Ameny stepped aside and invited him in. "No, what makes you think so?"

Hori plopped onto a stool like a sack of corn. Fresh fear overwhelmed him.

"He's disappeared!" he blurted. "Didn't come home. You think...? Could it be...?" He dared not speak his suspicion.

Ameny placed a calming hand on his shoulder. "Slow down. Where did he want to go? And what are you afraid of?"

"He went to the temple as we'd agreed, but we must have missed each other. You and I were in the garden for some time. The curse!" Hori jumped up. "We have to go to the temple and look for him. He might be lying there somewhere, all alone." The prospect was too horrible. He grabbed Ameny's wrist. "Come on!"

Ameny didn't budge. Growing despair showing in his face, he shook his head. "The temple's locked, the gates are barred. Just before dawn, the guards will open them again. You know that."

Helpless sobbing seized Hori, "Stupid guy why? Should have waited " Then he protested, "You're the top prophet! Do something! The king!"

Nakhtmin's father-in-law sank onto another seat and buried his face in his hands. "Just what I feared," he murmured. "Too dangerous. I shouldn't have dragged you two into this!"

And Hori realized it was hopeless. Ameny couldn't do anything for Nakhtmin right now. Only the pharaoh had the power to order the temple gates opened at night, and not even Ameny dared to request it at such a late hour. Slowly his tears dried up; determination conquered despair, and he managed to think clearly. "It's not your fault. We were involved in the investigation early on when nobody suspected where it would lead. But we're getting close to the treacherous priest. Maybe we can expose him tomorrow and force him to lift the curse from Nakhtmin."

Ameny looked up. "My daughter will never forgive me!"

It was dark. Dark and stifling. Where was he? Nakhtmin had no idea. Was he experiencing the same thing as Neferka, who'd been enveloped by darkness toward the end? The shadows! His head hurt, and he sat uncomfortably on hard ground. One hand clutched something, a small bag. Memories rushed back at him, and he groped around. Was he still in Hemiunu's room? Sure seemed like it. Through the slightly lighter rectangles of the ventilation slits a star twinkled. Which departed pharaoh might send his sympathies? There'd been a lamp on the table, and the table was right here—ouch! Nakhtmin rubbed his knuckles, then reached for the lamp again and found it. That didn't help him, though, since he couldn't light it. Would they keep torches burning in the corridor? He felt his way to the door, not without tripping over scattered objects he'd tossed from the chest. The head of the hemu-netjer hadn't bothered replacing anything. There was the door. He rattled the knob. Locked! Incredible. Again and again he tried, but the wood didn't budge. Hemiunu had locked him in.

Nakhtmin hammered against the door and screamed for help until he could only croak. Futile! He was alone in the temple; nobody could hear him. In his despair, he slid down the wall to the floor and stretched out his legs. Hemiunu wouldn't return until morning—to do what? Finish what he couldn't do earlier: eliminate him as well? Nakhtmin's heartbeat sounded far too loud in the silence.

What rotten luck had caused the fat one to return to his office? Did he want to fetch more of the poison or have a snack since the first day of mourning was over? Quite dangerous to keep the poisonous seeds among the sweets. He might acci-

161

dentally grab the wrong thing. In Hemiunu's place, he'd have stored the stuff somewhere else, maybe with the clothes or in one of the far back honeycombs of the shelves.

Hold on! What if someone had placed the seeds with Hemiunu's snacks so he'd poison himself? Nakhtmin had been taught they tasted nice, which of course enticed children to chew them, but the burning sensation on the tongue quickly showed how unbecoming they were. No, that didn't make sense, and the letter claimed Hemiunu was the perpetrator. Or...? Maybe someone found the principal's secret stash, recognized the castor beans and drew the same conclusion he did, which might be completely wrong. Who'd know of the lethal effect of those shiny, pretty seeds except a physician or someone who studied poisons?

But if the fat man was innocent, why did he attack him? Nakhtmin groaned and touched the aching back of his head. Moist and sticky. Blood? That reminded him of Hori's injury. By the gods, Muti! She must be worrying herself sick because he hadn't returned home. Nobody knew where he was. If only he'd left the note in Ameny's room, but now Shu-Ra had escaped with the incriminating evidence. All kinds of thoughts performed a wild dance in Nakhtmin's heart. Why hadn't the principal killed him right away? Or did he leave him for dead when he saw the blood? He couldn't hope to hide a corpse in his office. Would have been the best time to move him somewhere else, where nothing connected Hemiunu with the deed. No, he hadn't thought him dead. And what did he hope to gain by locking him in here? Then realization struck him like lightning: a head start. Now that his guilt had been revealed, Hemiunu was on the run.

His heart calmed down a little. He didn't need to fear the killer's return with murderous intent in the morning but could simply wait until someone found him. And he even had food. However...he'd rather not touch Hemiunu's stash. The snacks might be poisoned after all.

Nakhtmin jerked from uneasy slumber. Was there a noise? Darkness seemed more penetrable now; morning dawned. He rose from the writing mat he'd used as a pad and pressed his ear against the door. Nothing. Nevertheless he pounded against the wood until his fists hurt. No use overdoing it! Couldn't take much longer now. But what if Hemiunu opened the door? When the contours of his surroundings became clearer, he searched for a weapon he could use against the fat priest. The ebony box containing canes he deemed most suitable, so he grabbed it and positioned himself beside the door.

Now he certainly heard footsteps outside in the corridor—and voices. Again he knocked and called for help. And they heard him! Someone tried to open the door but didn't seem to have a key. Muffled by the wood, he made out Hori's voice shouting his name.

"Yes!" he hollered. "Hori, it's me!" He laughed and cried at the same time. He could really rely on Hori. Would Ameny be with him? He'd surely have spare keys for all locks in the building.

Time passed without anything happening. And now he needed to pee. As soon as he realized that, the urge grew stronger. He started shifting from foot to foot. What was taking them so long? In his predicament, he glanced around for a vessel to use as pisspot. For lack of anything better, he dumped the candied fruit from the earthen bowl and relieved himself into it. Ah, yes, that felt better. And at long last, the unmistakable noise of a key turning in a lock. After quickly shaking off the last drops, he adjusted his shendyt.

Immense relief flooded Hori as he saw Nakhtmin unharmed and apparently uncursed. "I'm so glad! We've been sick with worry!"

Nakhtmin grinned sheepishly. "That's nothing compared to the fears I suffered! Did you catch fatso?"

Hori exchanged an astonished look with Ameny, who'd entered the room behind him. "What do you mean?" Then he noticed the stain on the opposite wall. "Is that blood?"

"Oh, that. You." Nakhtmin turned around and showed Hori the back of his head. "I owe that to Hemiunu. He caught me here, so I faced him with the proof I'd found. He locked me in here, and by now he's probably cataracts away."

"Proof?" Ameny chimed in. "You mean Hemiunu is actually the perpetrator? I'd never have-"

That moment Nakhtmin emitted a muffled cry of jubilation and bent to pick up a papyrus. "He's left it here! Read this!" He handed the sheet to Ameny, who skimmed it with a frown before passing it on to Hori.

"Lo and behold," he said and clicked his tongue. "Where did you get this?"

Nakhtmin rubbed his head and grumbled, "Someone had pushed it under Ameny's door. I found it there when I was looking for you and thought I might as well take a look at Hemiunu's office."

"How could you be so inconsiderate!" Ameny exclaimed. "You know what we're dealing with! I'd never have dared to look in my child's eyes again if something had happened to you."

Nakhtmin at least had the decency to look stricken with guilt. "Was Muti awfully worried?"

"I managed to convince her you'd gone to Ameny and forgot to send word to her. Brace yourself for a welcoming harangue at your return."

"If that's all. Thank you! By the way, I did use caution, waited for Shu-Ra to head for the evening ritual. Of course I didn't expect him to return. Why should he?"

"Now I'd really like to know what you found," Hori said and scanned the room.

Triumphantly, Nakhtmin handed him a bag. "Castor beans! We were mistaken. Not a curse but poison. This proves it. I found them in there under a false bottom among Hemiunu's treats. Then he returned, and I confronted him with the evidence. That was when he attacked me and locked me in here. The head of the hemu-netjer is our man."

How could Nakhtmin be so wrong? Hori stared at him in disbelief. "Boy! I told you only yesterday that it must be a curse! Did you forget everything our teachers taught us? The symptoms don't fit with poisoning by castor beans." He could barely refrain from shaking Nakhtmin, who looked confused.

"They don't? Dizziness, cramps, that's what the men suffered."

"Yes, but no diarrhea, which is the most distinct sign. No throwing up or stomach cramps either. I thought we'd all agreed that we must be dealing with a conjuration of the dead." He was growing so irritated because of the anxiety he'd gone through during a sleepless night that he almost overlooked the most important thing. "Now I actually know for sure that Hemiunu isn't the perpetrator!" he exclaimed. "Furthermore, I know who it must be."

"How come?" Ameny asked.

At the same time Nakhtmin said, "Tell us!"

Hori got so excited the words gushed from his mouth. "Yesterday we told one man that the prophets considered promoting Hemiunu."

"Setka!" Nakhtmin interrupted.

He nodded. "Exactly. And the fact that we received an anonymous tip and found poison among Hemiunu's things proves Setka must have planted both because nobody else would have expected Shu-Ra to get in his way. After we talked to him, Setka had to assume we were looking for poison and he had to fear Hemiunu would snatch the coveted position from him. When Ameny gave his speech, he realized how he could get all he wanted with one strike: rid himself of Hemiunu and present the prophets with the murderer."

"Ha!" Nakhtmin exclaimed. "You missed something." He looked very smug.

Hori lifted his eyebrows.

"The poison was in a secret compartment. How could Setka have known about it?"

Hori snorted a laugh, and Ameny chuckled. "Everyone knew that!" the prophet said. "Hemiunu was probably the only one who regarded his stash a secret. The young priests had great fun pilfering some of his treats, while Shu-Ra suspected mice in his rooms."

Sulkily, Nakhtmin pushed out his lower lip. "Well, then…"

Ameny wrapped an arm around each of them. "Let's get out of here. It smells quite unpleasant." He glanced at a bowl holding yellow liquid and shoved them out the door. "Maybe there are indeed mice around. Besides, I'm sure you could both use a bite to eat. I, however, must hurry to the morning ritual."

Nakhtmin balked. "Shouldn't we arrest Setka before he curses someone else?"

Hori stopped as well. "Yes!"

"As much as I'd like to do that, I'm not completely convinced. If we arrest the wrong person…" He shook his head. "I better announce that Hemiunu is our suspect. That should put the perpetrator at ease." He locked the door to the principal's rooms with the spare key. "He gave you pretty bump, my boy. Hori, why don't you take care of the wound?"

He nodded. "Yes, let's go to the House of Life."

Nakhtmin strode ahead, as if he wanted to leave this part of the temple as soon as possible. Ameny and Hori followed at a slower pace. "You think Hemiunu will show up today? I wonder why he did that, knock out Nakhtmin and lock him in. It doesn't make much sense. He's innocent after all."

Ameny cast him a sideways glance. "I know the man. As soon as he read the accusation and saw Nakhtmin's 'evidence', he must have panicked, thinking he'd be charged with murder and seeing no way of disentangling himself. Hemiunu isn't brave. The attack on Nakhtmin was probably pure instinct of a trapped creature. Seeing the blood must have scared him even more. He believed himself doomed the moment Nakhtmin passed on his discoveries." He sighed. "So he locked him in to gain time."

"And he fled," Hori assumed.

"I'm afraid so. The poor man. Nakhtmin put him in an awful quandary, and now I guess I'll have to find a replacement for him, too. For a long time, I overlooked his shortcomings, because he made up for them in other areas. When his intellect failed, he knew where to get help: from his right hand."

"Another life Setka destroyed!" Hori exclaimed. "Maybe you can find a position for Hemiunu at one of the Amun temples in another town, where nobody knows what happened here."

Ameny nodded. "I'll try. With regard to Setka, I can well imagine he planted the poison and wrote the note. However, that doesn't necessarily imply he performed the conjuration."

Now Hori looked at him in astonishment. "What else could it mean?"

"That the guy's driven by pathological ambition. He might have thought presenting us a perpetrator he feared as a rival would grant him top position in the queue."

Hori groaned. "And since he doesn't know of the curses, he believes himself safe from the real killer as long as he watches out for poison. By the gods, you're right." In his rage, he kicked a door frame they passed and howled in pain when the tip of the sandal gave and his toe hit the wood full on. Limping, he followed Ameny through the still deserted corridors. Soon priests on their way to the morning ritual would bustle in the hallways, and they had made no progress at all!

THE PAPYRUS

Day 23 of month Ipet-hemet in Shemu, the season of the harvest

Nakhtmin wasn't ready to forgive Hemiunu so soon, particularly since he still fumed at Hori for berating him like that. 'Should have known that we're dealing with a curse,' he mimicked Hori in his mind. As if! He was the last to get enlightened, and how could he know what the mer-ut based his judgment on? Hori had kept that to himself. However, he wasn't totally blameless for his predicament, Nakhtmin had to admit. He'd obsessed over contributing something significant to the hunt for the killer, and thus he eagerly went along with the poison scheme without giving it much thought. Actually, he'd prefer a poisoner by far since he could be arrested. Those shadows, though, had no faces and couldn't be caught by mere mortals.

Fortunately, his head wound only needed two stitches to close it. Albeit, he couldn't hope Muti would overlook the injury. Instead of grabbing a bite with Hori at the temple, he had to think up a new lie for her. What a rotten day and it had just begun! He passed the gate and braced himself against the rage about to hit him.

His darling wasn't in the garden. Strange. Usually she ate her morning meal under the pergola at this time of day. Inside the house, he caught Inti loitering in the hall and wanted to vent his anger at him.

The servant beat him to it. "Oh, master, I'm glad you're back. The mistress isn't well, and I didn't know where you were."

A scorching jolt of terror struck Nakhtmin. His feet practically flew up the stairs. He found Muti lying on the bed in their sleeping chamber, pale and sweaty. An elderly woman bent over her and wiped her forehead with a wet cloth.

That didn't look like normal morning sickness. "My heart! What ails you?" Hopefully, she hadn't fallen ill—or... "Dear gods, have mercy! Is something wrong with the child?"

Instead of his wife, the woman answered, "I'm Geheset, midwife. Your servant called me in the first hour of the day, and since then I've been taking care of her. However, it's not the babe that plagues her, but a fever. She rather needed a doctor. They tell me you're one?" She glared at him reproachfully.

Nakhtmin wanted to protest in indignation, but the woman didn't know why he hadn't been home, and there were more important things to do. "Is it the fever of the hot days?" This far south such cases were rare.

Geheset shrugged her round shoulders and stepped back. If she ever resembled the gazelle she was named after, that must have been a long time ago. Nakhtmin touched Muti's forehead, which was very hot. More than anything else, it scared him that she didn't react to his voice at all. She mumbled something in her sleep; her hands nervously swept over the sheet. "Did you give her any medicine? An enema to bring down her temperature?"

"Am I the doctor or are you?" the midwife griped. "Call me again if she loses the child." With that she waddled off.

Nakhtmin groaned in agony. How could she say something like that? And he'd gotten himself locked away like a doofus, causing Hori to be absent as well last night. He'd certainly have been able to do more for Muti than the old crone. His child must not die, Muti either! "Inti!" he yelled. "Send Baketamun up with sweet beer, oil and honey!" He hurried into the adjoining room where he kept his stock of herbs, prepared remedies and stored his instruments when he wasn't at work. Soon the cook brought what he'd asked for, and he mixed an enema. Clean intestines procured a long life, as every inhabitant of the Two Lands knew. Anyone who could afford it, cleansed his body once a month from mucilage in the metu. Additionally, the procedure helped to lower the body temperature. For Muti he also added willow bark. After pouring the liquid into an animal bladder, he took the bull's horn with a hole drilled into the narrow end and inserted the tip into Muti's anus. Then he untied the cord sealing the lower end of the bladder and swiftly shoved it into the horn and squeezed the fluid through. While doing so, he spoke a ritual prayer to calm the fever demons

Even before her bowels were purged, she came to. "Nakhtmin?"

He moistened her chapped lips with honey water. "Can you get to the chamber pot?" he asked. Otherwise he'd have to catch her excrement in a bowl.

She gave a faint nod, but he lifted her up and sat her on the earthen vessel. In the meantime, Inti changed her sweat soaked sheets, so Nakhtmin could lay his beloved into a clean bed soon after. Within an instant, she dozed off again. He checked the going of her heart and the temperature of her skin. Both had improved but it was too early to relax. Was it really the fever of the hot days? One thing eased his fear: her hair hadn't turned white.

"Inti, go to Hori's place and tell them to send him over as soon as he returns. Or bring him along if he's already back."

At home a message from Nakhtmin awaited Hori, asking him to come right away. He groaned since he wanted nothing more than to fall into his bed. The night of worrying about his friend was taking its toll. Did Nakhtmin want to discuss all their findings once again? That certainly could wait.

At the neighboring estate, he found the staff in great concern for their mistress. Hori cringed with guilt. She hadn't looked too well yesterday, but because of his more urgent fears for Nakhtmin, he hadn't paid much attention. That wasn't good in her condition. Like the pinion feather of a passing bird, the thought grazed him she too might have fallen victim to the curse. Impossible! He fended off such foreboding. Why should the villain strike at her? His breath caught. Because she was Ameny's daughter! Muti had been there when all the high-ranking priests gathered at the prophet's estate. Was the perpetrator now planning to endanger the lives of Ameny's relatives to force the prophet's hand in his favor? He dashed up the stairs and into the bedchamber. When he saw Muti, he released the breath he'd been holding. "Thank Horus, it's a fever!" he cried.

Nakhtmin jumped up from a stool beside the bed and snarled, "Have the gods struck you with insanity? What's good about that?"

Heat rose to Hori's face. "Didn't mean it like that. I feared…the curse."

To his relief, Nakhtmin managed a faint smile. "Yes, that was my concern as well, but it's indeed 'only' a fever. Still, no reason to jubilate."

"No, you're right. What can I do?"

Nakhtmin reported how he'd treated her so far. "What do you think, could it be the fever of the hot days? I'm not sure."

Hori examined Mutnofret, who didn't wake at his touch. She felt hot, not dangerously so, but enough to weaken her. If the temperature had been even higher before... No, he couldn't say that aloud. Should it really be the tertian fever, they faced a fierce battle, and Muti likely wouldn't be able to keep the child. Nakhtmin knew that too, so he'd certainly want to hear something more positive from him. "Did she complain about stomach pains? Diarrhea? No? Man, you know the symptoms! We can't be sure, but to me it looks like a less dangerous fever."

Nakhtmin's face brightened like the rising sun, and Hori could only hope he hadn't given his friend false hope.

"Do you have bark left? I used up all mine for the enema," he asked.

"I'll fetch my medicine bag."

When he returned, Nakhtmin had already concocted another clyster. Hori poured the content of his bag onto Nakhtmin's worktable and quickly found what he needed. "I don't have much left either. I've used a lot, tending to the four priests. How do you feel about an incantation?" Among all the sacks and containers, he'd found a piece of papyrus.

"Definitely!" Nakhtmin exclaimed. "Can you recall one against fever demons?"

"Several. How about:

'I walk about by being healthy. Should one of Sakhmet's arrows hit me, while I am healthy? I have seen the bale, the fever. Do not seize me. Stay away from me.'

"Or: 'Hail to you, Horus. I come to you and praise your beauty. Destroy the evil in my limbs.'

"That might be better, what do you think? Oh, I know another one:

'Begone, you demons of disease. I am Horus who walks past the victims of Sakhmet. Horus, Horus, healthy despite Sakhmet! I am the only one. I die not at your hand.'"

Nakhtmin nodded enthusiastically. "How can you remember all that?"

Self-conscious, he shrugged. "Where are your writing utensils?"

While Nakhtmin fetched them, Hori lit an additional lamp to see better. "Oh, something written on the back?" he murmured and held the scrap to the light. Only a third of the original scroll had survived, but the sheet had been torn in the direction of the lines, so a cohesive section was still intact. He read a few words, then his gaze was drawn to something sending a shiver down his back. Now he studied the text more intently from the beginning. What he read made Hori's juices curdle in the metu. The sheet slipped from his trembling fingers, and he had to hold on to the table top lest he collapse. Where did the papyrus come from? Then he remembered: from Wenen's house! Rushing noises muffled his ears. As if from a far distance, he heard Nakhtmin call, "Hori? Hori?"

His friend reached for the papyrus. No! He must not! Hori's hand slammed down on the sheet before Nakhtmin could grab it. "Don't read this! No one should!" Slowly, his heartbeat calmed. He crumpled the scrap into a ball, the writing facing inward, so the ink wouldn't touch his skin, and hid it in his fist. "I must go."

He skipped down the stairs, Nakhtmin's outraged cries trailing him, but this was more important. At the jetty behind Nakhtmin's house a boat bobbed in the low waters, so he jumped in. The oar, he needed an oar! Dammit, Nakhtmin hid it somewhere so that nobody could steal it so easily. Jumping overboard with a splash, he waded to his pier. In his own dinghy, punt pole and oar lay at hand. Catching a breath of relief, he pulled himself aboard, stuffed the papyrus ball into his waistband and set off. Fortunately, the embalming compound lay north of his premises, and the slight current favored his progress. It didn't take him long to reach the weryt jetty and tie up the boat.

The guards were as strange to him as he was to them. "Stop! What brings you here? No living must enter this place!"

Oh, right, the king must have substituted the men after the irresponsibility of the old garrison soldiers came to light. "I'm Hori, the weryt physician. I have permission to pass from the king—life, prosperity and health—and the venerable mer-ut."

The two men exchanged glances, then one of them nodded, "All right, we've been informed." He banged against the gate. "Open up, you've got a customer!"

They'd developed a sick sense of humor pretty fast. Fine with him if it helped to ease the discomfort... When the gate opened, he slipped in and called to a servant, "I must speak to the mer-ut, quick. Where do I find him?"

The man tilted his head as he thought. "Probably in the storerooms."

Hori hurried in the given direction. The immense storage halls of the weryt held everything the little community needed, food, dishes, clothes and more, as well as what the dead needed: ointments, oils, resins and wood shavings, linen and most of all salt, natron salt. He spotted Hut-Nefer at the shelves which held precious amulets.

The head of the weryt looked at him in astonishment. "Hori? What's up?"

Out of breath, he leaned against a wooden strut and held his side. Then he fumbled the wad from his shendyt and cautiously opened it with the tips of his fingers. "Tell me if this is what I think it is," he gasped.

The mer-ut took the sheet from him and stepped into the light streaming in through the entrance. Holding the signs at arm's length, he began reading. After a short time, one arm sank down. "Where did you get this?"

Hori wiped sweat from his forehead. "So it is what I feared?"

Hut-Nefer nodded grimly. "A part of the directions to conjure the shadows. Most of it is missing, but even this bit in the wrong hands... What's wrong with you?"

"May the gods have mercy! We wrote healing spells on the back and added them to the potions for the sick men who'd been struck down by the curse!" They couldn't have done anything worse. The magical power of the words had been transferred to the medicine and with it the far stronger force of the curse. Never again would he use a scrap without checking the backside first! His only consolation was that probably nothing and nobody could have saved their patients.

With a flick of his hand, Hut-Nefer dismissed the additional torture of the four priests. "More important is the question of where this stems from? Did Nebkaura learn the conjuration by heart, or did he remove a script from our library, which he keeps copying over and over? Among the texts in his home, we did find secret incantations but nothing so dangerous. Either way we must find the treacherous lector priest! Come on, let's not talk about it here."

After the door to Hut-Nefer's office closed behind them, Hori reported all he knew. "Wenen is dead; we can't question him. Even more astonishing that we found the conjuration in his house. That makes him look guilty although he's a victim. The wanted man or an accomplice within the Amun temple could have planted the papyrus in Wenen's house when they didn't need it anymore, to direct suspicion at him…"

Pensive, the old man stroked his chin. "Possible. However, something different may have happened. To deal with such matters of the darkest knowledge is very dangerous. One error and the curse can turn against the one who speaks it, with double the impact. No mortal can control the forces of the shadows. I fear your friend unleashed something extremely dangerous and became its first victim. And we'll have to contain it. Did you find an ushabti in his house?"

Baffled, he looked up. "No, I'd have noticed. On the other hand, we didn't really search the house thoroughly. What about it?"

"I can only tell you this much: the conjuration addresses any shadow, but if spoken over an ushabti figurine with the name of a deceased, it calls that specific one."

During Hut-Nefer's words a thought sparked in Hori's heart but vanished before he could grasp it. Wenen evoking dark powers? That didn't fit at all with the image he'd formed of the young man. Oh dear, Nakhtmin! "I must go!" he exclaimed for the second time today and jumped up.

Nakhtmin was too relieved when Hori returned to get really upset with him. "Unbelievable! Runs out on me when I desperately need him!" he ranted anyway. "Muti is still asleep, but I think her temperature is rising again." Something in Hori's expression stopped him short. "By Seth's testicles, what was going on with you earlier?"

"The papyrus in Wenen's house, remember? On its back was written what we've been searching for all that time, the incantation."

Nakhtmin gaped until he'd digested the information. "The curse?"

"Exactly."

"Dear gods!" Then it hit him why all the patients had started that dreadful howling after they'd imbibed the potions with the healing spells *and the conjuration*. Hori fidgeted like a fish caught in a net, but Nakhtmin couldn't focus on their mission. His wife concerned him most right now. "First you write down a spell for Muti, then we'll give her another enema, and after that we can talk," he said with determination.

Hori nodded his acquiescence and got to work, but not without first looking at both sides of the sheet he handed him.

Nakhtmin exchanged a guilt-stricken look with him. "We screwed up pretty bad, didn't we?"

His friend only snorted.

After the clyster Muti fell asleep again right away. Nakhtmin ordered Inti to watch at her bed and ushered Hori out the room. "She must not learn about any of this."

Hori smiled sympathetically. "Then let's stroll through the garden and down to the river where no one should be around at this time." As soon as they'd settled in the lengthening shade of the reeds at the riverbank, he burst out, "Tell me all you know about Wenen!"

Nakhtmin lifted his eyebrows in surprise, then revisited every encounter with the young priest for Hori, trying to remember every detail. When he mentioned the tragic fate of Wenen's father, Hori interrupted him.

"Hold on, that's it!"

"What do you mean?"

"The mer-ut suspects Wenen might have accidentally brought the curse onto himself as he spoke the incantation. So I wondered why he'd toy with such dangerous things at all. Now it dawns on me. Could he have tried to conjure the shadow of his father?"

Nakhtmin considered this. The afterlife of his father had certainly troubled Wenen. Pretty much every time they met, talk got around to that topic. "He even had an empty grave erected for him."

"Right, he told me that as well when we were waiting for you."

Yikes, if only he remembered more than half of what Ameny explained to them about ka, ba, shut, ren and such. How did all that fit together? Was it possible to provide a dead man whose mummy got lost with an afterlife by calling its shadow, maybe lure its ba to a grave with the name and images on it, as well as a statue for the ka...? "I guess the important question is if *he* believed he could do it," he mumbled.

"You didn't see an ushabti at his place, did you?"

He shook his head. Such an answerer figurine would have caught his attention.

Hori cursed under his breath. "How did your friend get his hands on that papyrus? Where did he meet Nebkaura?"

That was indeed a good question. Where would *he* sell something stolen, forbidden? He'd certainly not offer it at a market booth. "Oh, I'm such a dumbass!" he exclaimed as he remembered that evening when he searched for the young priest. "The man in the tavern!"

Hori stared at him. "Explain yourself."

"Once I was looking for Wenen at his favorite watering hole, *The Apis*. But when I got there, he and a stranger sat together and talked austerely, heads close together. I didn't feel like making new acquaintances that night so I moved on. Could that have been the fugitive heri-heb? Since Wenen spent his evenings either there or at home, he could only have met someone at *The Apis*."

Hori exclaimed, "Of course! Where else but in the harbor district can stolen goods be sold so conveniently, particularly if they are of such delicate nature. I too paid the innkeeper there with incense so his good-for-nothing son would take my message to you when I escaped from the weryt for the first time."

All too well, Nakhtmin remembered the strange message and their eerie meeting in the dark. Then he remembered something else. "You think that was the reason why Wenen's pantry was so empty? I found that strange since as a hem-netjer he should have enjoyed generous provisions from the temple, but we found neither wine nor grains and oil, no bales of linen or anything valuable. Could he have given Nebkaura all his possessions?"

"Actually, that's quite likely what happened. Investigating further, we'll likely find out your friend recently traded plenty of things for deben. I doubt the heri-heb wants to lug lots of stuff around when he leaves the residence for good. We can only hope he hasn't hightailed it yet. Would you recognize the man?"

"I guess," he said but wasn't really sure. The only other person who could identify him and was allowed to leave the weryt was the mer-ut, but if he stuck his jackal snout into the tavern…not a good idea. "How could I have been so wrong about Wenen?"

"He deceived us all. I liked him, even Muti did."

Nakhtmin lifted his head. "Yeah." He didn't feel so foolish anymore. "And he never meant to harm any of us. How could it happen that he cursed his three colleagues instead of summoning the shadow of his father? As a hem-netjer of the second order, he couldn't hope to become prophet."

Hori snorted. "I suspect something else, and that takes us back to Setka. He must have found out somehow what Wenen was up to. Maybe he was also at *The Apis* that evening and observed the deal? Doesn't really matter. I think he forced him to do his bidding. First the poor guy had to sing his praise, then the bastard used the conjuration to curse his competition."

This time Nakhtmin snorted. "You don't really believe he would dirty his own hands. Never ever!"

"Yeah, you might be right there. Then it must have been even worse: Setka forced Wenen to become the most vicious murderer of all times by cursing the three hemu-netjer. Poor guy, indeed."

"Yes." Nakhtmin tried to imagine how Wenen must have felt: do Setka's bidding and become a criminal or get executed for possession of forbidden scripts— without the chance of a burial and afterlife. Would have been unbearable for him. "He must have felt horrible!"

Hori gave a grim nod. "That's probably why he messed up in the end. When Wenen wanted to summon his dead father, fear and guilt must have caused him to make a mistake. Thus the curse fell onto him, and as Hut-Nefer revealed to me, with double the force. That's why Wenen died first."

With each of Hori's words, the picture became clearer for Nakhtmin. Now he understood what Setka meant when he said, 'He caused his own demise.' What a hypocrite!

THE TRAIL LEADS TO THE HARBOR DISTRICT

Day 23 of month Ipet-hemet in Shemu, the season of the harvest

Nakhtmin ran to the palace. Now that they knew where the fugitive heri-heb might be found, there was no time to lose. Too bad only he'd seen the face of Nebkaura, not Hori. If it had actually been the weryt traitor he'd seen in the tavern with Wenen. All their speculations just now were built on that assumption. Nevertheless, *he* had to report to the king and accompany the search party combing the harbor district although he'd much rather stay with his wife. It had taken him some effort to dissuade Hori from coming along. Leaving Muti without a physician at hand? Unthinkable! Just before reaching the double gates, he slowed to catch his breath as he walked toward the two palace guards in the light of the sinking sun.

"The queen again?" one of them asked. "Physicians aren't to be envied either."

It seemed an eternity since he'd last been at the House of Women, so the question surprised him at first, but only a few days had passed. He shook his head. "The king."

The eyes of both men widened. "Did his majesty send for you?"

"No, but urgent matters need his attention." He wanted to pass, but the guards blocked his way.

"His majesty is receiving an ambassador from Retjenu. Come back tomorrow."

Oh, these fools! They surely had their orders, but he had to ignore them. "Then I need to speak to the vizier," he said although he didn't intend to settle for Sobekemhat. "Is he in the Great House?"

"The tjati is also present at the meeting."

Nakhtmin groaned. He should have expected that. Who else could he name? Oh, Hori's brother. "What about treasurer Teti?"

One of them shrugged, the other grumbled. "The treasurer's left the building."

"By the ennead of Iunu!" Nakhtmin blurted. "Let me pass, or you'll regret it, I promise. This matter is of utmost urgency! It's about the wanted man."

That finally got their attention. "You mean that Nebkaura fellow? Why don't you go to the Medjay right away. You think his majesty will jump to it and arrest the man himself after you talked to him?"

Nakhtmin blushed. "You're right. I'll do that." He really should have thought of that. The king would find out soon enough once they'd caught the fugitive. He trotted off.

The Medjay's quarters lay close to the harbor district since the law men were mostly needed there, and in case their duties called them to places outside the residence, they'd reach a boat fast. Nakhtmin cursed himself. If only he'd come here straight away, he wouldn't have wasted so much time in such a pressing matter. Finally the whitewashed brick building towered in front of him, garrison and prison at the same time. Here, two armed guards also barred his way, but they listened intently as he blurted his reason for coming here.

"The wanted Nebkaura? I'll take you to the commander," one of them said.

Senankh, the head of the Medjay, had been a long-serving veteran in the campaigns of Senusret's father, as everyone in the residence knew. He was enjoying a meal when Nakhtmin stormed in with the guard. His companion apologized for disturbing him. "This man claims to know something about the fugitive whose arrest is so important to the pharaoh—life, prosperity and health."

With one wave, Senankh managed to dismiss his subordinate and invite Nakhtmin to sit. "Speak!" An old school soldier, his words were just as efficient and sparing as his gestures.

Nakhtmin admired the man and attempted to copy his demeanor. "A few days ago, I saw a man in the tavern *The Apis*, who might have been the fugitive Nebkaura."

Across the table, bushy eyebrows rose. "When was that? Was it definitely the wanted? Would you recognize the man again?" He wiped the bowl with a piece of bread and ate that.

Since Nakhtmin didn't feel like telling the man the whole tangled story of their investigation, he simply nodded. "Quite sure, and yes, I believe I can." Then he counted the days since his trip to the tavern. "About a week ago."

Senankh grunted. "And you're telling us now? In the meantime, he's probably fled the city."

"Back then I didn't know anything of the matter," Nakhtmin justified himself. "Only today I realized who that man might have been. He might still be hanging around the harbor. To get the funds for his escape, he needs to sell things hard to trade."

"You know a lot now, considering that you knew nothing before." Senankh rose and scrutinized him with distrust.

Nakhtmin's face grew hot at the unspoken allegation showing in the man's gaze that he himself might have been one of Nebkaura's buyers of stolen goods. The man appeared as if he were already taking his measure to pick a suitable cell. Oh dear, he didn't exactly look respectable in his spotty and crumpled shendyt, and he'd forgotten to wear his insignia or a collar. "The king himself consigned this investigation to me," he said with as much dignity as he could muster. "And in the name of his majesty, I ask you to give me some of your men to search the harbor district."

The commander took a deep breath. "Why didn't you say so right away instead of babbling on and on?" He stepped to the door and hollered into the hallway. "Men! Assemble!"

That was easy! A short time later, Nakhtmin had selected a group of four Medjay. More would attract too much attention, he thought. With their dark skins and the bright red belts, ends dangling to their knees over their short shendyts, and the batons they carried, anyone recognized them as law men from afar. Nebkaura shouldn't get wind of their search lest he run off and disappear for good. If he hadn't done so already. Nakhtmin ground his teeth. Too bad he hadn't considered Wenen's drinking buddy to be the lector priest any earlier. "Let's go, men!" In vain he attempted Senankh's dashing tone of command.

Soon the typical odors of the harbor filled Nakhtmin's nose, and he began to scrutinize every man they passed. The fugitive probably did not only frequent *The Apis*. To be honest, he hoped they'd find him somewhere else since the innkeeper's impertinence still rankled. On the other hand...the scoundrel deserved to get in trouble for sheltering a criminal. At that pleasant notion, a grim laugh escaped his mouth, and he headed for the skewed house with the bull. "Let me go ahead and see if the man's there," he instructed his troop. "If so, I'll fetch you to arrest him."

The innkeeper paid no attention when he entered as he was serving at a large table fully occupied. Nakhtmin sneaked into one of the many dark nooks and carefully scrutinized every patron. Then he changed position so he'd see the faces of those who'd been sitting with their backs to him. Last time he's seen the supposed Nebkaura, the man had been wearing an ill-fitting wig. Underneath, his scalp must have been shaved as was appropriate for a priest. By now his real hair might have grown back enough, and he'd look different. In his place, Nakhtmin would certainly have gotten rid of the lice-infested thing as soon as possible. Nakhtmin groaned to himself. If he were on the run, he'd try to change his appearance. Nebkaura'd surely be smart enough to do so.

Nothing about the guy had been remarkable, except his dirty clothes. Hold on, one thing distinguished him from the other riff-raff in this area: the shaved eyebrows wouldn't have fully grown back yet. Likely Nebkaura painted them to hide that fact. That alone would draw attention in a district where apart from all the foreigners only common people lived, worked or went about their business. And those only lined their eyes with kohl, if at all, but didn't paint false brows on their faces. Now he knew what to look for. The wanted man definitely wasn't at *The Apis*.

Muti groaned and stirred. The wooden headrest clattered to the floor. Hori jumped to her side as she opened her eyes. Her temperature had gone down significantly, she looked much better than a few hours ago. "How do you feel?" he asked.

She licked her chapped lips. "Thirsty. And exhausted."

"Here you go." He gave her the mug with willow bark brew sweetened with honey, and she drank greedily.

"Oh," she whispered. "My head hurts, and I had awful dreams. Where's Nakhtmin? Wasn't he here a moment ago?"

A moment? His friend had left a while ago, and Hori grew impatient awaiting his return. He'd have loved to go along on the hunt for the villain who sold the secrets of the weryt and brought on such disaster. What did the man hope for? Even if he'd have a son with another woman, he wouldn't pass the Judgment of the Dead with the burden of such vicious crimes on his heart. Maybe he planned to fudge the tests somehow. As if one could cheat his way into the heavenly realms! Maat won't be tricked, and he preferred serving the goddess of justice to deceiving her. Therefore, he had no reason to fear the devourer.

"Nakhtmin went to the House of Life to get more medicine for you," he lied and felt ashamed right away. What was that about 'serving Maat'? Hopefully, the goddess wouldn't hold it against him since the lie served a good purpose. "Say, do you have aches in your abdomen, cramps, bleeding, any indication that you might lose the child?"

She seemed to listen into herself. "No, all seems well. I'm hungry."

He smiled. "A very good sign! I'll get word to Baketamun, but knowing her, she probably has a broth ready for you."

And he was right. To his relief, his patient fell asleep again soon after, but this time, it wasn't the unconsciousness brought on by fever. Mutnofret was on the mend.

Together with his Medjay, Nakhtmin had searched almost all nooks and crannies of the district. Night had fallen, and it became more difficult to study the faces of the idlers. Which eyebrow was real, which painted on? His hope to find the wanted man dwindled. Most likely, the cursed priest had already left the residence. His companions started to grumble.

"You really think we find the guy?"

"Yes," he said with more confidence than he felt. "He's here somewhere!"

They turned into an alley lined by beer halls and brothels. "We've been here already," one of the Medjay complained.

Nakhtmin cursed, but then the sight of the houses of pleasure gave him an idea. Hori mentioned Nebkaura being unhappy in his marriage and beating his wife. What a bastard! Outside the weryt, he'd have been punished for that alone. Why did Hori's esteemed mer-ut tolerate such behavior? He cast a glance at the western shore. Did they live according to different laws than the living? Anyway, a man unable to satisfy his desires felt pressure to do so, maybe even paid for relief. "Let's ask in the brothels," he suggested. "Maybe one of the women remembers the priest." In this area, an hour with a girl cost little. The fugitive wouldn't have shied from the expense.

At the first house of love the whore keeper claimed, "Priests are not served here because it's forbidden. Don't want trouble with those guys." He pointed at Nakhtmin's companions.

Of course, priests became impure when they had sexual intercourse and had to perform an elaborate cleansing procedure before they could enter their temples. Even coitus with their wives required purification, among other things by swallowing natron pills. Were whores regarded as so unclean that priests were not at all allowed to lie with them? Nakhtmin had no idea until now. "The man we are looking for is no priest anymore. He lets his hair grow. Has someone like that frequented your house?"

The man shook his head. "Try the *Temple of Bastet*. They don't look as closely as I do, if you get my drift."

Grinning, Nakhtmin nodded. They bent the rules. The name alone should be forbidden. Temple of Bastet—what an insult to the goddess of love! He handed the man a piece of copper for the information.

"Thank you, noble sir. By the way, strangers can even rent rooms there."

Hm, that was interesting. Leaving the place, Nakhtmin asked the Medjay, "Do you know that whorehouse?"

"Sure. It's like he said," the spokesman of the group confirmed, while his colleagues remained tight-lipped. "It's a big place. I doubt we'll find the guy there."

"Lead the way, we have to check it out anyway."

They showed little enthusiasm.

The house with the cat goddess painted on was indeed very large for the area and even had a second floor. The facade was three times as broad as the neighboring houses, and it looked like it might have several wings built around a small courtyard. They'd certainly have quite a few rooms to let. Nakhtmin grew excited. This was exactly the place where a fugitive would hide. His Medjay though acted strangely reluctant.

Then it dawned on him what troubled them. The *Temple of Bastet* must have an arrangement with the Medjay. In exchange for certain benefits or compensations, the law men turned a blind eye on possible violations of rules. Hiding a man wanted by the king went too far though. He glared at them. "We're hunting a murderer and evildoer who caused much harm and suffering. The keeper of the *Bastet* can't offer you enough to ignore that!" At the sight of their shocked expressions, he asked in an even sharper voice, "Does this rathole have more exits?"

The spokesman cleared his throat. "Only this one and a small gate to the jetty," he mumbled.

Well, well, even a private jetty! Probably for rich clients who didn't want to be seen or not befoul their feet in the dirt of the harbor district. "Then you'll go there. Don't let anyone leave, no matter who it is."

Hanging his head, he trotted off, and when Nakhtmin felt confident he must have reached the backdoor, he entered through the front gate. The keeper was a bull of a man and looked like a foreigner, probably from Retjenu. Astonishment showed in his face when he noticed Nakhtmin's escort.

"Let me take care of it, sir," one of the Medjay said and pulled the man aside.

"They call him the cat king," one of the two other Medjay murmured.

Nakhtmin almost burst out laughing. Instead, he settled for, "Meow."

The whispers between keeper and Medjay grew more agitated, but at some point the brothel owner resigned himself to the inevitable and turned to Nakhtmin. "How can I serve you, sir?"

"We're looking for a fugitive. Do you know a man fitting this description: about forty, a priest until recently and now let's his hair grow back?" he asked sternly.

The cat king's gaze darted left then right, then he nodded. "He's living in a room upstairs, which he hasn't left yet today. Take him away without making a fuss. You're harming business. Ishtar will show you the way. Hey, Ishtar!" he yelled and a delicate girl of fourteen years at most appeared. "The bald old fart on the upper floor is your customer, right? Lead these gentlemen to him."

She nodded, and for a moment the corners of her mouth drooped. She must have hoped for a client not an errand, which might rob her of a regular customer. Despite the exotic name, she was definitely Egyptian. "Follow me," she chirped and gyrated her hips lasciviously. Except for a belt with strings of pearls dangling down, she was naked. "What do you want from Khepri?"

Nakhtmin's breath caught. My little beetle, she called him, the endearment of Kheper? Maybe this was the wrong man. No, Nebkaura wouldn't be so stupid as to use his real name. Wasn't Hori's friend among the embalmers named Kheper? The dung beetle who recreated himself from feces was the sacred symbol of rebirth. If this guy really sought afterlife, he couldn't have picked a better name. "You like him?" He didn't want her to give the fugitive a warning and allow him to escape. "Don't worry it's only about an unsettled bill at one of the watering holes."

She snorted. "I also have something to settle with him. The dog hit me yesterday. None of us has to put up with that! Up there." She stepped into a narrow staircase.

Pricking his ears, Nakhtmin followed. Sure sounded like they had the right man. Ishtar sashayed on light feet ahead of him, and he too tried to make as little noise as possible. His three companions, though, stomped up the stairs like a herd of elephants. Hopefully, Khepri-Nebkaura didn't suspect anything. There might be another stairway reachable from this corridor, and he only had positioned a man at the back, not the front. Might turn out a bad mistake!

Ishtar stopped at one of the numerous doors and knocked.

Nakhtmin heard a shout from inside, and the girl opened. He pushed into the room behind her and hoped the three Medjay would cover his back. Before him stood a stubble-haired man gaping at him in astonishment until he spotted the Medjay and paled. Was this the man he'd seen with Wenen? He couldn't say so with absolute certainty, and in the twilight he had difficulty determining if there were real eyebrows under the paint. So he asked frankly, "Are you Nebkaura?"

An expression of horror flitted across the brothel guest's face, but he caught himself fast. "I'm called Khepri. Who are you to burst into my room?"

"People may *call* you Khepri, but it's not your name, and I heard you place a lot of importance on that, Nebkaura. Mine doesn't matter, but that of the king, in whose name you're arrested." He beckoned his men. Two jumped to it and grabbed the guy.

He screamed and writhed in their unyielding grips. "You're making a mistake! No! I didn't do anything wrong! I'm not who you're looking for."

Ishtar charged at him and slapped his face hard enough his lip split. "That's for yesterday, you bastard!"

"Help! Keep that wildcat away from me! I didn't do anything!" Khepri lamented.

Nakhtmin caught Ishtar's wrist midair and wondered if this heap of misery could really have committed those abominations. He had to make sure. Grabbing the oil lamp, he rummaged through Nebkaura-Khepri's belongings. Nothing but clothes. Irritated, he emptied his travel bag onto the bed without finding anything valuable. "Impossible!" He even turned the sack of straw inside out and pulled the bed from the wall.

The guy gloated, "I told you so, you've got the wrong man." He tried again to wrestle free of the Medjay.

Nakhtmin was convinced of his guilt, but he'd feel much better if they found evidence. Desperate, he looked around, then at the girl. "Hey, how did he pay for the room or your services, Ishtar? He has no Deben and no valuables to trade."

She shrugged. "He pays the cat king, none of my business." The tip of her tongue pushed between her lips. "Oh, if I were him…" She eased down onto her knees and began knocking on the floorboards.

"Hey, stop it. What are you doing? Bitch!" the prisoner clamored.

Nakhtmin laughed. The girl probably had a similar cranny in her room to hoard her meager earnings without customers snatching them. "Lo and behold, do we have a concealment somewhere? Is it here?" He stomped a foot and stepped aside. "Or here? Look how he's sweating. Oh, this sounds hollow."

The girl crawled over and slipped her thin fingers into the cracks until she found the loose board. Nakhtmin squatted beside her and held the light to the opening. Deben of copper and silver shone back, a small fortune. In addition, he'd stored a few sacks and scrolls there.

He only cast quick glances into the bags. "Incense, myrrh. All stolen." A sigh of relief escaped him. "We've got our man. Off with him to the jail, where he can't cause more damage!"

ONE CAUGHT

Day 24 of month Ipet-hemet in Shemu, the season of the harvest

At long last, Hori heard his friend return.

"We've got him!" Nakhtmin called. He practically burst with pride. Then he told him in all details how he'd tracked the fugitive.

Hori exhaled a sigh of relief. At least the secrets of the necropolis were safe now. That had been his biggest concern. "Well done! Muti woke up a little while ago. She's doing better," he said to his friend. "Listen, the thing with the ushabti still puzzles me. You don't need me anymore now, right? I'd like to check Wenen's house again."

"Sure, off you go. And thanks for holding the line."

Hori slapped his back and left the sickroom. A little later, he set out for the craftsmen's district equipped with a torch. His doubts whether he'd be able to find Wenen's house again vanished when he reached an intersection with a well that looked familiar. Then he stood before the door of the priest. Someone had painted an udjat eye with coal on it to fend off demons. Very considerate. Would that help him if shadows still lurked in the house?

He entered, lit an oil lamp and pushed the torch into a holder mounted to the wall. Darn, the flaxen wick was almost burnt down. Maybe Wenen had a new one in his pantry. Hori stuck his nose into the room. He was lucky and even found a second lamp, which he filled with oil and wick, before lighting it. Then his gaze swept over the fairly empty shelf boards. Nothing here resembled an ushabti. He lifted the lid of an earthen jar containing grain, dipped his arm all the way in without finding anything. He quickly dismissed the downstairs room as of little interest. Wenen would have conjured the shadows upstairs, where no one could surprise him. His bedroom only warranted a quick peek as well. He'd spent enough time there to notice such a figurine. In the other room, a faint scent of cold incense hit him. How did Wenen get his hands on something so precious? Purchased from the heri-heb as well? The room contained only a table, on which sat an earthen bowl with remains of something burnt and two wooden slats used to keep papyrus unrolled. Hori stepped closer. In Wenen's stead, he'd have performed the ritual right here, and the remains of a fire pointed in that direction. Nakhtmin must have found the scroll here. He closed his eyes and imagined the scene: the spell in front of him, next to it the ushabti. Maybe Wenen would have held it in his hand. As a stand-in, Hori picked up one of the slats. "Mumble, mumble, summon, summon, and then—what happened then, Wenen?" he asked into the silence. Did the curse strike down the blasphemer right there? He assumed so and dropped the wooden stick. As he bent down, he spotted something under the table and crawled to it. Two fragments of a clay answerer figurine.

The next morning, Hori waited impatiently in the antechamber for the king's arrival since he was interrogating Nebkaura. Eager to show yesterday's find to the pharaoh, he was even more curious to learn if the fugitive confessed. Finally footsteps sounded in the corridor and he peered through the opening. King and mer-ut were back! Filled with anticipation, he jumped up and stretched out his arms at knee-height. "Your majesty! Life, prosperity and health! Venerable mer-ut…"

"Hori. Skip the formalities and come in." Senusret rushed past him into his office.

They all remained silent until a servant placing refreshments on the table had left. The boy had looked keen to escape the presence of Hut-Nefer. Grateful, Hori sipped the clear, cool water flavored with blossoms.

"We've got the culprit," Senusret began. "The mer-ut identified him as Neb-kaura, so the prisoner's initial denials came to a quick end."

Hori nodded. Although he hadn't expected anything else, he felt relieved. "What else did he confess?"

"He needed some encouragement from the flogger." The pharaoh's lips formed a thin line.

Hori could imagine what that encouragement had looked like. The Medjay called 'floggers' carried the title for a good reason. Not too long ago, Hori had been in their hands and got close to getting a taste of their efficiency. Under the painful blows any tongue would loosen, he imagined. "Um, but the weryt," he replied. "Didn't Nebkaura reveal secrets nobody should've heard?"

"My personal flogger is deaf," Senusret said. "I trust my Medjay, but some interrogations regard state secrets."

Good idea.

"Nebkaura in the end admitted that he observed you diving under the wall. That sparked the wish in his heart to reach the other side of the river and begin a new life with a woman who could bear him children."

At these words, Hut-Nefer's jackal snout bobbed up and down. "Just like you thought, Hori." He lifted the mask enough to drink from his mug. "He stole resins and other valuable ingredients to sell on the eastern shore. But since he could only leave at night and search for customers among shady characters, he found selling his booty at an appropriate price harder than he'd expected. Nevertheless, he'd already decided to leave the weryt for good and try his luck in the south when he met a priest in one of the taverns."

"Hold on," Hori interrupted. "What about Rahotep and removing his heart? Didn't he say anything about that? And how did he cross the river?" Hori'd been lucky back then to find a leaking bull-rush boat in the shrubs along the western shore. Luck or divine intervention? Either way, he managed to brave the river in it. How did Nebkaura do it?

"Right," Hut-Nefer's deep voice droned. "When Nebkaura wanted to escape the weryt for the first time, he encountered the guard. Both were shocked, he claimed, but he regained his wits quicker. Rahotep probably thought him a ghost."

Hori snorted. Understandable.

"A scuffle ensued; the man fell. In his despair, Nebkaura picked up a rock and bashed his head in."

"That fits with the injuries." Hori shuddered as he imagined the scene.

The mer-ut took another sip. "Nebkaura maintains it was an accident, but he feared the dead man's ghost would take revenge on him if he left him unburied. That's why this lunatic used Rahotep's dagger to open his abdomen and remove the heart, which he wanted to prepare for eternity, then return it to the body for its final journey."

"What idiocy!" Hori blurted. "He didn't even know the man's name, how could he hope…? His reason must have floated down the Nile without him." How many lashes had Nebkaura needed before he spilled all this?

"Pretty soon he recognized his error, and when the heart was discovered so quickly, he knew he had to leave for good. He'd wandered upstream to the temple of Anubis, where he'd borrowed a boat the first time. For his return trip, he stole a small boat on the eastern shore and towed the borrowed craft back to the temple, so it wouldn't be missed. The other one he hid among the reeds on the riverbank."

Hori shook his head. "The man acted pretty smart. If he hadn't stayed away, who knows if we'd ever caught him…"

The king waved dismissively. "Instead, he encountered you on his final escape and might have killed you like the guard."

"Yes, that was close," Hori confirmed and stroked the spot on his head were now only a scab bore witness to the attack. Nebkaura'd acted like a cornered animal. Understandable if he considered how important his afterlife was to the man. He knew all too well what punishment awaited those who betrayed the secrets of the weryt. "Back to the meeting between heri-heb and Wenen, at least I assume Nebkaura ran into him?"

Senusret nodded. "Your friend Wenen desperately wanted to conjure a dead man—for whatever reason—and Nebkaura saw his chance to get enough funds in one fell swoop to start a good, new life. Otherwise he wouldn't have returned that night but would have sold off the remaining stolen goods, and you'd have a scar less to boast. Anyway, he did come back and took secret scripts from the library."

"Wenen was Nakhtmin's friend," Hori mumbled. "And the deceased whose ghost he wanted to summon was his father, a papyrus maker who'd been killed by a crocodile. He probably hoped to provide him with an afterlife somehow."

"Oh," the king said, and all three of them fell silent.

Then Hori remembered what he'd brought along. "Here, this proves it." He emptied the bag onto the table between them. "Last night, I found this ushabti in Wenen's house. Probably broke when he messed up the conjuration of his father's shadow."

"How come three more priests of the Amun temple were struck by the curse? Ameny already told me his suspicions, but I'd like to hear your opinion since I found them hard to believe," the king demanded, propped his elbows onto the table and put the tips of his fingers together.

Hori considered this. He didn't really know how the three hemu-netjer became victims of the shadows. It was one thing to speculate with Nakhtmin but a completely different matter to accuse a man of heinous crimes in front of the king. That might ruin his career and likely cost his life. Again he reported in great detail what their investigations had revealed but restrained from drawing conclusions. "Nakhtmin suffered nothing worse than a bump on the head and a night locked up at the temple," he concluded. "As to Hemiunu's whereabouts, I have no clue."

"Ameny sent a message earlier. The head of the hemu-netjer has been found dead in his garden," the pharaoh said. "His physician deems it death of natural causes. He'd suffered from a weak heart for quite some time."

He sighed in relief. At least not another curse victim, though that wouldn't make it any easier for Nakhtmin when he heard about it. Hori could well imagine how shocked the fat principal of the hemu-netjer must have been when he saw the 'evidence' against him. Then the struggle—Hemiunu had good reason to take flight. But it was too much for him. Responsible for his death was definitely Setka, only he had cause to lay a false trail to the fat man. And he'd personally hold him accountable for that, Hori promised himself, but wouldn't share his thoughts. Far more interesting was what the king made of all this. Thank the gods for a pharaoh smart enough to see beyond the obvious!

"The poison in the chest must have been a diversion," Senusret deducted. "Hemiunu was supposed to take the fall for the deaths, therefore the note without a signature. You only told one man that the principal would be appointed fourth prophet, right? What was his name again? Ah, yes Setka That priest presumably wants to improve his position in life urgently?"

Hori could only nod. It felt like the king had crept into his heart and read all his thoughts. "He thinks it's his due because he stems from a noble family," he croaked and raised his mug. Empty. The pharaoh gestured for him to help himself. Hori also poured more for the king and the mer-ut.

"Which family would that be?" his majesty wanted to know.

Hori concentrated to remember. "The uncle is first prophet of Ptah in the City of the White Wall, the father was-"

"First prophet of Ra in On, and another uncle is nomarch of Men-Nefer," the king added and turned slightly paler around the nose. "No matter. Setka will pay for his insidious deed, even if that means one of the truly great families will turn against me," he announced.

Hearing this made it easier for Hori to share the rest. "What I'm telling you now I cannot prove." He described Wenen's original take on Setka, then the sudden change of mind and his suspicion Wenen might have been forced to do Setka's bidding.

Hut-Nefer pushed the mask up so that Hori could see his sweaty face. It had to be unbearably hot under that thing. "With your permission?" he asked.

The pharaoh made an inviting gesture. "Within this circle, sure. Should someone enter, you must cover your face again, though."

"Correct me if I'm wrong. You think Setka forced your friend Wenen to render the incantation to him?" the mer-ut asked.

Hori found it annoying when people called Wenen his friend when he'd barely known the man, nevertheless, he felt obliged to defend him. "Or he forced him to curse the three priests. Wenen wasn't a bad guy. On purpose, he wouldn't harm a human being unless he found himself in dire circumstances."

"Be it as it may, that leaves one question: how did Setka know Wenen harbored such knowledge if your friend hadn't told him?"

Hut-Nefer was right. Hori sat there as if struck by lightning. "I haven't even thought of that yet!" He leaned toward the two men sitting across from him. "What if Setka observed Wenen when he tried to conjure his father's ghost? Maybe the fool took the papyrus to the temple with him, where Setka caught a glimpse. Initially, I thought the pompous snob put pressure on Wenen because of his preference for men, but maybe he had something worse on him."

King and mer-ut nodded. "A convincing hypothesis," Hut-Nefer murmured.

"This Setka appears to be a cunning villain. Doesn't dirty his hands and still gets what he wants."

Hori started. Did the pharaoh mean he couldn't prosecute the treacherous priest even if they found evidence for the scenario he'd described?

"He will receive his punishment though," Hut-Nefer growled. "The worst form."

All morning, Nakhtmin had felt as if two water buffaloes pulled him in opposite directions. On the one hand he wanted to stay with Muti and tend to her, on the other, he wanted to be at the palace with Hori and find out what the interrogation brought to light.

"You're restless like reeds in the wind," Muti complained. "Why don't you allow me to get up, then we can indulge ourselves in the garden. I can't bear this stuffy room any longer."

He jumped to her side and felt her skin. No, she wasn't hot any longer, but when he thought of how sick she'd been only yesterday, he didn't want to take any risks. "You'll stay in bed. Doctor's orders."

"I can't stand my doctor," she griped.

He raised his eyebrows. "Is that so? And you, poor thing, married him!"

She stuck out her tongue, and he seized the occasion to study the organ. Coated with a little white but much better than yesterday. He smiled. "Maybe Inti and I can carry you down later. You're right, it is rather stuffy in here."

"'Later' as in 'right now'?" she begged.

Why not, he thought. It wouldn't hurt her, and when Hori returned, he could leave her in the care of his servants for a short time.

As soon as he'd made Muti comfortable on cushions in the shade, Inti announced a visitor. "The Lady Isis."

Great! Company and supervision for Muti. Good thing he'd sent Inti over to Ameny's place yesterday to let her family know how his darling was doing. Grinning, he went to greet his mother-in-law. "Welcome! You'll find her on the mend. I've just brought her to the garden, and she'll be happy to see you."

Instead of rushing to her daughter, she took him aside. "My husband requests your presence at the temple of Amun. It's urgent. Go, I'll take care of Muti."

Nakhtmin's heart skipped a beat. The gods had listened to his wishes and granted them. To leave nothing to chance, he gave both women copious instructions until Muti actually waved him off with a shout. "Begone! The man thinks us imbeciles, Mother. As if you didn't know what to do when your child's sick."

More than happy to leave, he wondered what this was about. Why had he only sent for him and not Hori as well?

The Amun temple's courtyard was unusually busy. Hemu-netjer and wabu poured in like the other day when Ameny gave his speech. Nakhtmin squeezed through the crowd to the atrium since last time Ameny had stood on the steps leading up to it. There he spotted Hori between the columns and ran to him. "What are you doing here? What's going on? Tell me."

"Later. I'm glad you're here and just in time. Simply play along."

In time for what, Nakhtmin wondered. What was this about? He hated it when he was left in the dark. That moment he detected Ameny and the other two prophets and—the king, in full regalia with the striped Nemes headcloth. Above Senusret's forehead rose the two goddesses Nekhbet and Wadjet, the vulture-shaped deity of Upper Egypt and the cobra of Lower Egypt, protection for the king and threat to his enemies. And he wore the ceremonious beard, as well as crozier and scourge. Nakhtmin gulped. Even the dumbest heart understood the king was here on official business. He wanted to bow, but Hori grabbed his arm and dragged him into the sunlight.

When king and prophets lined up beside them, the assembled sank into a low bow, and Nakhtmin saw only brown backs instead of faces. He could've strolled over them all the way to the pylon without his sandals ever touching the ground. A sense of power and dignity gripped him. But when the moment extended in silence, he felt uncomfortable and glad he didn't stand down there. His heart would have turned to water by now.

Finally, Kagemni thundered, "Rise!"

Like a hippopotamus breaking through the surface of the river, the monotonous brown landscape of backs broke into colors and shapes. Expectant faces of men and women stared up to them.

"A few days ago, I talked to you," Ameny commenced. "I told you then, the king won't appoint a fourth prophet before the murderer among you has been revealed, the man who killed Wenen, Bai, Sehetep and Neferka." He let the names roll over his tongue like thunder and paused before he continued, "Many of you shared your suspicions with us, and today I can announce we're quite certain who did it." His gaze swept over the heads of the assembly, whose tension seemed almost tangible.

Ameny's words baffled Nakhtmin. When Hori left in the morning, nothing had been for certain yet. Had later developments brought new insights or...? Judging by the look of his friend, he'd cooked up something again. Hori's fingers fidgeted with his collar. A trap?

"Hemiunu is dead," whispered Hori. "Probably his heart."

"No...!"

Ameny's voice prevented further musings. "However, the crucial lead came from someone who didn't dare to show his face—out of fear or maybe cowardice. Without this priest stepping forth to explain his reasoning, we cannot give credence to his accusations, nor point a finger at the man who is a murderer. Thus ruled his majesty, the supreme judge of the Two Lands."

Oh, now he understood what they were up to. They wanted to entice Setka to confess to incriminating Hemiunu. Very smart. Would that also prove who placed the poisonous seeds with Hemiunu's snacks? Maybe not, but at least they'd be able to charge him with giving false testimony. Again he looked to Hori, whose hand clenched around a fold of his shendyt. What did Ameny wait for? The audience turned restless, too. At a loss, people glanced at each other.

The prophet unrolled a papyrus and held it up: the note that accused Hemiunu of the poisonings. Nakhtmin gulped. If only he'd never found it! The poor principal might still be alive.

"Whoever wrote this message and shoved it under my door, come forward now, or else the killer walks free."

Nobody stepped up. Where was Setka? What was he waiting for? The crowd stood unmoving, no one pushed through the tightly packed bodies. Nakhtmin sighed in disappointment.

"May the devourer scrunch his heart!" Hori hissed. "I didn't think him so cowardly."

Cowardly—or cunning? Maybe Setka smelled the trap.

Ameny rolled up the papyrus. "Well. This means nothing then." He tore apart the anonymous note, nodded at the prophets and the king, then they all headed into the temple. Hori also stepped into the shade of the colonnades and pulled Nakhtmin along. "Come on!"

Only now did Nakhtmin notice the two Medjay emerging from the shadows of the columns and following the group of dignitaries. Hori and he trailed after them to the offices of the prophets, where Kagemni and Duamutef excused themselves and returned to their duties. Hori entered Ameny's rooms after the king, and Nakhtmin followed with the Medjay.

Leftover snacks on a small table hinted at Hori and the pharaoh having sat here with Ameny before. Nakhtmin sank onto one of the offered chairs and couldn't wait to learn more, but for a while nobody spoke a word.

At long last, Ameny sighed. "We should have reckoned with this. Too bad, though."

"I'd really like a solid reason to pick up the man for interrogation," the pharaoh growled. "If he turns out innocent, his family will protest. Among Setka's relatives is the nomarch of Men-Nefer. That city bears unrest like a rabbit bears kittens. We can't take a risk in this matter, though, since the man may have gained knowledge..." He glanced at his soldiers. "...um, forbidden knowledge. These two Medjay will take Setka into custody today. He'll open up to the flogger. Go into the adjoining room, men, and wait there. The following isn't for your ears," he ordered and the law men retreated.

"What if he didn't do it?" Nakhtmin dared to ask as soon as the door closed behind the two guys. At a loss, he looked to Hori for help. "I mean, can we risk arresting the wrong man and warning the true perpetrator?" They'd chewed on that risk over and over again.

"Only Setka had reason to believe Hemiunu would snatch the position from him," Hori said.

Nakhtmin retorted, "He could have told someone else. Besides, it could have been pure chance that Shu-Ra was blamed. Ameny had openly announced the men were poisoned, so anyone might have seized the opportunity to get rid of the less-than-popular principal."

"Stop it!" Ameny slammed his hand onto the table hard enough that the knock at the door went almost unheard.

Nakhtmin rose. "Shall I?" At Ameny's nod, he opened the door.

"Setka!" Hori called.

"Enter, priest," the king ordered. "I assume you have good reason to interrupt this meeting?"

The hem-netjer bowed and rose again without waiting for the ruler's permission to do so. "Yes, your majesty. You and the prophets asked the author of the letter to come forward. Here I am."

Nakhtmin had to fight hard against a broad grin trying to conquer his face. He'd fallen into the trap after all.

"Why did you step into the light only now?" Ameny demanded to know.

Setka put on his arrogant smile. "Venerable prophet, how could I have done that in front of all my fellow priests. Nobody loves traitors. What would they think of me?"

Now that was something. Nakhtmin snorted in disgust.

"It would have shed a much more favorable light on you if you hadn't tried to hide your authorship at all," Ameny stated dryly.

"Prophet, majesty, I didn't dare. Hemiunu is a powerful man, and I feared for my life. He who poisons once may develop a taste for it and show even fewer scruples next time." His eyelids flittered a little. "As I haven't seen the principal at the temple since yesterday, I assume he has been arrested, and I'm safe."

While the king gazed at the priest, showing no reaction, Ameny waved the implicit question aside. "How did you know where Hemiunu hid the poison? Did you see him administer it to the four men? Do you know which poison he used?"

Again, Setka's lids twitched. He rubbed his nose and pursed his lips. "Have I seen him poison his victims? No." His gaze wandered to the right corner of the room as if the correct answer were written there. Then he gave an artificial laugh. "I wanted to partake of his provision of nuts and, on that occasion, I saw the bag with the castor beans. Those two—" He pointed at Hori and Nakhtmin. "—and Ameny said the four men were poisoned. I was lucky to recognize them and know how dangerous they are! I could have been his next victim, so I had to let you know."

As if Setka pinched sweets. Who'd believe that? Nakhtmin certainly didn't. From the corner of his eye, he glanced at the king, who didn't know Setka's character or his habits. And it wasn't impossible. Darn, in front of the Kenbet this little rat might wriggle free of the charges, and it might be difficult for the judges to convict him.

Ameny steepled his hands. "Yes, you had to and should have trusted we'd protect you. That is, if you'd spoken the truth. However, it was a lie, wasn't it?" He looked at Setka like a cat playing with a rat.

"But it's true!" the hem-netjer shouted in agitation. "You must have found the poison."

"Oh, we certainly found it," Hori interrupted Ameny's interrogation. "Only we weren't looking for poison."

Setka swayed slightly, his eyes widening. "But…you did say…"

Senusret took over. "We already knew what killed the men and so do you. Otherwise you wouldn't have used the opportunity to blame your crimes on someone else who died because of your malicious action."

While his gaze darted here and there, Setka made a step back toward the door.

"Watch out, he's trying to get away!" Nakhtmin shouted and blocked his way.

Hori dashed to the door to the adjoining room and summoned the Medjay. "Quick, arrest him. We've got the villain!"

The two men stormed in and charged at Setka. Within moments they had his wrists tied behind his back. "In the name of the pharaoh, you are arrested."

"No!" Setka roared. "You must not do this! You have no idea who I am. My family will never tolerate something like this!" He kicked and writhed in the relentless clutches of the Medjay.

"Get him out of my sight," the king ordered.

The next morning, a messenger from the Great House called on Hori. "Come with me."

To his surprise, they weren't heading for the palace. When they approached the harbor district, it dawned on him where they were going, to the headquarter of the Medjay. An area he'd usually avoid. His mouth felt parched. Memories of the days when he was held there under the charge of murder were still too fresh. Today, Setka would probably be interrogated. Still hesitant, he forced his legs over the threshold. As much as he wanted to know if the hem-netjer confessed, he shied from watching the torture. The deaf flogger might not hear the screams of his victim, but Hori would.

The messenger took leave, and a Medjay led Hori to the interrogation rooms, where king, mer-ut and Ameny awaited him. He bowed and looked around in curiosity. In the middle of the room stood a wooden post. Didn't look like it served to hold up the ceiling. He swallowed.

"Ah, Hori, how fast are you with the stylus? We need a scribe to record the confession," the pharaoh said.

Of course, Thotnakht or any other royal scribe must not hear the secrets of the weryt. "Tolerable, I guess."

"That'll have to do," Hut-Nefer's voice droned from the mask.

Now he wondered who'd taken care of it when Nebkaura was interrogated. The mer-ut's eyesight wasn't the best anymore. He settled on the writing mat, took a sheet of papyrus and spread it over his taut shendyt.

There came the flogger with the prisoner, whose wrists he tied to two loops protruding from the post, so that the man stood with his back to them. Setka turned his head to face the interrogators, features tense. Yes, now you're afraid, Hori thought. Suited the presumptuous guy better than his usual arrogance.

The king started questioning him. "Did you give false testimony when you accused Hemiunu of poisoning four men?"

Curious, Hori listened for Setka's answer, albeit none came forth. The guy pressed his lips together as if to prevent even one word spilling out. Ameny cleared his throat ostentatiously and gave Hori a sign. By Thot, he had to take notes! Quickly he scribbled the sentence and looked up again.

That moment, the king signaled to the flogger, who swung his pliant crop at Setka's back. The prisoner's nostrils flared, his eyes sprung wide open, but no sound escaped his mouth. Only the fifth hit made him scream. At the sixth, his skin cracked, and blood flowed. Before the flogger could strike again, he gasped, "Yes, yes, I confess. It was so."

Senusret stopped his deaf assistant with a gesture. "What was so?"

"I wrote the letter accusing Hemiunu."

Hori's cane stylus flew.

King: "Did you also place the poison into the chest to substantiate your imputation?"

Accused nods.

King: "Say it!"

Accused: "I placed the castor beans into the chest."

King: "Why did you do it?"

Accused: "I hate Hemiunu. He was supposed to become fourth prophet, but I'm entitled to that position."

King: "What was your part in the other four deaths? Neb-Wenenef, Neferka, Sehetep and Bai?"

Accused: "No part at all. I swear by Maat!"

Hori glanced at him. Could that be true? He certainly wouldn't lie in his position, and definitely not swear a false oath by the goddess of justice. However, he had no idea what sentence Setka would get for the crime he'd already confessed. A flogging was one thing, but eternal damnation...

At Senusret's sign, the crop lashed Setka's back three times although he'd started begging for mercy after the second. Hori couldn't watch and fixed his gaze onto the papyrus.

Accused: "Stop, please stop, I'll tell you everything!"

King: "Did you force the hem-netjer to do your bidding? If so, how?"

Accused: "I caught him stealing something from the temple storerooms. Incense. When I searched him, I found, in addition to the stolen goods, a powerful conjuration, which I knew he'd never be allowed to possess. And the incense he needed for the ritual. I confiscated the text. From then on, Wenen had to do what I told him."

King: "Did you use the secret incantation to curse your competitors for the position of fourth prophet?"

Now Hori did look up again. This certainly interested him. He thought he caught a brief glimpse of cunning cross Setka's face.

Accused: "No, that would have been far too dangerous."

King: "So you coerced Wenen to do it for you?"

Accused: "I never demanded something like that from him. He must have thought to fulfill my wish by doing so."

King: "How could he have done so when the spell was in your possession?" King orders three more lashes.

Accused: "Yes, I told him to do so. Stop! Stop!"

King: "And the man readily agreed to commit the murders for you?"

Accused (snorts in disgust): "The coward! He only wanted to find the shadow of his father and guide him to his grave. For days, he balked. So I told him he'd only get the text back after he'd cursed the three. In addition, I threatened to summon a shadow to haunt him if he didn't do it. And in case he got some funny ideas like cursing me instead, I promised to return as a shadow and haunt him myself." He licked his lips.

King: "Why did you have these three men killed in such a dreadful manner? State your reasons."

Accused: "I'll tell you everything, have mercy! Sehetep had just been appointed as Djedefra's successor. He had to go. Neferka—Wenen was stupid enough to consult him with regard to some of the things in that conjuration. He grew too curious and had to go. Bai, the rat! He nosed around everywhere. He found out that I released the snake at Djedefra's threshold and wanted to extort favors from me. *Me*! He had to go. I did not have a hand in Wenen's death. I was there when he cursed himself, that dolt. I hotfooted it."

King: "I've heard enough. Based on your confession, you're charged with the following crimes: extortion, murder of the fourth prophets of Amun, Djedefra and Sehetep, as well as the hemu-netjer Neferka and Bai, false testimony against the head of the hemu-netjer, Hemiunu, which led to the man's death, foremost however, sacrilege against the gods."

Hori looked up. Yes, now the guy didn't grin anymore. But wait, was that spite on his face?

Accused: "That's a lie! I didn't do anything except a little extortion and giving false testimony. Wenen committed the murders."

King: "Keep silent! The wish of *your* heart caused all these crimes, yours alone."

He signaled to the flogger by lifting both hands and splaying all fingers. Ten lashes? Hori gulped and averted his gaze. Setka's back was already drenched in blood. Since the three men rose, Hori assumed the interrogation was over and jumped to his feet. For quite some time, Setka's screams echoed in his ears.

THE CURSE OF THE SHADOWS

Heri-renpet I, first leap day

"Have they been convicted yet?" Hori asked. After days without news from the palace or temple, Ameny had come to him and Nakhtmin today. They'd left Mutnofret in the company of her mother and retreated to Hori's estate.

Ameny shook his head. His face looked ashen and gaunt. "Won't take long now. Both men, Nebkaura and Setka, will face a tribunal of the gods."

He knew what that meant: the first prophets of the major gods of Kemet would decide together with the pharaoh how the evildoers would be punished. "Good."

"The verdict must conform them to the harshest punishment the law provides: burning alive. That's the only way to destroy all evil."

Hopefully that was the case. Last year those whose names must not be spoken had met the same fate, and it would put Hori's heart at ease if he knew their evil was purged by fire. When Nakhtmin had to take a leak, Hori asked Ameny, "Have the adepts arrived in the meantime?"

"Yes. Tomorrow, we will perform the ceremony. To do so, we'll have to cross the river to the Beautiful West."

Of course, where else but in the realm of the shadows. And court could convene right after the ritual since the adepts were also the first prophets. Hori would feel great relief to see the secret knowledge go up in flames together with Nebkaura and Setka.

Nakhtmin returned from the privy. "What are you talking about?"

"Death by fire awaits the two murderers," Ameny replied quickly, as if he didn't trust Hori to keep his mouth shut about the ritual tomorrow.

Fortunately, Nakhtmin didn't dig deeper, but asked something else, "I wonder why Wenen stole the incense. Nebkaura could have sold it to him."

"Maybe Wenen couldn't afford that after he'd traded all his goods for the incantation," Hori guessed. "Or he simply didn't know because the villain didn't offer any." Dear gods, what would happen to Wenen's corpse? He couldn't imagine that his body would be prepared for eternity at the weryt. More likely it would be burned with Nebkaura and Setka, and he'd share his father's fate. A nameless shadow... He'd better not mention any of this to Nakhtmin.

Ameny gestured impatiently. "Maybe, but this is idle thinking. From that moment, he was in Setka's clutches. When he finally tried to summon his father's shadow, something must have gone wrong."

"Bad conscience or guilt," Hori murmured. Even though the horrible events could never have happened without Wenen, the poor guy didn't mean to harm anyone. He could empathize with his despair although he deemed his actions foolish and irresponsible.

Ameny grimaced. "What struck me as most alarming during the interrogation was that Setka seriously believed he hadn't done anything he might be convicted of, because he never dirtied his own hands. The temple is bereft of its best men only because of the selfishness of that one priest! It will be tough to make up for the losses."

Hori heard voices and glanced toward the house. Usually his servants slept already at this time of night. "What's going on there?" he asked himself rather than Nakhtmin or Ameny and rose to check.

His servant Sheser came running toward him. "Master, a palace messenger. It's urgent. Physician Nakhtmin must come as well."

Was the ritual to be performed now? No, then the messenger would've asked for Ameny, not Nakhtmin. Oh, *physician* Nakhtmin—a medical matter. By the gods, the queen! With everything else going on, he'd almost forgotten about her. And they were both summoned? Then it really had to be serious this time. "Nakhtmin!" he roared into the garden. "Quick, to the palace."

Alongside his friend, Ameny came running.

The messenger stepped up to them and confirmed his fears. "The queen needs your help. It's the Horus in the egg."

"They want us both. Nakhtmin, get your stuff. Ameny, I'll see you tomorrow," Hori exclaimed.

While Nakhtmin dashed off, the prophet grabbed Hori's wrist. "Not that on top of everything else! I'll come with you."

Hori gave a quick nod. "Your help will be more than welcome. I'll pack my things; you tell Muti and Isis. We'll meet on the street."

Thanks to the messenger, they passed through the palace gates without bother and hurried to the House of Women. Even in the great hall with the swimming pool, Hori sensed that something was wrong. Too many concubines sat around for such a late hour, but the really eerie thing was that they were so silent. The door to the queens' chambers stood open; maids carrying jars of water and cloth hurried back and forth. The pieces they carried out were stained with blood. That looked really bad. He exchange a worried glance with Nakhtmin before entering Nofrethenut's room.

The queen arched under a contraction. A horrific scream poured from her throat. The royal midwives had already brought the birthing chair—no, that couldn't be happening. Far too early! The Horus in the egg couldn't survive yet... He stood paralyzed while Nakhtmin bent over Nofrethenut and examined her. The scream ended in gasps.

"Hori!" Nakhtmin called. "Come here and help me!" He waved some of the women surrounding the queen aside. "Give us some space!"

Blood, there was so much blood! When he stepped close, he felt like he saw the scene through the eyes of his ba floating above it all. Something dark enveloped the woman in labor...the wings of death? The next moment, the strange image vanished, and he stood at Nakhtmin's side. The queen's eyes pleaded with him to do something. But what? Help her save her child, which was beyond help? Then those eyes rolled up until only the whites showed, and a new contraction shook her, back arched high enough he could have slipped through under her swollen belly propped up in a grotesque fashion. Like an archway into the realm of the shadows...

Like Wenen...like Bai and the others. "No," he whispered. "That must not happen!" He looked to Ameny, who stood there and kneaded his shendyt in helplessness.

"You're just standing in my way," Nakhtmin scolded. "Go prepare a drink to stop the bleeding. And you, Ameny, call the gods' blessings onto her. We must fight for her majesty!"

Hori shook himself, and his numbness eased up a little. Walking outside, he pulled Ameny along and down the corridor until they left the wing of the queens. As the door of the herb chamber closed behind them, he hissed, "A shadow! I saw it! It has seized the queen."

"What are you saying?"

"Those cramps—same as with the others. Ameny, do something or else both are lost!"

The prophet shook his head in disbelief. "But how-? Dear gods, the heriu-renpet! The curse must be contained, and fast! During the leap days, the shadows, once summoned, can transcend the borders between this world and the hereafter. We have to perform the ritual now. I'll notify his majesty." He stormed out the door.

Hori's hands trembled. What a nightmare! Had he been afraid to attend the incantation before, the thought of performing it at night when the power of the shadows reached its peak paralyzed him. But he must not waver. The queen needed medicine or else she'd bleed to death—with or without ritual. He crushed dried leaves of the Nile acacia, sage and poppy seeds and soaked them in wine sweetened with honey. Nofrethenut's screams carried through the ventilation slits, which made him hurry even more. Ameny returned just when he'd finished the remedy. "Quick now. His majesty has sent for the adepts. As soon as the first prophet of Anubis has arrived, we need to set out."

How fortunate that everyone had reached the residence already! He didn't dare to think what unimaginable horrors might befall them otherwise. "I'll get this to Nakhtmin and let him know." He hastened back to Nofrethenut's bedchamber.

The women had heaved the queen onto the birthing chair since the contractions came in short intervals now. The silvery shine of her hair drenched in sweat was not only due to the light reflected in it. White strands were among the short, black curls.

"Hori, finally!" Kneeling before the queen, Nakhtmin wiped sweat from his forehead and rose.

Hori handed him the jug, and he sniffed and nodded. "Good, give her some."

He squirmed. "Listen, I've got to leave. You'll have to fight this battle on your own."

Nakhtmin stared at him in shock. "Have you lost your mind?" he shouted and drew curious gazes from some of the women.

Hori took him aside and whispered. "It has to be. Don't you see it? She too suffers the curse of the shadows. Wenen's incantation has lured them, and on the leap days they can cross the river."

Nakhtmin's eyes widened. His head jerked around, and then he too noticed the white strands. "Dear gods!"

"Shhh. The king, Ameny, I and…a few more people have to…by the gods, I must not tell you!"

This one time, he asked no questions and didn't sulk. "It's all right. Go."

To Hori's astonishment, Ameny didn't lead him to the royal jetty. Oh, right, they had to go to the Beautiful West! He shuddered. At the riverbank, several people had gathered already, some of them women but mostly men, of whom he only recognized the pharaoh and the unmistakable jackal mask of Hut-Nefer. They all wore bracelets on their left upper arms: the adepts.

When Senusret spotted him, he rushed to his side and grabbed his shoulder. "How are they?" Worry was etched into his face.

Hori couldn't hold his gaze. "The Horus in the egg won't live. Nakhtmin is still fighting for your wife's life. I'm so sorry…"

The king sighed, then said, "Against these forces, all physicians of the Two Lands are powerless. I don't blame you or Nakhtmin. Maybe we can stop the curse before it takes…" His voice cracked since deep down, even the pharaoh was only a loving husband. "Are you pure?"

Hori nodded. He'd performed the prescribed cleansing in the evening and also shaved his head to be prepared. Fortunately, he hadn't touched Nofrethenut's expulsions.

"Good. Let's hurry."

One prophet after the other boarded one of the two boats. When the first was full, it departed under strong strokes of the oars—one of the speed boats. "How far is it?"

Hut-Nefer joined him. "You know the place since you've been taken there before."

The Osiris sanctum where he'd been initiated! All too well did he remember the potency of that place. Hopefully, their efforts would succeed there. "Is there anything I need to know?" he asked. "An incantation or spell?" He climbed over the second vessel's side and held out his hand to Hut-Nefer. They were the last to sit down. The seamen set the sails and took their seats at the oars, and the boat sped into the darkness.

"You'll have everything you need when the time comes."

How, Hori wondered, but he knew the old man well enough. He wouldn't learn more right now, so he had to trust his judgment. He felt the air stream past his face. What amazing speed! He'd never traveled so fast before. "How long can they keep up the momentum?" he asked. The sail billowed in the strong northern wind. Shu, the god of the air, was with them.

"As long as necessary. It's not far."

They headed south, maybe for Nen-nesu and its prominent Osiris temple. That would be more than three iteru, quite a distance even at this speed, and they were running out of time. "The shadows," he blurted. "Did you know this would happen?"

"Mh," he grumbled through the mask. "I guessed, feared, didn't know. There are no records of anything like this ever happening. These past days, I studied the scrolls in the library intensely. Your friend Wenen would have brought on disaster for the inhabitants of the residence even if he'd done everything right. Unfortunately, he made the mistake to call the shadows of the damned when he meant to summon the ghost of his father. I sensed them. Oh, those shadows have been lurking for a long time! I hear them in the wind howling from the mountains. I see them in the dark crevices. I feel them on my skin when I leave the walls of the weryt."

Hori shivered and made the gesture to fend off evil. The damned—among them, the two whose names must not be spoken. "Do the shadows remember those they knew when they were still alive? I mean…could one of them try to take revenge for a perceived injustice?" A drop of Nile water splashed from an oar onto his face, and he wiped it away.

"Definitely. When the body's destroyed, shadow and ba stray aimlessly. They are confused and search for their home, but the shadow also contains the dark side of a soul and knows everything the living person once knew and felt."

Just great! Hori didn't want to imagine how gloomy the dark side of that woman without name might be. She'd been malignant enough while still alive. "Can the shadows be eradicated? Is there a way?"

"That's what we'll have to do: deliver them to the devourer of shadows so that the evil spirits will be destroyed forever."

Why hadn't that been done right away? Why did the mer-ut allow something so dreadful to happen? Before he could ask, the old man answered the question.

"The rite poses great danger for those performing it. Furthermore, innocent shadows might get devoured if their bodies had not been properly buried."

"Like that of Wenen's father! Could his plan have worked, could he have led the shadow to the empty grave he'd had erected for his father?"

"Probably not. Without body, a shadow remains a lost soul."

Hori leaned back and watched the silhouettes of vegetation and occasional habitations on the riverbank slide by. Barely a light could be seen except for those in the sky. Behind a river bend, he detected torches on the western bank. They reflected on the water, and the oarsmen headed toward them. Osiris was the king of the realm of the dead, and therefore his temple was in the Beautiful West, over which he ruled.

One after the other, the passengers alighted. Did they feel as uneasy as he did? Hori wished himself far away to the world of living light. Here was only the harrowing silence of the lurking shadows. Unbearable appeared the darkness to him, like a firm wall with nothing but blackness behind it.

In silence, the procession marched through the pylon and crossed a dark courtyard with torches mounted to walls they couldn't illuminate. Then they entered a brightly lit chamber inside the temple. On long shelves lay the regalia and masks of the deities whom the prophets would represent today. One after the other took what belonged to him or her and transformed before Hori's eyes. Only the king and he remained who they were. Fear clutched Hori's throat. He too would have loved to seek shelter behind the power of a god, but that was denied to him. Why did he have to be here anyway? He asked Ameny, who already balanced the large two-feather crown on his head.

"The secret is shared with each adept, therefore all adepts must gather to recreate it in its completeness," Amun said.

Of course! Last but not least, they all removed their bracelets and exposed the signs of life. Leaving the room, each took a sip from a goblet Anubis handed to them. Hori tried to taste what the liquid contained but failed. An intoxicant that opened the hearts to the worlds of myth?

Single file, the adepts descended stairs leading to a room illuminated by wall-mounted torches. In its center rose a low underground burial mound—the grave of Osiris! The adepts formed a circle around it and held hands. At the head, the prophets of Osiris and Anubis took position. Hori stood pretty much across from them, while Senusret stood next to the king of the underworld.

"Osiris, Osiris, Osiris!" chanted the gods, and Hori joined in. Three times they sang, then fell silent.

"Worship to you, Osiris, divine master of eternity, sublime god, judge of all things, beautiful to the eye," Anubis intoned.

"Anubis, keeper of the gates, guide of the souls, take the shadows from my ba!" Osiris called. "Black jackal, escort my soul over the threshold and through the gates protected by ghosts and powerful magic. Anubis, opener of gates, purge my senses, free my heart from shadows, guide me to the light of my soul!"

Then Anubis recited an incantation in a language Hori didn't understand. Ancient and gloomy the words sounded to him. He shivered. Had it grown colder? The goddess by his side—the prophet of Bastet—gripped his hand firmly. Strange, but it consoled him that she too felt anxious. Still the jackal god spoke sentences, louder now, more urgent. Their power dimmed the light as if darkness expanded and crowded it out. Hori felt dizzy, and the room seemed to spin around him.

All of a sudden he believed he saw the darkness concentrate in one spot and take on shape. He blinked and the apparition disappeared. Only his imagination? No. More and more shadowy blurs bustled within the circle of adepts. At the feet of Anubis, an abyss had opened, and from it emanated horrible noises, like from a cross-breed of snake and crocodile. Anubis stretched out his hand and thus beckoned one of the shadows, which took on the shape of a man. "Shadow without body, you're nothing. You don't exist in this world, nor in the afterworld. Begone! The devourer of shadows awaits you."

"Am-shut, Am-shut, Am-shut!" the gods chanted and Hori, too. Did they really utter the words or did they simply resound in his heart?

Hori barely trusted his eyes. It looked like the shadow was sucked into the abyss while releasing a horrific scream curdling the juices in Hori's metu. Then it was gone.

Anubis summoned the next shadow in the shape of a woman and repeated the words until she too departed. One shut after the other fell prey to the devourer and was annihilated until only one remained. When it took form, Hori recognized the figure of a woman.

"Shadow without body, you're nothing. You don't exist in this world, nor in the afterworld. Begone! The devourer of shadows awaits you."

"Am-shut, Am-shut, Am-shut!"

The shadow shape laughed. "You can't destroy me, Anubis, because I know my name. United with my ba, I've only begun to take revenge. A son for a son. A son for a son. A son for a son. I'm not done yet!"

A cold shiver crawled down Hori's back. Anubis's body tensed. He lifted his was-scepter and thundered, "Oh ghost, shadow, arcane, hidden, who was once in the flesh. See here, I've brought you excrement to eat."

Osiris handed the jackal-headed one a bowl of excrement. The shadow retreated, searched for an escape route but couldn't leave the circle. All of a sudden, the shape was right before Hori and again released that dreadful disembodied laughter! Oh, no, what happened to him? The shadow penetrated him, flooded him. His heart darkened as if there was neither light nor joy in the world...

"Beware, hidden one, take care, lurking one, relinquish the bodies of the living! Ki-ki-ki-mi-na-ja-ti. Instead, enter me, Anubis, keeper of the gates, to become an akh and experience the power!"

Hori felt as if he were ripped apart. Something dragged and tore at him, and if the gods to his left and right weren't holding him, he'd flow with the dark specter to the jackal-headed and the abyss gaping at his feet. Then it ended and the shadow took form again.

Anubis thrust the excrement at it. The dark one charged and tried to enter the jackal god, but the power of the scepter kept it at bay. The shut screamed in rage as it slid down the smooth staff when Anubis lowered it toward the relentlessly sucking abyss. Albeit it could neither disengage nor prevent its inevitable obliteration. With a last bone-chilling howl the malicious shadow disappeared.

Anubis tapped the floor with his scepter, and the gaping hole closed. At once the room grew warmer and the torches managed to glow brighter again. Hori's hands were slick with sweat, but he didn't dare to loosen his grip and break the circle of the adepts.

"Anubis, who overlooks the necropolises from his mountain. You freed my ba of dark shadows," Osiris sang.

"Anubis, Anubis, Anubis!" the other gods chanted and bowed to the ruler of the underworld and his crown prince.

Together, Osiris and Anubis lifted the ankh sign of life, and the ceremony ended.

When Bastet let go of his Hand, Hori crumpled to the floor. His legs didn't follow his command anymore, then his senses dimmed.

Smeared with blood and birth fluid, the Horus slid into Nakhtmin's reaching hands. Bent and tiny, he fit on his palm. This falcon would never spread its wings and fly since the umbilical cord lay around his neck like a noose. Nakhtmin cut it and placed the corpse into a basket padded with the finest linen. Instead of beginning his life, his journey would only lead to the realm of the dead. Nakhtmin forced himself to shake off his grief. He could still fight for Nofrethenut. Again he gave her some of the potion to stop the bleeding, while the midwife massaged the queen's womb to speed up the release of the afterbirth. A short time later, Nofrethenut squeezed out the bloody chunk between her thighs. How she did that was a mystery to him because she'd been unconscious for quite a while now. With her eyes rolled back, she dwelt in a different, dark world, like the other victims of the curse had. Nakhtmin carried her back to the bed, then hurried to the herb chamber to crush more poppy seeds. If nothing else, he wanted to spare her majesty the horrors of the last moments, which Wenen, Sehetep and Neferka had suffered.

In the chamber, he realized to his surprise that a new day dawned. It didn't seem right for the sun to shine when the shadows ruled over the residence. Or was there hope still? The potion was done and he ran back.

Women surrounded the queen's bed. Maids, midwives, all bustled about the patient, even the Great Royal Wife and queen mother Weret, who he'd sent away as a precaution lest the malicious shadow attack them as well.

"What's going on here?" he called.

A midwife turned around to him. "Just look!" she exclaimed and stepped aside.

Nakhtmin didn't trust his eyes. Nofrethenut sat upright among the pillows, eyes open, skin pale but not ashen like a moment ago. Tears streamed down her cheeks. "My son! Where's my son?" she cried out to him.

Nakhtmin set the jug down and waved the maids away. "Your majesty, the Horus in the egg has begun his journey to the Beautiful West."

Queen Sherit embraced the young woman, and together they mourned for the dead child. Nakhtmin, however, rejoiced so much in the unexpected improvement of his patient; he wanted to break out in cheers. Was her recovery owed to whatever Hori and Ameny left for? It certainly looked like they succeeded. "Thank you, gods!" he whispered.

A maid entered and headed to him. "Nakhtmin, there's a messenger outside, asking for you."

A messenger? Probably sent by the king, who wanted to know how things stood. Nakhtmin quickly gave instructions, but he'd better take the potion he'd just prepared with him. Weak as Nofrethenut was, the strong drug might kill her if someone accidentally gave it to her.

At the gate of the House of Women no royal herald awaited him but Inti. "Master, something terrible has happened... Come quick!"

Nakhtmin's hand clutched the doorpost. "Muti?" His servant nodded, and he wanted to dash to her, but his legs refused to move. The jug slid from his hand and shattered. Red as blood, the wine poured onto the floor. Paralyzed, he stood torn between worry and duty. "The queen-"

The guard at the gate grumbled, "You go, I'll tell them to send for another doctor."

And his feet grew wings. He couldn't think of anything but the horror he'd just lived through. Please, great Taweret, tutelary goddess of childbirth, don't let her suffer the same, he pleaded silently, while his sandals rhythmically pounded the mud road. In his heart, though, he knew it was happening. Tears blurred his vision.

He found his beloved pale but conscious and responsive. Her mother was with her, as well as the midwife Geheset. He rushed to Muti's bed, unable to squeeze out a word. Nobody needed to tell him what had happened. Among Muti's dark hair, a white strand shone forth.

When Hori came to, he sensed gentle rocking. Where was he? On the primordial water Nun, from which everything came forth? He opened his eyes and gazed into a gorgeous sunrise and—the king's face! Senusret sat beside him. Hori studied the harsh contours of his face. Fear and lack of sleep made it look more worn out and worried than ever. Someone squeezed his hand. Anubis, he wanted to say, but no sounds came from his mouth. He sat up, and Ameny smiled at him.

How'd he get on the bark? They must have carried him. No one aboard spoke, not even the oarsmen. Likely they all felt the same trepidation, which still clutched Hori's heart. What a harrowing sensation when the shadow possessed him! As if he'd been thrust to the horrors of the Duat. Had Wenen and the others undergone the same, and for hours? He couldn't have borne it a moment longer, and he hadn't even been fully in the shadow's power.

Gradually, the words of the dark shape returned to him—had he felt them in his heart, or had everyone heard them? What did she mean: a son for a son for a son for a son? Goosebumps popped up on his skin, and he glanced at Hut-Nefer, who put a finger to the jackal snout. Silence. Yes, that was for the best. Hori closed his eyes and dozed until the slowing strokes of oars announced they approached their destination.

The palace still cast a shadow onto the royal pier when they tied up the boat. The other one followed right behind them, and two servants hurried over to give the alighting passengers a helping hand. Thus, king and prophets stepped onto firm ground in a dignified manner. Without their help, Hori wouldn't even have gotten on his feet, wobbly as his legs felt. The pharaoh was the first to speak and only to order palanquins, for Hori as well, which he truly appreciated. Before they went separate ways, each of them placed a finger to his lips. Hori understood. Never must they talk about what happened tonight. He certainly didn't feel like reliving things by talking about them although many questions pressed on his heart. Some things were too horrific for mere mortals.

On legs that felt like sticks of wood, he crossed the front yard to his estate when he heard running feet behind him and turned around. One of the gardeners...Mesu, right. The boy who wanted to marry Heqet.

"Master, come quick, Heqet! She's bleeding."

A miscarriage? Well, that happened fairly often and was usually no cause for worry, but the guy looked white as chalk. Maybe the little maid was in danger, his playmate of lonely nights. He took a deep breath. "I'll check on her," he said although he wanted nothing more than to sleep and forget. What a night!

In Heqet's room he found not only an old woman, probably a midwife, but also Baketamun, Nakhtmin's cook. The woman made room for him and he stepped closer. The girl was as pale as the linen around her, but what really shocked him were the white strands in her hair.

"What is it with you physicians?" the crone bleated. "If you're needed in your own home, you're never available."

That jerked him out of his stupor. "What are you talking about? And where's Nakhtmin? If Heqet's condition is serious, why didn't you call him?" That moment he remembered that his friend probably hadn't left the queen's side even if there was no hope left for the Horus in the egg.

Baketamun sobbed. "What a disaster! My mistress lost her little one as well. A boy."

"Your mistress? Mutnofret?" And then Hori understood. She whose name must not be spoken—she had three sons. One of them he killed, the others turned away from her and cursed her memory. A son for a son for a son for a son. He sank onto a stool and buried his face in his hands. What unrelenting depravity! The final horrifying scream of the shadow reverberated in his ears, but now the memory filled him with satisfaction and relief.

Epilogue

Day 5 of month Wepet-renpet in Akhet, the season of the inundation

Hori studied his reflection in the mirror and touched the spot on his scalp where white stubble grew, a permanent reminder of the night of horror. But that lay behind him, behind all of them. The queen as well as Muti and Heqet had recovered from their miscarriages thanks to the powerful conjuration by Anubis. However, being possessed by the vengeful shadow had left traces on them all, and not only on the surface.

Occasionally, he imagined he saw the abyss before him and sensed the darkness touching his heart. At night, he jerked awake from horrendous dreams. Losing his heir had hit the king as hard as his wife, but at least he didn't have to physically experience that horror. Senusret planned to send Nofrethenut to their estate in the delta for recuperation. Hori hoped with all his heart the change of scenery would help to heal her majesty's wounds. Heqet too had changed. She'd quickly grasped that he had something to do with what happened to her, and that made her feel bitter toward him. Actually, that wasn't such a bad thing because when her heart closed to him, it could open to Mesu. To somewhat ease the heavy burden of his guilt, Hori wanted to keep his promise and buy them a house even though he wasn't obliged anymore.

He left his abode and strolled into his garden. Nakhtmin joined him. "Now that the king has granted us some free time, I'm considering taking Muti on a journey, maybe heading south to Khent-min. What do you think?"

"Excellent idea!" Like Nakhtmin, he worried about Mutnofret's emotional state since all cheerfulness seemed to have abandoned her. Naturally, he could empathize, but he had the advantage of understanding what happened, while she must feel like a random victim of terrible forces. He couldn't imagine what fears his two friends would have to live through when she got pregnant again. If only he were allowed to explain what happened and that the danger has been banished, forever…

"Will you accompany us to Ameny tonight?" Nakhtmin asked. "He promised to tell me how things are at the temple, and I guess that interests you, too."

Hori nodded. "Sure."

When the women retreated after the meal, the men sat under the canopy of stars and enjoyed the silence for a moment. Then Ameny cleared his throat. "As you know, the temple of Amun has suffered some hard blows. Therefore, his majesty and I decided that the king alone should fill the positions of prophets anew—that includes mine." He paused.

Hori gulped. Ameny wanted to withdraw from office? Of course, in the end, the pharaoh always appointed his representatives in the temples of the Two Lands, but it had been common practice for a long time that the prophets succeeded each other. Did they abandon that custom now to avoid further scheming of ambitious priests? Soon Iriamun would be buried, and then the most powerful temple of the Two Lands needed new leadership. Hori peered at Nakhtmin, who looked just as baffled and shocked.

"Albeit the king assured me he couldn't wish for a better first prophet than me." Ameny smiled mischievously, having tricked them both. "However, I won't have to worry about the succession of the other prophets any longer. His majesty will decide. All hemu-netjer of Amun who have reached the highest order will assemble in the residence in a few days, so he can form his own opinions about suitable candidates. Oh, by the way, Hori, you remember that I ordered the temple to be searched?"

Surprised, Hori wondered where this would lead since everything had been resolved. "Yes?" he answered hesitantly.

"The Medjay also rummaged through the premises of the House of Life, and when I inspected the scripts they found there, I came across this document." He pulled a papyrus from the waistband of his shendyt

Hori unfolded the squashed scroll and moved closer to a torch. A letter from the head of physicians in Waset to Imhotepankh. Why should that concern him? Then he spotted the name Ouseret, and his heart skipped a beat. Imhotepankh had requested information about the female doctor from his colleague and thus learned her father was also a physician and had just been charged with and convicted of medical malpractice, which caused the death of a patient. So that was the reason why the old man had sent off his beloved. He clenched his fists. That explained a lot, though not everything. "Nakhtmin, I think a little journey would do me well too," he said. "You and Muti surely wouldn't mind if I tagged along, would you?"

Appendix ~ Egyptian Deities

Amun – *the hidden one*. Originally the local god of Waset (Thebes), he gained importance when the city became the capital of the 11th dynasty. First he was the god of wind and fertility, displayed as a human with a feather crown. Since the ram was his holy animal, he was also depicted as a ram-headed god. Later the deity merged with other gods of the Egyptian pantheon (syncretism). As Amun-Ra, he incorporated the characteristics of Amun, Ra and Min.

Anubis – *the crown prince*. Jackal-headed god performing the rituals for the dead. He has special significance at the Judgment of the Dead when the hearts of the deceased were placed on scales and weighed against the feather of goddess Maat. This procedure assumes good deeds make the heart lighter, while bad deeds literally burden it. The dead recite all the things they did not do in their lifetime, for example lying, stealing, killing. If the scales tipped to the side of the heart, it was fed to the devourer. Since the Egyptians thought mind and memory resided in the heart, this meant a second and ultimate death. If the deceased passed the test, they were granted eternal life in the underworld.

Apis – Holy bull of god Ptah in Men-Nefer. The Apis was a black bull with a triangular blaze on its forehead and a crescent white spot on his right side. An independent cult developed around the animal, and he was mummified after death.

Horus – *the distant one, who is above*. Falcon-headed god of the sky, mythical son of Isis, who conceived him when she transformed into a sparrow hawk and mated with the mummy of her husband Osiris. Horus was one of the most important deities of the Egyptian pantheon and strongly associated with the kingdom.

Isis – *seat, throne*. Mother of Horus and sister as well as wife of Osiris. She was patroness of mothers and lovers and depicted in human form with a throne on her head.

Maat – *justice, truth, world order*. Maat is a concept rather than a goddess. The word's meaning is a mix of justice, order and truth and signifies the ideal course of the world, where the sun rises every day anew and people treat each other fairly. The feather was her symbol, which she wore on her head as human-shaped goddess.

Min – God of procreation and fertility, who was always depicted in human shape with an erect penis. He was also called Min-Kamutef, bull of his mother, which refers to the insemination of his divine mother. Min is father and son at the same time; he can create himself.

Monthu – Falcon-headed god. Originally, he was the main god of Waset (Thebes) before Amun surpassed him in significance. As the god of war and protector of weapons he was particularly worshiped in the 11th dynasty, which also influenced the names of pharaohs.

Nut – Goddess of the sky. Egyptians imagined Nut arching her body over the earth represented by the god Geb. Every evening, she swallowed the sun, which then traveled through her body to be reborn from her womb in the morning.

Osiris – *seat of the eye.* The god of the dead, depicted as a mummy with a feather crown. According to legend, Osiris was murdered by his brother Seth, who begrudged him his throne as ruler of the world. Additionally, he chopped up the corpse and spread the parts all over the earth. Osiris's sister and wife Isis succeeded in finding all parts, and reassembled them. She reanimated the corpse and conceived their son Horus. From then on, Osiris ruled over the underworld and was depicted as a mummy. Abydos (Abdju) was the sacred place of this deity, and pharaohs as well as common people wanted to be buried there—if only in the form of a cenotaph, an additional, empty tomb. The myth of Isis and Osiris meant a lot to Egyptians.

Ptah – Human-shaped primary god of Men-Nefer, the patron of craftsmen and creator god. He took part in the ritual of mouth opening and was depicted as a mummy.

Ra – or Re. Sun god and father of all gods. The cult of the god, worshiped in On (Heliopolis), was strongly associated with the kingdom. The solar disk adorns this human-shaped god.

Sekhmet – *the powerful.* The lion-headed goddess was responsible for war, diseases and epidemics but also for healing.

Seth – *creator of confusion.* God with the head of a fabulous creature, brother of Osiris. He's regarded as the god of the desert and all foreign lands, of evil and violence, but also as patron of the oases, god of metals and god of the dead, who picks up the deceased.

Shu – *emptiness.* God of air and sunlight, father of Nut and Geb, as well as heaven and earth. The Egyptians viewed the sky as an ocean, and Shu was responsible for keeping it away from the earth, so people could breathe. He was often depicted as kneeling on the earth and pushing up the sky.

Sobek – Crocodile-headed god of water and fertility.

Thot – God of the moon, magic and knowledge. The Egyptians believed Thot had brought them scripture. He was depicted as ibis or baboon.

Appendix ~ Places and Regions

Abydos (Abdju) – The city of Osiris, the god of the dead, was located on the western shore of the Nile, about 100 miles north of ancient Thebes. In addition to the pharaohs of the first dynasties, many Egyptians arranged for their burial there or at least had a stele, a stone slab with inscriptions or reliefs, set up to become part of the resurrection ritual of god Osiris.

Khent-min – Today Akhmim, was about 125 miles north of Thebes and the main cult site of the god Min.

Itj-tawy – *encompassing the Two Lands* – Amenemhet I erected the city between the delta and Upper Egypt. The exact location is still unknown, but most likely it was close to the necropolis El-Lisht, where the first two kings of the 12th dynasty were entombed.

Kemet – *the black*. That's what Egyptians called their country.

Kush – or Nubia, the land south of Egypt (today Sudan). The territory starting at the first cataract (granite barriers in the Nile) was called Kush. Because of its rich gold deposits, the pharaohs undertook many expeditions and military campaigns into the southern neighbor's country.

Men-nefer (Memphis) – also called Inbu Hedj, the white walls. With a strategic position at the Balance of the Two Lands, Men-nefer was the capital of Egypt during the Old Kingdom. At the Sed festival run, the pharaohs had to circle the white fortification walls and thus prove their strength. Throughout Egyptian history, the city played an important part, among other things, as cult site of several important gods.

Sekhet-hemat – *salt field*. Today the wadi Natrun, a group of oases west of the delta with extensive salt fields, which were already exploited in the time of pharaohs.

Waset – (Thebes, today Karnak/Luxor) The capital of the 4th Upper Egyptian nome gained major importance when it became capital of the Two Lands during several periods of the Middle and New Kingdoms.

Appendix ~ Glossary

Akh – The transfigured, an ancestor's spirit, the part of the human soul created after death. Ba and ka are part of the soul while a human being is alive. At death, they leave the body. When they return to it, they merge and create the third component of the human soul, the akh. Nevertheless, they still exist individually. The akh, the spirit soul, ascends to the sky and turns into a star. Together with the sun god, it travels through the underworld. The akh is as good or evil as the deceased had been while still alive. It can influence the world of the living and harm these. Therefore criminals were denied a proper funeral to prevent their components of the soul creating an akh.

Ba – The ba is also called the excursion soul or free soul of the Egyptians. It's the part of the soul depicted as a bird with a human head. During life, it's confined to the body, but when death occurs, it can separate from the body and fly around. However, it stays connected to the body and unites with it from time to time. The Egyptians believed the ba could be caught, injured and even killed.

Khet – The body which turns into a sah, the mummy. Only in this form, the body could harbor the components of the soul after death.

Deben – Ancient Egyptian weight unit, its value varying in the Middle Kingdom. A copper deben was twice as heavy as one of gold. Besides barter trade, these pieces of precious metal served as a means of payment and for determining the value of goods. Deben were shaped in bars or rings, which allowed one to break off smaller bits.

Decade day – Tenth day of the week. Egyptian months consisted of thirty days split into three weeks of ten days each. On the last day of the week people had off from work. Additionally, work ceased on important religious holidays.

Dung beetle – Sobriquet of the scarab, which was worshipped as scarabaeus sacer under the name Kheper. It symbolized reincarnation since the beetle seemed to recreate itself from its excrement, and also represented the sun on its recurring journey across the sky.

Duat – Name of the netherworld. It consisted of the subterranean region and the celestial realm named Aaru. The two touched each other at the horizon. While the dead had to face various horrors in the underworld and needed to pass their judgment, they could reach the heavenly realm of Aaru afterward and enjoy a kind of paradise. Unlike in the garden of Eden, they had to work, though, farming the fields among other things. To avoid manual labor, Egyptians had little figurines called ushabti entombed with them. These 'answerers' were to jump to work in their master's stead at the gods' summons.

Eye of Horus – Symbol of the god Horus. In their fight over the throne of Osiris, Seth ripped out his nephew Horus's left eye. The god Thot healed it, and since then it symbolizes medicine. In addition, mathematical fractions were based on the proportions of the eye, and these ratios were used for dosing the ingredients of remedies. Painted onto the hull of a boat, the eye was supposed to protect against dangers lurking in the water.

False door – An element of Egyptian graves that looked like a door. They were either a relief or painted on and allowed the ka soul of the deceased to leave the tomb.

Going of the heart – Egyptian expression for the pulse, which they believed were caused by air and the life energy of a human being.

Great House – In ancient Egyptian, pr-aa referred to the seat of the king. In Greek times, the term became synonymous to the king, who from then on was called pharaoh.

Hem-netjer/hemu-netjer – Priest/priests. This group of priests ranged above the wabu and was divided in orders of initiation. From the highest order of priests, the hemu-netjer-tepi, the prophets of the gods, were selected.

Heri-heb/heriu-heb – Lector priest/lector priests. High-ranking priests who played an important role during mummification and funerals since they recited ritual texts, litanies and songs.

Hin – Egyptian measure of capacity equal to about 17 ounces.

House of Life – One might call it a kind of university, where the higher professions like scribes, physicians, artists and priests were educated. It also provided rooms to cure the sick as a sort of walk-in clinic.

Ib – The heart. The Egyptians didn't realize what function the brain has and considered it useless. The seat of reason and soul they assumed to be the heart, which in consequence played a major role in the cult of the dead.

Ibu – Place of purification. First stop for the deceased in the embalming process. There's no archeological evidence for these constructions. Judging by the few surviving paintings, they were made of light wood and mats.

Imi-Ra – Head of a profession.

Inundation – The Egyptians counted years by inundations since the Nile floods were a yearly recurring event and therefore offered a fixed time frame. To specify a particular year, the regency of the king was given (year 3 of Amenemhat).

Iteru – Egyptian measure of length equal to about 6.5 miles.

Ka – A part of the soul. The ka leaves the body of the dying and continues to exist independently. As a double of the deceased, it serves as its guardian spirit. It inhabits a statue erected specifically for it in the tomb of the dead and feeds on the sacrifices placed before the statue.

Kenbet – Board of judges, which consists of dignitaries with jurisdiction over property claims and crimes. Besides these local courts, there was the Great Kenbet with the vizier and the pharaoh as chairmen.

Mastaba – Arabic word for bench. The kings of the first dynasties established the tradition to erect these large structures as their tombs in Sakkara. Starting with Djoser, pharaohs chose pyramids as their burial chambers. Until the Middle Kingdom, officials and noble people were entombed in these so-called bench graves, which were rectangular structures built with adobe or stone. Inside lay the dead. During the New Kingdom, graves were dug into rock, likely because then they couldn't be robbed so easily.

Medjay – Law enforcement, mercenary soldiers from Kush or the desert tribes.

Mer-ut – Head of the embalmers.

Metu – *Vessels*. The Egyptians believed the body to contain tubes, the metu, which transported blood, water and air from the heart, the central organ, to all other organs. They imagined it in analogy to the Nile with its web of channels to water the fields. The metu were also responsible for the disposal of excrement: mucus, feces, semen, urine. It was important for those canals to not clog up and form a 'sand bank' so that all juices could flow unhindered. This is why Egyptians had regular enemas to cleanse the metu. At the same time, floodings of the organs, for example with blood, were deemed unhealthy.

Middle Kingdom – After the First Intermediate Period, the family of the nomarchs of Waset asserted itself under the rule of Mentuhotep II, and unified the torn country. During the Middle Kingdom, Egyptian culture blossomed. Most works of literature, which survived, were written in that period.

Necropolis – City of the dead.

Neshmet bark – Festival bark of Osiris. In its cabin, the god journeyed to the yearly poker feast from his grave in the temple of Abdju to be reborn. Deceased Egyptians were transported to the embalming compound in an imitation of this bark so they could join Osiris in his resurrection.

Nome – Administrative division in ancient Egypt. There were 22 nomes in Upper Egypt and 20 in Lower Egypt, which were ruled by nomarchs. Their borders probably derived from former tribal territories of prehistoric times. The nomarchs were responsible for law enforcement and tax collection but in a fairly autonomous way. In the course of history, whenever the central power weakened, some nomarchs expanded their fiefdoms and tried to usurp power.

Poker feast – Annual festival of Osiris in Abdju. The god's statue was taken onto the Neshmet bark and traveled from the temple grave of Osiris to his divine birthplace (today Umm el-Qa'ab) to return reborn.

Pylon – Large gateway made of stone, built in front of temples.

Ren – The name. It was absolutely important for the afterlife because without the name, the various aspects of the soul couldn't find their way back to the corpse.

Sedge and the Bee – (Nesw Bity) Part of a pharaoh's title. The bee symbolized Lower Egypt, the sedge Upper Egypt. A pharaoh had five different names in total. The nesw bity name was the throne name a pharaoh chose in addition to his birth name. Another name, the nebty name (the two mistresses) also showed the dualistic attitude of the Egyptians: the vulture goddess Nekhbet represents Upper Egypt and the snake goddess Wadjet Lower Egypt. Both animals adorned the pharaoh's crown to protect the king. Additionally, the king chose a Horus name and Golden name.

Shut – Shadow. Each living being casts a shadow, and thus it is proof of a physical existence. The Egyptians believed it also contained part of a human existence. After death the shadow disengaged from the body, but usually returned to it. If the mummy was destroyed or the body never mummified, the shadow strayed freely and could cause harm to the living.

Senet – A board game depicted in numerous murals since the first dynasties. Two players tried to place their pawns on a certain field on a board of thirty squares.

The Romans adopted the game. It might be a precursor of backgammon.

Strong bull – The king was often equated with a bull since the animal represented virility, power and strength.

Sunu/Sunut – Male/female physician. Even women could become doctors but seldom trained in that profession.

Sycamore – also called sycamore fig or mulberry fig. With its protruding canopy, the tree made for an ideal shade dispenser in Egypt, where few deciduous trees prospered. Many parts of the sycamore were used as food or cures, and in Mennefer (Memphis) a holy sycamore was worshiped as embodiment of the goddess Hathor.

The Two Lands – Upper and Lower Egypt. Even in prehistoric times, the fertile Nile valley had been a popular place for different cultures to settle. The population of the marshy delta in Lower Egypt had been a different one than that of Upper Egypt. The mythical king Menes, however, managed to unite the two kingdoms. For Egyptians, this event retained immense significance throughout history. Their language reflects the duality in many ways as a consequence of previous individuality. Particularly in imagery, the unification was symbolically reenacted over and over again.

Tjati – vizier.

Udjat eye – see Eye of Horus.

Ushabti – *Answerer*. Figurines in human shape made of clay, wax, wood or stone, often varnished or painted green with inscriptions and the name of the deceased they were to represent. They were placed into the graves since Egyptians believed the heavenly fields needed to be farmed, and the gods might call the transfigured to any other tasks. Should this happen, the answerer figurines were supposed to jump up and shout, "Here I am and will go wherever you order me!" Then they'd take care of any work deemed too menial for dignitaries.

Ut/Utu – Embalmer. Little is known about this professional group, neither where nor how they lived. Presumably, the art of embalming was so secret that hardly any information was passed on. The sparse knowledge mostly stems from Greek authors of the Late Period, who had their own particular view of a culture so strange to them.

Wab priest – The wab priests were the largest group within the priesthood of a temple. They ranked below the prophets in the temple hierarchy and took care of a major part of the daily offering services.

Weryt – Embalming hall. What the weryt looked like or how its interior was made up is fairly unknown. In Memphis, an embalming hall for Apis bulls was discovered, and it can be assumed the weryt for humans was designed in a similar fashion.

CALENDAR

Early on, Egyptians had a fairly exact calendar based on the annual Nile floodings. Additionally, they observed the course of the stars. When the morning star Sirius, Sothis in Egyptian, rose with the sun, the Nile floodings were about to begin. This marked the start of the year. The Sothis year and the solar year diverge slightly. Every 126 years—approximately—a one-day difference needs to be figured in.

One peculiarity is that the first month of inundation started earlier in the south than in the north, because the floods arrived there about two weeks later. I've used the later dates in this novel, because Itj-tawy was located quite far north. Egyptians knew three seasons with four months of approximately 30 days each,

Akhet (inundation)
Wepet-renpet – June 19
Tekh – July 19
Menkhet – August 18
Hut-heru – September 17
Peret (emergence/winter)
Ka-her-ka – October 17
Shef-bedet – November 16
Rekeh wer – December 16
Rekeh nedjes – January 15

Shemu (harvest/summer)
Renutet – February 14
Khonsu – March 16
Khenti-khet – April 15
Ipet-hemet – May 15

Heriu-renpet – *between the years*, the five leap days, June 14 to 18.

The day was divided into 24 hours, with 12 attributed to the night and 12 to the day. The day began at sunrise and ended with sunset. This close to the equator the hours of daylight varied far less than farther north or south. A week encompassed ten days, the year consisted of 36 weeks, plus five leap days called Heriu-renpet. In early times, these were regarded as dominated by demons, later they were dedicated to the gods. These leap days came right before the new year. Julius Caesar adopted this very exact calendar, and it formed the basis for the Julian calendar. Thus our calculation of time, to a large extent, goes back to the calendar of ancient Egypt.

Postscript

In this story, Egyptian beliefs of the afterlife and supernatural forces take up a large space. Surviving medical texts of the time show how firmly these notions permeated everyday life of the inhabitants of the Nile country. As advanced as Egyptian medicine was, just as strange seem the incantations supporting the treatments of patients. Particularly infectious diseases, whose causes were still unknown, were attributed to divine actions (Sakhmet's arrows) or demonic influences. Thus, amulets were often prescribed as cures or a magician was called in. Magic spells unfolded their effect when the ailing ate or drank them in accordance with the belief that writing held magic power. In fact, prayers might aid recovery if the recipient believes in them.

The destruction of a corpse, as it happened to criminals, did not only serve as punishment by robbing the ostracized of an afterlife but also prevented the deceased turning into an akh, who then might harm the living. Nevertheless, certain aspects of the soul or the spirit survived, the shut and the ba, but without grave and mummy, they roamed the western shores in confusion. Not much is known about the shadow, so I had to resort to my imagination to a large extent. For Egyptians, the danger of lurking shadows was absolutely real, and the incantation of ghosts must have been secret knowledge kept under lock and seal.

And on a side note, from the New Kingdom on, people who drowned or were eaten by a crocodile were regarded as blessed. Their bodies didn't need mummification, because they were chosen by the god. During the Middle Kingdom, however, no such ideas had developed yet, and relatives of such an unlucky person had to mourn eternal death—an unbearable notion for a people whose thinking was so focused on the afterlife.

I hope to have provided readers with an enthralling and interesting glance into the world of ancient Egypt. More adventures of Hori and Nakhtmin in Maat's service should follow.

Kathrin Brückmann
Berlin, January 2016

Made in the USA
Middletown, DE
21 February 2019